THE PIPER

In this bone-chilling tale of terror, a devoted mother must confront the paranormal forces that have cursed her family.

When Olivia James receives a phone call just after midnight, she recognizes her brother's voice. But there's a problem: her brother has been dead for the past nine weeks. Moving back to her old childhood home in Tennessee – the place where her brother has just died – her young daughter Teddy seems troubled, telling her mother that she's being visited by a menacing ghost. When another tragic death occurs and her daughter disappears, Olivia must confront the demonic force that has cursed her family.

THE PIPER

Lynn Hightower

Severn House Large Print
London & New York

This first large print edition published 2013
in Great Britain and the USA by
SEVERN HOUSE PUBLISHERS LTD of
19 Cedar Road, Sutton, Surrey, England, SM2 5DA.
First world regular print edition published 2012 by
Severn House Publishers Ltd., London and New York.

British Library Cataloguing in Publication Data

Hightower, Lynn S. author.
  The piper. -- Large print edition.
  1. Haunted places--Tennessee--Fiction. 2. Suspense
fiction. 3. Large type books.
  I. Title
  813.6-dc23

ISBN-13: 9780727896568

Severn House Publishers support the Forest Stewardship Council™
[FSC™], the leading international forest certification organisation. All
our titles that are printed on FSC certified paper carry the FSC logo.

MIX
Paper from
responsible sources
FSC® C013056

Printed and bound in Great Britain by
T J International, Padstow, Cornwall.

For Robert, my Frenchman

ACKNOWLEDGEMENTS

To the usual suspects, Alan, Laurel, and Rachel.
And David & Arthur, Wes, Katie and Isaac.
Rebecca and Brian.
To the French side of the family, Arnaud, Julien,
Elda, Miria, Ernest.
For Sheila, and Lindsay.
And Matt, as always.

'It is ten years since our children left.'

Town Chronicles, Hamelin, Germany
Eyewitness account, recorded by
Decan Ludde, 1384

ONE

They call us, you know, the dead do. The ones we've loved, the ones who've passed. Someone you know has received a call – maybe it was you. They call to tell us they love us, to tell us they're okay. And sometimes they call us to warn.

For Olivia James, the phone call came through on the last night that she and her daughter, Teddy, spent in the California house. Olivia's brother, Christopher James, had been dead for just nine weeks. Olivia immediately recognized his voice.

The radio alarm had been set for seven a.m., but it went off just after midnight, at 12.12 precisely, waking Olivia with a song she had not heard since she was a little girl – 'Heart and Soul', that old romantic standby from the nineteen forties. Like every other child in America, Olivia had played the song on the piano as a duet, sometimes with her brother, Chris, but most often with her big sister, Emily, before Emily disappeared. Twenty-five years ago, when Olivia was only five. Six years later her mother died, from what Olivia always secretly thought was a broken heart. Both parents were dead now. It had just been Olivia and Chris, for the last ten

11

years, expanding their little circle to spouses and kids of their own. Olivia and Chris and the ever present hope that someday their sister Emily would miraculously return.

Heart and soul, I fell in love with you –
Heart and soul, I fell in love with you –
Baaaabyyyy...

Olivia's cell rang on *baby*. The land line had been cut for months.

Olivia was immediately awake. She was a bad sleeper, particularly these last few months, when the money worries had been extreme. She heard static, and rubbed her forehead, then frowned over the distinct echo of chimes. Wind chimes, she thought. The voice, so familiar, so longed-for, brought her sitting up and trembling in her bed.

'Livie? Do you know who this is?'

It sounded like her brother. But it couldn't be her brother. Her brother was dead. The death verdict had been bizarre. SUNDS. Sudden Un-explained Nocturnal Death Syndrome. A rare, mysterious death that worked like an adult form of SIDS. People died in their sleep and no one knew why.

'Chris? Is it really you?' Olivia gripped the phone so hard her fingers ached. As if she could squeeze her brother out.

'I tried to hang on, Kidlet. But it just wasn't meant to be.'

The voice was her brother's, but different somehow, in a way Olivia could not quite figure out. But only her brother called her Kidlet. Her brother who was dead but talking to her on the phone.

'Chris, if it really is you, somehow, I love you, okay? I miss you.'

Static again, and Olivia got out of bed, pacing toward the front window, the connection was always better there.

'—sten to me, Livie, I don't have ... ong.'

'Chris?'

The silence came like a vacuum, the voice gone. Olivia dodged the boxes that were stacked to the ceiling. The movers had taken ten long hours to get everything packed up, and were due in the morning first thing to load. She pinched one of the slats of the blinds and looked outside. The *For Sale* sign in front of her house was slightly twisted. There were lights in her neighbors' houses, and the blue of television screens glowed in every house in the cul de sac, though everyone was sealed up tight. Californians lived behind closed doors and did not hang out on porches, like Olivia remembered from Tennessee.

She saw the glow of a cigarette, and a woman in a dark tee shirt, walking her tiny dog. The woman lived three houses over, usually wore sandals with rhinestones, and she always turned away when Olivia said hello. Olivia made a point of saying hi whenever she saw the woman, in the way of southerners who use courtesy to mess with people under the cover of being polite. People who did not grow up in the south never understood they'd been insulted on the sly. Olivia had learned early that you could say any

13

nasty thing that came to mind so long as you preceded it with *bless your heart*, and said it with a smile. Teddy's father, Hugh, called it her southern bullshit.

Olivia's throat was tight enough that swallowing hurt. She had just decided the call was nothing more than a dream when she heard the chimes again, and a crackle, as if a lost connection had been restored.

'...warn you, Livie.'

'Warn me about what? Chris? Warn me about what?'

'I had to pay the piper. You have to know it's been taken care of.'

'I don't understand. What's been taken care of?'

'...my fault. Don't let him ... after you.'

'Who's coming after me?'

'The *Mister Man*.' Static again. '...ove you, Livie...'

'Chris?'

Silence like forever in her heart.

The Mister Man.

Olivia stumbled across the hall, dodging the boxed up pictures that were stacked next to the wall outside the bathroom. She peered into Teddy's room, heart beating hard until comforted by the visible curl of her little girl, sleeping on the wrong side as usual, head at the foot of the bed, wrapped in the pink chenille bedspread. Olivia and Teddy had their peculiar habits of sleep, Teddy wrong side up, and Olivia always on top of the bedspread, because she hated the slippery sensation of sheets.

Winston, the golden retriever, lifted his head and groaned because his bones ached, but dutifully padded out to the hallway to nuzzle Olivia's knee.

Olivia and Winston settled side by side at the top of the steep stairway, Winston with his muzzle in Olivia's lap, smelling like old dog and comfort.

The Mister Man. Sibling code for the nameless, faceless unknown that made Emily disappear. Olivia knew that it was her imagination, but ever since her sister went away, Olivia had often felt the ongoing, unsettling sensation that she was being watched.

He is three million, eight hundred years old and counting. He is six hundred sixty years since renewed. In the flesh, he leaves the footprint of the goat, though he can leave the footprint of the man, if he chooses.

Tonight he walks behind the woman with rhinestone slippers, watching with his lazy yellow sated lion eyes. Her tiny little dog looks anxiously over its shoulder, but the Piper's business, his hunger, is not for the woman or this miniature guardian. The little dog strains the leash, hard enough for its tiny heart to burst, how delicious, yet the woman only frowns, no appreciation at all, too busy talking on the cell phone to her married lover. The Piper turns his connoisseur's nose up at the reek of her, ennui on the hoof, no thank you – too easy, too tainted, too dry.

It is the face he sees at the window that rouses him. Heart shaped and full, those fleshy pink lips, flower petal soft, the thick hair a man could wrap round his hand to pin her down, the juicy rounded body, contours where he could sink his teeth and chew. This one stirs his loins, and sings like an ache of exquisite pain in his blood. He tastes her, shudders at the strength of her yearning, though she hardly seems to know, truly, what it is she wants, only thinking of it as home, the hungry grief for the ones she has lost. Now hunger – that is one thing the Piper understands. And when they fall away into the dark, as some of them always do, the Piper is there to catch them. One more into the fold.

But he yearns most particularly for the special ones, craving the warmth and throb of their light, wrapping himself around it tighter and tighter until he chokes it off for good.

The Piper looks up at the window and smiles. She does not see him, oh no, she will not see him unless – until, *dare he say it – she chooses that he be seen. The very best games have rules. But she can't keep him from stalking, and she is sensing him, smelling him, he prickles now on the back of her neck. He knows her sweet spot, her little Teddy. The Piper can always taste the salty red meat of their hearts.*

He howls with pleasure, has watched her such a long time, licking at her heels, and he is after her now, like a dog digging up an old buried bone, but then he stops. He listens.

A scent, perhaps? Merely instinct?

Something makes him hesitate, stops him mid stride, chokes off the flow of pleasurable pain. He hears it very faintly, the voice that calls his

16

name – not Decan Ludde, not Duncan Lee, the Piper has so many names, and he loves them all, like little treasures. This is the old name that knows him, that puts him in his place, and he feels the nasty anger that burns. He does not like being distracted from his pleasures, but he is a wise old hunter and he knows when to put the pretties aside and concentrate on the smells.

Nothing he can see yet, just the feeling, which is knowledge enough. She will not be easy prey, this one, she is not alone. They never are alone, if only they knew it. And how little they do know, how innocent and simple their delusions. It makes them that much more delicious to hunt.

He looks back up at the window. She is no longer there, but he feels her. Olivia. He knows her name and she'll soon learn his.

Next time he will leave her a calling card. A tiny pool of water, no bigger than your average blood stain, maybe by the bed. He likes water, it makes him strong, it travels, and he drowns them like rats in the water.

Let me in, little girlies, let me in.

This is how it begins. Again.

TWO

Olivia was barely aware when the movers arrived at nine forty-five a.m. instead of eight, and though she was a veteran mover and knew better, she supervised very loosely while they loaded the furniture and boxes. They were grateful for the Gatorade (electrolytes), the bananas (potassium for muscle support) and cashews (protein) that she always provided. They worked up a serious sweat and took smoke breaks, and, as usual, never stopped for lunch. By six p.m. the house was dirty, empty, echoing.

Olivia did her final walk through, with her phone jammed into the front pocket of her jeans, where it had sat, silent and uncomfortable, all day.

She had kept the phone line open for an hour last night before she hung up. Then she'd checked the record of incoming calls. It had been there, twelve twelve p.m., lodged, inexplicably, as voice mail. No number to trace.

The Mister Man.

Olivia was upstairs in Teddy's empty bedroom when she heard the front door open and Teddy shout for Winston. She headed down the stairs, smiling hard.

Teddy's khaki shorts were crumpled and stained with something orange, little round glasses loose on her nose, fine brown hair limp from the heat. Her toes were dusty in the sandals, and she had a Nancy Drew book tucked under one arm. Right now it was *The Secret of the Old Clock.*

'The truck's gone, Mommy. How come you didn't call? I'm hungry and Dr Amelia's taking us to the Wolf Creek Grill. I ate a bite of Winston's dog chow. It really wasn't bad.'

'I promise you she got to the dog chow before I could stop her.' The red of Amelia's hair had a harsh glint, like a bad dye job, though Olivia knew Amel paid several hundred dollars a month for that particular shade. Her eyes were brown, slanty and kind, and she wore black cat glasses on a chain around her neck.

Olivia had toyed with the idea of going red herself, maybe a rich auburn instead of her natural color of mud brown, but constant coloring was expensive so she settled for blonde streaks when she was in funds. She kept her hair shoulder length and layered to set off the rounded shape of her face, the Kewpie doll lips. On good days she looked at that face in the mirror and thought Botticelli angel. On bad days she thought fat.

Amelia had changed out of the usual white coat and scrubs into blue jeans and a tee. She was a physician's assistant with her own practice in conjunction with a family services clinic in Valencia, and she had been Teddy's pediatrician since the Los Angeles move.

'Teddy and I stopped and got your last bit of mail. Don't let me forget to give it to you.'

Amelia patted the green crocodile purse slung over one shoulder. 'It's in the bag. So, are you hungry? Did you even eat today?'

'I had a mustard sandwich for lunch. Teddy, did you thank Dr Amelia for letting you hang out at her office all day?'

Teddy was shy around moving men. Packing up the house always upset her.

'Thank me?' Amelia said. 'I should be thanking her. She organized my store room, sorted and threw away all the old magazines, then curled up and read her book for the rest of the day. If I'd known how useful she was, I'd have kidnapped her a long time ago.'

Olivia gave Amelia a grateful look. Things had been going badly with Teddy since the divorce. Badly enough to scare both Olivia and Hugh into setting their inevitable hostilities aside, so they could present a united front.

The most infuriating thing was the lies – not big ones, defiant ones. When it came to the big stuff, Teddy seemed to have the strong moral center she'd had since she was a little girl. No, the lies she told were stupid ones. Obvious ones. Like a little girl begging to get caught. Things like eating cookies for breakfast and saying she'd had toast and jelly, when there were Oreo crumbs spilling down her shirt. Or saying that Hugh had given her permission to pour beer into Winston's water bowl.

Hugh and Olivia had instituted the policy of same rules, both households, had sat down together all three of them to explain all boundaries.

Teddy had responded by ignoring her work at

school – going so far as to stand on the back of the toilets in the girls' restroom after lunch every day, folding her arms and refusing to come out, much less do her school work. Teddy was doing things that made Olivia want to laugh and punish her at the same time. *My outrageous daughter* was what Hugh called her now. But even when Olivia and Hugh laughed, they knew it wasn't good.

'Teddy, take Winston out, okay? He needs to pee.' Olivia waited till the sliding doors opened and closed. 'Amelia, what's wrong? You've smeared all your mascara off. And there are wads of tissues hanging out of your pocket.'

'Maybe I've known *you* too long,' Amelia said. Olivia was famous for leaving a trail of tissues wherever she went. 'And couldn't I just be sad because my best friend is moving all the way to Tennessee? Or tired because you called and woke me up in the middle of the night?'

'Why don't you just set that shit on fire and tell me what's up?'

Amelia tucked her hair behind her ear. 'Marianne Butler. More fluid in the lungs and Alexis and Jack won't let her go. They want another round of chemo while Marianne gags like a baby fish on a hook. Don't ever let anybody tell you drowning is painless.'

Olivia squeezed Amelia's hand. Little Marianne Butler, in and out of hospitals with leukemia for most of the three short years of her life, haunted Amelia in her dreams.

Amelia and Marianne's mother, Alexis, had been college room-mates, together during all the

21

major milestones, graduation, Alexis marrying Jack, Amelia opening her practice. Four years ago they'd gone to Santa Barbara for a couples weekend, Alexis and Jack, Amelia and Brandon, for a miraculous forty-eight hours that ended with two unplanned events – Amelia and Brandon in a spontaneous wedding resulting in a marriage that lasted eighteen months, and the conception of Marianne.

Olivia had learned to slough off the little geysers of envy when she saw Amelia and Alexis together. A friendship, lasting through the years, stronger than your average marriage, was not an option for a nomad like herself.

'Look, let's skip dinner. You go ahead to the hospital, Amel.'

'I can't do it anymore, Livie. I won't. Alexis is a brick wall when I try and talk to her about it, Jack is a zombie, and the oncology team is dead set on prolonging the agony – there's nothing I can do. Let's go have dinner and a drink. Or two.'

'You're sure?'

'We absolutely have to talk. I've been googling all afternoon. I'll tell you over dinner, Livie, but there are entire websites devoted to this stuff.'

'This stuff?'

'Phone calls from the dead.'

THREE

The Wolf Creek Grill specialized in hamburgers grilled with melted blue cheese, portabella mushroom sandwiches, wood fired pizzas and house brewed beer. Amelia ordered the Asian Sesame chicken salad, which came with a side of fruit, and Olivia was not surprised that Amelia had been continuously stealing shoestring French fries off Olivia's plate. Olivia had ordered the Swiss mushroom burger, and set the bun aside, eating onions, mushrooms and meat. She was not in favor of salad for dinner, and did not care for any fruit except mangoes. She was happy to share her fries. She would have preferred mashed potatoes, because mashed potatoes, mustard sandwiches, and bread and butter pickles were her particular comfort foods, but the Wolf Creek Grill had none of these. It was hard to find bread and butter pickles anywhere but the south.

'Mama?' Teddy said. 'Ashley just texted me. She and Amber are going to the Marble Slab. Can I go over there too? Like a goodbye thing? I've had all I want to eat, I promise, I'm full, and it's right next door, so I'll be safe.'

Olivia glanced at Teddy's cheeseburger. Three bites, maybe four, but little ones. She'd made

23

inroads on the fries. 'Okay, but you stay there, in the ice cream shop, till I come over and get you. Don't go *anywhere* else. Here.' Olivia dug her wallet out of her purse. 'Here's five bucks.'

Amelia shuddered. 'Five dollars for ice cream. The world has gone mad. And while we're digging in purses, let me give you your mail.'

'Amelia, I'll be right back. I just need to walk Teddy—'

'*Mother*. I can walk next door by myself.' Teddy stuck the money in her pocket, and headed out, then turned back. 'Thank you, Mama.'

Olivia watched Teddy walk out of the restaurant, craning her neck a little when her daughter went out the door.

'Southern children are so polite.'

'Only if you beat them.'

'Seriously. How is she doing?'

'Up and down. More down than up. Nothing I can't handle.' Olivia did not mention that she was unable to sleep anymore, and lay awake at night, doubting every decision she'd made. Should she and Hugh have stayed married no matter what? Would moving yet again make things better or worse? There was no question that what Teddy needed was stability. To live in one place, to go to one school, to end the constant moving that was an integral part of life with Hugh. Neither she nor Teddy could get any traction in their lives living this way.

'She's struggling, Amelia, and it breaks my heart. She wants to be good, but something inside her wants to be bad too. I hate that term, *acting out*, but it's exactly what she's doing. So.

24

She needs stability and she needs limits, and that's what she's going to get.'

'Stability?' Amelia said. 'You're moving again.'

'One last move. So we can go home and stay put.'

Amelia set a small stack of envelopes on the table by Olivia's plate and took a sip of her Grey Wolf Ale. 'Just keep in mind that things may get worse before they get better. And by the way, when did you cave and let her acquire the cell phone? I mean, come on, Livie, she's *eight*.'

'Lose the pursed lips. It was a gift from Hugh.'

'You're familiar with the *no* word?'

'Yes, Amel, and he asked me first, we talked about it. Teddy's had a lot of separation anxiety since the divorce. You know how connected she is to her dad. It's supposed to be a special phone just to talk to Hugh.' Olivia shrugged. 'But yes, you're right, it's starting to get out of hand. Suddenly her friends are texting from their mothers' or siblings' phones, and it's going off all the time. I'm going to let it be until we get settled in Knoxville, then slowly phase it out.'

'That's what they all say, but Pandora couldn't put it back in the box.' Amelia looked over Olivia's shoulder and tilted her head, pointing toward the television mounted in the corner of the bar. 'Will you look at that. Talk about karma. That couldn't be a coincidence.'

Olivia twisted to see the screen – football players in white and orange against blue and white. The first game of the season, a grudge match between the University of Tennessee and

25

Western Kentucky State.

'Don't go all woo woo on me, Amel, I'm pretty shook up. I *recognized* his voice. That was definitely my brother last night on the phone. My brother, deceased.'

'Supposedly this is an actual known phenomena.'

'You got this off the Internet, remember.'

'You're the one who got the call. You look pale, Olivia.'

'Pale or sunburned. There's no in between for me.' Olivia leaned back in the booth and stuck her feet out. She was short so they didn't go very far. Her feet were very small.

Amelia leaned across the table. 'Evidently, it's happened to a lot of other people. There are some very distinctive patterns on how this ... *manifestation* works.'

'I love how you make it sound like science.'

A waiter with lovingly spiked hair and a honey mellow voice offered refills on the beer, and a box for Teddy's burger.

'We'll let the burger go,' Olivia said. 'But the beers are a really good thing.'

The waiter hesitated, eyebrows scrunching.

'She means yes,' Amelia said.

'Thank God I'm going home where I'm not going to need a translator.'

'Hey, they just don't get the music of your speech.'

Olivia began shredding her napkin. 'So what are these patterns on the calls from the dead?'

Amelia leaned across the table. 'They divide it up into categories.'

26

'Who is they?'

'I don't know. The Internet people. First up are the calls that come right after the person dies – eight hours to two days. Usually before they're even buried. And the one who gets the call – most of the time, they have no idea the caller is dead. They only find out later. Think about that.'

'I think it's creepy.'

'Maybe it's just sweet. I wonder if children ever call people after they die.'

'What do they say? In these calls?'

'Most of the time just hello, I love you, I'm okay.' Amelia cocked her head. 'Now, the next group are the calls that come in the first week after the death. After that – now get this.' Amelia jabbed her finger on the table. 'Nobody ever gets a call in the time period between eight and thirty days after the person has died. Your brother has been dead how long?'

'Two months, give or take.'

'There you go.'

'That's weird. That time period of silence. So why is that?'

Amelia waggled a hand. 'No telling. But after that, twenty-two percent of the calls come between two and six months after death. Just like yours.'

'They actually have percents?'

'I think your brother's call would fall into the category of a *crisis* call. That runs to twenty-seven percent.'

'A crisis phone call? The crisis is over. Chris is dead.'

'Not him. You.'

'I'm not *in* a crisis. That's all done.'

Amelia put out her hand. 'Look, I—' The waiter arrived with the beers, and Amelia paused until he was out of earshot. 'Don't take this wrong, and get that mouth of yours all fired up. But maybe this whole thing is some kind of stress reaction. You haven't slept for months, Liv. Sleep deprivation causes all kinds of ... reactions. And no wonder. You almost lost everything when you got laid off.'

Olivia made finger marks on the condensation of her glass. So Amelia had noticed when the car disappeared. She figured people did notice these things, but were too polite to bring it up. In the last few months the thought of being homeless had joined her list of lifetime fears, which included drowning, earthworms and being buried alive. If it hadn't been for Hugh giving her his battered up Jeep that he kept for off-roading, she'd have had nothing to drive, a virtual death sentence in California.

A prince among exes. What was that thing he'd told her? That you take care of your child by taking care of her mother. She'd been warned by at least two girlfriends that men were nice like that during the separation if they were hoping you'd change your mind, but to watch out when things went to court.

'It worked out, though, Amel. I sold the house. I'm taking a new job back in Knoxville, and that's like a dream come true. I'll be the rain-maker, the broker, building up my own business instead of working in the back office because I move all the time. I'm going home and I'm

28

going to stay put. I'm happier now than I've been in years.'

'But it's been hell for you, Livie. And this whole time you're worried sick about your brother in Tennessee, who is clearly in the middle of some kind of psychological meltdown. How many pounds did he lose before he died?'

'Sixty. At least.'

'Acting weird, not sleeping, making his wife and daughters move out of the house. All that worry, coming just a year after you and Hugh got divorced.' Amelia sat back in the booth. 'Still here, Liv?'

'You're saying I imagined it.'

'You said you were asleep. Maybe it was part of a dream.'

Olivia flipped her cell phone open and texted over to incoming calls. 'Is this a dream?'

Amelia took the phone, and pulled the glasses up on the chain, using them like a magnifying glass to study the screen. 'Are these things getting smaller, or am I just getting ... Jesus, Liv. Twelve twelve p.m. exactly, just like you said. But there's no number here. It says voice mailbox.'

'I don't think they have a category for ghost.'

'So okay, then, maybe the crisis is now, Livie.'

Olivia put her elbows on the table, avoiding a smear of catsup next to Teddy's plate. 'My take is he was trying to tell me something about my sister. He said *The Mister Man*. I think maybe it was just a ... a sort of guilt call. Making amends. He said something about it being his fault, and that it was okay he died, because he paid the

29

piper. Maybe he was just reassuring me about that SUNDS thing. You know damn well I've been wondering if it wasn't a suicide.'

'It was a pretty weird diagnosis for the coroner to make. SUNDS is a pretty fucking rare diagnosis. The general consensus is it doesn't exist.'

'So maybe that's why he called, because it didn't make sense. He wanted to reassure me. To tell me he didn't kill himself. What is it, Amelia? You've got that look.'

'No look.'

'Come on.'

'Well, okay, but be logical here, Livie. If he didn't kill himself, why does he feel guilty? Why does he need to make amends?'

'He always felt guilty. About Emily.'

'Why?'

'God only knows. We all did, a little bit.'

'Could Chris have had anything to do with it?'

'Hell no, Amel. He was seventeen. He was in Louisville, Kentucky on an overnight trip with the wrestling team, some kind of national competition, he was totally absorbed in that.'

'And they never found out anything? About what happened to your sister?'

'Nothing. My mom and dad were out with friends, playing bridge. They called to check on us a little after eleven. Emily was babysitting, I was five and she was fifteen. I was asleep on the couch, and she told my dad she was taking the dog, Hunter, outside for his late night wee wee, and then she would tuck me into bed. My parents get home and there I am on the couch in my little jammies, sound asleep. The back door is un-

30

locked, the gate is open in the backyard, and Emily and Hunter are gone. Both of them. And Hunter was no ordinary dog. He was a German shepherd, and very protective. People were scared of him. So they figured she took him out like she said, and never made it back in the house. And both of them disappeared. Just like they say. Without a trace.'

Amelia had heard it all before but she listened as if for the first time.

'We named him The Mister Man – whoever it was who took Emily. That's what Chris and I always called him. And that's what he said in the call. To watch out for The Mister Man. You know, that's actually strange.'

'The whole thing is strange.'

'No, I mean, if you saw a picture of my brother after it happened. Well, all of us. We looked ... sad. But Chris, he'd been this kind of hefty guy, I mean, he was on the wrestling team and he was big boned and bulked up. But after Emily disappeared he started losing weight, just like he did this last year. If you look at pictures, before and after, you can't even recognize him. Emily was gone three years before he stopped looking like he'd spent his life in some kind of con-centration camp.'

'Didn't you say that Chris said he wanted to warn you?'

'There was a lot of static, Amel, it was hard to understand. Maybe I heard it wrong.'

'Maybe you did. They did mention that, on the website. Bad connections, and sometimes the sound of bells.'

31

'Bells? Really? I heard that. Like wind chimes, but a long way off.'

'Yeah, well, if it was your brother, it *was* a long way off. It's just—'

'*What?*'

'I can't help but wonder what he meant by *warn*.'

FOUR

No one was expecting them, when Olivia and Teddy took the I-75 split and headed north into Knoxville, one day ahead of schedule, arriving in that last magnificent blaze of sunlight and breezy coolness that comes at the end of fading summer days. For Olivia, it was a *moment*. She had been homesick for such a long time.

Back in the day, Olivia had left home willingly, unaware how hard it would be to get back. Hugh's work in the manufacturing management of anything metallic and noisy led them to more places than Olivia could remember, the highlights being Fort Smith, Arkansas, Madison, Wisconsin, a short stint on the outskirts of Memphis, followed by a living hell called Endicott, New York.

Hugh had talked a lot about the work ethic of Americans, the only people in the world who dropped family, friends and homes without a second thought, moving regularly and willingly

32

for the sake of a job. He talked about it like it was a religion, but Olivia had come to the conclusion that this corporate culture was a scam. In the early days, Hugh had changed jobs at the beckoning dollar signs dangled by the headhunters, but more and more lately he'd been skewered by the dreaded *work force reduction* – the corporate term for *we're going to fuck up your life.*

California had just been another stop along the way.

Olivia had planned to spend a night in Memphis, but the city had been dark, and hot, and industrial along the interstate. They were ahead of schedule, and Olivia was on a roll. Teddy and Winston had been deep asleep, and Olivia, restless and anxious to be home, fueled by coffee and sugared gummy worms bought just outside of Little Rock, had blown through Memphis on an impulse thinking she would stop somewhere along the way. She made it into Nashville at three a.m., too close to falling asleep behind the wheel to get the rest of the way home. They took a room and she slept past noon, not getting up and running until three, missing the hotel checkout time, which meant an extra night's charge.

They'd stopped at a McDonald's in Harriman, no longer noticing the rank long car trip odor of fast food and sweaty socks, overlaid with the whangy aroma that had permeated the cab since Winston had tangled with a pimento cheese sandwich and lost. It was cool out, a relief from the hot days of the trip, and they opened the doors to the breeze, and Olivia ate French fries, and drank a big Coke, Winston had his own order of Chicken McNuggets, and Teddy ate a cheeseburger and kicked her heels against the seat. The heat would be back, likely tomorrow, today was just a tease, like one of the crisp cool days they'd get around Halloween. Olivia had that good fall feeling – fresh starts, new things, a little hum of excitement because she was almost home.

She had one of those too rare glints of awareness, as she sat in the Jeep sharing fries with Teddy and Winston. This was it. This was happy. Whoever that was who said you couldn't come home again was totally full of shit. From here on out things were going to be good. They had been through the wars, her little family, but now they were over the hump.

Olivia would remember this one, truly perfect moment, before she and Teddy took their very first look at the house. Blaming herself, later, for being dazzled and distracted by the joy of coming home, was entirely unfair.

They rolled into Knoxville right at dusk. It was a strange feeling, being back home, where the streets were familiar but so distant in memory. Two months ago, home for her brother's funeral, Olivia found her way around by instinct, only getting confused when she tried to consciously think about which way to go.

She headed north on Kingston Pike, late enough that the after work rush had died away.

'Look for a street sign that says Westwood,' she told Teddy. 'It should be on our left. Do you

34

want to run by and see your new school? It's on the way.'

Teddy shrugged and stared out the window. Her hair was half in and half out of a ponytail, and her little round glasses were smudged. She had chosen to wear socks today with her sandals, for no particular reason, different colored socks, sliding and bunching at the ankle.

'You want to go see it?' Olivia said.

Teddy's voice was a whisper. 'That's okay.'

'I know how much it sucks to have to go to another new school, Teddy. But remember, me and Uncle Chris both went to Bearden when we were kids. It's friendlier here than in California.'

'I like California.'

'I know. But after this, Teddy, no more moving and no more changing schools. This time we're going to stay put.'

Teddy's hand strayed to Winston, who was straddling the middle trying to get his head in the front seat. He licked each one of Teddy's fingers, and she wiped them on her shorts. She sat forward and pointed.

'There it is, Mommy. See the sign? West-wood.'

Olivia put on the turn signal.

'Are we almost there?'

'One minute away.'

Teddy smiled and sighed deeply, and the dog put a paw in her lap. 'It's a pretty house, Winston. Uncle Chris used to live there and it's cool.'

Olivia turned right on to Sutherland Avenue, watched for the landmarks, the line of little bungalows she'd known from childhood.

The front porch light was on, which was comforting, though it was not yet dark. As far as Olivia was concerned, the stone Tudor cottage defined home. Charlotte and Chris had let the yard go to hell, but even behind the overgrown magnolia and berry bushes, the clumps of dried leaves and moldy chestnuts that littered the ground, the house struggled to welcome her back. She loved the wood battens and diamond paned windows, the waist high stone wall and black iron fencing, the thick hedge of snarled honeysuckle and forsythia that shielded the boundaries of the property on all sides.

For Olivia, a house was a love affair. She loved arched doorways, wood floors and casement windows, but when she had been married to Hugh every move meant the inevitable decision between living in older, edgy neighborhoods and beige carpeted suburbia. Olivia's preferences were always trumped by crime rates and good schools.

And though she kept her secret curled tight inside, she allowed a private wish. Because coming home meant a revival of hope for that tearful reunion Olivia dreamed about, where her sister Emily would knock on that front door, with a long story that no matter how horrific, would be calmed and healed by the joy of returning home. When Olivia had been a little girl, she had sat on those stone steps out front, waiting and waiting. Even now, twenty-five years later, when those stories broke on the news of a miraculous reunion and return, a missing child come home

36

at long last, Olivia had hope that it would happen in her family. She had never given up. Neither had Chris. She missed having someone to hope with.

And just as Olivia turned left into the steep driveway, and eased up the broken and buckled asphalt, thinking how much she missed her dead brother, she recognized Chris's Ford Explorer parked to the side of the garage. The driver's door hung open, the way Chris always left it, when he was absentminded and in a hurry to get where he had to go.

Olivia jammed on the brakes and sat forward in the seat.

'There's somebody here,' Teddy said.

FIVE

'Teddy, you and Winston stay in the car. Just for a minute. I'll be right back.'

'We've only *been* in the car two hundred million hours.'

'Then another few minutes won't hurt.'

Olivia looked in the pickup when she walked by. Chris's orange UT ball cap was there, crammed into a corner of the dashboard.

The backyard was bound with a privacy fence, the gate slightly ajar, and Olivia thought she heard a voice. She listened, just for a moment. Crying, someone crying softly, and the hair rose on her arms, because it sounded so much like her mother. When Emily disappeared, there had been a lot of crying in that house.

She pushed the gate open, remembering how Hunter the German shepherd had been Lord of the Backyard, and King of the Mountain on the sloping hill. It would be good for Winston, too, a safe, fenced place to run. Not that Winston ran a whole lot these days.

The crying stopped. But Olivia saw her, a woman sitting on tiles beside the koi pond and fountain, cross legged, head in her hands, only now starting to turn and get to her feet.

Charlotte. Of course, Charlotte, her sister-in-law, driving Chris's Ford, it made perfect sense.

Charlotte was one of the best things about coming back to Knoxville. She and Olivia had always hit it off, but lived too far apart for a true, intimate friendship. Olivia was home now, and she and Charlotte could be close. They could take care of each other when they missed Chris. Olivia had precious little family left.

'Olivia?' Charlotte was coming down the hill. 'Did I get the day wrong? I thought you weren't due in till tomorrow. I was just going to call you.'

'I'm early. It's me that needs to call you. Oh, honey, you've been crying. Are you missing Chris?'

Charlotte enveloped Olivia in a hug. She smelled like something sweet and lemony, and there was sweat in the creases of her neck, and mascara running down her cheeks.

Olivia felt better, like she always did, when-

38

ever she was around her sister-in-law. Charlotte was the kind of woman people gravitated to, her dinner invitations were never refused. Physically, she somehow managed to add up to more than the sum of her parts. Reddish gold hair, chin length and blunt cut. Brown eyes, skin a bit rough and pitted, generous in the hips and waist. The longer you knew her the more you noticed how pretty she looked.

Chris had always said that Charlotte's only fault was that she fed their children oatmeal for breakfast, which both Chris and Olivia found grotesque. Olivia was not sure when she and Chris had developed their oatmeal prejudice. In truth, Olivia loathed almost all breakfast foods, and started her own days with microwave popcorn and coffee, feeling that life was too short for anything with bran.

Charlotte also drank white wine, another serious strike. Olivia felt that wine should only come in shades of red, but she never said anything about this to Charlotte. There was a need for diversity in the world, and there were people who found her own love of mustard sandwiches weird.

'I came over to do some work on this yard before you saw what a mess it was.' Charlotte held up a pair of pristinely clean gardening gloves. 'You can see how much I've accomplished.'

'Don't worry about the *yard*, Charlotte. Don't worry about any of this. You've got enough on your mind these days.'

Chris had been madly in love with Charlotte

(in spite of the oatmeal) from the first moment he'd seen her, saying there was something sparkly about her, though she had lost a lot of that sparkle now. They had been one of those touchstone couples everybody else had envied, which made it all the more upsetting four months ago when Chris had insisted Charlotte and the girls move out of the house, and leave him there alone. Neither Chris nor Charlotte would talk about it, though they'd sworn the marriage was sound and intact, and Olivia had wondered but not intruded, aware the little family was in trouble, and watching helplessly from the sidelines, hoping things would work out. Things had been very wrong, and neither Charlotte nor Chris would tell her why.

Olivia noticed that Charlotte would not look her in the eye. There was none of the usual calm steadiness that was like an anchor for everyone else.

Charlotte ran a hand through her hair, and looked up at the fountain. 'I meant to get things taken care of. I really did. It's pretty awful. And look – see? Both of the apple trees are dead.'

'It doesn't matter. You know I don't eat fruit.'

'But Livie, that's not all. Come look, come on, up at the fountain.' Charlotte tugged Olivia's hand and led her up the hill. 'I didn't want you to see this, it's horrible. All the fish are dead.'

Olivia followed Charlotte up the hill, the uncut grass itchy on her ankles. The circle of tile and stone was chipped and broken, and there was a coating of dark green where the water had once spilled in a spray from the stone lion's mouth into the little pool. The pond smelled like the river at low ebb, and Olivia saw lumps of floating things. Bloated koi, in advanced decay. The fish had been dead for months.

Olivia nudged Charlotte back down the hill. 'Let it go, Charlotte.'

'The truth is, Livie, I still need to clean out the freezer, and scrub the bathrooms, and it's ... it's a mess and I can't...' Charlotte put a hand to her face, wiping the tears and makeup into another smudge. 'How long before your moving van gets here?'

'Four days. Don't agonize about this, Charlotte, I'll take care of things myself.'

'I just don't want you to think I'm upset about you taking the house. You understand I'm okay with the trust? I always thought it was great that your parents paid the house off and left it for you and Chris.'

'And Emily.'

'And Emily, of course. I don't want you to think this is sour grapes on my part, because I had to give up the cottage. Because I promise that's not it, Chris found us another house, right before he died, and it's pretty and it's new, so you have to promise me that you won't think it has anything to do with that.'

'Charlotte, I do feel bad about taking the house—'

'No.' Charlotte put both hands on Olivia's shoulders, pressing down hard. 'I don't want this house. I *hate* this house. I spent all afternoon trying to get the nerve up to go inside and do some cleaning, and you know what? I made it to the

41

back door, and couldn't even put my hand on the knob. Look at my hands.'

Charlotte held her hands out. They were shaking.

'Charlotte, come on, look, it's okay to have a meltdown, anybody would with all you've been through.'

'No, *listen* to me. The fish are all dead. Chris is dead—' Charlotte looked over Olivia's shoulder and froze.

Teddy had gotten tired of waiting in the Jeep, and come to find her mom, and neither Charlotte nor Olivia had noticed her, standing close and listening in. How much had she heard, Olivia wondered.

'Mommy?' Teddy pushed her glasses back on her nose. 'Did Uncle Chris die in this house?'

'He died in his sleep, Teddy,' Olivia said. 'He was sick. I told you that, remember?'

'But was it *in this house*?'

Charlotte put a hand on Olivia's arm, but Olivia shook it off. 'Yes, it was in the house. That's normal, in older houses. Families live there for years and years and it's a natural part of life. He was very sick, and he went to sleep, and he didn't wake up. It was very peaceful.'

'But which room was he in? What made him sick?'

Olivia looked at Charlotte, who bit her lip.

'A grown up sickness,' Olivia told her. 'Something that kids can't get, so you don't have to worry. Teddy, where is Winston?'

'He won't come out of the car.'

Hours later, at Charlotte's new little house,

42

when Teddy and her cousins had been fed, taken baths, and been tucked into bed, when Winston had relieved himself, stretched his legs, and sniffed through every interesting smell in Charlotte's raw and new backyard, Olivia and Charlotte huddled together at the kitchen table. The dishwasher hummed, and they opened a bottle of pinot noir. Charlotte was no doubt being polite, because Olivia had seen a bottle of chardonnay, already open in the fridge.

The house was a mix of rosy tan brick and white aluminum siding, small, one level, brand new, in a subdivision off South Peters Road, three miles past the Baker Peters Jazz Club where Olivia and Hugh had their second date – a quirky, old brick southern mansion with a dental practice in one wing, a restaurant where Olivia could not afford to eat out front, and a jazz club and patio on the roof. The parking lot adjoined a gas station on one side, and an insurance office on the other, and there was a hive of suburban tract houses fanning out on either side.

Charlotte was calm now. Her hands had stopped trembling about halfway through making her trademark macaroni and cheese casserole, which Winston had tried and approved to the admiration of Teddy's cousins, who sorely needed a dog of their own.

'Where is Winston?' Charlotte said, chin propped on her hand.

'Sleeping with Teddy. Is it okay with you, that he's up on the bed?'

'Sure, this is a dog friendly household. I was just thinking, you know, how he wouldn't get out

43

of the car. Before. At that house.'

'*That house?* Charlotte, that house was your home for the last, what, twelve years?'

'I know. Are you sure you want to move in there?'

'Charlotte, I grew up there, it's my home. Not to mention that it's paid off, there's no mortgage, and I love it there. I get, you know, that Chris died there. I can understand that it brings up bad memories for you.'

'It does. It was so weird. I was going to go in there and clean. Put some flowers in a vase in the kitchen. But when I was all set to go inside ... it was like I panicked. I couldn't make myself go in.'

'Chris died there, Charlotte. Don't you think it's like an association thing? Because bad things happened when you lived in the house?'

Charlotte rubbed her forehead. 'We used to be so happy there. But we've had a bad couple of years.'

Olivia put her palms on the kitchen table. 'Charlotte, were you and Chris getting divorced?'

Charlotte looked up and frowned. 'No, of course not, why would you say that?'

'I just don't get what was going on. Why Chris had you move.'

'Chris was not ... himself. But it wasn't about the marriage.'

'Then what was it about? Charlotte, he lost sixty pounds before he died. When did this thing, whatever it was ... when did it start?'

'When does anything start? It just creeps up on

44

you, that's what it does.'

'Give me your best guess.'

Charlotte folded her hands in her lap. 'I guess ... really, I think it all started with Janet.'

'Janet?'

Chris's oldest daughter. Tall for her age, big boned like Chris, but thin and tiny waisted, where her father had bulk. She had been dry eyed and angry at her father's funeral, the first eruptions of adolescent acne making bumps along her chin.

Olivia took a sip of her wine. 'What did Janet do?'

'Do? What do you mean by that?'

'I'm sorry. I don't mean anything. I don't know why I said it.'

Charlotte ran a finger on the side of the table. 'Janet didn't *do* anything. Janet got sick.'

Olivia gripped the stem of her wine glass.

'It started in the middle of the night. She would get these horrible attacks – high fevers, vomiting. They ran tests and found all kinds of weird stuff. But nothing would really add up. First her liver enzymes were sky high. Then they were normal. Then they thought her gall bladder was shot.'

'At her age?'

'I *know*. And then...' Charlotte put her face in her hands and her voice caught. 'Then a malignant tumor on her liver. Then it was a *pancreatic* tumor. An automatic sentence of death. Chris and I were just ... we were so worried, so scared for her. We were literally just hanging on.'

'But why didn't you tell me?'

45

'We told *no one*. We didn't want to talk about it to anybody until we were sure. And then – then it was nothing at all. All those scary test results were some mysterious mistake. We got a clean bill of health for our little girl. I was so ... grateful. So relieved. I used to stand outside her bedroom door after she and Annette and Cassidy fell asleep, and literally cry from happiness. I thought how good life could be. Back then.'

'And?'

'And ... it seemed to affect Janet. She was *different* somehow.'

'Well, come on, Charlotte, she'd been sick, all those tests.' Olivia gentled her voice. 'No matter what anyone told her, she's a smart girl, maybe she was afraid she was going to die.'

'But that's just it. She wasn't afraid *she* was going to die. She was worried about everybody else. And it wasn't just Janet. It was Chris. *He* was more affected than anybody. He stopped sleeping. Stopped eating. Started having dreams, horrible dreams, about – how did he put it? *Something evil sitting on his chest*. And he would wake up choking, saying he couldn't breathe. I thought it was some kind of stress reaction. I dragged him to the doctor, they tested his heart. Everything was normal, everything was fine. But he was so different. Our little girl wasn't sick anymore, but instead of feeling the joy he was so ... sad. He started losing weight. And then Janet started having nightmares, terrible terrible dreams that made her scream. She said someone was watching her. That it whispered to her when she was alone. It got so bad that she was afraid to go to sleep. She said if she didn't keep watch, something bad was going to happen. First it was the fish. She was convinced that something was going to kill all the koi in the pond. And then the fish died. All of them. Just like Janet said they would.

'And after that she started worrying about Annette. She could not sleep, she had to do certain things, or something awful would happen to her little sister. She was frantic some nights sitting up in her bed, rocking back and forth, trying to stay awake.'

Olivia put a hand on Charlotte's arm. 'Don't you think it might have been some kind of aftershock, from being so sick, having to go to the hospital for all those tests? From being afraid she was really sick, that she was going to die?'

Charlotte nodded. 'I did think that. For a while. I wanted to take her in for counseling, but Chris said it wouldn't do any good. He stopped talking to me, he just kept losing weight, then ... then one night, we were all asleep, and the attic fan came on. It was so weird. It switched on all by itself in the middle of the night.

'We were all creeped out, but Janet was *hysterical*. She said it was some kind of a warning, and something was going to happen that was really bad. That there were voices that told her horrible things when she was alone. Chris sat up with her all night, she didn't want me, just her dad. Janet said that only her father understood. And he held her, and told her over and over that it was just a glitch in the electrical switch of the attic fan, that she was not to worry, that he would

47

take care of things, that everything would be okay. The next day he went out and found us this house. And he made us move.'

'Did he explain at all?' Olivia said.

'He said he was a danger to us. Which was crazy, it didn't make any sense. And when I tried to push him on it he ... he *cried*.'

'Chris never cried,' Olivia said flatly. 'Not even when he was ten years old and dropped a manhole cover on his foot.'

'He cried, Livie. So I said fine, we'll all go together. But *he* wouldn't come with us. He said he had to deal with things. That afterwards, we could all live together again.'

'After what?'

'*He never would say.*' Charlotte ran a hand through her hair.

'And Janet? Is she okay now?'

'She's fine. Perfect health, no more nightmares. The only thing is when we were at the visitation, right before Chris's funeral. I found her in a corner, by herself, crying, and she told me it should have been her who died.'

Olivia put her arms around Charlotte and gave her a long hard hug. 'Charlotte, what a terrible terrible thing for all of you to go through. No wonder you're upset. No wonder you can't bear to go inside that house.'

Charlotte pulled away. 'Chris was so happy when he found out you were coming home to Knoxville. He was so upset when you and Hugh got divorced, so worried about you on your own, and losing your job. I know you were worried about him, I know you were coming home to

48

look after Chris, but *he* wanted to look out for you. He'd want *me* to look out for you too.'

'Which you're doing, Charlotte. By letting us stay with you till we get moved in. By offering to pick Teddy up after school when you get your girls, and letting her stay till I get off work. You have no idea what a relief it is for me, to have family here, and not be so alone.'

'It's a relief for me too. I'm so glad you came home, Olivia. It helps to have someone here who misses Chris like the girls and I do.'

Olivia nodded and smiled and thought about the phone call. She had always planned to tell Charlotte about it, thinking it would be a comfort, but that would have to wait. Her sister-in-law was too emotional, too frayed, too raw. Charlotte might look okay on the outside, but clearly, she was still a mess.

'Listen to me, now, Charlotte. Before Janet got sick, were you and Chris okay? Were you happy in that house?'

Charlotte looked very tired. 'Yes, we were, and I get what you're telling me.'

'You had a rough year. Your daughter got sick. Your husband died. It isn't the house, it's just ... life. Don't forget I grew up there. That for me, it's my childhood home.'

Charlotte cocked her head to one side. 'Were you never afraid there, when you were a little girl?'

'Never. Not once.'

SIX

Olivia spent the next week moving into the house, getting acclimated to the new office, and, in the little spare time she had, roaming the city like a ghost, haunting her past life. In the evenings, just before dinner, after she picked Teddy up from Charlotte's house, they would take small detours into the past on their way back home. Standing on the sidewalk in front of the Bearden Kroger's with a little half smile, telling Teddy how her family had done the weekly shopping there every Friday night, buying sausages in the deli, and each of them picking out their favorite box of cookies. Chris, invariably, Pecan Sandies, Emily, the powdery white wedding cookies, Olivia always dithering between Oreos and Devil's Food.

She took Teddy down to the river and showed her the tree where she'd gotten stuck when she was four, the hood of her little blue jacket caught on a branch while she dangled what seemed an enormous distance over the ground. Olivia had loved trees then and she loved trees now, and she had always been better at climbing up, and bad at climbing down. She had driven her siblings crazy on walks in the park, insisting on hugging her favorite trees.

Chris had pushed at the bottom of her little red

Keds – even then she had loved red best – threatening to dislodge her hood from the branch and catch her when she fell, but she had not cried. Nor had she threatened to *tell*, the usual power base of the youngest child. She was not above such things, but she was not stupid, and crying or telling would mean that the next time something interesting happened, she might get left behind. Her mother swore her first word had been *mine*, the second *move*, and her first sentence *wait for me*.

With the carefully honed wisdom of the baby child, Olivia had simply said she was fine where she was, thank you very much, and clasped her hands, and sung quietly to herself, until Chris had finally climbed the tree, grabbed her roughly around the waist, and passed her down to Emily. They kept it to themselves, the three of them. Even in those days, when children were left to themselves in cars while their mothers shopped and allowed to roam the neighborhood, they were not supposed to be in the park.

There were strangers in the park. *The Mister Man.* The childhood bogey who had come true one day and taken Emily away.

Far from being bored with these mundane nostalgic trips, Teddy egged Olivia on, so that each night they arrived home later and later. Almost as if Teddy dreaded going home.

At night, after Teddy went to bed, and sometimes, quite honestly, at the office when she was supposed to be doing her work, Olivia roamed the Internet, haunting the paranormal websites. She found a wealth of phone call incidents, personal accounts of relatives calling after they were dead, some of it linked to electronic voice phenomena, most stories more comforting than anything else. Whether you believed them or not, the calls seemed to be about telling people that death was not the end, that their loved ones were somehow still close.

Olivia knew that she was one of legions of people roaming the Internet late at night, paying psychics for readings, talking to priests, haunting bookstores and libraries, all of them wanting the same thing – relief from a pain that stretched on forever, some alternative to the brutal severing of someone you loved from your life, an unwillingness to accept how bad it could all feel. The research was dangerously seductive. It felt more important than the drudgery of day in and day out things. Olivia had spent more hours than she liked to tally up, reading story after story, crying a little over the grandmothers who reached out from beyond the grave to troubled teenage grandchildren, the aged parents who sent comfort from the afterlife to grown children in stress. The children who had died but wanted their parents to know that it had been their time and their plan, and they would all be together some day. Those were the stories Olivia liked reading. She hadn't run across any stories about a warning call from the dead, though she had not tried all that hard. Having that call from Chris, knowing he was somehow and some way okay, had given her a peace she had not thought pos-sible. Peace was all she wanted right now, she craved comfort and nothing else.

Olivia found the holy water after they'd been in the house for a week, when she was down in the basement, changing over the laundry.

The basement was the only part of the house she hated. Footsteps echoed on the backless, dirt encrusted steps. The light switch was weirdly located halfway down the wall, the traditional horror story naked bulb hanging from a wire in the center of the room. Orange rust stains on the floor let you know where the water trailed in during heavy rain, and the heating and air unit was older than God, with a metal filter she would have to take out and wash by hand.

The layout was a maze of half walls put up by Chris and her dad many years ago, when the foundation started to sag, creating crawl spaces and dark corners. Chris and Charlotte had left a variety of junk, including an old washer and dryer that weren't hooked up to anything, but created a nice ambience along the back section of the wall.

Olivia had her back turned when a stack of boxes toppled and fell with a crash, three of them splitting open and spewing her collection of old tax records onto the damp concrete floor. Something had broken, Olivia heard the shatter of glass.

She stared at the boxes, and set her laundry basket of dirty towels on top of the washing machine.

'Mommy, are you okay?'

Olivia jumped and looked up. 'Teddy? What are you doing down here? I thought you were in

53

the backyard, with Winston.'

'I was.'

'I didn't even hear you come down.' Olivia looked at her daughter, who pushed her glasses back up on her nose and clasped her arms behind her back. 'Why were you rooting in those boxes? Those are old financial records, you don't need to be getting into those, and now look at this godawful mess. And I am sick and damn tired of packing and unpacking boxes.'

'*I didn't do it,*' Teddy said.

Olivia put her hands on her hips. Closed her eyes and counted to ten.

'I think something broke,' Teddy said in a soft little voice, bunching the hem of her shirt in a fist.

'I heard it,' Olivia said.

She headed for the mess, looking for the shine of broken glass. The movers had stacked the boxes neatly on wood pallets, in the only corner of the basement that was swept clean. Olivia saw the wet spot near the water heater, and saw the glint of a thick shard of glass. She crouched down to take a look.

The boxes had knocked over a jam jar of clear water someone had set behind the stairs. The front of the jar had a label on the front where someone had handwritten *Holy Water*.

Olivia sat back on her heels. She was not a Catholic, and as far as she knew, neither were Charlotte or Chris. It was a nervous thing, finding this jar of holy water hidden away in her basement. Who would put it there, and why?

'What broke, Mommy?'

54

'Nothing. Have you finished your homework, Teddy?'

'Everything but math.'

'Then go and do the math.'

Teddy trudged away, then sat down heavily on the bottom step and put her head on her knees.

'What's the matter, Teddy? It's okay, I'm not mad at you about the boxes.'

'It's scary here, without a daddy in the house.'

'Why don't you get your homework finished, and then call your dad?'

'Janet says this house is *haunted*. Janet says it's not safe.'

Olivia gritted her teeth. 'Janet is telling you stories to scare you, which is mean, but it's something big kids do. I'll talk to Charlotte and make her stop.'

'I didn't touch those boxes, Mommy. There was no reason for them to fall down. Are you scared here, Mommy?'

'No, I am not.'

SEVEN

When Olivia tried to kiss Teddy good night, Teddy pushed her away.

'No good night kiss?' Olivia asked.

'You think I knocked those boxes over, don't you? You think I tell lies.'

'And do you?' Olivia heard her phone ringing

downstairs. 'We'll talk about this later,' she said, running down the steps. Since the mysterious call from Chris, she had been frantic not to miss a call. Her phone was on the table in the sun-room, Amelia's number on the caller ID.

'Amelia,' Olivia said.

'You sound out of breath.'

'I had to run for the phone. Is everything okay with you? How's Marianne holding up?'

'She's losing ground inch by inch, but they're still keeping her propped up. How is it going for you?'

'Bad day. Teddy told me a lie about knocking over some boxes, and she's upset anyway – her cousins are telling her creepy stories about the house.'

'That's mean.' Amelia sounded distracted.

'What's up with you?' Olivia said.

'The thing is, I've been doing more research. On phone calls. Like you got from your brother.'

'Yeah, me too. Are you as obsessed with this as I am? I'm spending way too much time on the Internet with this.'

'Did you find the one about the Metro link crash?'

'No.'

'Okay, listen. Do you remember when that Metro link commuter train in LA collided with the freight train? It was 2008, September, I think.'

'Oh, God yes, the Chatsworth crash. Didn't you go into the ER that night?'

'Yeah, everyone did who could. There are only two trauma centers in the San Fernando Valley,

56

and they were swamped. Twenty-five people were killed in the crash, something like a hundred thirty injured.'

'I remember that. The engineer missed a signal, right, because he was texting?'

'Who knows what really caused it. The thing is – there was this passenger on the train – he worked for Delta in Salt Lake City, and was in Los Angeles for a job interview, because his fiancée lived in California and he wanted a transfer. She was actually on her way to pick him up at the Moorpark Station when she heard about the crash.'

'God. How terrible.'

'He called her, Livie. It's all documented. He had two grown sons, and his family was together waiting to find out if he survived the crash. We're talking about a fiancée, two sons, a brother and sister, stepmom. The first call was to the fiancée, I think.'

'The *first* call?'

'The caller ID showed this guy's number. And when his fiancée answered, all she could hear was static. And then one of the sons gets a call. Then all their cell phones start ringing and eventually all of them get calls. They try to call him back, because all they get is static on the line, but when they call back, the calls just go to voice mail.'

Olivia shivered. Please tell me this ends well, she thought. 'So he was injured then? Calling for help?'

'That's what his family thought. So they get with the rescue workers, who start tracing the signal from his phone, trying to locate him in the wreckage. It's carnage there, remember. The emergency services are overwhelmed. But for a period of eleven hours, this family keeps getting his calls. Thirty-five calls in all, Livie, all documented. Then at three twenty-eight a.m., all the calls stop.'

'Did they save him?' Olivia said.

'They found him one hour after the calls stopped, twelve hours after the crash. According to the coroner, he died instantly, on impact – the Metro link engine car got shoved back into the first passenger car, he never had a chance.'

'Are you telling me he was dead when he made the calls? Because maybe he was hurt and called till he died, or somebody else was using his phone.'

'Nope. They traced the phone signal to where his body was, in the first car, so nobody else had the phone. And the autopsy confirmed that he wasn't alive after the crash. All of the calls came in after he died.'

Olivia paced the living room. 'I don't know, Amelia. It sort of has that urban legend flavor.'

'Look it up yourself. I found stories in the *LA Times*, and the whole incident has a *true and authenticated* status on SNOPES.'

'SNOPES?'

'That website, Livie. You know, the one that checks out urban legends and those dumb-ass warning emails people forward. But they authenticate this story. And I think this guy was trying to tell his family goodbye, that he loved them and all that jazz.'

Olivia sat down. 'Yeah, I hear you. And I do think you're right – I've been doing my own research and I can believe he was telling his family that he was somehow okay, trying to comfort them and give them peace. Don't you think that's why Chris called? To comfort me, and let me know he's okay?'

'Partly. But he was warning you too, Liv.'

'Yeah, I know, you told me, and I wish you'd just let it go.'

'Let it go? Don't go into that southern denial thing, Livie. Think about what he said – The Mister Man. That was your nickname for who-ever took your sister, twenty-five years ago. Maybe he's around.'

'After twenty-five years? You know what, Amelia, I don't tell people about Emily, and this is the main reason why. To you, it's a scary story, to me it's real life and real hell.'

'That's not fair. I *do* understand. And I'm a good enough friend to tell you what you *need* to hear instead of what you *want* to hear.'

'The Queen of Tough Love. If you want to be a good friend, Amelia, don't bring Emily up again. It's private and it's painful and unless you've been through it you can't know anything about what it's like.'

'Oh, come on, Livie. When you ask me about Marianne, do I rub your nose in that *nobody knows how I feel* kind of shit?'

Olivia's voice went small. 'No.'

'Sorry. Really, I'm sorry, I didn't mean to be such a bitch.'

'It's just – I'm finally home, okay? And it feels

59

good for me here. I just want to be happy, I'm not looking for trouble. I've got my hands full making a living and raising my kid. Things are looking better for me. Or are you going to tell me I should never have come home?'

'No, that's *not* what I'm saying. The call from Chris came when you were in California, remember? It would have happened no matter where you live. I just wish I understood what your brother meant, don't you? Doesn't it worry you at all? And hearing about this Metro link thing – it just makes it feel more real. More like you better pay attention. The phone call *was* a warning, Olivia. Don't turn your back.'

'Fine, then, Amelia. What is it you suggest I do?'

'I don't know.'

'Exactly. I just need to remember not to be happy because something bad is going to happen and I better watch out. That sum it up?'

'I'm not saying don't be happy.'

'Well, hey. Thanks for that.'

EIGHT

Olivia was restless after Amelia called. Upset over their fight.

She went to the kitchen to unpack a box, but found she did not have the heart or the energy to open it up. She opened the refrigerator and looked inside. Nothing interesting to eat.

Finally, she went to the sunroom, opened her briefcase and fired up her laptop. It was dark out, lights from houses down the block reflecting in the window panes. She wondered why Chris and Charlotte didn't have any blinds or curtains or shutters in the sunroom. Of all the rooms in the house, this one had the most charm. Olivia wasn't quite sure why she didn't spend more time here. It had been the heart of the house, when she was a child.

She took her laptop and curled up on the couch in the living room, where all the windows were tightly shuttered. She felt more private here, more safe. In the sunroom she felt watched.

She pulled up a search engine, and entered *phone calls from the dead* plus *warnings*. She looked over her shoulder, while the screen began to fill, and tapped a finger on the edge of the keyboard. She wasn't sure she wanted to do this, look at her brother's phone call this way. But Amelia, annoying as she was, definitely had a point. Maybe she was hiding in southern denial.

Olivia looked over at the fireplace mantel, at the picture of Chris and Charlotte and all three of his kids. An old picture, Cassidy was just an infant. The picture had actually been taken here, in front of the fireplace, and Chris looked happy, unshadowed. God, she missed him. They had had the usual family squabbles and irritations, but there was no one quite like a sibling, someone who had lived so much of your life. So easy to ignore a big brother when you lived hundreds of miles away. To take for granted that you could visit, share a meal, go for coffee and talk. Little things you never thought about until you couldn't do it anymore, and then they seemed more important than anything else in the world.

Thinking about the afterlife and ghostly visitations was fine, Olivia thought, as long as the thoughts and experiences were good. As long as the experience was a spiritual comfort.

When it went south to the dark side, Olivia wasn't sure she wanted to know. She had enough problems just dealing with everyday stuff.

But she went to the search engine, and found a chat room, not joining or signing in, just lurking, reading old posts that came up under *warnings from the dead.*

TORN & IN LOVE (posted eighteen months ago): But he's perfect. I never expected to find a man like this. My daughter lives in San Francisco, but she came down for Easter, and they hit it off. He charmed her, that's for sure. He never loses his temper, like my first husband. He cares about me. I've been happier the last six months than ever in my life. I can't help feeling like I deserve a man like this. I can't imagine not having him in my life. It would be crazy to throw a relationship like this away, over something this, well, vague.

WORRIED IN PHOENIX: But TORN, when your mother called you, did she actually use his name?

TORN & IN LOVE: Yes. That was what's got me so scrambled up inside. She said 'stay away,' then there was static, and then she said 'Clark.' And I know it was her voice, it was unmistakable.

She sounded good, she said she loved me. God, I miss her so much.

WORRIED IN PHOENIX: How long has your mother been dead?

TORN & IN LOVE: Two years last Christmas.

WORRIED IN PHOENIX: You can't be sure what she meant. With the static and all. Maybe you should just go slow with the relationship, sort of keep a watchful eye.

TORN & IN LOVE: Yes. That's good advice. The thing is, he's asked me to marry him. He got me a ring. He has this whole destination wedding-honeymoon planned, and my God, it's so cold here, I'd go to Jamaica with him just to get warm.

WORRIED IN PHOENIX: You should come live here in Phoenix, you'd have all the warm you want. Where are you?

TORN & IN LOVE: Vermont. It's still snowing at the end of April.

Olivia kept scrolling. Nothing else from *TORN & IN LOVE.* She pulled up a new search window and typed in various combinations of *Vermont, Clark* and *weddings.* Nothing. Well, women rarely put a wedding notice in the paper for a second marriage later in life. No surprise. On a whim she added *San Francisco,* hoping for some smalltown newsy item that included a daughter coming in for a wedding from out of town. She came up with a notice then – but not a wedding announcement. An obituary from the *Burlington Times.*

Burlington, May 21st: Juliana Hargreaves Cavannaugh, aged forty-nine, known to friends and family as 'Jules', died yesterday of an apparent heart attack in her home. Her body was discovered at 2:00 PM by her husband, Clark Cavannaugh, who returned home from work concerned when Mrs Cavannaugh did not show up for a lunch date the couple had planned. Mr and Mrs Cavannaugh had recently been married at a destination wedding in Ochos Rios, Jamaica, returning from their honeymoon just one week ago. Visitation will be held from four to six tomorrow, at the Grayson Funeral Home, with burial at the Burlington Cemetery on Tuesday, at 3:00 PM. Ms. Cavannaugh is survived by her husband, Clark, a daughter and son in law, Mr & Mrs Vaughn Melrose of San Francisco, and two grandchildren, Cary and Silas, aged six and three.

Olivia set the laptop on the coffee table, and put her head in her hands, feeling sick to her stomach and sad. There was no doubt in her mind that *TORN & IN LOVE* was dead. She had a name now, Jules, and she was a presence in Olivia's mind now, whether she liked it or not.

Juliana Hargreaves Cavannaugh had received a phone call from the dead too – a warning call, told by her mother to *stay away* from *Clark*. Now she was dead, one week after marrying the guy. Had Jules somehow been murdered by this Clark, who had given her a drug or something to fake a heart attack? Olivia would never know. There was nothing she could do for Juliana, who was now dead, no way she would know for sure if it was at the hands of her new and perfect husband, Clark.

But the lesson was there. And Chris had told her to be careful of the mysterious *Mister Man*. Shit. How exactly was she going to do that?

NINE

Olivia's work day was a total loss. One canceled appointment, a lot of phone calls that brought her annoyed customers and no sales. Her mind had not been on the job, her thoughts divided between warning phone calls from beyond the grave, and, on the practical side, how she was going to approach Charlotte about Janet telling Teddy scary stories about the house. She considered what she was going to say as she passed through the second light on Ebenezer, on her way to pick Teddy up. She was threading the suburban maze when her cell phone rang.

As always, now, she tensed, but it was Hugh's name that came up on the caller ID. She hesitated, then said hello, pulling to the side of the road. She was not one of those people who could talk and drive at the same time. Not when the caller was her ex-husband.

'Olivia? Look, is this a good time for you? Are you somewhere private, where Teddy can't hear?'

The hum of the car's air conditioner was noisy. Olivia shut the engine down. It was a hot day, the car full of afternoon heat, and the coolness seeped quickly away.

'What is it, Hugh? Is something wrong?'

'That's what I was going to ask you. I have three missed calls from Teddy today, and a weird text message, all between eleven fifteen and noon. Is she sick? Did she go to school?'

Olivia knew that tone of voice. She could picture Hugh, running a hand through the thick, graying black hair, pacing and light on his feet like a thoroughbred horse, nervous energy to spare. 'Of course she went to school, and no she's not sick. That's her lunch break, eleven fifteen.'

'Surely you're not letting her have the phone at school?'

'*No*, Hugh, I'm *not*, but I'm not in the habit of searching her backpack, either, every morning before she leaves. What do you mean by a weird text?'

'It said, let me see, I wrote it down. It said *provoking malign troubles.*'

'What? That doesn't make any sense.'

'No, and it doesn't seem like something an eight year old would say just out of the blue. I wondered if maybe someone got hold of her cell phone.'

'I don't know. I'll check. Look, Hugh, I know your heart was in the right place, but the phone thing just isn't working out. She's too young for a cell phone.'

'Yes. That was a bad call. Look, let me be the bad guy on this, since it was my idea. Have her call me tonight and I'll tell her we decided together to take the phone away. I need to talk to her anyway, she was pretty keyed up last night when we talked. Are things going okay at the new school?'

'She seems to be settling in pretty well – better than usual.'

'She seemed really upset last night on the phone.'

'She was mad at me. We had a little incident in the basement, did she tell you about that? She knocked over a stack of boxes, then lied and said she didn't when I bit her head off over it.'

'Well, you did the right thing, calling her on it. This lying thing will probably get worse before it gets better. We're going to have to tough this out.'

'Yes, my thoughts exactly.'

'I take it you're sure she lied?'

Olivia unclipped her seatbelt and twisted in her seat. 'No, I'm not *sure*, but she was standing right there, and there was no reason for those boxes to go over.'

Hugh sighed. 'I miss you guys, Olivia. I wish to *God* I'd taken that job in Knoxville. I get that I made a mistake.'

'A mistake? How about a *betrayal*.'

'Yes, all right, a betrayal.'

'On so *many* levels, Hugh. I moved with you God *knows* how many times, and when you had the chance, when we could have come home, all of us, together—' She choked on it. She always did. 'You betrayed me and violated my trust.'

'And I've apologized a million times. But in my defense, Olivia, don't you remember when we first got married? You couldn't wait to get out

67

of that town. You said it oppressed you there, you wanted to be free.'

'What are you talking about? Free of what?'

'Oh, hell, you know. The family. The past. Whatever.'

'That's not an excuse for deceit, Hugh.'

'No, of course not. I don't want to fight about this, Olivia.'

'And anyway, that was years ago, Hugh. Years ago. You know damn well I changed my mind. Sometimes you have to leave your home to appreciate what you've got.'

'Yes, yes, I know, you're right. I should have taken the job, or at the very least, discussed it with you when they offered.'

'We might still be married if you had.'

'And we might still be married if you hadn't read my emails.'

'I don't want to talk about it anymore.'

'I'm still sorry, Olivia. About that, about all the constant moving.'

'I'm a big girl, Hugh. I could have said no.'

'Look, about Teddy. Something she said last night really bothered me. Is there any good reason she's *afraid* to go to sleep?'

'She actually said that to you? That she was afraid to go to sleep?'

'Yes. I didn't know if she was just, you know, being dramatic and up to her tricks. But she seemed so sincere. And I wondered if it might be something to do with your brother. Him dying in the house.'

'That, and maybe one of her cousins. Saying things to scare her. Listen, Hugh, what about

68

Teddy coming to see you in California for Labor Day? That would give her something to look forward to, a familiar place to go, to see her old friends.'

'I won't be here. I was going to tell you. I've accepted a job in Seattle.'

'You're moving again?'

'Yes.'

'Of course you are. Goodbye, Hugh. I'll have Teddy call you before bedtime. On *my* phone. I'm taking the other one away.'

TEN

There were no blinds or curtains to block out the sun on the Palladian window in the living room of Charlotte's L-shaped house. The garage doors were open, Charlotte's Honda SUV on the left, and Chris's Ford Explorer on the right.

Olivia pulled into the driveway, left her briefcase on the front seat, and paused by her brother's car on her way up the walk. She ran a finger across the layers of pollen and dust on the hood. Her brother's UT ball cap was still on the dash.

For some reason, the orange appealed to her. Olivia had opinions about color, and she went through phases. Although all the clothes she owned, except blue jeans, were always either black or white. Just lately she had been attracted to the color of Italian blood orange. It felt like the onset of a completely new phase.

She was on the front step when she heard soft sobbing coming from an open bedroom window in the front of the house. She frowned, and rang the bell. Saw Charlotte, through the window, motioning her to come in.

'Maybe I lived in Los Angeles too long, but you ought to keep that front door locked.' Olivia set her purse down in the hall and kicked off her shoes. Several months of unemployment meant she was going to have to get used to being in heels again, rebuild those calf muscles. She cocked her head to one side. Heard nothing but the faint noise of a television from one of the bedrooms at the back of the house. 'Which kid's been crying? Yours or mine?'

Charlotte frowned. 'I didn't know anybody was crying. I don't hear anything.' She had a pencil tucked behind one ear. She wore khakis today, and an oversized man's white shirt, probably one of Chris's. She worked from home, architectural scut work for the firm that laid her off but kept her going with contract work. 'You look tired. Bad day at work?'

'My assistant is a bitch and the last financial advisor left the clients in a mess, but God am I glad to have the job.' Olivia unbuttoned the snap on the side of her skirt. Her work clothes had gotten mysteriously tight.

Little girl screams brought Charlotte's head up. 'That can't be good,' she said, leading Olivia down the hall.

Charlotte was one step ahead, and Olivia ran behind her, vaguely aware of the short, beige

70

carpeted hallway, the beige walls, the whole beige beige beige that she always hated in every new house she'd ever lived in with Hugh.

They passed Charlotte's bedroom first, door open to reveal a double bed, neatly made, blonde oak furniture, solid and dull, and on the walls, more beige. The next bedroom was painted lavender, and little Cassidy was curled up on a white canopy bed, sucking her thumb, watching cartoons on the television propped on the little white dresser. Olivia curled her lip. She refused to allow Teddy a television in her room, and she had a horror of pastel walls.

The screaming stopped.

The door to the third bedroom was closed. No noise, no light. Charlotte opened the door.

Three little girls were sitting in a circle, holding hands, a lit candle flickering, next to Teddy's pink cell phone. Teddy's face was tear streaked, and her cousins, Janet and Annette, looked solemn and wise.

'What's going on here?' Olivia flipped on the light.

'*Mommy.*' Teddy, the baby of the group, scrambled to her feet, and grabbed Olivia around the waist.

Charlotte snatched the candle up and blew it out. 'Janet, what the hell are you doing? Where did you even get matches? What are you girls doing with a candle burning? You know better than that.'

Annette pulled her knees to her chest, pushing hair from her eyes with trembly fingers. 'You got to have a candle, it's a seance.'

Charlotte opened the blinds that were shut tight against the light, and closed the window, snapping the lock. 'A seance? Are you kidding me? Why were you screaming?'

Teddy looked up at Olivia. 'Janet says our house is haunted. She says the house killed Uncle Chris. She says we have to stay *here*, because it's not safe to go home. We need to go and get Winston, Mommy, he's there all alone.'

'*Janet*,' Charlotte said. 'How could you?'

Janet straightened her back and folded her arms. Her hair looked oily and unwashed. Unhappy girl, Olivia thought. Unhappy and angry and sad. She needed to be patient with Janet. Chris's little girl who had almost died.

'It's *him* again, Mama,' Janet said. 'It's just like I told you. He's after Teddy now. He'll get her, too, if we don't watch out. Once he starts watching you, it's hard to make him go away. So we were asking Daddy to come and help. But Daddy didn't come. *He* came instead.'

Charlotte pressed both hands down on Janet's shoulders. 'I cannot believe you would pull something like this after everything we've been through.'

Olivia watched her niece, waiting for the tears. There were none today and there had been none at Chris's funeral. Nothing but pale, thin-lipped anger.

'I'm not pulling anything and I didn't make it up. Somebody has to take responsibility here. Somebody has to fight back.'

'*Janet*.'

'He was here. He texted us. Look at Teddy's phone.'

Olivia folded her arms. 'I don't know about you, Charlotte, but I'm feeling old. Remember the good old days when people used a Ouija board for this stuff?'

'This isn't funny, Livie.' Charlotte had the phone and she was pushing buttons, studying the screen. Olivia put a hand on Teddy's shoulder and looked over Charlotte's shoulder.

I AM HERE

daddy? ??? who r u?

DL I AM HERE

what u want

THERE IS ALWAYS REPRISAL THERE IS ALWAYS REPRISAL TORMENTS ILLNESS POSSESSION OF YOUR HOUSE

Vile words, Olivia thought. Vicious, childish and malign. She snatched the phone from Charlotte and looked down at Janet. Her hands were trembling. 'Did you do this, Janet? Did you set this up to scare Teddy?'

Janet folded her arms. And turned her back.

'Charlotte?' Olivia said. 'Will you talk to your daughter?'

Charlotte rubbed her forehead. 'Janet, you and Annette go in with Cassidy and watch TV for awhile. Go, now, we'll talk later on. Olivia. Look, I'm sorry, but I think the best thing right now is for you and Teddy to leave. Teddy, hon, get your book bag, okay, your mom needs to take you home.'

'But we're not safe at home,' Teddy whispered.

Olivia picked up Teddy's book bag and took

73

her daughter's hand. 'Of course we're safe. Your cousins were playing a dirty trick, to scare you.'

Charlotte looked over her shoulder at her daughters, trudging down the hall. 'Olivia, I just – I need to think.'

'Don't worry about it, Charlotte. If you want us to go home, we'll go home.'

'Livie, you don't understand—'

'I understand you've been through a really rough year.' Olivia led her daughter through the house, snatched up her shoes, and paused at the front door, Charlotte trailing behind. 'Teddy, thank your Aunt Charlotte for picking you up from school today.'

'Thank you, Aunt Charlotte.'

'You're welcome, hon.' Charlotte bent down and gave Teddy a long hug. She looked up at Olivia. She was crying and mascara was beginning to run around the edges of her eyes. 'Would you go on and get in the car, Teddy, I want to have a quick talk with your mom. Okay, baby? Good girl.'

Olivia watched her daughter head for the car, clutching her book bag to her stomach, shoulders slumping, chin tucked into her chest.

Charlotte stood up, pushed her hair out of her face. The pencil slid from behind her ear and hit the sidewalk. She did not bend to pick it up.

'Livie, I'm sorry. Really, really sorry.'

'It's okay, Charlotte, just talk to Janet and tell her—'

'No, that's not what I mean. I can't ... I can't have this ... this *business* starting up all over again. Livie, I'm sorry, but this arrangement we made isn't going to work. I won't be able to pick Teddy up from school anymore.'

'*Charlotte.*'

'I'm sorry, please believe me.'

'Fine.' Olivia dug her car keys out of her purse. Her hands were shaking, but she managed to get her sunglasses and the keys, slide those high heels back on her feet. 'Whatever you say, Charlotte. You're right, I won't need you to get Teddy after school. Teddy and I can take care of ourselves.'

'Livie, I'm sorry. I'm so sorry.'

'Stop apologizing, Charlotte.'

'I feel like I'm abandoning you. Please understand I ... I can't let this start up again. I have to keep my children safe.'

'Your daughter needs help, Charlotte. So do you.'

'You're the one that needs help, Livie.'

'*What did you say?*'

'I know you don't believe me. And I'm sorry for you. I am. I hope things don't happen to you the way they did to us. Because once you've seen it with your own eyes, Livie, your life will never be the same.'

Charlotte stepped back in the house and shut the door in Olivia's face.

ELEVEN

It was Olivia, not Teddy, who cried on the way home. Olivia's fingertips trembled on the steering wheel.

'Are you scared to go home, Mommy?' Teddy asked.

'No, I am not.'

'But you're crying.'

'Aunt Charlotte hurt my feelings, that's all.'

'Maybe we're not safe without a daddy in the house.'

'We're safe.'

'But I'm scared. Do you believe in ghosts, Mommy?'

'Sometimes. But the kind of ghosts I believe in are family. I think my mama and daddy are watching over us. And so is Uncle Chris. But that doesn't scare me, that makes me feel safe.'

'Do you think they're in the house?'

'I don't think it has anything to do with the house, Teddy. I just think that when people who love you die and pass over they keep an eye out. To watch over you, like guardian angels. You're not afraid of guardian angels are you?'

'No. Is that what we have in our house?'

'That's what I think.'

'Then we don't need to be scared?'

'No, Teddy, we don't need to be scared.'

Olivia signaled left and turned onto Westwood, then took a right on Sutherland to her childhood home. She put the turn signal on, waiting for traffic to clear before she turned left into the driveway. There was a lot of traffic here now, they'd have to keep a close eye out on Winston and keep him out of the street.

It was full dark now, and the porch light was on and comforting.

Olivia had a sudden memory of herself at Teddy's age, hiding behind the azalea bushes, playing kick the can. There were plenty of good memories here in this house. Lots of happy times. She still had the old Mystery Date game she and Emily used to play. Stuffed in a box somewhere. She and Teddy had been looking for it since the last two moves.

'Teddy, you left your bedroom light on again. I know I told you to turn it off.'

'But I did, Mommy, I checked special before we left.'

Olivia pulled the Jeep up into the driveway that circled the side of the house and parked outside the sunroom window, near the backyard gate. The garage was rotting and unsafe. For now she kept it locked.

Teddy jumped out of the car and ran to the darkened window, rapping on the glass and calling Winston's name.

'Winston, are you in there? Winston, are you okay? I think I see him, Mommy. He has his paws on the glass.'

The light in the sunroom flicked on. Olivia

dropped her car keys. Winston had his nose to the glass, making snout marks, wagging his tail.

Everything was in place. The round black iron table with Italian tile that Hugh and Olivia had bought in Santa Barbara, covered in the yellow cotton table cloth, an open bottle of wine by the fruit bowl, that never held any fruit, just as they'd left it that morning. A charming room. The happiest room in the house.

Teddy was quiet, save for the noise of her deep, panicked breaths. Her hands were fists tucked under her chin.

'Mommy. Do you think a guardian angel turned on that light?'

'You know what I think, Teddy? Here's what I think. I bet your Uncle Chris and Aunt Charlotte had one of those timers set up. You know, the ones that turn lights on and off automatically.'

'Like we had in California? So bad guys won't know when you're not home?'

'Yeah, Teddy. Like that. And when Aunt Charlotte got everything out of the house, she probably just forgot it. Like those plates we found in the cabinet over the refrigerator. Every time you move, you usually leave something behind.'

'Mommy, do you think we should go back to California? Do you think you and Daddy could just make up and get married again?'

'No, honey, we can't. This is our home now, Teddy. Come on, let's hold hands.'

TWELVE

There was a bad moment with the back door when it almost seemed as if the house would not let them in.

Teddy touched Olivia's arm. 'How come the key won't work?'

'It works, hon. Old houses have personalities and so do the doors, so you just have to baby it.' Olivia gave the door a push before she twisted the key, and the lock released. The door was tacky, though, the wood had swelled into the frame, and Olivia had to shove.

The entry way was old warped linoleum, water damaged, avocado green. Olivia went in slowly, inhaling the moldy scent of old house. She flipped the light switch, the illumination so dim it was hard to know if the light was on. Chris and Charlotte had installed energy saving mercury bulbs all over the house, and the lights came on gradually, as if they needed to warm up.

Olivia and Teddy crept hand in hand into the kitchen, like Hansel and Gretel crossing the threshold of the witch's cottage. The kitchen floor was red brick tile, dark with age and old stains in the grout. The appliances were stainless steel, the countertops old yellowed Formica, but the ceilings were white plaster with old beams of wood, Chris had just installed mahogany wood cabinets, and a lovely arched doorway led into the little sunroom that faced the driveway and the side of the house.

Winston rushed them the minute they were through the door, and both Olivia and Teddy were relieved to find that he was quite okay, happy to be hugged and kissed on the head, and ready for dinner after a quick whiz in the yard.

The first thing Olivia did was check the outlets in the sunroom.

'Teddy? Come here and look.'

Teddy peered in from the kitchen, as if she were afraid to come into the room.

'Come on, honey, see that? It's a timer, just like I said. That's why the light came on like that. Okay? Now go take your book bag upstairs, then come back down and feed Winston.'

Olivia turned on the television in the living room, to give the house a sense of mundane normality. She and Teddy liked to watch boxed sets of old television shows, so they could see as many episodes in a row as they liked, with no commercial breaks. Teddy liked westerns and was mad at Olivia for not letting her watch *Deadwood*, because of the cursing. But Olivia stood firm. It wasn't just cursing, it was violence and sex. Teddy was way too young for the good stuff.

Olivia was relieved when Teddy headed upstairs, no protests or hesitation, with Winston right behind, carrying his squeaky yellow chicken. It was not long before the aroma of leftover meat loaf warming in the oven and the scramble of Winston's toenails on the wood floors gave Olivia the sense that they had regained their dull, suburban edge. She and Teddy ate side by side on the couch in the living room watching TV, instead of at the tile table in the sunroom, which is where Olivia had imagined them taking their meals. Comfort was all she wanted. Comfort was easy to achieve.

Teddy took her dirty dishes into the kitchen, scraping her leftover meat loaf into Winston's bowl. The dog hesitated over the catsup, then gobbled the meat and the rest of the kibble in the dish. Teddy was being quiet and obedient enough to make Olivia nervous.

'Bath time,' Olivia said.

'Can I take a bubble bath and read Nancy Drew in the tub?'

Olivia checked the clock on the stove. 'I don't know, Teddy, it's getting late. And I'm not sure the bubble bath is unpacked.'

'I found it in a box in my bedroom. And I got all my homework done. Mommy, please, I've been waiting and waiting to take a bubble bath upstairs, like you and Aunt Emily used to do.'

Olivia nodded. 'I'll get the water running, you get me the bubble bath out of the box. And your homework is done? All of it? Even the math?'

'Even the math. Can we fill the bathtub all the way up?'

Olivia tried not to think about her utility bills. 'All the way up.'

It was the perfect bathroom for bubble baths, and Olivia turned the taps on the claw foot tub and poured in a full cup's worth of Ragin' Cajun

Strawberry Foam. Chris and Charlotte had refinished the tub, and put dark tile down on the floor and in the glassed in shower stall, but been wise enough to leave everything else alone. The mahogany bead board around the pedestal sink was clouded with moisture, as it had been when Olivia was a little girl, brushing her teeth at that very same sink. She sat on the edge of the tub, swirling her hand in the water, encouraging the bubbles, just like her sister Emily had done for Olivia when she had been a very little girl. The candy sweet scent of strawberries filled the room.

Olivia kept an eye out for Winston, who appreciated a nice hot bubble bath as much as she and Teddy did. He had been known to jump into a tub full of water when he got the chance.

'Winston?'

The dog whimpered, and sat at attention in the hallway outside the bathroom door. He turned his head to Teddy, who was wandering naked down the hallway with her nightgown in her hand.

'Is it ready, Mommy?'

'Just be careful, the water's hot.'

Olivia left Teddy soaking with a giant sponge, finishing up *The Whispering Statue*, her latest Nancy Drew. She pushed the overflowing clothes back down in the hamper, and headed for the laundry room.

'Mommy? How come Winston won't come into the bathroom?'

'Hang on, Teddy, I think I hear my phone.'

Olivia let the wicker hamper bump down the

steps behind her, holding onto the rail because the wooden stairs were slippery. She headed for the sunroom, where she'd left her phone. She wondered how long it would be before her hands stopped shaking every time it rang.

The caller ID showed Amelia's number. Olivia snatched a wine glass out of the kitchen, and sat at the sunroom table, filling the glass half full.

'Amelia?'

'Hey, Olivia. I just wanted to call and see if we were still mad.'

'No, I don't have the mind space to argue with anybody right now.'

'You sound funny. You are still mad at me, right?'

'No, honest, I'm just a little shook up. I had a weird run-in with my sister-in-law today. It seems she doesn't want Teddy at her house in the afternoons after all.'

'What, just out of the blue? Didn't she offer to take Teddy after school?'

Olivia took a sip of wine. Told Amelia everything, beginning with Charlotte distraught over the dead fish, and telling her not to stay in the house.

Amelia listened, then laughed.

'You think it's funny? This from the woman who was freaking about warnings from the dead?'

'I'm sorry, Olivia, I know it's not funny, but this is like every stereotype I've ever heard about the south. Holy water in the basement? Really? Is there a picture of Jesus taped to the fridge?'

'If there was, Charlotte took it with her. But

83

don't let that disappoint you. I still drink Jack Daniel's whiskey straight from the bottle, went barefoot as a kid because my parents couldn't afford shoes, and they use rattlesnakes at the Sunday afternoon services at the Baptist church down the road. Oh, and don't forget that I was an unwed mother in a high school teeming with racial unrest, while I lived in a trailer home and fucked my cousins.'

'Just so long as your cousins were cute. Listen, maybe your brother was warning you about his crazy wife.'

'That's not helping, Amelia.'

'Okay, the doctor is in. Tell me about this niece of yours. Janet. How old is she?'

'Going on thirteen.'

'Well, there you go. She's going to be in a bad mood for the next eight years. Bottom line, Livie – your sister-in-law lost her husband, these little girls just lost their dad. They're angry and they're grieving and looking for something, *anything*, to blame.'

'How about scared, Amelia? They were really afraid, Charlotte and Janet both. And it wasn't just this afternoon. They were both pretty strange at Chris's funeral.'

'Think about it, Livie. If somebody you love dies mysteriously in his sleep, you might be afraid it could happen to you. Or your sister or your mom.'

'That's a good point. Though I have to say I agree with you about that SUNDS diagnosis. I don't believe people just die in their sleep. Charlotte says Chris got his heart checked out a few weeks before he died. Maybe it had something to do with that.'

'Look, if it would make you feel better, I can take a look at your brother's medical records and autopsy report. They may be a little tricky to get hold of, you'll have to get Charlotte's permission.'

'I have a friend who might get the autopsy report for me, without going through Charlotte.'

'A *friend* in that tone of voice sounds like a man.'

'Old boyfriend who's a local cop – one of those good old boys who has connections every place you look.'

'*The* McTavish? That one you're always talking about?'

'I'm not always talking—'

'You should definitely give him a call.'

'Why are you whispering all of a sudden, Amel?'

'Little Bit was stirring in her sleep. She's pretty drugged up, but she responds to my voice.'

'Little Bit? Are you in the hospital with Marianne?'

'Just checking in and giving Alexis and Jack a chance to grab a late dinner. It's hard to get them to leave her, even for a second, but they do have to eat.'

'Bad?'

'She was scheduled for surgery this morning, but they're going to have to hold off until her white count goes back up. All I can do right now is sit here and watch her struggle for every single breath.'

'Have *you* had anything to eat today, Amelia?'

'Two hash brown patties from McDonald's for a dollar, it's a hell of a deal. Look, I was thinking about coming out for a visit, Olivia, when things here ... sort out. I could use a break, but I know you're just getting settled in.'

'You're welcome anytime. Always.'

'Thanks, kiddo. In the meantime, get me that autopsy report. Maybe I can figure out something that will make everybody feel better, so the kiddies won't be afraid to go to sleep.'

'I'd sure appreciate it.' Olivia heard noises, coming from upstairs. She put her wine glass down. 'Look, I have to go. Some kind of thumping sounds coming from upstairs, sounds like all hell is breaking loose. Teddy's upstairs taking a bubble bath, so I better go check.'

THIRTEEN

Olivia heard Teddy's voice as she scrambled up the stairs.

'Are you OK, Winston buddy? Are you all right? How is your head, let me kiss it. Good boy.'

The bathroom door was open. A flutter of cobweb hanging from the attic fan in the hallway caught Olivia's eye. The attic fan was the one thing Olivia had never liked about the house. When she was a little girl, she had always won-

86

dered if there was something up there, watching her behind the grill. She thought about Charlotte's story. The attic fan coming on in the middle of the night. Could some kind of intermittent connection cause something like that? Maybe Janet had turned it on herself.

'Teddy? Are you okay?'

Teddy was out of the tub, naked and dripping and squatting beside Winston, who was covered in the chunks, shards and powder of shattered plaster. A two foot square of the bathroom ceiling had caved in, landing right on the dog.

Olivia grabbed a thick white towel and wrapped it around Teddy, pulling her daughter to her feet.

'Don't worry about me, Mommy, worry about Winston. The ceiling caved in on his head and he cried really loud.'

Olivia crouched down to pet Winston. No cuts, no obvious damage, just plaster in his fur. Olivia took a bit of tissue and wiped grit from his eyes. He stood up and shook like he did when he got his bath.

Teddy put her fists up under her chin. 'It's my fault, Mommy. He was scared to come in and I made him and then the ceiling came down on his head. Do you think he knew it was going to happen?'

'Teddy, Winston follows you everywhere, it's not your fault the ceiling caved in. Stuff like that happens in an old house. It usually means a water leak.' Olivia craned her neck and stared up at the ceiling, thinking about the runaway cost of repairs. There was no sign of the telltale yellow discoloration that meant water collecting behind the scenes. Just wood slats and dirt, and an exposed support stud that looked, oddly, as if there were burn marks in the wood.

'Teddy, is that stepladder still in your room?'

'Want me to go get it?'

'No, I will, you get your nightgown on and brush your teeth. And pull the plug in the tub so the water can drain.'

There were still boxes in Teddy's room, and the ladder was in front of the built in bookshelves that Olivia and Teddy had been filling with Teddy's entire collection of stuffed animals and Nancy Drew. Olivia took the ladder into the bathroom, kicking away some of the plaster. She was aware of Winston and Teddy, watching from the hallway, the sound of water draining in the tub.

'Teddy, do you still have that flashlight under your bed?'

'Yes, Mommy. Want me to get it?'

'Please.' Olivia was aware of the patter of bare feet on wood floors, as Teddy ran to her room, and then back.

'Here you go, Mommy.'

'Thanks.'

Olivia pointed the light into the gaping ceiling. The burn marks in the wood were letters. Burned in, like a brand. Some of the edges looked charred, and she thought of fires. Chris had smoke alarms all over the house. Had he been worried about fires?

'Teddy, go back out into the hall with Winston, in case more of this plaster falls.'

'What are you looking for, Mommy?'

'Water leaks.'

'Is that what made the ceiling crash?'

'That's the usual suspect.'

But there was no water, no dampness, no blue black sign of mold. Olivia touched the wood stud, found it dry to the touch. She climbed to the top step of the ladder for a closer look, shining the flashlight to study the burnt letters in the wood. Names. Some of them written sideways, some upside down. Two of the names she did not recognize – *Allison. Bennington.* But the other two she knew. *Emily*, her sister. And *Jamison.* McTavish's cousin who'd suffered a debilitating closed head injury in a car accident, not too long after Emily disappeared.

Olivia played the light up and down the wood. And found one more name, a bit further up. This one looked different. This one looked new. The letters were so deeply branded that she could trace the grooves in the wood. Her brother's name. *Chris.*

FOURTEEN

Normally, Olivia would have called Charlotte first thing to get the name of a plumber, she needed to find someone fast, but she wasn't sure her sister-in-law was speaking to her right now. She was in her office, finding comfort in carbohydrates after five hours spent calling everyone on the client list to introduce herself and say hello. She and Teddy had stopped off at Panera's for breakfast on the way to school, and Olivia had bought an apple pastry for her lunch.

There was precious little comfort to be had. There were a handful of clients who viewed a change in broker as traumatic as a divorce, and enough of them had such an unrealistic view of their investment portfolio that Olivia knew her predecessor had played them and made promises no broker could keep. Now the funds weren't panning out, and she was going to take the blame.

The intercom alert dinged on Olivia's computer.

Message from Robbie: Gentleman here to see you. Want me to blow him off or are you coming out of the cave? I know you didn't want to be disturbed.

Message from Olivia: Name, Robbie? And ask him what he wants and if I can call him back.

A pause. Then:

Message from Robbie: He says he wants a brown eyed girl. Do you know this guy?

McTavish. Olivia fluffed her hair and thought about lipstick. She heard the voice before she'd slipped back into her shoes. He was singing as he thundered down the hallway. He would be, he'd serenaded her with 'Brown Eyed Girl' since the first time she'd turned him down for a date.

'Hey, where did we go? Days when the rains came. Down in the hollow. Playing a new game.'

90

Olivia opened her office door and peered out into the hall.

He still had it. The presence. Barrel chested in the way of ex-football players, thick brown blond hair waving just past his collar, mud green eyes. He wasn't bad looking. But that wasn't what turned heads. Maybe it was the boom of his voice, the way he loved to sing when he couldn't carry a tune, or just the way that he engaged in the moment. When McTavish was smiling, you warmed at the fire.

Confidence, but not ego, not these days, and Olivia knew the secret – the high level of his intellect, the precision of his mind, cloaked by the crowd pleasing athlete, illegitimate, fatherless, everybody's favorite son but no one to call dad. He and his mother shunned by their family because she had not gotten married, not had an abortion, not given up her child, just raised him, quietly, happily, right out in front of God and everybody, putting the lie to the pronouncements of doom.

The family had resisted the curly headed, chubby baby boy who would have toddled happily into their arms. By the time they were anxious to welcome the lauded football player, it had been too late – McTavish had been polite and distant, with everyone except Jamison. Jamison had been his hero, the cousin who loved him with the rough affection of a big brother until the accident, when their roles were cruelly reversed.

'Brown eyed girl,' McTavish said to Olivia, giving her that smile that always made you think he was up to something.

'McTavish,' Olivia said.

He opened his arms and folded Olivia into a hug that almost took her off her feet.

Olivia's assistant, Robbie Arliss, followed down the hallway, and stared at McTavish as if she'd seen him somewhere before. She was tall and rangy, her look more Washington DC and political committees than Steel Magnolia. She'd let her fine soft hair go entirely white, and it aged her. Her face was tan, lined and thin, and she wore the kind of clothes favored by Republicans, right on down to the string of pink pearls. Olivia would bet money that she had a credit account at Talbot's. She was just drifting away when she looked back again at McTavish, and put a hand to her mouth.

'You're Vince Modello.' Robbie put her hands on her hips and actually smiled. *'Vince Modello.* Quarterback for UT.'

'That was years ago, my dear. Today I'm just a lovesick fool.'

'Stop it, McTavish,' Olivia said. 'He's kidding, Robbie, he's not lovesick. He's married.'

McTavish shook his head at her. 'No, ma'am, he's divorced. How about you? What happened to that damn metrosexual from New York?'

'San Diego. Hugh and I got divorced a year ago. I have a daughter—'

'Named Teddy, and an old dog named Winston.'

'Let me guess,' Robbie said. 'High school sweethearts?'

McTavish shook his head as Olivia pushed out of the hug. 'We didn't date until college, after I

92

blew out my knee. Olivia wouldn't go out with football players, no ma'am, she wasn't into jocks. But back in high school, Livie and I had a deal. I wrote her theme papers for English class, and she helped me cheat the math exams.'

'Until I found out he was having Annabelle McClintock do the work. He never wrote a single word. She lived to serve, like all the rest, but if she'd known those English papers were for me, she'd have fired your lazy southern ass.'

McTavish gave Olivia the sideways smile. 'Still jealous after all these years?'

'You wish, McTavish. This is Roberta Arliss, by the way. My office manager.'

'Call me Robbie. I saw every game you play-ed. Still never miss. My husband has box seats.'

Vince shook her hand gently, careful of fragile, bird sized bones. 'You bleed orange then, just like me.'

'So tell me, why does she call you McTavish?'

Olivia did not particularly like being called she. As if she were not standing in spitting distance of them both.

'Only Livie calls me that, and don't bother to ask her why, she won't tell you.'

Robbie edged closer to McTavish, giving Olivia her back. 'You know, Greg always said you should coach, after what happened to your knee.'

'Only in my wildest dreams. I'm pretty happy with Knoxville PD.' McTavish absently touched the back of his belt where Olivia suspected he holstered his gun.

'Still homicide?' Olivia said. Vince's dreams of

93

the military life had died with the knee, so he'd moved on to the next best fraternity of men.

He nodded. 'We've had some bad ones here, Livie.'

'I know. Charlotte told me.'

'You be careful at the house. Crime rate around there is picking up.'

'McTavish, I just moved here from LA.'

He grinned. 'That's a point. So, you got a minute, Livie? I've got that paperwork you asked for.'

'I'm actually on my way over to pick Teddy up from school. She's going to Bearden, can you believe it?'

'Just like you and me.' McTavish glanced at his watch. 'How about I drive you over? That sound good?'

Olivia nodded, fighting the urge to throw herself into his arms and tell him it sounded better than good. McTavish magic. She would have to watch herself with this guy.

FIFTEEN

McTavish was parked out front and Olivia laughed. 'What is it with men and Cadillacs?'

'Yeah, I've turned into an old fart. Is school really out this early?'

'Not for half an hour yet. I just needed to get

94

out of the office.'

'You want to get a cup of coffee?'

'Would you mind if we just go over to the school parking lot and wait? I promised Teddy I'd be there early. She's got some issues with school phobia, and I want to keep her feeling secure until she gets settled in.'

'We'll park right up front, and get in before all the soccer mommies and SUVs.'

The school was no more than a three minute drive. McTavish looked across at Olivia and smiled. 'It's good to see you, babe. Outside of funerals, and all.'

'You too.'

'How are Charlotte and the girls holding up?'

'They're having a rough time. How's your mom?'

'Turning into an old lady. Eating breakfast at Long's everyday.'

Long's Drug Store was known for fluffy pancakes, three dollar breakfasts served on foam paper plates, and their loyal geriatric customer base.

'Hey, be nice. Teddy and I have been there twice.'

'Did you see my mother, adding up her bill with a little calculator, digging in her coin purse for a tip?' McTavish eased the Cadillac into a slot at the front door of the school. He flipped off the engine, then reached for a brown envelope on the back seat. 'This is it, Livie. Chris's autopsy report.'

Olivia reached for the envelope, but he pulled it away. 'First you have to agree to go to dinner with me this week. Some place special, so dress up.'

'Bad idea, McTavish. Considering our history and all.'

He waved the envelope. 'You're the one calling in favors. Come on, Livie. Eleven years is long enough to hold a grudge. Time to let it drop.'

'I don't want to leave Teddy alone.'

'My mom already agreed to come to the house and keep an eye out while we're gone. And you know that even if you don't love *me*, you love my mom.'

'I do love your mom. So long as you get that you're paying, and it's not a date.' Olivia snatched the envelope, and ripped it open. 'I really appreciate this, by the way.'

'Is there something about your brother's death that has you worried?' McTavish turned sideways, draping an arm across the back of the seat, his hand close to the collar of Olivia's blouse. 'Because you want to be careful there, Livie. About stirring things up.'

'Don't choke on it, McTavish, what's on your mind?'

'Just that it was a stroke of good luck, for Chris's wife and kids, having a definitive verdict like this. Your brother's insurance policy was less than two years old, which means it doesn't pay out for suicide.'

'You think my brother killed himself?'

'It crossed my mind. Yours too, right? Isn't that why you wanted the report?'

'Maybe.'

96

'Look, I talked to the ME about it this morning. Unofficially, by the way. He genuinely *doesn't* think it was a suicide.'

'How does he explain the SUNDS thing? I've never heard of it before. My best friend in LA is a PA and she's never seen a case.'

'The ME says he looked into your brother's medical history. Talked to a doctor who treated Chris before he died. Initially, he was looking for heart disease, but when he opened your brother up – sorry – he said his heart was in beautiful shape right up until his death, the arteries over-sized and clear, like you'd expect from someone who had been a nonsmoker and an athlete most of his life. He also said the medical records show your brother lost seventy-six pounds between that last medical visit and his death.'

Olivia nodded. 'I know.'

'So the ME was thinking maybe thyroid or stomach cancer. But there was nothing. Your brother was in good health, other than the strain on his system from the sudden loss of weight. Mainly his gall bladder was about to pop. There was also a huge build-up of cortisol and other stuff – the specifics are there in the paperwork. ME was thinking it looked like prolonged stress and sleep deprivation, which would dovetail with the sudden weight loss. But here's the weird part. According to the records, your brother was diagnosed with night terrors and sleep paralysis before he died.'

'Sleep paralysis? That's a diagnosis?'

'It can be. According to the ME, sleep paralysis can be hereditary. Did anybody else in your

97

family have a history of this sort of thing?'

'Not that I know of. And I don't get how something like that could kill a healthy guy like Chris. I don't even get what it is.'

'The way the ME described it, the victim—'

'Would you mind not calling my brother *the victim*?'

'Sorry. The patient feels awake, but he can't move or talk. The ME gave me a lot of technical blah about *nonreciprocal flaccid paralysis*, but all it means is that the brain prevents a person from acting out their dreams, something or other to do with motorneurons, which is basically a defense mechanism that keeps you from jumping out a window if you dream you can fly. It comes down to this – the patient feels awake, but he can't move or speak. But it's real. What happens is the person wakes up before the brain sends the signal to activate muscle contraction, which means you can't move your body, thus the paralysis. Evidently, it's very common to have hallucinations in this state. The hallucinations can be pretty ... horrific.'

'Horrific?'

'Demons. Ghosts. Satan on your chest.'

'Right. Nightmares, in other words. But that doesn't kill you. My brother is dead.'

'What happens with SUNDS is that things go one step further. The victim has no body movement – extreme muscle atonia is what they call it – and it can get so severe the cardiac muscles and the diaphragm paralyze. And if that was happening to your brother while he was awake, it would explain the histamines they found in the

98

toxicology blood work.'

'Histamines? What does that mean?'

McTavish touched her shoulder. 'When someone dies in extreme pain or fear, the body produces histamines. Think of it as a stress measure of what a person goes through before death.'

'Lay it out for me, McTavish. No pulling punches here. I want to know exactly what it was like for my brother when he died.'

McTavish rubbed his forehead. 'The bottom line is this. Your brother was in a state of extreme fear and agitation right before he died. And while he was lying there paralyzed and afraid, he was experiencing myocardial infarction and severe breathing difficulties. There's no way to tell which killed him first. He either strangled, slowly, or his heart gave out.'

The school bell rang, and Olivia was vaguely aware of the fleeting pause of quiet before the scramble of footsteps.

'Livie? Livie, honey, come on, take deep, slow breaths.'

McTavish was opening the door on her side of the car. Unstrapping her seat belt. Coaxing her to one side and making her put her head between her knees. Olivia heard the mingle of childish voices and the occasional call of an adult until she heard the right flavor of *mom*. She sat up straight.

Teddy was running, holding out an oversized flap of paper that was clearly artwork still damp to the touch. She had that smile that reminded Olivia so much of Emily – if she remembered one thing about her big sister, it was that way

Emily had of tilting her chin, squinting her eyes and letting the smile spread all the way across her face.

'There she is. I noticed it at your brother's funeral, you know? How much she looks like Emily,' McTavish said.

'Yeah.'

'Hey.' He turned to look at her. 'You steady, sweetheart? I'm sorry, I should have handled that better. I've been a homicide cop too long. You going to make it there?'

'Need a minute.'

'Wave at her,' McTavish said. 'That's good. You sit tight, and I'll go round her up.'

Olivia watched them, saw Teddy stop and squint up at McTavish, the sun in her eyes. McTavish pointed at Olivia and she waved again. Something McTavish said made Teddy laugh, then Teddy ran to the car.

'Hey. Kidlet. How was school?'

Teddy was climbing into the back seat. 'You were right, Mommy, it is friendly here.' She looked over the headrest at McTavish. 'Did you know my teacher is a *man*?'

McTavish was climbing back into the car. 'Is he old and ugly and mean?'

'Mr Oswald?' Teddy ducked her head and looked sideways at a boy kicking a soccer ball as he headed toward the circle of buses. 'He's younger than you.'

'*Teddy*,' Olivia said.

McTavish shrugged. 'He must be a baby, then. I'm surprised they let him teach school.'

'He's really good, he teaches us a lot and he

100

makes it fun. And you'll never guess what. The whole third grade is going to do a play. But Annette says Aunt Charlotte won't let her be in it.'

'Your cousin can't be in the play? How come?' McTavish started the car. 'What play are you going to do?'

The Pied Piper of Hamelin. I get to be a rat. The rats are the narrators so it's an important part. I've already learned some of my lines.

'Hamelin Town's in Brunswick.
By famous Hanover city;
The river Weiser, deep and wide,
Washes its wall on the southern side;
A pleasanter spot you never spied;
But, when begins my ditty,
Almost five hundred years ago,
To see the townsfolk suffer so
From vermin, was a pity.'

SIXTEEN

Olivia tried to call Charlotte before she went to bed. She felt bad about their fight, but no one picked up the phone. She left a message, asking Charlotte to call her about hiring a plumber. A mundane request, and a perfect way to break the ice.

Olivia curled up against the pillows, thinking of Chris saying he *paid the piper*. Imagining him lying in his bed in the dark house, afraid and unable to move, strangling in his sleep, the words *hereditary condition* echoing in her mind. She drifted in and out of sleep, until the sound of a barking dog brought her fully awake.

She sat up in bed, listening.

And there it was again. The deep throated huff of a big dog, somewhere close by the house. It sounded like Winston. What was he doing outside?

Olivia sat up, wide awake now, and switched on the lamp by the side of the bed. The bedroom, dormer windows and dark woodwork, was still unfamiliar, but it was her bed, and her lamp. She swung her legs over the side of the bed, and slid as soon as her feet hit the floor. She went down on one knee and grabbed the mattress to break her fall.

The floor was wet. She looked up at the ceiling, thinking there might be a leak. The ceiling was dry. Olivia turned on the overhead light, saw that the water trailed across the room toward the hallway, as if someone had left wet footprints, as if someone had come in from a bath.

She thought about Teddy getting up in the middle of the night, taking a bubble bath, then wandering around the house. Preposterous, but what else could it be? Maybe whatever caused the bathroom ceiling to come down was causing the water on the floor. She would call Charlotte again in the morning about a plumber. Or go on Angie's List and look.

The dog barked again, sounding hoarse and frantic, and Olivia headed out into the hallway, turning on lights as she went. She had left that hall lamp on, hadn't she? Maybe the bulb had burned out.

But Winston was inside, not out, pacing and restless outside of Teddy's room, lifting his head and whining. Teddy's door was closed.

Olivia felt the thump of her heart. 'What's going on, Winston? What are you doing out here?'

Because Teddy always slept with her door open, comforted by the stream of light coming in from the lamp they always left on in the hall. And Winston slept on the bed beside her, taking his half out of the middle. Teddy complained that he hogged the pillow, but Winston had been sleeping beside her since the night they brought him home from the pound.

The door creaked as Olivia pushed it open. It was dark inside the bedroom, the last unpacked boxes stacked in front of the window so that even the moonlight didn't relieve the pitch blackness inside.

Teddy was quiet, and very still and at first Olivia thought she was asleep. Until she saw her daughter's eyes, wide open, shining like a possum's eyes did in the dark.

'Teddy? Teddy, are you okay?'

Olivia hit the overhead light, and felt tears come to her eyes when she saw her daughter move. She wasn't sure what she had thought. Teddy had been so still in her bed.

'Mommy. You came.' Whispering. But wide awake. Teddy's face was pale, her little freckles standing out against the blanched whiteness of her skin.

Winston bounded into the room and jumped up on the bed. Teddy sat up and hugged him and she trembled, though it wasn't cold.

'Teddy, are you sick?' Olivia put a hand to her daughter's forehead. Warmish. Maybe yes maybe no on a fever, possibly something on the way. Which made perfect sense, new school, new germ pool. 'What's going on, Teddy? Why was Winston out in the hall?'

Teddy's lower lip trembled. 'I don't know.'

'What do you mean, you don't know?'

Winston groaned and put his head on Teddy's knee.

'Teddy, don't lie to me, tell me what's going on.'

'I can't.'

'What do you mean, you can't?'

'He won't like it if I tell.'

'He? Who is he? Teddy. Who is *he*?'

'Duncan Lee.'

'Who the hell is Duncan Lee?'

'The one that texted me. At Aunt Charlotte's house, you remember, that day in Janet's room. He talks to me now since you took the phone away. He likes to sit on my bed. But he doesn't like Winston. He says that Winston can't come in my room anymore.'

'Teddy.'

The tears came suddenly, a downpour, and Teddy sobbed hard as Olivia wrapped her in her arms.

'He said something bad would happen if I let Winston come in anymore. He said I had to lie in bed and be still and very quiet and I wasn't allowed to wake you up, or tell you. He said if I didn't do what he said that he would hang Winston from the attic fan with a red leather belt. *Oh, Mommy, I was so afraid.* How did you know? How did you know to come?'

SEVENTEEN

Olivia told herself that she was humoring Teddy when she agreed to take Winston to work the next morning. Her daughter had seemed happy when Olivia picked her up from school, checking carefully that Winston was safe in the car. She had news of Mr Ogden, who had brought in an aquarium and introduced them to a gecko named Eduardo. It would appear that geckos ate crickets and worms, loved honey, communicated with chirps and had special toe pads to help them walk across ceiling tiles. Mr Ogden was very hands on when it came to science.

'Because,' Teddy said, 'Mr Ogden says that science is how you understand the world.'

Olivia looked up from her computer screen at her daughter, who was curled up reading. Teddy's color was good, there was no fever and she seemed her usual self except that she had refused her after school snack. Even McNuggets from McDonald's didn't tempt her.

Olivia's office was shaping up. It was good to have her own desk, photos of Teddy on the wall, and the special client chair that Teddy helped pick out in the far left corner of the room.

Teddy had seemed so afraid, in the night, but back to her usual self today. Was it possible that once her cousin Janet planted the ghost stories in Teddy's mind, she was using them to get attention from her dad?

Olivia knew the attention seeking was fallout from the divorce, but she missed the old Teddy, the quiet child who entertained herself. When she was little she had spent hours quietly coloring, using two crayons only, pink and yellow. Olivia herself had gone through a pink and yellow phase at the same age – she wondered if that kind of thing could be genetic.

She did not like not trusting Teddy, did not like wondering if Teddy was sliding away into lies and drama. Olivia reminded herself that Teddy was only eight years old. That this was the third time she had changed schools. It was the adults who were having the drama. Teddy needed structure, patience, and a firm but loving hand. She needed stability in her life.

Robbie gave them a cold glance from the hallway as she headed toward the shredder in the back.

The figures on the screen began to waver and jump, which always happened when Olivia got tired or stressed. 'Shut the door, will you, Teddy?'

Teddy folded a page of the book and set it on the floor. 'Good idea. That person doesn't like me.'

'What person?'

106

'Mrs Arliss. She gives me funny looks.'

'If she doesn't like it, too bad.'

'Yeah, 'cause you're the boss.'

Olivia smiled but her stomach was tight. She was on very shaky ground. Kids at work were questionable enough, but dogs were strictly against corporate policy, and Olivia wondered if having Winston in the office could get her fired. Robbie had been very unhappy when Winston had chugged through the back door with her that morning, though he had been good as gold and only barked once. Robbie did not seem to be an animal lover. Admittedly, there was a certain amount of shedding, but that was what vacuum cleaners were for. Olivia wondered if putting Winston in a UT football jersey would help.

'Can we go back to California, Mommy?'

'No, Teddy, we live here now.'

'I miss Daddy.'

Olivia nodded. 'I know you do. Why don't you call him tonight, after we get home from work.'

Olivia's cell phone rang.

'Maybe that's Daddy. Maybe he knows I needed him to call.'

'No, it's Dr Amelia. She told me she wanted to talk to you today, when you got home from school.' Olivia handed Teddy the phone.

'Hello?' Teddy stood at attention right by Olivia's desk. 'Yes. Yes. Okay. Uh huh. His name is Mr Ogden.' Teddy turned pink. 'You might say so.'

Olivia wondered what Amelia had said.

'We have a lizard in our class room, his name is Eduardo. No, he doesn't have a last name, or if he does, Mr Ogden didn't tell us. What?' Teddy crossed the room and picked up her book. 'No, it's *The Ghost of Blackwood Hall*, I finished *The Secret of the Old Clock* ages ago.'

Teddy slumped suddenly, shoulders sagging, little tummy poked out. 'No, ma'am. No, ma'am. No, there aren't any red leather belts in the book. *They don't hurt animals in Nancy Drew.*'

Teddy snapped the phone shut and slammed it down on the edge of Olivia's desk.

'Didn't she want to talk to me?' Olivia asked.

'I hung up.'

'*Teddy.*'

Teddy grabbed her Nancy Drew book and threw it at the wall.

Olivia stood up. '*Teddy.* What's the matter with you?'

'You told her, Mommy. You told Dr Amelia about Duncan Lee and she said it was all a dream. It was supposed to be private, just between you and me, and now we're all going to get it, *because he told me not to tell.*'

EIGHTEEN

Tuesday night was the spaghetti special at Naples Italian Restaurant, so Olivia told Teddy they'd have dinner out. It would have been a matter of five minutes to stop at the house and drop Winston off, along with Teddy's backpack, to give Olivia a chance to put on a pair of jeans. But somehow, they didn't. Olivia told herself that her fantasy of cuddly dinners with Teddy in the little sunroom off the kitchen would have to wait until all the kitchen boxes were unpacked, and they were better settled in.

Naples was a block down the road, on Kingston Pike, and their parking lot was half full. Olivia and Teddy giggled about how close the restaurant was. They'd done a lot of driving in LA. They parked the Jeep on the left hand side of the restaurant, and left the windows down a double snout length. Winston seemed content to curl up and sleep and Teddy promised him a share of her spaghetti for later on.

The restaurant was small, and had not changed, which made Olivia feel nostalgic and relieved. This was where she'd celebrated birthday dinners as she grew up, where she and Hugh had their first date. She and Teddy could smell garlic sautéed in olive oil, and freshly baked bread. Wooden booths with red upholstery, darkly papered walls, two tiny alcoves in the corner for private, intimate dinners – a traditional family Italian restaurant right down to the wine bottles along the wall.

Olivia and Teddy slathered herb studded butter on warm bread from a basket, ate spaghetti with meat sauce, and ended by splitting an order of tiramisu. Normally Olivia would have had a glass of Chianti or Shiraz, but for some reason it didn't seem wise. She was glad, later, that she had passed.

Teddy ate a good dinner. Olivia was relieved.

They took the leftovers with them for Winston. But eventually, they had to go home.

Olivia was sure she had left a light on in the kitchen, but the house was dark when they pulled into the drive. The dog was barking again, the one Olivia had heard the night before. Winston stuck his head in the crack of the window and growled.

'Mommy, do you hear that dog? I think he's trapped in that yard, where that house is for sale.'

'Which one, Teddy? There are a lot of houses for sale.'

Teddy pointed. Past the trees to the privacy fence, the tangle of bamboo, honeysuckle and forsythia that shrouded them from the house next door.

Olivia shook her head. 'That house is empty, Teddy, nobody lives there.'

'But listen.'

Olivia stepped out of the car. Teddy opened the door for Winston, who jumped out and headed straight for the woods that divided their yard from the one next door.

'I don't hear it anymore, Teddy. The barking's stopped,' Olivia said.

'But what if the dog is in there, trapped in the backyard?' Teddy pushed her glasses up on her nose and her eyes seemed to glint in the dark.

Olivia had an image of the way her daughter had looked last night, so still and afraid in her room.

'People do that, you know. They move away and leave their animals, I heard it on the news. Please, Mommy. Can't we just look? If they left

110

him in the backyard, he'll starve.'

Olivia left her purse and briefcase on the front seat of the car. The truth was the barking *had* seemed to come from the fenced in backyard. 'Okay. We'll take a quick look.'

Teddy went first, calling to Winston, who led the charge. Olivia lagged awkwardly in her heels. She trudged behind Teddy and Winston, past the koi pond that was now full of dead decaying fish, and the old brick barbecue grill gummed up with the dried, charred remains of cookouts past. Chris and Charlotte had left things in a bad way. Olivia knew she needed to clear things out, but she didn't have the energy right now.

But it reminded her of how things used to be, and she liked thinking about those days, the early ones in particular, when they were all there and safe, Emily, Chris, her mother and father and Hunter the dog. They played Monopoly every Saturday night, and cooked barbecued chicken outside on the grill, and sometimes on cold weekend days her daddy built a fire in the fireplace. The images were good ones, a timeless loop she liked to play in her head.

The *For Sale* sign next door was crooked. It had been up a while. The windows of the house were dark, with the bereft glaze of vacancy, no shutters, curtains or blinds. The grass was high and weedy, wet and itchy on Olivia's ankles. Slats of wood had fallen from the side of the house. Someone had heaped branches and grass clippings in a pile that was too close to the house for the garbage men to pick up.

Olivia hesitated in the driveway. Teddy and Winston charged ahead.

The wood gate that led into the backyard was not locked. It swung inward with ease. A security light on the utility pole in the back made spotlights and shadows. Olivia went in first, with Teddy at her back, and she took Teddy's hand as Winston rushed past them. He covered every inch, running in a zigzag, following scents, nose to the ground, investigating every tree, every dip of ground. The yard was terraced, tangled with neglect, and lonely somehow. There was no dog to be seen.

'I know I heard him, Mommy,' Teddy said.

'I heard him, too. He's just a neighbor dog, honey. Maybe he lives over there,' Olivia pointed. 'Or even across the street.'

'The barking came from here.'

Olivia didn't argue.

'I can prove it. Let's come back tomorrow, when it's daylight, and look for poo.'

'Come on, Kidlet. You need a hot bath and I want to get out of these shoes. OK, Winston, here boy.'

Olivia was careful to close the gate behind them. She noticed, as soon as they turned back for home, the light in the kitchen was on now, just the way she'd left it that morning.

Olivia knew that she was tired. She knew she was stressed. And she knew the house had been dark ten minutes ago when she and Teddy drove up.

Olivia kept an eye on Winston. If someone had broken in, he'd tell her.

NINETEEN

Olivia put it down to imagination, but the house did not seem to welcome her anymore. It seemed distant somehow, and strange. When she looked at the stone fireplace, the wide planked wood floors, the high ceilings in every room, the aura of magic was gone. They were just rooms. Her rooms. As long as she lived.

Winston charged in first, heading for his food bowl. Teddy chucked softly in her doggie voice, and filled his bowl with kibble, then dumped the leftover spaghetti on top. Olivia wondered if Winston would even notice an intruder if there was spaghetti to be had.

'Go get your bath, Teddy. It's almost time for bed.'

'Can I take a bubble bath?'

'Not tonight, Teddy. You need to take a really quick bath and get to bed. It's already a half hour past your bedtime.'

But Teddy did not move. She squatted beside Winston and did not look up. 'Mommy, can we play boat tonight?'

Boat. The game where everyone piled in the same bed, dogs included, and the bed was the boat with water all around.

Olivia rubbed her forehead, wondering how

much sleep she'd get with Teddy in the bed. Then she thought about SUNDS and changed her mind.

'Okay. But you and Winston have to get on the boat ahead of me. You need to get to sleep, and I have some boxes to unpack.'

'Will you run the water for me?'

Olivia looked over her shoulder at Teddy, who was still squatting beside Winston, and would not meet her eye. Clearly, Teddy did not want to go upstairs alone. This whole damn thing was getting out of hand.

'Fine then.' Olivia dropped her briefcase on the sunroom table and kicked off her shoes. 'Come on, let's get moving, and get you tucked into bed.'

Olivia went first up the stairs, but Teddy and Winston scrambled ahead. Teddy was at the turn of the staircase when she stopped and cocked her head.

'Mommy, do you hear that?' Teddy said.

'Hear what?'

The three of them paused on the landing at the top of the stairs, and Olivia flipped the wall switch, felt relief when it actually came on. Teddy took a step forward, but Olivia touched her arm.

'Hang on a minute, Teddy, I do hear it. Did you leave the bathroom faucet running this morning when we left?'

'No, Mommy, I promise.'

Olivia went down the hallway, eyeing the grill of the attic fan. The mercury light in the hallway was dim, but growing slowly brighter. The sound of running water was unmistakable, and the bathroom door was closed. Olivia opened the door. Switched on the light.

The hot water tap for the claw foot tub was turned full blast, and the tub was full but not overflowing, the drain working overtime.

'*Teddy, come in here.*' Olivia twisted the tap shut, and turned to look at her daughter, who hung in the doorway, her backpack sliding down one shoulder. 'Did you do this? Leave the water running all day? Do you have any idea what our utility bill's going to be like? Teddy, we don't have the money for this kind of thing.'

'Mommy, I didn't do it, I promise.'

'Teddy, if you tell me *honest*, then I believe you. But just don't lie. I won't be mad at you if you tell me the truth. Did you leave the water on, Teddy? Just answer me, come on, will you, I'm tired. Did you leave it on or didn't you?'

Teddy would not meet her eye.

'Teddy?'

'I don't remember.'

'You don't remember or you did it and don't want to say?'

'I don't know.'

'I don't know isn't a good answer.' Olivia moved swiftly, so fast that Teddy stumbled backward when she took her arm. 'Look. I just need to know the truth about what happened here. Because either you left the water running or it came on by itself. Are you telling me it came on by itself? Or are you going to tell me *Duncan Lee* did it?'

Teddy folded her arms and stared at the floor.

'Maybe I did do it.'

'*Maybe* you did do it? That's just great. You know what, just brush your teeth. There's not going to be any hot water anyway, so forget the bath. Get your pajamas on and get into bed.'

'Can we ... can we still play boat?'

'*Fine*. Just get on with it, Teddy, I'm tired and I've had a long damn day.'

'You promised I could call Daddy. I need to talk to Daddy *tonight*.'

'*Teddy. Go to bed.*'

TWENTY

The North Shore Brasserie was in an upscale shopping strip off South Northshore Drive. The sign beneath the green awning promised Belgian/French cuisine, and announced a Sunday Brunch, from ten until two. McTavish guided Olivia through the double doors.

The floors were dark hardwood, polished to a shine. A chalk board of features was propped on an easel in front of the bar, which was on the right, quietly elegant, with high wood tables, a granite top, two big screen TVs, and a head spinning assortment of interesting bottles and Belgian beer on tap. A hostess led them to the dining room on the left, settling them at a table/booth combination, comfortably tucked in the far corner of the room.

In Europe, a brasserie meant a working man's price, but Olivia knew it would be just the opposite in the USA. She and Hugh had eaten at countless restaurants like this, but the last two years of financial pressure made Olivia dread opening the menu, even though McTavish was paying and seemed comfortable in his wallet.

McTavish reached across the table, touching her hand. 'You okay?' There was a range of dress in the restaurant, jeans to Ralph Lauren, and McTavish looked good in the starched white shirt and black sweater.

'I'm fine.'

'Uh oh. *I'm fine.* A southern girl's code for anything from I really am happy to fuck you, bud.'

Olivia smiled.

'I like your perfume,' McTavish said.

'Thank you.'

'And your dress.'

Olivia nodded. The dress was an oldie but a favorite. The classic black sheath.

'Do you still turn your nose up at white wine – shall I go ahead and order a red? Or they have some good Belgian beer, if you'd rather.'

'Red wine sounds good.'

He frowned over the wine list. 'South African Shiraz or Spanish Rioja?'

'Shiraz.'

'Thank God. I love a woman who actually has opinions.'

'Then you ought to love me a lot.'

'I do,' he said, smiling.

'Stop,' she told him. Without a smile. 'Remember this is not a date.'

'The duck is good,' McTavish said, always good at disengaging from a fight.

Olivia read the description. *Duck Confit Salado, crispy with lavender honey glaze, mixed greens, roasted baby beets, toasted hazelnuts. Danish blu cheese, raspberry vinaigrette.* 'Is that what you're having?'

'Hard to decide. I think I'll go for the Guinness Braised Lamb. You?'

'The pork.' Two words that did not do justice to *Pork Tenderloin, Flemish style with hard cider and apple soufflé, glazed haricots verts, sauce charcutière.*

'Want to start with the frog legs?' McTavish asked, eyes full of smile.

'Hell, no.'

'Soup?'

'No thanks.'

'Brie? With warm fruit compote, toasted walnuts, and macerated strawberries?'

'I have no idea what a macerated strawberry is, but it sounds violent.'

'Let's order it and find out.'

The waiter was a foodie and he liked to talk, but he was as amusing as he was competent, and Olivia began to relax over Brie and wine.

'This is a wonderful place,' Olivia said. She felt good here. She liked the black and white photographs of Knoxville, the window into the kitchen, the striped upholstery on the chairs. Even French/Belgian restaurants were friendly in Tennessee.

'If I order you something chocolate for dessert,

118

can we finally put our eleven year standoff to rest?'

'So *that's* your ulterior motive. How disappointing.'

He put a hand on her knee under the table. 'Let's say I have two ulterior motives tonight.'

'Multitasking? Unusual for a man.'

'I'm a high achiever.' He leaned close, across the table. 'How about an official apology?'

'Just let it go, McTavish.'

'No, now, let's settle it once and for all.' He put a hand over his heart. 'I'm sorry, Olivia. Sorry I let Annabelle McClintock come between us when you very correctly pointed out I was turning into an egotistical pig.'

Olivia shrugged. 'Yeah, well, you *were* the quarterback. The whole city was worshipping at your feet.'

'Everybody but you. It was like being a mythical god, until I blew out my knee. And then the only one who stood beside me who didn't give a damn whether or not I played football was you.'

'I'm a gem. And still, you let Annabelle get between us a second time, even after she had dumped you on your ass. Once I can forgive, but never twice. Particularly because she wants whatever I have, and she *always* has. She gets it too.'

'Give me a break, Livie, she *did* tell me she thought she was pregnant. I thought there was a child involved.'

'And if I recall, I *did* tell you it was probably a lie.'

'You were right. I admit it. But when I tried to

119

sort it out with you, you drop kicked my butt to the curb.'

'No second chances, dude.' She gave him a cool smile. 'Honestly, McTavish, I'm just messing with you. I don't think about it anymore. I married Hugh, I have a daughter, and I've lived in about a million places. This is all old stuff.'

'Then what is it, Livie? I know you've got something on your mind.'

But she waved him off and he let it go, the way men always did, reluctant to delve into troubled waters without a push. It was Olivia's dithering over the chocolate pot de crème that made McTavish take her hand across the table and frown.

'I knew it. Turn down chocolate? It's that autopsy report I gave you on your brother, isn't it? Is that what's worrying you? I told my mother about it – she says hello by the way, and wants me to bring you and Teddy by for dinner sometime. She ripped me a new one, and told me I should have spared you.'

'I *asked* you for it.'

'Yeah. And my thinking has always been that what you imagine is worse than what you know. It wasn't a pretty way to go, I grant you, but it's over now. Chris is at peace.'

'I'm glad you gave me the report. I really did want to know the details.'

McTavish leaned back in his chair and narrowed his eyes. 'You're sure? You're not just handing me the old southern bullshit just to make me feel better?'

It occurred to Olivia that sometimes McTavish sounded exactly like Hugh. 'I know Chris is at

120

peace because he *told* me he was.'

McTavish cocked his head to one side, with the air of a homicide cop who was used to listening and letting out the rope for people who were ready to talk. 'Don't stop there. Because since Chris is dead, I was just wondering...'

'Seriously. He did. But something else came up that bothers me. I wasn't going to tell anybody about this, just Amelia knows—'

'Your buddy in LA?'

'The PA, yeah, that's right. But if I do tell you about it, you have to keep it between us,' Olivia said, in a low whisper, looking over one shoulder.

McTavish grinned.

'Never mind.' Olivia folded her arms. 'When you grin like that it makes me feel stupid for bringing it up.'

McTavish was out of his chair, scooting close to her on the cushioned bench on her side of the table. 'Sorry. Guys are assholes, you know that – it's why you need girlfriends. So just tell me what's on your mind, and spare me the agony of asking you what's wrong another eighty-seven times. I know that's the southern way, but it's godawful agony.'

Olivia rubbed her chin. McTavish was pragmatic and skeptical. Let him tell her she had nothing to worry about. It was exactly what she wanted to hear.

So she told him everything. The detailed version of the phone call from Chris. Her suspicions about *TORN & IN LOVE*. The worry about the Mister Man. As soon as Olivia touched on

121

Emily's disappearance, McTavish bent close and took her hand. He had always understood about Emily. The waiter filled their wine glasses and left them alone.

McTavish was frowning when Olivia finished what she had to say. He was quiet, which was not like him.

'So am I nuts?' Olivia asked. She tried for a light tone, but that only made her sound nervous. Olivia twisted the heavy cotton napkin in her fingers. She watched McTavish. He looked like a man who wanted to light a cigarette, except she knew he didn't smoke. 'McTavish?'

'Give me a minute to think.' He turned to get the waiter's attention, ordered coffee with cognac for both of them, not asking if she wanted any or not. Olivia tried not to think about the bill.

Finally, McTavish put a hand on her shoulder. 'No, I don't think it sounds crazy. Just the opposite. It creeps me out, if you want to know the truth.'

'Not exactly reassuring.' Olivia gave a little laugh, but her stomach was tight and cold. There was still time here for a save if McTavish said the right things. He could reassure her and she would sleep better at night.

'I heard about something along this line a couple of years ago. A friend of mine was involved – a cop, down in Nashville. I can tell you the story, if you want to hear.'

'Does the story have a happy ending?' Olivia asked.

'No.'

The waiter came with coffee – it had depth

without bitterness and an almost butter soft taste. Olivia, stalling, asked the waiter about it, smiling vacuously while he explained that each cup was made individually, with a press. McTavish said nothing. He seemed a long way away.

'So tell me about this cop friend,' Olivia finally said, cradling the coffee cup in her hands.

McTavish laced his hands over his stomach. 'So the guy who told me, Ramsey, I've known him five, maybe six years. We met at a training thing out of Memphis, stayed in touch over some murders for hire that spilled across the state. He's got his feet on the ground, methodical, smart. Doesn't take any crap, but isn't going to beat you over the head with his ego, either. No drama with this guy, nothing to prove. Just matter of fact, by the book, *normal*. Wife, kids, dog, loves the job, but it doesn't eat him alive. Kind of a poster boy for the balanced cop. OK?'

'Sure. In other words, he's not a nut.'

'Right. So he inherits this case – cop buddy of his out of Houston asks him to keep an eye on a vic, a woman – I'm going to call her Mary, okay? Not her real name. So this Mary was twenty-eight, worked in IT for an oil company in Houston, had a kickass job, nice life, and one big problem. Mary had a stalker who wasn't going to let go. Guy was seriously dangerous, and she had trouble, off and on, for, I don't know, maybe three, four years. She filed the reports, got the restraining orders, worked with Houston PD, did the drill. But this guy's a nightmare and he just doesn't quit.

'Long story short, he steps up the pace,

escalates, and Houston PD actually catches him in her apartment with a rape kit and a pretty sharp cleaving knife, if I've got the details right. But she has a gun, legal, registered, Daddy taught her to shoot. She wounds the guy, police pick him up. Goes to trial, son of a bitch gets put away. Should have been the end of it.'

'But it wasn't,' Olivia said, wondering what something like this could possibly have to do with phone calls from the dead.

'Guy started calling her from jail.'

'From jail? How did he do that? Don't they monitor those calls?'

'Honey, these days every con has a cell phone tucked under the mattress. They're contraband, but so is most everything else that goes on in jail. So he's calling her from a mobile, keeps tracking her down, until she decides to change her name, get the hell out of Texas, and make a fresh start. That's where Ramsey came in.

'She lands a job in Nashville, buys a loft in a converted warehouse downtown, starts to breathe again, you know? So she's fine for a few months, thinks she's home free. She's up and down in the building elevator several times a day, and the elevator has this emergency phone built into the wall and one night, she's coming home late from work, and the elevator's emergency phone rings. Mary picks up the phone, thinking what the hell, and it's him. She knows his voice by now, and anyway, he always says the same thing – *hello there, little darlin'*.

'Naturally, she freaks. Makes a police report which lands on Ramsey's desk. He doesn't really

124

believe her, thinks all the years of being stalked kind of put her around the bend. He checks in with Houston PD, but the detective who worked her case said no way, she's solid, so Ramsey checks, and sure enough the call is documented and shows up as coming in on the same cell number that the stalker used before. So Ramsey gets in touch with the prison warden, but come to find out, the stalker is dead. Some feud with another con, they worked together in the laundry room, I don't know the details, but he was beaten to death, found him with his head stuck in a dryer. And he'd been dead for something like three months.'

'And no one else had the phone?'

'Buried somewhere in a warehouse of police evidence. Houston couldn't track it down.'

'So what happened? Did he keep calling her?'

McTavish downed the last of his coffee. 'A couple of months after Ramsey told Mary this guy was dead, she either jumps or falls out of the bedroom window in her loft. He thinks it was a suicide. Happened in January, it was cold out, no good reason to have the window open.'

'Did he check the phone records on the elevator phone?'

McTavish nodded. 'Best he could tell, three more calls came in from the old cell number. Of course, as Ramsey says, it couldn't have really been the stalker, because the guy was dead. And this girl, let's face it, being stalked like that can do your head in.'

'So how does he explain it, the phone calls she got?'

'He doesn't. Can't make sense of it, which is why he told me about it one night at a bar when we were drinking sixteen year old Scotch.'

'Uplifting story,' Olivia said, raising a glass.

'My thinking is this, Livie – so hear me out. Mary would have been better off just going on with her life and not picking up that elevator phone. She didn't have to pick it up, right? Now you, you got this call from your brother. He gives you a vague warning you can't make any sense of, and you're turning yourself inside out trying to figure out what to do. My advice is don't mess with this supernatural stuff. I'm not saying it didn't happen exactly like you say. I'm just saying it makes good sense to leave it be.'

'Hey,' Olivia said. 'I'll leave *it* alone, if it leaves *me* alone.'

'There you go. Tell your buddy in LA to stop stirring things up. Feel good about your brother reaching out, if you really think it was him, if it gives you peace of heart. But stop researching this stuff and looking over your shoulder. Live your life in the here and now.'

TWENTY-ONE

Olivia did not sleep. The story about Mary in the elevator had kept her awake, ending the romantic dinner on an off note. She had refused to kiss McTavish good night or let him walk her

126

to the door.

Not sleeping left her restless, and she sat at the sunroom table the next afternoon, heavy eyed and depressed. The plumber had been scheduled to arrive first thing in the morning, she had not yet been in to work, and it was now almost one o'clock. She had been mystified that morning when a van with the Harrison Plumbing logo had pulled into the driveway just a few minutes after eight, but had inexplicably pulled back out and disappeared. She had called in to enquire and been left hanging.

Her phone had rung at eleven, McTavish on the caller ID, but Olivia had not picked up. Although Olivia had told him that her grudge over Annabelle McClintock was old dead news, the truth was, she had never actually forgiven him. Not for betraying her with Annabelle of all people – one of those girls who always had everything they wanted, wealthy parents who paid for cheerleading trips and uniforms, a new car when she was sixteen, full tuition and sorority fees when she went to college.

Olivia, on the other hand, grew up in the aftermath of a family whose financial back had been broken when her older sister disappeared. Extra monies went to the great white hope of private detectives who specialized in missing persons. So she had worked summers at a doughnut place to pay for her car, an ancient rusting Pontiac Le Mans. She'd moved up to retail jobs at the mall and taken on debt to get through school.

And yet, Annabelle had somehow minded. All the things she had were never enough. Annabelle

127

had set herself up in competition with Olivia from that ancient moment in elementary school, when Olivia had gotten the coveted role of Snow White in the first grade play. Annabelle had planned to be Snow White, and told everyone who would listen that Olivia had only gotten the role because the teachers felt sorry for her, because her sister Emily was a missing child. Which Olivia, who was no good at all in plays, she had to admit it, felt was very likely true.

Olivia thought that this might have been Annabelle's first experience of *no*. And evidently, Annabelle had really wanted to be Snow White.

Because from that day on, Annabelle went head to head with Olivia in every possible way. If Olivia took piano lessons, Annabelle took piano lessons. If Olivia joined a Brownie troop, Annabelle joined the same troop, making sure to cut Olivia out of the herd. High school had been a little better, with Annabelle kept busy with cheerleading, while Olivia spent her spare time working part time after school, but as soon as McTavish started getting handsome and playing football, and his friendship with Olivia got seriously noticed, the rivalry sparked.

Annabelle had obsessed over McTavish, suddenly jealous of the friendship between his family and Olivia's, flirting with him, keeping a distance as long as the relationship between Olivia and McTavish did not turn to romance. McTavish did have an unwed mom after all, which her parents didn't much like, and Annabelle wasn't quite sure was cool. But in that first year of college, when McTavish and Olivia began to date, the game was on.

Annabelle worked him hard, and at the first sign of trouble between McTavish and Olivia, she had scooped him up. The only satisfaction Olivia had was knowing that whatever happened, Annabelle was unlikely ever to play Snow White.

Olivia heard a truck pull into the driveway. She was gratified to see the encouraging presence of a ladder and built in tool boxes, and the Harrison Plumbing logo. Old houses meant late plumbers, and she felt she should count herself lucky someone had actually arrived on the scheduled day.

She watched out the sunroom window, and a man in a red denim shirt got out of the truck, saw her through the window and waved. She met him at the front door, Winston at her heels.

'Mrs James? I'm Con Harrison – you called about a problem with leaks in your bedroom and bathroom ceiling?'

'Come in,' Olivia said.

Harrison grinned at Winston. 'He friendly?' A rhetorical question since Winston was already nuzzling his head into the man's large, square palm. 'Good boy.' Harrison looked up. 'I'm sorry about my guy not showing up this morning. I'm the owner – I usually ride the desk these days unless we get slammed. We actually pride ourselves on showing up when we say, so since all my other guys are tied up, I thought I'd come on out myself, and make sure things get taken care of. When Lenny called in sick, it played hell with the schedule, or I'd have been here sooner.'

'He actually did show up,' Olivia said. 'I saw the van in the driveway around eight.'

Harrison's face darkened, and he looked embarrassed. He was big shouldered and slim, and he put his hands in his jeans pockets. 'Yeah, he did come out, but he called in – from your driveway, actually. He said he was feeling off all of a sudden, and needed to take the day sick.' Harrison shrugged. 'I really wanted Lenny out here, because he did the work for the last owner. They called us out several times.'

'That was my sister-in-law, Charlotte. She recommended you guys.' She hadn't. Olivia had found old plumbing invoices in a kitchen drawer.

'So, can you show me where the leaks are?'

'Up here.' Olivia headed up the stairs, followed by Harrison and Winston, feet and paws clattering on the wood. 'The worst is in here,' she said, leading Harrison into the bathroom. She pointed at the hole in the ceiling.

'Oh, man.' Harrison craned his neck and studied the hole, frowning, as if something did not make sense.

'And also in here.' Olivia went to her bedroom – she had made sure all the clothes were put away and the bed was neatly made. Strangers in the house meant the perfection façade. 'Right here, by the side of the bed. I keep finding little puddles of water. I can't figure out where they're coming from. I don't see any discoloration or leaks in the ceiling.'

Harrison crouched down by the floor, running a finger on the wood. 'I'm not seeing any damage. How much water are we talking about?'

Olivia put a hand to the floor. 'Right here. About what you'd find if you dumped a cup of water beside the bed.'

'Huh.' Harrison stood. 'Okay, let me go get my tools. I've got some paperwork in the truck – copies of the orders we did when we came out last year. I'll go over all the old work and take a look around. You got a ladder handy? If not, I'll bring one in off the truck.'

Olivia waited in the living room, checking emails, then setting her laptop aside and folding a basket of towels and sheets. Harrison clattered in and out of the house, went into the basement several times, muttered something about checking the gutters and the window flashing. He refused a cup of coffee with an air of distraction that made Olivia nervous.

She was wondering how much of her work day could be salvaged when she saw Harrison putting the ladder back on the truck and gathering up his tools.

He popped his head into the living room. 'I'll take that cup of coffee now, if you don't mind.'

Olivia filled a mug, and they sat together at the tile table in the sunroom for the dreaded talk. Harrison had armed himself with a clipboard and pen.

'So here's the thing, Mrs James.'

'Olivia.'

'Pretty name.' He flipped through a stack of stained and wrinkled paperwork. 'I went over all the work we did for your sister-in-law – double checked everything was holding up okay. Over the last eighteen months, we replaced the wax gasket on the upstairs toilet, replaced the joints to the sink, and we also had to go in and tear out the old shower pan and put in a new one. All of that looks solid. Then I went over everything else in the house.' He laughed a little. 'The good news is I can't find anything much wrong.'

'Okay,' Olivia said, knowing she sounded wary.

'Let's talk about that ceiling coming down. If the plaster had come out due to water damage, then there's going to be discoloration and mold, and there's nothing like that up there. And about that floor in the bedroom – there's no water damage to the wood, like you'd expect with an on-going problem. There aren't any pipes up under that floor. No window leaks upstairs, nothing with the flashing and the gutters. You're welcome to get another opinion from a different plumber, but you want to be careful, some guys might come in here and bullshit you, and run you up a big bill.'

'Then why did that ceiling come down?'

'Could be lots of reasons, I'm just saying it's not caused by a leak.'

'What about the water on the bedroom floor?'

'Again, no pipes, no leak. Nothing coming in from the ceiling, the windows or the walls. So my only thought is it could be rising damp. That might account for the problem in that bathroom ceiling too, but I'd expect to see some traces of mold.'

'Damp?' Olivia said. 'What am I supposed to do about *damp*?'

Harrison grinned. 'Rising damp comes from

one of two things. Water that's getting in – and I've pretty much ruled that out. So it comes down to water that can't get out.'

'But where does the water come from?'

'Condensation. From showers, baths and cooking – just normal living in a house. I noticed you have a vent in the upstairs bathroom, and it's working just fine. You do turn it on when you take a shower or bath?'

'Sometimes. It's noisy.'

'Yeah, my wife won't turn ours on either. But you need to run that thing, okay?'

'Okay.'

'Now the bedroom. That one's odd, but old houses are quirky. You could put trickle vents on the top of the windows, but that's going to run into some money. My suggestion would be to get a portable dehumidifier and run that, see if it does the trick. If it solves the problem, then at least you know it's an issue of damp, and you can just keep using the dehumidifier or see about the vents.'

'So the bottom line is, no big plumbing worries, run the vent in the bathroom, and get a dehumidifier.'

'Yes, ma'am.'

At least, Olivia thought, writing out a check for a hundred fifty dollars, Harrison had come up with a solution she could afford.

'Can I ask you one last question?' Olivia said, as she handed over the check. 'Is there any way a bath tub faucet could come on by itself?'

'I checked all the shutoffs, all the packing nuts. That faucet doesn't leak as far as I can see.'

133

'No, I don't mean a leak, I mean come on full blast.'

Harrison gave her a worried look. 'No, ma'am. Not unless you had a pipe bust on you. And then it wouldn't stop.'

TWENTY-TWO

Teddy had been cheerful that afternoon when Olivia picked her up after school, full of news about Mr Ogden and bringing home a sheet of directions that Olivia was to use for making the rat costume for the school play. Olivia studied the directions nervously. She didn't sew, wisely giving it up after trying to hem Teddy's little corduroy overalls, and sewing the little legs together one time too many. Teddy had eaten a good dinner, finished her homework on time, even the math, and had called her daddy on the phone right after her bath, begging for extra reading time after they'd hung up. The evening had been deliciously normal and calm, the only wobble cropping up when Olivia suggested Teddy sleep in her own bed. But she'd looked at the quiver in Teddy's chin and said never mind.

Olivia took a break from the unpacking. She considered a long hot bubble bath, but decided not to tempt plumbing and fates, and curled up in the living room and watched a dreary and para-noid German movie before she went to bed.

When Olivia headed upstairs, Teddy was asleep with all the lights on – the overhead light, along with the lamp by the bed, and the lamp and the light in the hall. Winston was curled up on the end of the bed, wide awake and keeping watch, when Olivia crept into the room.

She had not chosen the master suite for her bedroom, and she told herself that it was because the smaller room, Emily's room, had more charm. And that it did – T-shaped, with one dormer window, the ceiling rising into an arch, with a little alcove nook for the bed. The light was good. There were two big windows.

Chris had died in the master bedroom, and Olivia did not like to go in there. She told Teddy they would reserve the master bedroom for guests. Olivia knew that Teddy thought guests meant her daddy, and nothing Olivia said could change Teddy's mind. She also knew that the reunion fantasy was normal after a divorce. It would all take time.

Teddy was cuddly in pink and yellow pajamas, and she slept soundly, hair damp with sweat and sticking to her forehead. Olivia's cell phone lay on the bedside table in the event that her daddy might call, and *The Ghost of Blackwood Hall* was splayed on the side of the bed.

Olivia took the book and set it on the night table. Ghost stories were not the best idea right now. She pulled a blanket up over Teddy's shoulders, then sat on the edge of the bed, head in her hands, promising herself that she would not be short tempered with Teddy, even when she lied. She would be steady and strong, firm and kind,

135

the perfect mother. She did not really believe in the perfect mothering myth, but that did not stop her from trying, and maybe if she beat her head against the wall in private, she could seem serene and calm when Teddy made her want to scream.

Because the lies unnerved her. Her own little Teddy, standing with her arms folded, defiant in a way reminiscent of her cousin Janet, and lying right to her face. Maybe it was better that Teddy would not be spending the afternoons with her cousins. Maybe Janet was the source of some of this. Teddy was just the age to idolize a teenage cousin – Olivia remembered how captivated she had been by her sister Emily. Her grown up bras. The frosty pink lipstick that Emily used to dab on Olivia's lips to make her feel grown up too.

Olivia rubbed her eyes. She settled into what she tried not to think of as Hugh's side of the bed, and Winston crept forward, and stretched out by her side. The door was wide open. She thought about turning the lights off. Changed her mind. Maybe Teddy's fears were getting to her, but Olivia felt better with the lights on now, and Teddy curled up by her side. She did not want to think about why and she did not expect to sleep.

But sleep was not the problem. The insomnia that had dogged Olivia most of her life seemed to have mysteriously kicked into reverse. The problem now was waking up.

And she needed to do that, to wake up. The dog was barking, and Teddy was restless, crying softly, crying out for Mom. In her dream, Olivia was a little girl again, sitting on the front porch steps, waiting for Emily and Hunter to come home.

Olivia opened her eyes, reaching out instinctively, in a sort of panic, but Teddy was there, in the bed, muttering in her sleep.

'No, Mommy, don't touch me, it hurts.'

'Teddy?' Olivia was wide awake now, the lamp by her bedside was on the softest setting, but she could see that Teddy was sweating and shivering, her face flushed, fingers pawing the bedspread. Olivia touched her daughter's cheek, and she didn't need to go hunting down a thermometer to know the fever was high. Winston had abandoned the bed, and was stretched out on the floor.

When Olivia swung her legs over the side of the bed her bare feet met water. Again. She looked up at the ceiling. Still no leak. Should she call the plumber again and let him see the water? No, she'd just get the dehumidifier. It couldn't hurt.

The emergency kit of Advil, Band-aids, Ocilla and Robitussin was downstairs in the kitchen. Olivia followed the trail of lights she'd left on in the house, trying not to analyze her relief at finding them just as she had left them. The emergency six pack of Schweppes ginger ale was one of the few things in the pantry, that and a box of saltines. It had only taken one quick and dirty stomach virus during a move years ago to teach Olivia the value of preparing for Teddy to come down sick at awkward moments, as any child might.

Olivia piled everything she might need into a colander, the kind of odd thing that always came

137

up in the first kitchen box one unpacked, then headed up the stairs. They were steep, polished wood, and she held tight to the rail.

There was that bloody dog barking outside again, and now it sounded like it was in her yard. Olivia moved the wood slat aside in the upstairs hall window to take a quick look. And there he was. Pacing beside the backyard fountain. It was too dark to make out much detail, but he seemed to be limping, favoring the back left leg. Olivia wondered if he needed rescuing. If he was a stray. Even from the upstairs window he looked very big. A German shepherd, like Hunter. Olivia had a soft spot for shepherds. Maybe she would adopt him if he didn't have a home.

'*Mommy.*'

'I'm coming, hon.'

Teddy vomited it all up, the children's Advil, the child dosage of Ocilla, the tiny bit of ginger ale and cracker Olivia had given her to get the medicine down. After that came the pork chop and rice from her dinner, something unidentifiable that might have been her school lunch, then dry heaves and yellow bile. And the fever did not come down at all, if anything it was worse. Teddy was dehydrated now, shaking with chills, face so white her freckles stood out like noisy brown dots.

Winston paced and moaned in the hallway, and Olivia used a washcloth of lukewarm water to cool her daughter's skin. Teddy cried at every touch. She began to hold her head very still, and when Olivia asked her if her neck was hurting, Teddy whimpered and whispered yes.

Olivia slid into a pair of jeans, bundled her daughter in a blanket, and half carried, half walked her to the car.

Olivia wanted to take her to the University of Tennessee Medical Center, but Hugh's insurance meant the ER at St Mary's. An older hospital, on the other side of town.

Olivia sat on a round stool in an empty ER cubicle, awaiting an audience with the doctor. She felt chilled and vaguely nauseous, fatigue, she knew, the effect of too bright lights, old green walls and a bit of shock. Her daughter was no more than six feet away in the next cubicle, and though Olivia could not make out the words, she could hear the animated rise and fall of her daughter's voice as she chattered away to a nurse.

When the curtain rings slid aside without warning, Olivia jumped a little, on the edge of her seat. The doctor at last. Olivia felt a sharp flutter in her stomach. Good God. Now she really was home again. The doctor wore dark blue scrubs, and a white coat with a nameplate that confirmed she was indeed Annabelle Mc-Clintock, MD.

'I know you, don't I?' Annabelle said. She had the same sallow skin and sharp sideways look that Olivia had tried to forget.

She was as thin as Olivia remembered, arms sinewy with stringy muscles, blonde hair cut short, beautiful, almost violet eyes. Edgy, as always, in constant motion, moving across the room now and straightening the instruments on

139

the table, barely aware she was doing it, as ever OCD.

Olivia gave her a sideways smile. If that was how Annabelle wanted to play it, that would be fine. She wondered if she could ask for another doctor.

'*Olivia*. Oh, of course, it's James now, and Teddy is your little girl? But she's adorable.'

'Thank you. No doubt you have several children of your own by now,' Olivia said. Though she knew better.

Annabelle lost her professional smile, and her handshake was only borderline cordial, fingers thin, limp, and waxy with clinical chill. 'No, I went the professional route. Vince told me you'd moved back to town. We still talk, you know. We're very close. Eight years of marriage doesn't just go away overnight.'

'About my daughter,' Olivia said.

'Right. About your daughter.' Annabelle consulted her clipboard. 'She's fine.'

Olivia noticed that Annabelle's haircut was quite expensive, and she wore no rings, but the diamond studded earrings looked mighty fine. Olivia decided she'd rather have pearls.

'I know you were worried about meningitis, but her white blood count is normal. She wasn't happy about the IV, but she's fully hydrated now, and her temp is ninety-seven point eight, just a little under normal.'

'But that's ... that's unbelievable. She was so sick.'

Annabelle leaned against a waist high, stainless steel cabinet, and crossed one foot over the

140

other. She had a professional comfort that Olivia envied. She was likely a very good doctor. One of the rare ones, who had graduated from medical school without any debt.

'That's kids for you. One minute they're sick as a dog, the next they're playing video games and demanding TV. My guess is a stomach virus. Well, school just started, makes perfect sense. We won't need to admit her. If the fever comes back, let your pediatrician know because it might be good to dose her with some Tamiflu. The flu swab we took showed negative, though, so I think you're off the hook on that. My guess is she's through the worst. Keep her home from school tomorrow just to be on the safe side, and go slow on fluids until you're sure she'll keep them down. And I'd also—'

The beeper on her side went off. She checked it absently, then frowned. 'Can you hold here, just a minute? Someone will bring you some paperwork to sign, and then you can head out.'

Olivia settled back on the stool, and allowed herself to stop worrying. Just a virus, a bad one, gone like magic the way things often went with kids. She missed Hugh, just a little bit. He was good with hospitals and paperwork, and arranging things. If Hugh were here all she'd have to do was worry and hold Teddy's hand.

Olivia frowned when she heard Annabelle's voice – she had evidently been called next door to her daughter. Which meant Teddy was sick again. She'd let her guard down too soon. Olivia was up on her feet and around the corner, but Teddy did not look ill, just shy, and Annabelle

141

McClintock was bent over her, talking in a low and urgent voice.

'What's going on?' Olivia said.

Annabelle looked at Olivia over one shoulder, and motioned to a nurse, who refused to meet Olivia's eyes. 'I want to finish my conversation with your daughter, Olivia. Can you wait for me in the hall?'

'No, I can't. I'm her mother, and I want to know what's up.'

Annabelle straightened. 'Maybe you and I should talk in private then. Come with me.'

Annabelle led her down the corridor, no hurried meeting in a curtained cubicle this time. She was led into a small and private office. This meeting would be held behind closed doors.

'What's wrong with her?' Olivia said.

Annabelle tilted her head to one side. 'Nothing right now, as far as I know. Sit down, Olivia.'

'What's the problem here?'

Annabelle pointed at the brown leatherette chair as she settled herself behind the desk. 'Please.'

Olivia sat because it was silly not to. She put her purse on the floor and waited while Annabelle fingered the stethoscope that hung round her neck. Olivia's heart was thudding, and she felt very cold. Whatever this was, it could not be good.

'Your daughter—'

'Teddy.'

'Teddy has been saying ... she's had a rather disturbing conversation with one of the nurses.'

Olivia clamped her fingers around the edges of

the chair. 'Disturbing how?'

'The nurse was asking if any of her friends at school had been sick. Your daughter said she hadn't caught anything from anybody else, because *somebody made her sick.*'

Olivia sat very still in her chair. 'Somebody made her sick?'

Annabelle picked up a pencil and rolled it on her hand. 'That's what she said. The nurse wrote it up.' She flipped the paperwork in Teddy's chart. 'She said the *somebody* was mad, and wanted to hurt her because *she told on them*. And that she was *going to get it because she told*. According to the nurse, those were her exact words.' Annabelle McClintock looked at Olivia. 'Are you the *somebody*, Olivia? Was Teddy talking about you?'

'No, of course not. That's ridiculous.'

'Who does she mean, then?'

'I don't know. Look, we just moved home, and her older cousins have been telling her ghost stories, and she's been having nightmares. Her father and I got divorced a year ago – I think this is just some kind of adjustment thing.'

'I see.'

Olivia wondered what Annabelle thought she saw.

'So lots of pressure for both of you.' Annabelle rubbed a finger on the edge of the desk. 'Here's the thing. Your daughter asked the nurse if she could spend the night at the hospital. You understand we don't hear that request from kids with IV needles in their arms. All they want is to go home with Mom and Dad. But not Teddy. Teddy

143

said she was afraid to go home. Teddy wants to spend the night here. Can you explain that, Olivia?'

Olivia shook her head. 'Honestly no, I can't explain it, it doesn't make any sense. Unless it's some extreme form of school phobia. We had that once before, when we moved, and we had to change schools.'

'I'm at kind of a crossroads here, Olivia. I'm wondering if I should call Child Protective Services. Your daughter, is she prone to telling stories?'

'You mean lies? Look, Teddy's a very sweet little girl, who is having a hard time moving two thousand miles away from her father and changing schools for the third time in five years. But if you think she's in danger, then go ahead and make that call. I'm sure that no one would think you were exercising a grudge because your ex husband and I are dating.'

'So you and Vince are dating already. Really.'

'We're having dinner tomorrow night. My place this time.'

'He's going to make you cook? You should make him take you to the North Shore Brasserie.'

'He did.'

Annabelle went dark red. 'Look, I've got the nurse to back me up. About what Teddy said.'

'Then do what you have to do. But I'm taking Teddy home right now, and this conversation is over. And by the way, go fuck yourself. But I guess you'll be used to that.'

TWENTY-THREE

Olivia did not run down the hall, but she walked very fast, unable to resist looking over her shoulder for a security guard coming her way. Teddy was alone in the cubicle, and Olivia breathed deeply, grateful for the organized neglect that was the average hospital norm. She scooped her daughter up and settled her on her hip, and carried her straight to the car. Teddy was too big to be carried, and she protested all the way.

'That's not the way home,' Teddy said, fidgeting with the edge of her seatbelt and staring out the window. 'Where are we going?'

'I don't know where we're going. I'm just driving right now.'

'But why?'

'Because the doctor told me you were afraid to go home.'

Olivia swallowed hard and kept her attention on the road. She could cry later, in private. It was not good for Teddy to see her rattled so hard. And in truth, for the first time in her life, she did not even want to look at her own little girl.

'I'm sorry, Mommy. I'm sorry I told.'

'Teddy, I'm not mad at you.' A lie. She was mad. 'It's just – you have to understand.'

'Understand what?'

'Teddy, that doctor and that nurse. They thought I was the *somebody* that hurt you. Did you tell them that?'

Teddy gasped, and put a hand to her mouth. 'Oh, Mommy, no no no. I didn't tell them that. It was *Duncan Lee*. It's just I'm not supposed to say his name.' The tears came, sliding silently down Teddy's cheeks. 'I didn't say it was *you*.'

'It's okay, Kidlet. The main thing is for you to be better and to feel safe. Look, Teddy, we need to talk about Duncan Lee. Do you really think he made you sick or is this just one of your games?'

Teddy put her hands over her face. 'It's not a game.'

'You're saying he's real. He actually talks to you. Are you saying he's in the house? Because I don't see him.'

'Of course you don't see him, he only lets certain people know he's around. It isn't up to us, it's up to him.'

'Really? What does he look like?'

Teddy rubbed her eyes. 'It's hard to explain. He looks like the dark.'

'Like a shadow?'

Teddy nodded. 'Sometimes he stands over me, by my bed, and leans on me. And he's behind me, in the house sometimes. He creeps up. He watches us a lot. He doesn't like Winston. And he really doesn't like you.'

'Does he talk to you?'

Teddy nodded.

'In a regular voice?'

'It's just a *voice*, Mommy, like yours or mine, only he whispers a lot. Winston hears it too, it

146

makes his tail go down.' Teddy turned sideways toward her mother. 'I know what we should do. Let's tell them there's not a *somebody*. Let's tell them I made it all up. Let's tell them I did it so I wouldn't have to go to school. So we could go home and live with Daddy in California.'

'Oh, God, Teddy.'

'Please, Mommy. I didn't mean to make you cry. Let's just go home, okay? I want to see Winston. Please, Mommy, please.'

'Teddy—'

'I need to go home with you, Mommy. If I can have you and Winston, I'll be okay. I'm so sorry I got you in trouble at the hospital. Please don't be mad.'

'I'm not mad.'

'You seem mad.'

'I'm upset. But the person I'm upset with is me.'

'Why?'

For dragging you two thousand miles away from your father, Olivia thought. For yet another move. 'Teddy, *did* you make it all up or do you see a ... a dark man in the house?'

Teddy bit the knuckles of her fist. 'Which one do you want me to say?'

TWENTY-FOUR

Olivia was on her way to the airport when her cell phone rang. Clients had been calling in like crazy all morning, and she'd left an annoyed Robbie Arliss to hold them off. Amelia was coming. Olivia had called her in the middle of the night and she'd promised to take the first flight out. Her plane was due to touch down in thirty minutes.

Olivia knew better than to pick up the phone when she was driving, but she was idling at a traffic light on Kingston Pike, waiting to take the exit to 275, and it was McTavish on the caller ID.

'Hey, babe, I hear it's official that you and I are dating again. Oh, and I'm looking forward to that dinner at your place tomorrow night.' McTavish sounded amused and Olivia was glad she was alone in the car with her blush.

'I take it Annabelle called.'

'In the middle of the night. To confirm. How's Teddy? She okay?'

'Yeah, whatever it was, she got over it.' The physical part anyway, Olivia thought. 'What did you say to Annabelle?'

'What she already knows.'

'Which is?'

'That you're a great mom. That Teddy prob-

148

ably has school phobia just like you said, and your brother just died so for God's sake cut you some slack. And not to let her professional ethics be swayed by jealousy because I backed you up on our dinner plans tomorrow night. I'll bring a bottle of wine. Seven, okay?'

'I'd love to, but I can't. I've got a friend flying in from California.'

'What, some guy?'

'No, a girlfriend, she's also a PA, she was Teddy's pediatrician when we were in LA. I can't just run off and leave her.'

'She coming to check Teddy out?'

'Kind of.'

'So you're worried.'

'Are you going to discuss this with Annabelle?'

'I sure as hell am not. But that ain't no reason to cancel dinner, we'll just do it Sunday afternoon, after you girls have had a chance to catch up and stuff. I can meet your friend, you can cook the side dishes, and I'll bring some ribs for the grill.'

'That grill hasn't been used in God knows how long.'

'Then I better get there early to clean it out. Make sure the beer is cold. We'll have a big family dinner, like your mom used to do, on Sunday afternoons.'

'In that case you better bring Jamison. He was always there mooning after Emily.'

'I thought she was mooning after him. But I'll bring him and thanks for asking. He doesn't get invited out a lot.'

149

McGee-Tyson Airport was a hell of a relief after LAX. There was only one terminal and you could pretty much park next door, and it was free if you were in and out in half an hour. Olivia had visited Chris right after 9/11 and though the airport was swarming with National Guardsmen armed with machine guns like everywhere else, they had a tendency to smile and say hi.

Olivia checked the monitor, laughed a little because Amelia's flight was right on time and things were just simpler in Tennessee. She stood outside of security, next to the crashing fountain. Sun streamed through the glassed in walls, and she felt better already. Amelia was sensible, intelligent, confident and wise. She would figure out what was going on with Teddy, poke the notion that Teddy was being haunted by the mysterious Duncan Lee full of obvious holes, and make everything okay. There would no doubt be a handsome man helping her with her carry-on luggage, and she would have packed way too much stuff.

But Amelia was frowning when she came down the steep sloping hall, oblivious to the long looks she got from certain types of businessmen traveling on their own. When she saw Olivia she smiled, and her carry-on bag was bulging, as were her briefcase and her purse. Her hair was clipped in a knot of loose waves on her head, and she wore snug, worn Levi 501s and a black tee shirt that said *Yeah, what?* The black rimmed cat glasses hung from a chain around her neck.

Amelia dropped all her bags to the floor and

gave Olivia a big hug, and Olivia inhaled the familiar scent of Chance by Chanel and felt safe again.

'Livie, God it's good to see you.'

'I can't believe you actually came, Amelia. I know how impossible it is for you to get away. This means so much to Teddy and me.'

Amelia looked over Olivia's shoulder and out the windows. 'This airport is surrounded by *fields*. Please God tell me there's an actual town.'

'Yes, Amel, there is an actual town.'

'With shopping and everything?'

'With shopping and everything.' Olivia grabbed the handle to the rolling carry-on bag. It was hot pink with black trim. 'Come on, baggage claim is downstairs.'

'I didn't check any luggage.'

Olivia stopped. Turned to look at her friend. 'Really? I thought ... I thought you were going to stay a whole week.'

'I am.'

'But—'

'I left in kind of a hurry, remember? To tell you the truth, Livie, if you hadn't called me I was going to call you, and ask if I could come.'

'What's going on, Amelia?'

'I think I did something bad. I need to talk to you about it, but not right in the middle of an airport, okay? Can we go somewhere and get coffee or do you need to get back to work?'

'I already planned to take the day off,' Olivia lied. 'When's the last time you had a meal? There's a little place right near the house, home

151

cooked southern food.'

'I'm up for anything. I'm starved.'

Big Fatties was empty of clientele. A cheerful box of a restaurant, sharing a building with an adult bookstore. Two blocks down from Olivia's house, and around the corner from Teddy's school.

Amelia paused in the doorway, taking in the bright tile floors, the blond wood table and chairs. A guy who looked college age sat behind a table near the cash register, engrossed in an open textbook, making notes on a laptop. The shelves behind him looked like what you'd find in a messy house full of children – sweaters, shoes, books, toys. Family stuff, nothing that said restaurant. The boy looked up.

'Sit anywhere you want. There's menus on that table over there.' He jerked a thumb over one shoulder. 'The special's on the board. My name is Greg if you need me.'

They settled at a table as far away from Greg as they could get, right in front of a window, where they could see the car wash next door, and the traffic up and down the Pike.

'What y'all drinking?' Greg said from across the room. 'Sweet tea's good.'

Amelia looked across the table at Olivia. 'Sweetie?'

'Sweet. Tea.'

Amelia smiled at Greg over one shoulder. 'Bring us two.'

After querying Olivia on what was meant by *Meat & Three*, Amelia ordered the chili, and Olivia had the barbecued chicken sandwich with shoestring fries.

When Greg was in the back, seeing to their orders, Olivia leaned across the table and lowered her voice. 'Is it Marianne that's got you shook up, Amelia? Is she getting worse?'

'Yes and no. There's something I didn't tell you, Livie. I haven't told anybody, but I can't get it out of my head.'

Olivia realized that while she had assumed Amelia had come to provide moral support, she was actually there for help. 'I'm listening.'

Amelia clasped her hands together as if she were saying a prayer. 'It all started a few months ago. Marianne was having bad dreams. Dreams where she couldn't breathe, and couldn't call for help. So Alexis and I sat down with her, and talked it out. And we told her that Mommy and Daddy would always be there to look out for her, and that I'd be the backup, and I'd come when she needed me. And I gave her a special pager, it was an extra I had, and I set it up so that all she had to do was push a button, and it would buzz me day or night.

'Truth to tell? I just gave it to her for comfort value. Like a security blanket. Because the hospital staff in her peds unit is top notch. And Alexis and Jack – when Marianne's in the hospital, they're with her night and day, it's not like she's alone.

'I told Marianne the pager would show a special code so I would know it was her, but that she could only use it if she really needed me, because if I saw her special code come up, I was going to drop everything and be there as fast as I

153

could. We put the pager in her special lovee, this stuffed platypus she has – it has a little tummy pouch for platypus eggs, and we tucked the pager in there.

'Then one night, after Marianne was already starting what I call the downhill run...' Amelia took a breath. 'She was spiking a fever and having a hard time getting her breath, fluid building up in her lungs. I met all three of them in the ER, we got Marianne medicated and stable, and we were keeping her in a night or two for tests and observation, and then the oncologist was going to come in and tell us what was next.

'So. Middle of the night twenty-four hours later. I'm home, sound asleep, and something wakes me up. I don't know what. I come up out of a deep sleep, like someone has touched my shoulder or called my name. And I sit up in bed, turn on the lamp, and look at the clock. Three sixteen a.m. I'm yawning and rubbing my eyes, thinking it was maybe some noise outside, a neighbor coming home late, when the pager goes off.'

'Marianne's code?'

Amelia nodded. 'So I pull on my scrubs, pick up my cell and get peds on the line while I'm rounding up my car keys, putting on my shoes. Trying not to panic, there's a whole hospital staff there after all, and Alexis and Jack. I'm thinking maybe it was an accident or maybe Marianne was just lonely or scared.' Amelia swallowed hard, rubbed at her left eye. 'Night nurse tells me Marianne is coding, so I'm on the way.

'By the time I get there, Livie, the excitement

154

is over. Marianne is stable again, sedated, sleeping hard. Doesn't even twitch when I touch her hand. I look but the platypus isn't there. I ask Alexis about it, and she says they left it at home, because the hospital wouldn't let Marianne have it in the ICU.

'So. Alexis and I have been friends a long time, right? I have a key to the house. The dog, Harry the Hound, he and I are old buds. So on my way home I stop by. Harry is sleepy but glad to see me, and I fill up his water bowl and take him out for a pee.

'Then I head upstairs to Marianne's room, Harry on my heels, wagging his tail. There's a nightlight on in the hallway, and I go in. And it's like the lair of a little princess. White canopy bed, pink quilt. Tiny little desk and bookshelves filled with Dr Seuss. Everything in miniature, fluffy, white, gold and pink. And the platypus is on the bed, laid out on the pillow. I open up the belly – it's Velcroed shut, and sure enough, the pager is right there. It shows me being paged at exactly three sixteen a.m. Only Marianne and her parents have been in the ER for the last thirty-six hours. So who set off the pager? The next day I look at Marianne's chart. She coded at two fifty-eight a.m., and lost all vital signs at three sixteen right on the nose.'

Olivia felt a chill begin at the top of her arms. 'Sometimes those pagers just go off.'

'At the exact same time Marianne's vitals are lost?' Amelia leaned close across the table. 'So you can see now, when you got that phone call from your brother, why I was so, so—'

'Obsessed.'

'Okay. Obsessed.'

'So you haven't been researching this just lately. This has been going on a while.'

'Right.'

'Look, you have to be careful with this, Amelia. You can't let it take over your life.'

'You're telling me to back away, when a little girl's life is involved? I know I need to help her. I'm trying to find my way. What do *you* think it means, Livie?'

'I don't know, Amelia. I don't think it means anything bad. Maybe Marianne needed you, and was somehow able to ask for help.'

'*Exactly*. In a hospital full of qualified doctors and nurses, and her parents just a few feet away, she wants *my* help. Because she's drowning with fluid in her lungs, and she doesn't want to be on the ventilator.'

'You can't be sure that's what it meant.'

But Amelia did not seem to hear. 'And I can't seem to get her parents to understand that prolonging things is torture, and the end game is not going to change, it's only a matter of how much their little girl is going to suffer before she dies. Sometimes, Livie, there are things worse than death, and a lot of those things are in hospital rooms.'

Olivia put a hand to her throat. 'What did you do, Amelia? Tell me you didn't pull the plug on that little girl.'

'*Pull the plug?* Livie, number one, if I was going for euthanasia, I wouldn't have to do something quite so crude. And second, I did take

156

an oath. It's not my decision to make.'

'Sorry, Amel. It's just ... the look on your face when I picked you up at the airport.'

'It wasn't that. It's what happened later. When Alexis and I had our talk.'

Greg swooped in from the kitchen with their orders, setting the plates down on the table, refilling their tea.

'So?' Olivia said, when Greg had gone away.

'Livie, I think he can hear us. This room echoes.'

'It does not echo and just talk soft. You said at the airport you did something bad, now you tell me what you mean.'

Amelia looked at the cornbread. 'They put butter on it.' She broke off a piece and crumbled it in her fingers. 'I just ... I was talking to Alexis, late in the night. Jack was sitting with Marianne, and Alexis and I went down to the cafeteria to get some coffee. The doughnuts are delivered hot at three a.m., and I was trying to get her to eat. We were both so tired we didn't know which end was up. And out of the blue, Alexis starts going on and on about the afterlife, about children going to heaven and how could you be sure they would be okay. Who would take care of them, when they were dead.'

'Is she religious?' Olivia asked.

'She seems to go back and forth. I thought she was finding her way to letting Marianne go. She was pretty shook up, Marianne had been having a horrible night, gasping for every breath, and Alexis asked me point blank what it felt like, what Marianne was going through, and I told her

157

the truth. That her little girl was drowning in air.'

'*Amelia.*'

'Yeah, I know, it was a rough thing to say. I thought it through before I said it. But somebody needs to wake her up. She's right there, she can see how bad it is. I'm not going to let her off the hook and give her platitudes. Marianne might survive another surgery, she might not, but the chemo is making her sick and miserable, it isn't helping, it's just making her death slower and more agonizing. Alexis and Jack have to make the call, but it needs to be an informed decision.'

'I don't think that's bad, Amelia. I think it's tough, but true. I think Alexis needed to hear it.'

'But that's not all I said. She just seemed to want to talk about it, what happens when you die. Like we can know, right? So I told her about your phone call from Chris. That your brother actually called you after he died. And he said it was all right, that everything was okay. I thought it was going to be like one of those Hallmark television specials, where Alexis would be comforted, and get the strength to man up and let her little girl go. Instead we go straight to the paranormal channel, where she accuses me of having demonic influences, and trying to manipulate her into – how did she put it? *The sin of euthanasia.* She freaked out on me, Livie.' Amelia put her hands over her face and tears streamed through her fingers and into the chili. 'Sorry, Livie. I didn't mean to cry.'

'How are things between you now? How'd you leave it?'

'Alexis went to the attending and had me

158

barred from Marianne's room.'

'Good God, no wonder you're upset. What a horrible thing for her to do.' Olivia tried to ignore what felt like a tiny betraying twinge of satisfaction. Shameful. She had always been envious of Amelia's friendship with Alexis. She tried to push it down. 'And how long have you guys been friends?'

'Since college,' Amelia said. 'And I love Marianne like she was my own. And Alexis knows that. She and Jack *know* how much I love that little girl. I was in the damn delivery room when she was born. I thought ... I thought I was *family*.'

Olivia put a hand on Amelia's shoulder. 'You're still family, Amel. Their daughter is dying, they're not going to be all that rational. Look, remember the other night on the phone when you said Charlotte and Janet were looking for someone to blame? I know it's not fair, but that's all this is. You were talking to a friend, you were honest, you tried to help. You didn't do anything wrong. Alexis has her back to the wall and she's looking for somebody to be mad at and someone to blame.'

'I know. I know you're right. It's just not fun being the one.'

'Hey. I've got news to distract you. I'm cooking a big dinner tomorrow afternoon. You're going to get to meet the famous McTavish. Only you have to promise not to let him fall in love with you, so keep the charm on medium, because I'm calling dibs on this guy.'

TWENTY-FIVE

The dinner had almost gone off the rails when Jamison refused to come into the house. Olivia, who remembered the blond heartbreaker her big sister Emily had idolized, saw nothing of that boy in Jamison the man. He was tall still, big shouldered like McTavish, but stooped now, with an uncertain, sideways cant to his walk. He wore stiff, off brand jeans and a short sleeved plaid shirt, a UT ball cap, and Timberland boots that looked brand new. He was in his forties, but he looked older, and the shiny blond hair had dulled, showing gray. He was freshly shaved, jeans creased. He wore his clothes as if someone else had picked them out.

'Go ahead, Jamison. You want me to go first?' McTavish headed through the arched front door, pausing on the stoop.

'Maybe he's shy,' Amelia said.

Teddy pushed her glasses back on her nose. 'Shy people don't like it when you say that, Dr Amelia. Are you scared, Jamison? See Winston, his tail is wagging, and there's lots of people around. *You know who* only watches when there are so many people around. It should be safe if you go home before dark.'

Olivia looked at Amelia, who slid the cat glasses up on her nose and stared at Teddy.

160

'Who is *you know who*?' Amelia said.

Teddy frowned. 'It's better if you don't say his name.'

Olivia looked at Teddy. Considered saying something, then decided to deal with it later, in private.

'Come on, Jamison,' Teddy said. 'I'm icing brownies, want to help? You can wear an apron, like me.'

Jamison followed Teddy across the threshold and back to the kitchen. He did not look right or left, but focused on Teddy, like a man walking through the woods and whistling in the dark.

Teddy tied Jamison into an apron and handed him a table knife, and the two of them iced the brownies while Amelia drank a dirty martini, three olives, and critiqued their work. But Olivia could see that Amelia was watching Teddy, and sipping steadily, as if unaware there was high octane vodka in her glass. Olivia was watching Teddy too.

McTavish breezed past them after grabbing a beer. 'You handle the brownies there, Jamison. I'm going to tackle that grill.'

Olivia made potato salad and baked beans, and McTavish grilled fresh asparagus along with the ribs, brushing them with the Bone Sucking Barbecue Sauce Olivia had found at Earth Faire. Olivia had to hide in the hallway just before they sat down to eat to wipe the tears out of her eyes. It was ridiculous, of course, but in her mind's eye she imagined Chris, elbows on the table, eating ribs, and that knock at the door she had listened for all of her life, where they found Emily and

161

Hunter waiting on the front porch, home at long last. Olivia was flooded with that mix of happy and sad that comes to those who move away and come back.

They ate in the sunroom, a late dinner as the sun went down. McTavish was sweaty in his tee shirt and jeans, the hairs on his arms smudged with the blackened grease he'd cleaned out of the barbecue grill. McTavish drank Killians, and Olivia had martinis with Amelia, and Jamison and Teddy had bottles of lemonade. By the second martini Olivia had forgotten to be mad at Teddy for acting weird. They would talk later, when their guests were gone.

They left the mess in the kitchen and piled into the living room. McTavish and Amelia amused themselves at Olivia's expense by swapping Olivia stories, trying to mesh the Tennessee Livie with the Livie in LA.

'I'm the same no matter where I live.' Olivia threw an olive at McTavish, which he caught in midair.

'Well, yeah, Livie, that's kind of what's so funny. The fish out of water, and *Innocents Abroad*. I need another beer. You ladies want to really go for it with a refill? One more martini and Livie's going to sing.' McTavish was heading past the staircase when he stopped and cocked his head. 'Do you hear that?'

Amelia had just asked Olivia in a whisper if she'd bedded him yet. 'Hear what?' she said, talking loud.

They went quiet, and Olivia turned the music

down. Sobbing, soft sobbing, distinctly masculine, coming from upstairs. She looked at once for Teddy, who had curled up in the red leather chair with *The Sign of the Twisted Candles* and fallen asleep. Teddy looked exhausted all the time now. She did not seem to sleep much at night.

'Where's Jamison?' McTavish said. He glanced around the room, then headed up the stairs, taking them two at a time, Olivia and Amelia right behind. 'Jamison? Where are you, buddy? You okay?'

The bathroom door was shut tight, and Winston was scratching at the door, whining softly. McTavish knocked once, then went in. *'Jesus, man.* Are you okay?'

Olivia looked at Amelia.

'You need help or privacy?' Amelia said.

'He's decent. But Olivia, you better look at this.' McTavish pushed the door open wide. 'I noticed you had a big hole in the ceiling when I was up here earlier, but—'

'Oh, hell,' Olivia said.

Jamison had clearly been washing his hands after using the bathroom, and a section of the ceiling had come down on his head. He had plaster in his hair, and blood running down his temple from a gash on his scalp.

'Let me look at that,' Amelia said.

But Jamison backed away. Pointed up to the ceiling. 'Waverly,' he said.

'Will he freak out if I clean up that cut?' Amelia said to McTavish. 'It looks like it might need a stitch or two.'

163

'Jamison doesn't cry when he gets hurt, do you buddy? Jamison is the King of Stoic. He only cries when he's scared. It would have scared me too, buddy, if the ceiling came down on my head.'

Jamison looked at McTavish and frowned. His face was flushed and there were beads of sweat mixing with the run of blood. *'Waverly.'* He pointed up into the ceiling. 'Names.'

'What names, buddy?'

'His name *is* up there, in the ceiling,' Olivia said. 'But I don't know how he could see that from here.'

McTavish picked chunks of plaster off of Jamison's shoulders and tossed them in the trash. 'What are you talking about, Livie?'

'Just what I said. There are names up there. Look, I can get you a stepladder and a flashlight and show you.'

'Jamison, why don't you go back downstairs, and maybe you and Teddy could watch a movie.'

Jamison folded his arms and put his back to the wall, shaking his head. He had barely spoken all day – McTavish said that was the norm – but he was talking now, repeating *Waverly* over and over.

'Okay, Jamison, I get you. Olivia, darlin', better get me that stepladder and flashlight. He's not going to stop chanting till I take a look.'

Amelia matter of factly fished peroxide out of the medicine cabinet, and wet down a wash rag, then wrung it out. 'Come on, Jamison, let me clean that cut while the two of them check the ceiling out for leaks.'

'If you've got a plumbing problem, Livie, I know a guy. I'd do it myself but I'd probably flood the house. Remember my mother's kitchen?'

'There's no leak up there, McTavish, I had a plumber out already. I have no idea why that ceiling is caving in. Or why there are ... names.'

McTavish was already up the steps, and his head and shoulders disappeared up into the ceiling. They heard the click of the flashlight, saw him twist and shift as he played the light.

'This is weird,' McTavish said.

Jamison watched him, barely noticing when Amelia cleared the blood and plaster from his forehead, not even flinching when she dabbed the cut with peroxide.

'You can get by without any stitches,' Amelia said. 'If you don't mind a scar. But this is a nasty little gouge.'

'Did you *see* this, Livie?' McTavish said.

'You mean the names?'

'Yeah. Jamison, Chris, Emily. Allison, Bennington and Teddy.'

'*Teddy?*'

'Yeah.'

'Get down, McTavish, let me look.'

Olivia took the flashlight, and McTavish steadied her arm as she scrambled up the stairs.

'You see?'

Olivia was trembling so hard she wasn't sure she could keep her footing on the ladder. Teddy's name was written on a stud, just below *Chris*. But not burned in, like the others. This was new, written in what looked like blue chalk. Olivia

165

touched the letters, smudging the *y*.

'Yeah, you're right, McTavish, Teddy's name is here. But it wasn't there before. It's new.'

'How could it be new?' McTavish said.

'*I don't know*. Seeing as how it's up in the goddamn ceiling. I don't like it either.'

'Waverly,' Jamison said.

'Do you know what he means by that?' Amelia asked.

'Yeah,' McTavish said. 'I kind of do. It's that place in Louisville, Livie, you know.'

'You mean ... that *institute*? That crazy place? It's an old abandoned tuberculosis hospital, right? The haunted one?'

'Yeah. Chris never told you about it?'

'Told me what?'

'About what happened up there. At the Waverly. When they were all up in Louisville, you know, at that wrestling competition. Remember?'

'I was five then, McTavish. But I do sort of remember the wrestling competition. Because that was when Emily disappeared.'

TWENTY-SIX

Olivia settled Teddy and Jamison in front of the television set with a movie, an old favorite of Teddy's, *Return from Witch Mountain*, while she and Amelia and McTavish huddled around the

166

sunroom table looking at the screen of her laptop.

The Waverly had a website. And webcams up and down the dark corridors of the old empty buildings. Amelia was hunched over Livie's laptop, scrolling. 'This place is all over the Internet.' She began to read aloud.

'"The Waverly Hills Sanatorium in Louisville, Kentucky is known as The Holy Grail of the Paranormal."' Amelia looked up at Livie, then back down to the screen. 'It looks like the land was bought for a school and named for Scott's Waverley novels. Evidently the hospital kept the name when they opened in 1910.'

'The place is massive,' McTavish said, looking over Amelia's shoulder. 'They had beds for over four hundred patients.'

'They treated thousands of tuberculosis patients, over the years,' Olivia said, reading. 'They called it the white plague. Almost none of them survived?'

'No antibiotics then,' Amelia said. 'Look at the treatments they had. Fresh air and bed rest. Good nutrition and diet. Heliotherapy. So basically they kept the windows open even in the winter and sat the patients outside to soak up the sun. Looks like they used sunlamps too.'

'But didn't they get pneumonia or something?' Olivia said.

'Keep reading, it gets better.' Amelia squinted at the screen. 'Their cutting edge surgical treatments were brutal. Collapsing parts of the lung. Removing rib bones, one or two at a time. Sweet Jesus God, they've got pictures of the doctors performing this stuff.'

Olivia looked at the pictures. Tiled rooms and men draped in white bent over patients who did not have a chance.

'It looked like Frankenstein's lab without the technology,' McTavish said looking over her shoulder.

'Medical science in the dark ages,' Olivia said.

Amelia covered her eyes with her hands. 'I'm not sure we're any less barbaric today.'

'Listen to the part about the Body Chute, guys.' McTavish put a hand on Olivia's shoulder and squinted down at the screen. 'It was an underground tunnel for transporting bodies so the living patients wouldn't be upset. They went under the hospital and down the hill and the hearses were waiting for them when they came out. Five hundred feet long, and it wasn't wired, so there was no electricity.'

'Five hundred feet in the dark?' Amelia said.

'I guess they had lanterns,' McTavish said. 'And some kind of rail and winch system to get the bodies through.'

Olivia closed her eyes, imagining the dark tunnels, the echoes. Then she looked up at McTavish. 'What does the Waverly have to do with all those names upstairs? What does this have to do with Jamison and Chris?'

'What I know is kind of hazy, Liv.' McTavish ran a hand through his hair. 'Remember how little you and I were at the time, right? But Jamison talks about it sometimes, he has nightmares. From what I can piece together, from things Jamison has said to me over the years, they went there. Jamison, Bennington and Chris.'

'There? At Waverly Hills? And who was Bennington?' Olivia asked.

'He was one of the guys on the Bearden High School wrestling team. They were the stars, you know, the A-Team. There were eight of them that made the trip. It was for the National High School Wrestling Championships – which were pretty new then, but now they're the crown jewel of high school wrestling. I mean, these days, they cover it on ESPN, and bring in wrestlers from all over the US and Europe.'

'But what's that got to do with the Waverly?'

'They went there, the three of them. Snuck out of their hotel room because they were teenage guys and goofy, and thought it would be cool to see the notorious haunted sanatorium. These days you can go on a ghost tour, but back then it was strictly No Trespassing.

'Jamison talks about the Body Chute sometimes, when he has bad dreams. The impression I get was that he was actually in there. That the three of them went down some kind of vent shaft to get inside the tunnel. Something bad happened, I just don't know exactly what. Jamison never really makes sense when he tries to talk about it.'

'But what's the big deal?' Amelia said. She was clicking her way through the website. 'Did it make them freak out and lose the wrestling match?'

'No, just the opposite. Championship wins for all three. They all got big fat scholarship offers from the NHSCA.'

'Look at this,' Amelia said. 'It's a web cam, set up at the edge of the Body Chute. There's stuff written on the walls.'

'They'd have graffiti in hell,' McTavish said. 'For a good time call six six six.'

Amelia peered close at the screen. 'What is that? Decan Ludde. Is that a name?'

McTavish sat forward. 'Does it really say that? Decan Ludde?'

Amelia pointed. 'See, right there, at the edge of the screen.'

'How weird. Jamison used to say that over and over, in his sleep.'

'Decan Ludde,' Olivia whispered. Thinking how close it sounded to *Duncan Lee*. 'Google it, Amelia.'

But Amelia wasn't listening. She twisted her head sideways, staring at something on the screen. 'So did they get their scholarships, and go to college and—'

'Live happily ever after?' McTavish said. 'Jamison didn't. He had his car wreck two days later, went through the windshield, closed head injury. It's taken fifteen years of daily therapy just for him to be able to walk, and talk, and live on his own. For Jamison, after the accident he had, being able to hold down a job stacking shelves at Long's Drug Store, and volunteering at the animal shelter are genius level. This for a guy who had it all. A star athlete who scored in the ninety-ninth percentile across the board. I mean, he was going to have a future. Now he has a life.'

'What about Chris?' Amelia asked.

170

Olivia shook her head. 'No, he didn't take the scholarship, and my parents were furious with him, I remember a lot of arguing.'

'But why not?'

'Because. The night they came back. That was the night that Emily disappeared and our whole family just fell apart. Chris didn't want to go to college until they found her. He said he wouldn't go until she came home. My parents tried threatening him, then they moved to bribes, they even promised to buy him a car if he'd go. But he wouldn't. He just dropped out of everything – barely finished his last year of high school. Stayed home and around the house for the next couple of years. Lost about eighty pounds. I could show you pictures.

'But then he came out of it. We all did. We got counseling. We moved on. Chris went to UT and got a degree in science and education and started teaching at Bearden Middle School, even coaching the wrestling team. He married Charlotte and had three little girls. He was really okay, until about a year ago. When he started acting weird and losing all that weight again.'

Amelia rubbed the back of her neck. 'Why don't you—*shit*. Do you see that? On the screen?'

'What is it?'

'There. You see how there's something kind of dark, standing at the edge of the camera? Never mind, it's gone. Probably my imagination. I'm getting seriously creeped out with this Waverly stuff.' Amelia logged off the computer. Put the screen to sleep.

'So what about this Bennington?' Olivia said. 'And McTavish, do you have any idea who Allison is? And why their names are up there in my ceiling?'

'Not a clue. But I'm a cop. I could find out who they are. Why the names are up in the ceiling is anybody's guess.'

TWENTY-SEVEN

That night, Olivia dreamed of McTavish, who had doubled back to the front door after getting Jamison settled into the front seat of the car. He had kissed her under the porch light while Amelia took the empty bottles and glasses into the kitchen, and Teddy stumbled up the stairs, Winston trailing, to put on a nightshirt and sprawl back to front in her bed. McTavish had touched Olivia's cheek afterward and smiled, catching her hand for a quick squeeze before heading back down the walk to the car.

The martinis had put Olivia under in a deep, engulfing sleep, but she woke up instantly at the sudden flash of light streaming in under her bedroom door.

'*Stop.*' Amelia's voice from the next room. Sounding odd. The light went out. Then came back on again. '*I said stop.*'

Olivia swung her legs over the side of the mattress, pulled her sweat pants on. And again, her toes slid in yet another puddle of water, collecting at the side of her bed. She was going to have to get that dehumidifier ASAP. She tiptoed out into the hallway, and flipped the hall light.

Teddy was there, standing in the doorway of Amelia's bedroom. She was holding a worn stuffed Eeyore she had not pulled off the shelf since she was two and still taking naps.

'What are you doing out of bed, Teddy?' Olivia said. 'What's going on out here?'

Amelia was sitting up in bed, her red hair sticking up, her face pale and strange without the familiar makeup. She shoved the blankets off her legs. 'My light keeps going on and off. I would say a loose connection but hell, it wouldn't *keep* going off and on like that.'

'Teddy, were you messing with Amelia's light?' Olivia asked.

'It wasn't her,' Amelia said.

'I didn't, Mommy.'

'Somebody did, and you're the one standing there.'

'*I didn't do it.*' Teddy threw Eeyore and hit Olivia full in the chest. 'You always blame me for everything.'

Olivia took Teddy's arm. 'Come with me, right now, move it.' She led Teddy into her bedroom, looking over her shoulder. 'Hang on a minute, will you, Amel? I'll be right back.'

'Don't kill the kid,' Amelia called after them. 'She didn't do it. She wasn't even there when it started up.'

Winston followed them into Olivia's bedroom,

173

and Olivia shut the door.

'Sit,' Olivia said.

Teddy perched on the edge of the bed and looked at the floor.

Olivia folded her arms. 'Just tell me the truth, Teddy. I don't want *any more lies*. Were you messing with the light in Dr Amelia's room?'

'Nope.'

'Then what were you doing? You were standing right there.'

'He told me to get out of bed and watch.'

'Who told you, Teddy?'

'You know who. *He* wanted me to watch.'

'To watch what?'

'The lights. I don't know. He just told me.'

Olivia folded her arms. *'Who* told you, Teddy?'

Teddy's shoulders went stiff, and she looked at Olivia out of the corner of one eye. She lowered her voice, so much so that Olivia had to bend close to hear.

'He has lots of names. Duncan Lee. Decan Ludde.'

'Did you say Decan Ludde?' Olivia felt a flutter of strange fear in the pit of her stomach. Decan Ludde was the name in graffiti on the walls at the Waverly. Had Teddy overheard them talking? She'd been in the same room, watching a movie. Of course she'd heard.

'Don't say it, Mommy. Please don't say it. He knows about you and Winston. He watches you all the time.'

Olivia sat on the side of the bed next to her daughter. 'I don't know what to say to you, Teddy. I don't know what to think.'

174

'Do you believe me, Mommy?'

Olivia sat on the edge of her bed and put her head in her hands.

TWENTY-EIGHT

Olivia and Amelia headed down to the kitchen for coffee.

'You got any Advil, Olivia? I don't know what possessed me to drink all those martinis, but I'm paying for it now.'

'Maybe it was *you* turning the lights on and off.'

'It wasn't. And it wasn't Teddy either.'

The kitchen was still a wreck, and Olivia had to move glasses and sticky barbecue plates just to get to the coffee maker. She ground fresh beans, and Amelia rummaged through the cabinet over the microwave, looking for the Advil.

They slumped side by side in the sunroom, and neither of them started the conversation till the coffee was ready. There was almost too much to say.

Amelia stirred half and half into her cup, an oversized mug with paw prints on the front that said *Bark Less Wag More*. A Christmas gift from Teddy and Winston the year before.

'It wasn't Teddy messing with the lights, Olivia. She wasn't there when it started. I got woken up twice before I saw her standing by the door. And I heard when she got up. I sleep light.'

'Not after that many martinis.'

'There is that.'

'You were right when you told me things would get worse with her before they got better. So can you tell me when better will come? Because right now she's got me so tied up in knots. And it's getting serious now, Amel. Look what happened at the hospital. Her telling the nurse she was afraid to go home. I came that close to having Child Protective Services on my back. And what if there *is* something wrong with her, Amel. She keeps talking about this Duncan Lee like he's a real person. Only now she says he has another name. Decan Ludde.'

'The name I saw on the Waverly web cam? She said that?'

'Yeah.'

'Is that what she meant tonight when she was talking to Jamison about *you know who*?'

Olivia nodded.

'Because I have to tell you, that was kind of weird.'

'She's so convincing when she talks about this stuff. I can't tell now when she's lying or telling the truth.'

'The thing is, Olivia, she was right in the next room. She probably overheard us talking. My take is that her little cousins planted this Duncan Lee, ghost creepy thing in Teddy's head. And my guess is she sort of believes it and she sort of doesn't. Anything can seem real if you concentrate on it too much. Look, do you have good health insurance?'

176

'Minimal. And I'm going to have to move her off Hugh's and on to mine, but at least I've got it.'

'Has Teddy been having any headaches, visual disturbances? Her appetite is normal, she's eating okay?'

Olivia fiddled with the handle of her coffee cup. Her stomach was too nauseated for her to actually drink. She hadn't even gotten the Advil down. 'Nothing like that, other than that night she got really sick, and we wound up in the ER.'

'I think you should take her to a psychologist, Livie. Someone who specializes in children.'

'Yeah, Amelia, but you know that's going to get her labeled, and go on her health records, and cause her all kinds of problems later on. That's what happened to me and Chris.'

'Not if you handle it right. Describe the problems as anxiety and school phobia. Those are typical childhood problems that won't put up red flags. Do you know anybody? Because I can ask around, but most of my contacts are in California.'

'I do know somebody, yes.'

'Is she good?'

'*He*. Yes, he's good, if he's still in practice. He's the guy Chris and I talked to, after Emily disappeared. When my family was having so much trouble.'

Amelia put her head in her hands. 'Look, I'm exhausted, I need to go back up to bed. But why don't we do this. You get Teddy off to school tomorrow, like usual, and I'll sleep in. Tomorrow afternoon, I'll go and pick her up – make sure you tell her it will be me there, okay? Let's not spring anything on her at the last minute. That way I can spend some time with her, one on one. We'll go shopping, go out to this Long's place you guys keep talking about and get ice cream. Oh hell, I don't have a car.'

'You can have mine. My office is just around the corner, I can walk.'

'Walk? This from the woman who has extreme claustrophobia, but still takes the elevator rather than climb the stairs?'

'I'll walk, Amelia, it's not that far.'

'Okay, then. Be sure you make that appointment with the shrink. Especially after what happened at the hospital, with that Dr McClintock. She called my office, and checked up on you, Olivia, did I tell you that?'

'God. No, you didn't.'

'The bottom line here, Livie, is that you need to get Teddy in counseling for two reasons. One she really needs it, and two, you need to cover your ass. If that McClintock bitch took the step of calling my office, then there's an official record of what happened. So now there's a paper trail. You need to be seen as being a proactive, careful mom. Look, I'm dead on my feet, I'm heading up to bed. But before I head up, pull out your laptop and google that name, will you? Decan Ludde, wasn't it? I want to know if maybe Teddy is pulling stuff off the Internet.'

Olivia hunched over the laptop and keyed *Decan Ludde* into the search engine. Waited. Squinted at the screen. 'How weird. Look what came up. *The Pied Piper of Hamelin*.'

'That kid story?'

Olivia's fingers trembled over the keyboard. She began to read, bit her lip, and looked up at Amelia. 'OK. So evidently *The Pied Piper* was more than just some poem by Robert Browning. It was based on an actual event in Hamelin, Germany during the Middle Ages. When a whole village of children disappeared.'

Amelia grabbed Olivia's shoulder. 'But isn't that what your brother said in his phone call? You told me that, didn't you? That he paid the piper, so everything would be OK.'

'Yeah. Amelia, did I tell you what they're doing for Teddy's third grade play? *The Pied Piper*. Teddy's going to be a rat, she brought home the school instructions for her costume this week.'

'Take it easy, Livie, it's just a fairy tale.'

'Is it? Really? Maybe Charlotte has a point. She won't let Annette be in the play.'

'But doesn't it say anything about what happened to those kids? Surely somebody has theories.'

Olivia scrolled the computer screen. 'There's a theory that the Pied Piper was a psychopathic pedophile, kidnapping children and using them in *unspeakable ways*. Some of them were found dismembered and scattered, or hanging from the branches of trees. Or were never seen again.'

'So what they're saying is the Pied Piper of Hamelin was a serial killer? Why did it come up for that name, Decan Ludde?'

Olivia rubbed her forehead. 'Decan Ludde of Hamelin, 1384. It looks like he may or may not have been a *priest*. They can't trace him. But he supposedly had some kind of chorus book with a Latin verse giving an eyewitness account of what happened. There was a stained glass window in the church in Hamelin, circa 1300 – evidently a sort of memorial.' She frowned at the keyboard. 'Oh, God. Listen to this – it's in the town chronicles from 1384. "It is ten years since our children left."'

'That sounds so sad. And so creepy.'

'Put the pieces together, Amel. *The Pied Piper* is all about making deals. That's why they call it *paying the piper*. So Chris and Jamison and Bennington go to this haunted sanatorium the night before their wrestling match. They go into the Death Tunnel where all the bodies went, back when it was an active hospital. And in the most haunted place in America, this Death Tunnel is where they went. The center of paranormal activity.'

Amelia sat back down, staring out the window into the night. 'The next day they each win every match in their wrestling competition. They all get scholarships.'

'Right. They get what they ask for. And then Jamison has his car accident and suffers this closed head injury, so for Jamison the scholarship becomes nothing more than a cruel joke.'

'And your brother Chris?'

'Comes home in happy triumph only to find his sister has disappeared.'

'Because they have to pay the piper,' Amelia whispered.

'Right. And afterwards, my brother, Chris, is

wracked with guilt, like somehow it's all his fault. And he won't take that scholarship. Like maybe he doesn't deserve it. Or it's tainted.'

'So what are you telling me here, Livie? That all of them made some kind of deal with this Decan Ludde thing, whatever it is?'

'Look at the pattern, Amel. Say my brother made a deal, all those years ago, and learns a hard lesson. He gets what he wants but the price is too high. Then he leaves this thing he attracted somehow at the Waverly, whatever it is, he leaves it alone. But then. Then his little girl, Janet, is deathly ill.'

Amelia put a hand to her chin. 'So he's a desperate father who will do anything to save his daughter. You're saying he made another deal.'

'Look how it played out. Janet is suddenly okay, but Chris doesn't sleep, he loses sixty pounds, he has nightmares and can't sleep. He makes his family move out of the house.'

'He's afraid.'

'Right. He knows he's going to have to *pay*. Which is exactly what he told me in the phone call. He had to pay the piper.'

'I wonder what happened to the Bennington guy,' Amelia said. 'Do you think Charlotte knows any details about him?'

'I think she knows more than she's said.'

Amelia put a hard hand on Olivia's shoulder. 'You might want to keep some distance between you and this sister-in-law, Livie. Remember, all of this started up when this was *her* house.'

'That won't be a problem. She treats Teddy and I like we're ... infected.'

'Yeah. But Teddy picked up a lot of nasty ideas from that cousin of hers. Maybe they're the ones infected. Not you.'

TWENTY-NINE

For the first time since Livie had come home to Knoxville, she was able to clear her mind and concentrate on work. Having Amelia at the house made things better. Amelia was smart, and practical, she loved Teddy like her own, and she had a way of tackling problems that made them seem doable. Olivia did not feel so alone.

If Amelia thought that Teddy was going through a normal phase of adjustment, then Olivia would ride it out. It was parenting. It was life.

The day got off to a wobbly start when Olivia's assistant called in sick. Olivia had three morning appointments stacked one after the other, and she made a pot of coffee, her thoughts jumping from a tally of the commissions she was going to need to make her bills this month, to kissing Mc-Tavish on the front porch the night before, to imagining Amelia and Teddy having ice cream at the soda fountain at Long's.

But the office was more cheerful without Robbie's air of disapproval and Olivia relaxed and let the phones go to voice mail. One of the clients, a retired elderly teacher, had a windfall from a lottery ticket, and she wanted to invest.

'You ought to travel and have some fun,' Olivia told her.

But the woman shook her head. 'I'll be getting some new curtains for the kitchen. But I want a safe little nest egg for my grandchildren. Do you think I should play the market with all that short selling stuff?'

'No, ma'am, I think we should find you some safe and boring bonds or a guaranteed annuity.'

'That was a test question, young lady. You are now officially hired.'

Olivia's lunch hour came and went with no time to eat, but by two the clients had left satisfied and she had miraculously made her sales quota for another month. Time to savor the moment. She closed her office door, leaned back in her chair and closed her eyes, and had an entire ninety seconds of peace before the bells jangled on the front door. She reluctantly slid back into her shoes and stuck her head around the corner of her office, thinking she smelled pizza.

McTavish was heading toward her down the little hallway, smiling, hair mussed from the wind and a Red Onion pizza box under one arm. He wore gray flannel trousers and a French blue oxford shirt with white cuffs.

'I took a chance you might be free for lunch,' he said, then put the pizza box on the front counter and looked at her over one shoulder. He was giving her that half smile he had, and Olivia wondered if she'd been on his mind that morning as much as he'd been on hers.

Olivia flipped the *Open* sign to *Closed* and locked the front door. 'My stomach was growling so much during my last appointment I had to keep scooting my chair around to cover up the noise. I'm glad to see you. Come on back. I've got coffee, bottles of water, and Coke.'

'Coke it is.'

McTavish had put the pizza box on the side table next to her desk and was hanging his jacket over the back of a chair as she came out of the little kitchenette with two icy red cans of Coke. She could see the gun, holstered at his back. He took the cans out of her hand, and set them on the desk, then pulled her close and moved closer still to kiss her.

'I've been thinking about you all morning,' he said, voice low in her ear.

Olivia sighed as he planted nibbling little kisses up and down her neck. She pushed in closer, and kicked her shoes off. McTavish sucked her lower lip gently into his mouth and ran his hands down her back, then lifted her skirt.

'Christ,' he said, running a finger around the lacy top of her stockings.

He lifted her off her feet, and sat her on the edge of the desk, pushing her skirt up and out of the way, and pressing close, kissing her again, one hand moving up under her sweater and the other moving between her thighs.

'Oh shit, McTavish.'

'Oh shit yes, or oh shit no?'

'Oh shit yes.' Olivia caught her lip in her teeth, wondering if he was going to do that thing he used to do. She touched him through the cloth of

184

his trousers, and began to unbuckle his belt.

He had her bra unfastened, and the sweater up and over her head, and cupped her breasts in his hands as he put his head between her legs. Olivia bit the edge of the collar of his shirt, leaving little teeth marks where the point of the collar was securely buttoned down. She grabbed hold of his shoulders and shut her eyes tight, and he wrapped his arms around her waist so she could give herself over to the excruciating sweetness of the sensations that rippled like tiny little shocks making her legs tremble.

He grabbed her suddenly, roughly, and pulled her off the desk, turning her so he could take her from behind, thrusting and pulling out slowly, one arm around her stomach pulling her in hard and tight.

'This is really good pizza,' Olivia said. 'What's in the other box?'

'Baklava.'

They were sitting side by side with their backs to the desk, clothes back on but with the kind of telltale tangles and creases that could lead to speculation from co-workers.

McTavish rooted through the pizza box for another slice. 'You know that sweater you had on last night is pretty irresistible. I lay awake half the night thinking about you taking it off.'

'Really? What about the sweater I have on now. You don't like this one?'

'I thought it was the same sweater.'

Olivia winced and shifted sideways, reaching under her leg for whatever it was that was causing her pain, coming up with a white plastic fork. 'So this is a baklava slash pizza joint?'

McTavish nodded, chewing thoughtfully. 'Pretty much. They deliver, by the way, and they're just a couple of blocks from your house. Jamison and I order out there all the time. Oh, hey.' He reached into his pocket. 'I got some information for you. You know that guy you asked me to check out last night? That old buddy of your brother's? That Bennington guy?' He handed her a scrap of paper from a memo pad. 'Background check looks fine, he's married, got a couple kids. Here's his phone number. I called a couple times around noon, but no luck.'

'He's probably at work,' Olivia said.

McTavish frowned. 'Maybe.'

Olivia cocked her head sideways. 'What aren't you telling me?'

'It's nothing. Just that the first time I called somebody actually picked up, but didn't say anything. The second time, no answer. But, you know, sometimes people get freaked when they see Knoxville PD on the caller ID. Maybe *you* should call him,' McTavish said. 'Or better yet, just leave the whole Waverly thing alone.'

'Why?'

'Well, come on, Olivia. You're home, you got a new job. A beautiful daughter, and me bringing you pizza for lunch. What more could a woman want?'

Olivia stuck the scrap of paper under her desk blotter, thinking maybe McTavish was right.

McTavish was gone by three thirty, and though

186

Olivia unlocked the front door and turned the *Open* sign back around, nobody wandered in, and the phones were quiet. She waited till the market closed at four, imagining Teddy and Amelia at Long's Drug Store, digging into hot fudge sundaes. Something chocolate would be good right about now. Right about anytime, actually. If they were still there, she could join them. She'd pulled her weight in the office today.

But Amelia didn't answer the phone.

Olivia changed to her walking shoes, leaving her heels under the desk. Gathered up the trail of tissues she had somehow shed from doorway to desk. Long's was just a block and a half away. She'd surprise them.

She locked the office up, double checking both the front and back door, then headed down to the corner, waiting for the light to change. Her briefcase was heavy. When the walk signal came on, she hesitated. It bothered her that Amelia hadn't answered the phone. And she'd confiscated Teddy's cell phone, so she could not call her daughter direct. She dialed Amelia's number again.

The connection was jumpy – it was windy out, but the sky was clear. The phone rang six times, with no answer.

The light changed again, and Olivia went left instead of right, turning the corner and heading down the wide sidewalk to her house. She was being ridiculous, of course. Stupid to be worried on an afternoon when the sun was shining. A man walking a mastiff passed her by, and grinned and said sorry when the dog tried to put a nose up her skirt. Olivia thought about McTavish and felt her cheeks go pink. A man and a woman, both in motorized wheelchairs, swooped past her like lovebirds in flight. There were section eight apartments up the road, niches for the disabled, and those struggling with the recession and keeping their children fed on jobs that paid minimum wage. Jamison lived there, two blocks northeast.

Which meant McTavish would be close by quite a lot, Olivia thought.

Olivia passed the stone wall next to her house and hesitated. Her car was parked right next to the garage, canted a bit to the left, where she'd left it the night before. Olivia headed up the steep asphalt drive. Could Amelia possibly still be asleep? Had she remembered to pick Teddy up after school?

Olivia began to run toward the house, catching a flash of movement from the front porch. Maybe the stray dog she and Teddy had seen, but it was gone by the time she made it up to the door.

Which was closed, but unlocked.

Olivia went in slowly, warily. It felt somehow wrong in the house. Her heartbeat picked up and the mom fear, always a breath away, was making her stomach clench. Olivia could hear Winston barking in the backyard and the scrabble of his toenails as he whined at the back kitchen door. Teddy's backpack was on the floor next to the coffee table, along with her pale yellow sweatshirt, that had been wadded and tossed on the couch. She took a breath. So Teddy was home then. Home safe from school.

'Teddy?' Olivia said. 'Amelia?'

Olivia picked Teddy's backpack up, to set it on the couch, and something fell out of the side pocket and hit the floor. Chalk. A piece of blue chalk. Olivia thought about Teddy's name newly scribbled on the ceiling stud in the bathroom upstairs. Could Teddy have done that? How? Even with a ladder she wouldn't be tall enough.

The house was quiet, but oddly present. Olivia thought about what Teddy had said the night before, that she and Winston were being watched. She was glad for Winston's sake that he was out in the yard, but it was strange that Teddy had not let him back in. She dropped her briefcase to the floor and headed up the hardwood stairs. It was dim upstairs, no lights on at all. Amelia's orange flip flops were in the hallway, right outside the bathroom door. Amelia was obsessively neat. It was odd for her to leave her shoes like that, out in the hall.

Olivia thought to call out again, but didn't. She moved quietly. Not even a creak of the floor. She listened for voices. Maybe Amelia and Teddy had simply walked. It was, after all, a beautiful day. Maybe they'd forgotten Winston, and left him out in the yard.

Olivia paused in the hallway, listening. Something – the tiniest gurgle of noise, like water lapping against the side of the tub. The bathroom door was open.

It took a full moment for her brain to register and her mind to accept everything that she saw. Water on the floor, a lot of it, as if someone had struggled mightily to get out of the tub. Amelia, naked, twisted sideways, her head under water, her hair undulating gently. And Teddy. Standing at the foot of the bathtub. Holding tight to Amelia's feet.

'Oh my sweet Jesus God.'

Olivia's words broke the spell. Teddy began to sob and shake, and Olivia pushed her out of the way and stepped into the tub, the water drenching her shoes, her panty hose and the bottom of her skirt.

'Oh, Mommy, I'm sorry, I'm so so sorry. I think Dr Amelia is dead.'

'Call nine one one, Teddy. My phone's in my purse, it's in the living room downstairs.'

Teddy was wearing her monkey shirt today, a worn out favorite her father had given her, with a circle of chimps throwing bananas. Her hair was in pigtails and her shirtfront was drenched. Olivia was aware of every detail as she listened to her daughter's frantic scramble down the stairs.

Teddy was sorry. So so sorry. What had her little girl done?

It was going to be too late for Amelia. She was definitively dead, and Olivia knew it, though she strained and hauled Amelia up and out of the tub, wincing when she lost her grip and the body thudded and hit the floor. She tried CPR. The breath of life. But Amelia's skin was cold, her limbs heavy and unwieldy, as if they were filled with sand. There was a froth of white foam in her nostrils and mouth, and her eyes were rolled back into her head, showing white. Olivia listened for the sound of sirens, and help, aware when Teddy ran back up the stairs, aware when she stood in the hall outside the bathroom, staring.

'Did you make the call?' Olivia asked.

Teddy shook her head. 'I couldn't find the phone. It wasn't in your purse.'

'No, I said it was in my briefcase, Teddy.'

'I thought you said purse. Mommy, is she—'

'Teddy. Go into the bedroom. Just sit on the bed and I'll be right there.'

'I can bring the phone.'

But Olivia was remembering an old movie she and Hugh had watched. A movie where a man had murdered wife after wife, by running them a bubble bath, then creeping into the bathroom, jerking their feet to submerge them suddenly in water. There was some term for this kind of drowning, vagal inhalation? Her mind wasn't working right, she could not get the details straight. But Teddy had not seen the movie. Teddy would not know how to do such a thing. Teddy loved Dr Amelia. Teddy was just a little girl.

'No, Teddy. Don't do that. Not yet. I want you to tell me what you meant when you said you were sorry.'

Teddy went very still. 'Mommy, I'm afraid.'

'It's okay, Teddy. You need to know that no matter what happened, I love you. I'll take care of you, *always*. But you need to tell me what you did.'

'But aren't you going to call an ambulance? Will I have to tell the police?'

'Tell them what, Teddy?'

191

'Tell them what happened to Dr Amelia.' Teddy put her hands over her face. 'I think she drowned.'

'Teddy, why were you holding her feet?' There were red marks on Amelia's ankles. Teddy had been holding her hard.

'I don't know. He told me to.'

Olivia felt queasy. But she had half expected this was what Teddy would say. 'Who told you, Teddy?'

'You know who, Mommy, you know, and it's bad to say his name.'

'What else did he tell you, Teddy?'

Teddy took a step backward. 'He tells me lots of things, Mommy. I won't talk about it anymore.'

Olivia felt the last hope wither. There would be no more quiet joy, no pleasure in coming home. Her dreams for the job, her pleasure in the little stone house, were nothing, out of reach, her focus must be on only one thing. Teddy. Olivia loved her so much right now, maybe more than ever before, because the love felt so sad. She did not think for one moment that Teddy had hurt Amelia, she was too little, just a baby girl. But something had happened, and she didn't want Teddy within one mile of questions from the police. She wanted no rumors, no publicity, no locals speculating about the little girl who found the body in the tub. And clearly, Teddy needed help, counseling of some kind. Whatever Teddy had seen or not seen, done or not done, it had to be dealt with, but in private, on Olivia's terms, as a mother who knew the dangers of letting a child get chewed raw by officialdom and the system. Teddy was already fragile, and finding Amelia's body this way, on top of everything else, was too much for an adult, much less a little girl of eight.

'Teddy, I want you to come with me.'

But Teddy backed away. 'Why? Where are you taking me?'

'To your Aunt Charlotte's house. It's going to be upsetting here for a while, when the emergency people come. I want you to be safe with Charlotte, while all of that is going on.'

Teddy grabbed Olivia around the waist, and the tears came, with hiccups and sobs. 'Mommy, I feel so bad.'

'I know you do, Teddy. I feel bad too. We'll talk about this later. In private. Right now I only want you to discuss this with me, and a friend I'm going to introduce you to. His name is Dr Raymond, and he helped me a lot when I was a little girl. We can trust him, Teddy. He can help you too.'

Teddy looked up. 'Mommy? What if Aunt Charlotte won't let us in?'

'She's family, Teddy. Of course she'll let us in.'

THIRTY

Teddy was hiccuping softly when they pulled into the driveway of Charlotte's house. The garage doors were open, and both cars were there. Charlotte was home. Olivia took a deep and steadying breath.

'She wasn't there when I got out of school,' Teddy said softly. She had a hand on Winston's collar, as if she were afraid to let him go.

'Do you mean Dr Amelia?' Olivia asked.

'She was supposed to pick me up after school, but she didn't come. I waited and waited.'

'Did that make you mad at her?' Olivia asked.

Teddy gave her a puzzled look, and shook her head.

'Why didn't you call me, Teddy? How did you get home?'

'I walked.'

Olivia dug her fingernails into her palms. Waited. But Teddy seemed to have nothing else to say.

'Come on, Teddy, out of the car.' Teddy needed to be there with her, standing at the door. That would make it hard for Charlotte to turn them away.

But Charlotte was holding the front door open as they came up the walk. Opening the screen door. Beckoning them in.

'I thought I heard a car,' Charlotte said. She was looking at them oddly, taking them in, the two of them, desolate and desperate and on her front porch.

Olivia tried to pull Teddy through the open door, but Teddy hung back. 'Are you sure you want me here, Aunt Charlotte?' Teddy said.

Charlotte winced. 'Yes, honey, I'm sure.' Her eyes were circled and dark, and she crouched down to give Teddy a hug and pat Winston. 'We need a dog around this place to cheer things up and—*Teddy, you're drenched*. What happened?'

'Teddy, take Winston and go in the house,' Olivia said.

'The girls are in the backyard on the trampoline.' Charlotte waited until Teddy was out of earshot. 'I know you're mad at me, Olivia, and I'm sorry I didn't return your call about coming to dinner Sunday night. I've been thinking and – look, come on in the house and let's talk this out. I know I treated you like hell the other day. I panicked. I just didn't want ... I just didn't know what to do.'

'I can't come in right now, Charlotte.'

'Oh, come on, Olivia, at least hear me out. We can—' Charlotte paused and put a hand to her mouth. 'Your skirt is wet and you look like hell. Something's happened. What is it, Livie?'

'I *need* you, Charlotte. I need you to do what I say and not ask me any questions.'

Something in Olivia's voice made Charlotte go very still. 'So it's starting up again, isn't it?'

'Just listen to me, Charlotte. Please. For Chris's

195

sake, if nothing else.'

Charlotte put an arm around Olivia's shoulders. 'Come on in, sweetie.'

'I can't. Look. Teddy has been here, with you and the girls, all afternoon.' Olivia held up a hand. 'Don't interrupt, just listen. You picked her up from school. You were late, so she started home and you picked her up at the curb right at the stop sign at the intersection of Sutherland and Westside Drive.'

'Olivia, please tell me what's going on.'

'Amelia's dead. My friend from California? The PA?'

'Yeah. I met her, remember – but what happened? Was she in an accident?'

'She's been visiting us and she died at the house.'

'Oh my God. Another one.' Charlotte put a hand to her mouth. 'Did it happen in the night? Did she die in her sleep?'

'It happened this afternoon. Sometime in the last hour, I think. It looks like she drowned in the tub.'

'That's why you're wet? And Teddy?'

'Teddy was there when it happened.'

Charlotte reached for Olivia. Tried to give her a hug. 'Oh my God. Poor poor baby.'

Olivia took a step backward. For some reason it was harder not to cry when Charlotte was being nice. When it felt like they were family again, part of the same tribe. 'Look. I have to go and deal with things. I have to call nine one one.'

'You mean you haven't called them yet? She's still—'

196

'I got her out of the tub. She was beyond help, I promise. The thing is, *Teddy was there*, in the bathroom, when it happened. I don't want the police to know that. I don't want her questioned and traumatized anymore than she already is.'

'What is it you're not telling me?' Charlotte said.

'I'm protecting my daughter. That's all you need to know.'

'Protecting her from what?' Charlotte said.

'Honestly? Honestly, Charlotte? I have no idea. I just know that whoever it is, I'm scared.'

THIRTY-ONE

Every single light was on in the house when Olivia pulled up, so that for a moment, she wondered if the paramedics were there ahead of her. But the driveway was empty. The front door shut tight, the back gate snug against intruders. The cottage looked so pretty, the sweep of old stone and the twist of the double chimney. The azaleas, pink and white, were beginning to lose their flowers, and the dogwood trees along the side of the drive were on the verge of shedding their leaves. Olivia was afraid to go in.

The house was different now, she could feel it the minute she walked through the front door. It felt dense inside, as if the very air was heavy, a waking, breathing underwater feeling that made

197

Olivia's heart beat hard and her movements awkward and slow. She stopped in the living room, thinking there was something she needed to do. She felt thirsty and cold, and knew she was feeling the shock.

The backpack. Teddy's sweater. Olivia snatched them up and jammed them into the living room closet, stashing them behind a stack of pictures yet unhung. She looked carefully around the room, then started up the staircase, hesitating on the third step. She did not know why she listened. The house was very quiet now, but oddly aware.

Olivia began to tremble. She didn't have to go up there, not really. Did not have to go into that bathroom, and look at Amelia, lying dead on the floor. She could call for help from downstairs, here in the living room.

Olivia looked over her shoulder at her favorite red leather chair, where Teddy had curled up and gone to sleep, Nancy Drew book in her lap, just the night before. How long ago it seemed. She thought she'd had problems then, but now. Now her life could never be the same.

Best not to think that way. She would deal with things. She loved Teddy as much as any mother ever loved a child, and getting Teddy the help she needed would be the sole focus of her life.

Olivia headed up the stairs. Better to look. Check and make sure that everything was okay. She had the oddest feeling that the body would not be there when she went down the hall. She imagined how she would feel if it had moved.

But it was all just like she had left it. Water

pooled on the floor, Amelia, sprawled sideways, the water in the tub lukewarm, a skin of bubble bath residue on the surface. Olivia took care not to look at Amelia's eyes as she pushed through the bathroom door. Amelia's bathrobe swung gently from a hook on the back. Her makeup was lined up on the counter, so much of it that Olivia almost smiled. And with the smile came a rush of tears.

'I'm so sorry, Amelia,' Olivia whispered. She crouched down close to Amelia, and touched the cold white cheek, wondering how such a thing could have happened. It did not feel real. Olivia was flooded with an enveloping disbelief, because Amelia should not be dead and would not be dead if Olivia had come home sooner, or if Amelia had stayed in LA. Olivia wanted a reprieve, a second chance, to find a way to do the day entirely over. She could save them all, Amelia and Teddy, if she could start this day again.

Olivia took the phone out of her pocket, and grabbed for the tissue that spilled out as well, shredding it while she made the call. The routine 911 recording would catch the tremor in her voice. All she had to do now was wait. Should she go downstairs or stay up here? She felt guilt at the thought of leaving Amelia behind, but she did not want to be here anymore. Downstairs would be better, she'd have to let them in.

Olivia was at the top of the stairs when she turned back for one last look. There had been something odd she had noticed, but her mind was so full of noise right now, it was hard to think.

Amelia's right hand was curled in a fist. Olivia

199

bent over her, and peeled back the slim waxy fingers.

'Sorry,' she whispered. 'Sorry.'

Amelia had a button in her hand, and Olivia held it up to the light. Not a button. A little plastic eye, from one of Teddy's stuffed animals.

Olivia heard sirens and flinched. They were coming now, she should have searched the bathroom more carefully before she'd made the call. She looked under the wad of towels on the floor, into the hamper, stupid, yes, but she had to be sure.

She found it just as the flash of revolving lights hummed against the bathroom window. Eeyore, soaking wet and missing an eye, wedged in a space against the back wall, right at the bottom of the tub. Olivia ran to her bedroom, and tucked him into her dresser drawer, beneath a stack of tee shirts she never wore.

More sirens, the crunch of tires in the driveway, voices. She ran downstairs to open the front door.

THIRTY-TWO

Olivia knew she should cry. The paramedics had brushed by quickly, boxy cases of equipment in their hands, but the uniformed officer named Farrell who asked her questions kept watching her out of the corner of his eye, and she knew

200

that he was expecting tears, that he dreaded it, but that it would also reassure him that nothing odd was going on.

They had asked her if Amelia was depressed. Despondent over things going on in her life. If she suffered from seizures, was on any kind of medication. Adult women did not drown in the tub as a matter of course.

Farrell hadn't liked it, that Olivia had pulled Amelia out of that tub. She'd overheard him say something to his partner about things feeling *hinky*, and his partner had shrugged and told him not to be an idiot. It was perfectly normal to pull someone out from under the water like that.

That had seemed to reassure him and Olivia knew that all she needed to do was burst into tears to ease that last bit of suspicion, but somehow she felt tight inside and it simply was not possible to let go.

Until someone on the porch said *who called homicide?*, and McTavish walked into the room.

'Livie,' he said. 'I was down the street with Jamison when I heard the sirens. I just called in and they told me there was an accident – not Teddy, though, Amelia.'

As soon as Olivia saw him, the tears were unloosed.

McTavish crouched beside her and wrapped her in his arms. Olivia knew then that she had come home to feel safe. And though McTavish felt safe right now, the feeling wasn't going to last. She would never be safe until Teddy was okay.

He still had the blue shirt on. Olivia thought

about the two of them, together in her office, at the same time Amelia was drowning, of Teddy by the side of the tub. She shuddered and closed her eyes.

One of the officers tapped McTavish on the shoulder. 'Would you like to see the scene, sir, before we take the body away?'

'I'm here as a friend, Mike, but yeah, if you don't mind.' McTavish spoke over the top of her head. Olivia could feel the whisper of his voice in her hair.

'Did you know the deceased, sir?'

'I did, yeah. Just sit tight, okay, Livie? I'll be right back.' He squeezed her shoulders and whispered. 'Where's Teddy?'

'With Charlotte. That's where she goes after school, every afternoon.' Olivia had rehearsed those words and they sounded stilted.

'Right,' McTavish said, nodding his head as if he had no memory of their conversation the afternoon before, when Olivia had brought him a beer as he cleaned out the grill, and vented about how weird her sister-in-law had been. How Charlotte had backed down from her promise to watch Teddy after school. He followed the officer up the steps, their footsteps heavy and loud on bare wood.

They were gone a long time. One of the paramedics came downstairs and knelt beside her, told her his name was Art. Asking if she was okay, and would she mind if he checked her over. He was looking at her hands, the skin on her wrists and arms. Olivia held her hands up to cover her face. Go ahead and look, she thought.

You won't see any marks on me.

'I'm just upset, Art, and all I really need is a tissue to blow my nose.'

He made a note on his chart and gave her a sad little smile, but he seemed satisfied, like he'd done what he had to do. 'I've got bandages, ma'am, but no tissues.'

Olivia found a tissue caught between the cushions of the couch. She had stopped crying by the time McTavish came back downstairs. He nodded to one of the paramedics, who looked at his partner over his shoulder. There was the groan of hydraulics as someone wrestled a stretcher through the door.

'They don't want you watching, Livie, when they bring Amelia through. Let me take you up-stairs to your bedroom. You can change into dry clothes and pack a few things. You won't want to sleep here tonight.'

'I'm the one who found her, McTavish, why shouldn't I be here when they take her through?'

'It's protocol, sweetheart, so don't fight me on it.' There was a message in the tone of his voice, and the way that he met her eyes.

She shrugged, and let him lead her up the stairs, past the uniforms clustered outside the bathroom, and into her bedroom where he shut the door.

'Stay here until I come and get you. Make sure you change your clothes.'

'I'm not worried about being wet, McTavish, and they're almost dry anyway.'

He folded his arms, waiting till she met his eyes. 'That's right. They are almost dry. But

203

we're in luck because nobody else has noticed that but me, which is why you need to just go on and throw on some jeans or something like you want to be comfortable. Because if you'd really called right after you found the body, you ought to be soaking wet.'

'Oh.'

'Right. I'll be back,' he said. Then he was out the door, leaving her alone in the room.

THIRTY-THREE

McTavish was losing the argument and he didn't like it. 'You ought to go to Charlotte's house and be with Teddy. And if you don't want to go there, then come home with me.'

'This is my home, McTavish, there's no reason I can't be here.'

'I don't want to leave you here in this house.'

'Why not?'

'I don't know. It's got a weird feeling here right now. It's like that sometimes, right after a death. Look, please talk to me about this, Livie. I've got your back, but *tell me* what's going on.'

'I've told you everything.'

'Then why were your clothes so dry?'

'They just didn't get that wet, McTavish, don't cop me to death.'

He folded his arms. 'Okay, sweetheart, I'll respect your privacy on this, but let's go on record here as me knowing that's bullshit. If you decide you want to talk let me know. You sure you don't want to come to my place? I can cook us something. Open a bottle of wine. You look like you could use some TLC.'

Olivia did not allow herself to imagine it, safely tucked up with McTavish, drowning in a bottle of wine. 'I need some time alone, McTavish. I just lost my best friend.'

'If you change your mind.'

'I'll call.'

'Even in the middle of the night?'

'Even in the middle of the night.'

Olivia waited till she saw the headlights of his car disappear down the drive. She had no intention of staying the night, and did not want to be alone in the house, but at least she did not have to go back upstairs. She got Teddy's backpack out of the closet, and the yellow sweater and put them next to the small overnight bag where she'd thrown in a few things for herself and Teddy for tonight.

She watched out the living room window. McTavish, all the paramedics and patrol cars, they were gone. She thought she would feel relieved when they left, but she didn't. She just felt alone.

And then she realized she would have to go back upstairs one more time. She would get Eeyore out from under the stack of tee shirts, and then she could go. She would drop him off at a dumpster behind some shopping center – somewhere away from the house. Charlotte had called and said she'd cooked dinner and had a bed made up. She just needed to hang on a little longer, to make sure that Teddy would be safe.

Olivia headed up the stairs steadily, wondering if anyone had pulled the plug in the bathtub so the water could drain, unable to make herself go in and take a look. Eeyore was tucked in the drawer right where she had left him, soaking the tee shirts, and she put him in the garbage bag from the trash basket in her bedroom, and tied the top in a knot. She had just turned off the bedroom light when she heard the phone.

Not her phone, quiet in the pocket of her jeans. The ring tones were familiar and insistent – Amelia's phone, the ringing coming from Chris's bedroom where Amelia had spent the night. Olivia stood in the hall, trying to make up her mind about answering, when the ringing stopped. Better that way. She was just past the bathroom door when the ringing started up again. Olivia hesitated, then turned back.

Amelia's Blackberry was on the dresser top, next to a half filled mug of coffee. Olivia picked it up, absorbing the details of the room. Amelia had made up the bed. Been drinking a cup of coffee. A half eaten bacon sandwich was on a plate next to the coffee. And downstairs, the kitchen was pristine. So Amelia had been having lunch. Why had she taken a bubble bath in the middle of the day?

'Amelia's phone,' Olivia said.

A male voice. Worried. 'My name is Jack Butler and I need to speak to Amelia Wainwright.'

'I'm sorry, but Amelia isn't available right

now.' How calm she sounded, Olivia thought. Not the slightest tremor in her voice.

'Look, this is extremely urgent. My daughter, Marianne, is ... was ... is one of Amelia's patients.'

'Mr Butler, if you need a doctor, you need to call Amelia's service.'

'I don't need a doctor, I need her. Look, I'm not just some patient, Amelia is a close family friend. I need to talk to her *now.'*

'Mr Butler, forgive me, but are you calling with ... with news?'

He took a breath, and was quiet a long moment. 'I really have to talk to Amelia.'

'And I already told you she's not able to come to the phone.'

'Look. Can you get her a message?'

'I'm sorry, I can't.'

'Please. I get that she's upset with Alexis. I don't blame her. It was a damn fool thing to do, having Amelia barred from Marianne's room. Amelia's been so good to us, more than anybody can know. But something's happened, and – look, Marianne had surgery this morning, and she didn't make it through. Or at least that's what we thought.'

'I'm not following you on this.'

'Her heart gave out on the operating table. They had just put her under the anesthetic, hadn't even opened her up. I tried to call Amelia then, and I left a message, just so she'd know, okay? But then, a little while later, my wife and I are in with the hospital chaplain, kind of just taking it in, and one of the nurses busts in the

207

door, and says that the morgue called up, and Marianne, she's not dead.'

Olivia caught her breath. 'Mr Butler, I'm sorry for your loss, but—'

'That's the point, *it's not my loss*. Marianne is *alive*. Only Alexis, she's hysterical, she says it's not our daughter that came back, it's some kind of demon, that it's not right, that it's all a sin, and she starts talking about something Amelia said about phone calls from the dead. And I just wanted ... I just needed—'

'Amelia,' Olivia whispered. 'What did you do?'

'Ma'am, are you there?'

Olivia hung up the phone.

THIRTY-FOUR

Olivia sat in Charlotte's kitchen, trying to absorb the comfort of suburban normality while Charlotte checked on the kids. The kitchen floor was beige linoleum, the appliances stainless steel, and the round wooden table was exactly like a million others in furniture showrooms in every city of the United States. Olivia wanted comfort and was finding it hard to get.

Charlotte came in from the hallway, pausing behind Olivia to put a hand on her shoulder. 'I'm so very sorry about your friend. I know how bad you must feel. How shocked.'

'Thank you, Charlotte. Thank you for taking us in.'

'And look, I know you're worried about Teddy, and rightly so, she was pretty shook up when you left. But she was asleep when I checked the girls, all of them were. She's got Winston curled up with her on the pillow, and I left the hall light on. Look, you didn't eat anything. You want me to warm up that bowl of beef stew?'

'Sure.'

'Are you going to eat it?'

'No.'

'Then why do you want me to warm it up?'

'That's just in case you need something to do. So putter around all you want, Charlotte. Go check the kids three more times, and drink another twenty-seven glasses of wine.'

'You sound angry.'

'Not with you, Charlotte, sorry. Evidently I'm going through the stages of grief really fast and I've just fast forwarded to really pissed off.'

It surprised Olivia when Charlotte laughed.

'It isn't like that, one stage moving in a straight line to the other. You can go from shock to anger to denial then back to shock in fifteen minutes. I know, because I've done it. There's no fast way to get through it, Livie, I wish I could tell you there was.' Charlotte settled herself into the chair next to Olivia as if she were an achy old woman a hundred years old. 'But you know it as well as I do, don't you? Maybe better.'

'I do, yes. And I think next up on the agenda is going to be guilt.' Amelia would be fine if she hadn't come here. She'd be in California, alive and well.

Charlotte topped off Olivia's wine glass, though Olivia had left it untouched. 'For God's sake, Livie, lose the guilt, you're as bad as Chris. Ever since I've known your brother, it's been very clear that he felt responsible for what happened to your sister, Emily, so much so that it seemed almost pathological.'

'He had good reason to feel that way. In a way, it *was* his fault. Because of whatever it was that happened that night, when he went to the Waverly. You do know about that, don't you, Charlotte? It happened when he was a senior in high school, when he and his buddies were up in Louisville for a wrestling championship. How they all sneaked out to go ghost hunting at the notorious haunted sanatorium. He must have talked to you about it, Charlotte.'

Charlotte didn't answer, would not meet Olivia's eyes.

Olivia clenched her hands into fists. 'You know, Charlotte, I think I could handle anything. *Anything*. So long as Teddy was okay.'

Charlotte frowned and put a hand on Olivia's wrist. 'Teddy *is* okay. She *will* be. It's just going to take some time.'

'I don't think time is what's called for here.'

'Livie, I'm not following you on this.'

'Did Janet ... when she was having her troubles. Did Janet ever do anything ... *bad*?'

'*Bad*? No, she didn't. I don't like what I'm hearing here, Livie. There's nothing wrong with Janet and nothing wrong with Teddy, but something really wrong with that *fucking house*.'

'I got a strange phone call, Charlotte, after they took Amelia's ... Amelia away. Did I tell you that Amelia's goddaughter, Marianne, has been dying, she's very very sick. She's three years old.'

'That's terrible.'

'And evidently she died today at noon, and then, by some strange miracle, the morgue said there was some kind of mistake. She was alive after all, after they declared her dead. Does that remind you of anything, Charlotte? Like what you and Chris went through, with Janet?'

Charlotte pulled back away from Olivia, a hand to her throat. 'What are you saying?'

'I think you know. I think Chris told you every- thing, you guys were too close for him not to tell you what was going on. I think Chris made a deal with this ... this piper, and I think Amelia did the same damn thing, and somehow, Teddy got used, she was ... she was maybe the instru- ment, I mean *why*, Charlotte, why won't you let Annette be in the school play? Do you know what really happened? Did my brother make some kind of deal so Janet would be all right?'

Charlotte narrowed her eyes and put a finger to her lips, looking past Olivia's shoulder to the hall, and the bedrooms where their daughters slept. 'Okay, Livie. I don't know all the ins and outs for sure. But I'll tell you what I do know.'

Olivia waited while Charlotte gathered her thoughts.

'It was strange the way that Chris told it,' Charlotte said finally, tilting her head to one side. 'But the way he put it was that they—'

'They being he and his buddies. Chris, Bennington and Jamison.'

'Right. That they went down into that Body Chute at the Waverly, just as a sort of teenage prank, but that something there ... something *found them*. Then he said, did I know that in every haunting, there was a *heart*. A *focus* of activity or energy. And the heart, at the Waverly, was this Body Chute. He said ... so many strange things. That at first he thought that the fear was just his imagination. He said that ... how did he put it ... that when reasonable people are faced with the unbelievable, they have no defense. They can't protect themselves. He said that the three of them had been *infiltrated*. That's what he called it. He and Jamison and Bennington.

'He said that it had been given away like a gift – with them winning the wrestling match, and getting full ride scholarships. Just like a dream come true. But that the gift was really nothing more than a lure with terrible strings attached, like this thing was fishing for them, and hooked them on a line. And that he got what he thought he wanted, and Emily paid the price.

'So when Janet got sick, he went into things knowing that ... how did he put it? When you provoke malign troubles, you face retribution.'

'Provoke malign troubles,' Olivia whispered, thinking of the text message that Hugh had gotten from Teddy. She felt ill.

'Livie, my God, you just went white. What are you thinking? Did Amelia know any of this? Do you really think she made a deal?'

'I don't know, but it looks that way. Marianne

212

dies, then Marianne is miraculously okay.'

Charlotte sat forward. 'And Amelia, a grown woman, drowns that very afternoon in the tub.'

'There's no help then, is there?' Olivia said. 'I'm all alone with this.'

'That's not really true, though, Livie. Not according to Chris. Remember I told you I wanted him to leave that house, but he said no, that it wouldn't do any good? It wasn't because he was giving up and crawling off to die. He said he couldn't come with us until after he *dealt* with things. He said these things weren't happening to just us, there had been three of them there at the Waverly, and he didn't know about Jamison, but Bennington was in trouble too. And he kissed us all goodbye like he knew he might never see us again, but he said he and Bennington had put their heads together, and they had a plan, so not to give up hope. That when things worked out, he would come home to us again, because he and Bennington had found someone who might be able to help, but that first he had to make sure we were all safe.'

Olivia went very still. 'Did he tell you who that someone was?'

'A woman. A psychic, she lives in the neighborhood. Patsy Ackerman.'

'But – I've *heard* that name. Didn't they do a television special on her once?'

Charlotte nodded. 'She's kind of famous. Or she used to be. She stopped practicing, or whatever you call it, over fifteen years ago. But Chris and Bennington were wearing her down. Chris was positive she could help, but she was reluctant to get involved. He said she had good reasons to be ... afraid.'

'Patsy Ackerman,' Olivia said.

'Right. And that's it, Olivia, I've told you everything I know.'

'I wonder if she would talk to me.'

'Why, Livie? You don't need her. Look.' Charlotte slapped her palms down on the table. 'So maybe you're right, and Amelia made a deal. The bottom line is that Amelia paid the price. It is what it is, and it's over now. Whoever did what, whoever made deals, it's done. Stay away from it, Livie. We don't have to understand to know it was bad. Time to walk away.'

'But what if it's not over? What if Teddy is part of the price?'

'I know how scared you feel,' Charlotte told her. 'But Teddy is safe and tucked in her bed. Amelia's dead. It's done. All you have to do is stay out of that house.'

Olivia put her chin in her hands. Stay out of the house, Charlotte told her. Stay away from that sister-in-law, Amelia had said.

'I'm going to bed now, Charlotte,' Olivia said. 'Do you mind if I take the wine?'

Charlotte waved a hand. 'If you finish that off, there's vodka in the freezer.'

Olivia picked up the bottle and her glass. Vices to still the soul, she thought, heading down the hall.

214

THIRTY-FIVE

Chambliss Place was residential commercial, lined with what the realtors called Shrink Shacks – zoning laws forbade any kind of business that generated more than one or two cars an hour, which meant the little bungalows made perfect offices for psychologists, attorneys and brokers.

Dr Raymond's office was in a stone bungalow with a prime position on the corner, and the green sign with white lettering was a presence in the front yard. *Chambliss Psychological Services, Miles Raymond, PhD, Adolescents, Children, & Family Counseling.* Olivia's father had taken her to talk to Dr Raymond a few weeks after her mother died. Dr Raymond found out how much she loved iced brownies. They'd sat together at a weathered, old oak farmhouse table on every visit, and bonded over chocolate, while Dr Raymond eased her heart.

Olivia was alone in the waiting room. Dr Raymond's associates had gone home at four, and there was no receptionist, just a complex system where patients rang buzzers, and an answering service took the incoming calls.

Dr Raymond had taken her emergency call first thing that morning. He had known exactly who she was and she'd immediately recognized his voice. He sounded the same as he had when she was a child.

Teddy had been back in Dr Raymond's office for an hour and fifteen minutes now, which was already twenty-five minutes past the usual allotted time.

In all the years that Olivia had ranged far and wide, moving from city to city, Dr Raymond's office at Chambliss Place had evidently stayed the same. Dark wood floors in the waiting room, and the red Persian carpet with a hole in the middle, courtesy of Dr Raymond's cat. A masculine room. A comforting cliché.

Two tobacco brown distressed leather love seats had earned their lines and creases the hard way. A vintage silver ash tray on a stand split down the middle at the touch of a crank, even though if you smoked, you had to go outside. Pictures of horses in the hunt and dogs playing poker. A generous hodge-podge of books and magazines – everything that might appeal. Celebrities, vampires, wizards, women being carried off by muscular men who wore tight breeches and strategically ripped shirts. A little something for everyone, Dr Raymond always said. Dr Raymond always had the good stuff, and he never minded if patients or visitors looted the goods. He liked getting a book back for each one that disappeared, but it wasn't like there was a set of rules.

Waiting was hard. Olivia had client files in her briefcase, but she did not touch them. After a while, she got up and took the briefcase to the car. Locked it in the trunk. Then went back into

216

the waiting room to sit.

Dr Raymond's office door opened at five twenty-nine and Olivia heard Teddy's soft tread in the hall. She was half up off the leather couch when Teddy came around the bend.

'Hi, Mommy.' Teddy was rumpled as always. Her jeans sagged at the belly, her left shoe was untied, and her favorite, well worn pink sweater was untucked on one side. She also looked relieved, and Olivia knew then that the talk with Dr Raymond had been good.

'You okay there, Kidlet?'

Teddy smiled. 'You were right, I like him.'

'I wouldn't steer you wrong.'

'Dr Raymond says he needs a smoke break, and then the three of us need to talk.' Teddy went straight to the piles of books. Sorting. Rooting. Frowning. 'Nothing here but vampires.'

'There are more books in that little alcove next to the bathroom,' Olivia said.

Teddy disappeared for a while, and then peered back around the corner, waving a book in her hand. 'Nancy Drew. *The Secret of Red Gate Farm.* I knew he'd have one.'

'You can take it home with you,' Olivia said. 'Dr Raymond won't mind.'

As Olivia remembered, it was cigarettes and orange juice that got Dr Raymond through the day, and sure enough, when she heard his heavy footsteps on the wood, and saw him zoom into the waiting room with that almost kinetic energy she remembered so well, he reeked of tobacco, and there were stains on his sweater where he'd spilled the juice that he drank out of tiny cans

217

with a straw. He used to tell Olivia that it took talent to spill juice from a straw.

And no doubt he left the house tidy in the morning, but he was the kind of man who came apart at the seams as the day went on. He wore his clothes like a bear all dressed up for the amusement of humans, pants baggy and twisted at the waist, denim shirt he did not bother to tuck in, and sweaters, cuddly sweaters, he always wore those unless it was really hot.

And though his office had not changed, Dr Raymond had. Another forty pounds. Permanent circles under the heavy-lidded eyes that were creased with too much sun and gave him a woeful hound dog air. No brown in the hair now, all white and gray, but still thick. Huge hornrimmed reading glasses that he wore on a chain around his neck like some maiden aunt who tucked tissues in her sleeve. Olivia thought of Amelia and the way she wore her cat glasses on a chain and she had to bite her bottom lip not to cry. Later she would cry. *Later*.

'Livie, Livie, Livie. You're all grown up.' Dr Raymond smiled and opened his arms and gave her the kind of hug you'd get from a kindly giant.

Dr Raymond, she thought, help me take care of Teddy. Maybe Dr Raymond could make it all okay.

The three of them sat together around Dr Raymond's big oak table, like a family after a big holiday meal. His desk looked like a library after a hurricane, the wood chair pushed back. The trash can overflowed with papers and empty cans of juice, and a Styrofoam carton that still reeked of curry and chili chicken from the Indian buffet down Kingston Pike.

Dr Raymond leaned so far back in his chair, Olivia was afraid it would topple over. 'I was telling Teddy about the day you disappeared after school and gave your daddy heart failure, till he found you sitting on the front steps of your house.'

Olivia smiled. 'I don't remember that.'

'Oh, yes, your dad went to pick you up from school and you weren't there, and turned out no one had seen you since lunch. I guess they didn't count heads so good back then – you had a substitute teacher that day and she kind of lost track. Your dad was well and truly pissed about that. But as it turns out, you'd just gone home, in the middle of the day, and your daddy found you right there, sitting on the front steps. You said you were waiting for Emily and Hunter to come home. You don't remember that?'

Olivia shook her head. 'I don't remember leaving school. I do remember sitting there a lot.'

'It was right after your mother died. That's when your father started bringing you in to see me. It worried him, all the time you spent sitting on those front porch steps.'

Olivia chewed her lip. 'I thought we were here to talk about Teddy.'

Dr Raymond looked over at Teddy. 'Your mother was always impatient like that, even when she was eleven. She's type A.'

'Tell me something I don't know,' Teddy said. They seemed very cozy, the two of them.

Olivia folded her arms.

'Let's start with something we all know,' Dr Raymond said. 'That Teddy is afraid in the house. Go ahead and say it, Teddy. State your position.'

'I am, Mommy. I'm really scared.'

'I understand,' Olivia said, but she didn't. Dr Raymond seemed to be missing the point.

'There's a ghost there, Mommy, you have to believe me, there's a ghost.'

'Teddy—'

Dr Raymond held up a hand. 'Ladies, we're not dealing with the *why* of things today. The point right now is the fear. Can we all agree on that?'

He looked them both in the eye. 'So. A terrible thing happened yesterday, and you ladies lost a friend you both love. Anybody would be shook up and afraid. Now there are pills people can take to help handle their fears, but Teddy doesn't want to go on medication. She's been very clear with me on that.'

Now Teddy folded her arms. Jutted her chin.

'Nobody can think straight and feel better in the world if they're scared all the time where they live. So, Olivia. Teddy and I have a plan. This is an emergency solution that is temporary to take care of the fear. So Teddy can feel empowered and safe. We'll deal with the whys and wherefores later on. Tell her the plan, Teddy.'

'You say it.'

'Okay, the plan is this, Livie. When you and Teddy leave my office you go straight home. You park in the driveway, and Teddy stays in the car.

220

Right now I don't think Teddy should ever go into the house again until she's ready and until she feels safe.'

Olivia swallowed. 'Okay. But—'

Dr Raymond held up a hand. 'I understand that Winston the Wonder Dog is waiting in the car.'

'He is.'

'You could have brought him in. Melissa Kitty has passed on. Winston is welcome to come with Teddy when she's here to talk, so long as he knows how to behave. Winston is a big part of the plan. He stays with Teddy and doesn't go back in the house.'

'Mommy shouldn't go in either,' Teddy said.

'Yes, Teddy, but we talked about compromise. We're asking a lot from your mother right now. She needs to be able to pack her things and your things too. You're going to have girl stuff you need.'

'It's a bad idea,' Teddy said.

'But you agreed. Are you backing out?'

'No. I agreed.'

'So Livie, you go inside and pack a bag for Teddy and for yourself, and get Winston's food bowls and toys. And you have to agree not to go back in the house when Teddy is at school. You have to promise. For now, you and Teddy are going to stay in a hotel, just for a while.'

'We don't need to go to a hotel. We can stay with Teddy's Aunt Charlotte.'

Dr Raymond shook his head. 'Not a good idea right now, and you and I can discuss why later. I know a hotel is expensive, but can you swing it, Livie, for just a few days? Teddy said maybe her daddy would help pay the bill. She wanted to call and ask him, but I said we should check with you first.'

Olivia twisted her fingers in her lap. 'It's okay. If you really think it's necessary, we'll go to a hotel.'

'It's necessary.' Dr Raymond jerked a thumb at Olivia. 'See, Teddy? Your mom's on board. We're all three going to work together and sort everything out, just like I said. We're going to make sure you're safe.'

Teddy nodded.

'Okay, Teddy – this is the time for me and your mom to talk alone. Head on out to the waiting room, kiddo.'

'Yes sir.'

Dr Raymond shut the door after she went.

'We've got trouble, don't we?' Olivia said.

Dr Raymond turned around, and Olivia wondered if he was conscious of how he looked, running his hands through his hair, his back literally pressed to the dark oak door. 'Unless your daughter is a sociopath, and don't worry on that head, because I've worked with a score of sociopathic children, and that's one thing she's not. She's a great kid, Livie, and that's my professional opinion. But she believes one hundred percent in some ghost she calls Duncan Lee.' Dr Raymond folded his arms and frowned. 'This Duncan Lee is very powerful. It took me twenty minutes to convince Teddy just to say his name. Duncan Lee watches her, he watches *you*, he watches everyone in the house, even the dog. Sometimes he bothers her at school, but she feels like he's stronger in the house. Duncan Lee killed your brother, he killed your friend, Amelia, and he made Teddy and Janet sick. Now you and I know better, but Teddy believes this one hundred percent. And you and I are going to have to deal with that.'

Olivia put a hand to her throat. 'How?'

'One baby step at a time.' Dr Raymond squeezed her shoulder. He did not sit at his desk, but instead paced the room. 'The *images* in her mind. Did she tell you about the red leather belt?'

'She told me Duncan Lee threatened to hang Winston from the attic fan with a red leather belt.'

Dr Raymond headed for his desk chair and settled there, rocking from side to side. 'It's not Winston anymore. Now it's you.'

'Me?'

'You. That's why she wants to sleep with you at night, that game you have, called boat? That's why she wanted to stay in the hospital, because she knew you wouldn't leave her, that you'd spend the night in her room. She's trying to protect you. She's convinced that Duncan Lee is going to hang you with that red leather belt.'

'For God's sake. Nothing's going to happen to me.'

Dr Raymond pointed a finger at her. 'Don't underestimate the level of Teddy's fear. Whatever is behind it.' He sat forward in his chair. 'Livie, listen to me. Your daughter is terrified every minute of the day. We can't get to the heart of what's really going on until we get her to feel safe. Are you going to be okay with those hotel room bills? Because if not we might consider sending her back to her dad.'

'But isn't that catering to her fears?'

'Right now we cater. For the short term.'

'Her dad's not an option right now. Let's just do the hotel. But there's a limit on how long I can afford that kind of thing.'

'I understand. This is a sort of emergency measure. Let's see if she feels safe at a hotel. One thing we're doing is testing to see if this satisfies her, or if she just changes the nature of her fear. And for now, I want her to stay away from her cousins, what's the oldest one's name? Janet?'

'Janet. Yes. They've been telling her things.'

'So I understand. In time we'll see about getting Teddy to a point where she has defenses against that sort of nonsense, but for now, she's too suggestible, too vulnerable. So right now our only goal is that Teddy feels safe. Remember this is an emergency plan – short term, and we're taking drastic measures because frankly, your daughter is at a crisis level of fear, do you understand what I'm telling you?'

'I understand, but what do you think is going on, Dr Raymond?'

Dr Raymond opened his hands and shrugged. 'Too early to tell. No fast answers, here, Livie, but don't panic. She's a smart kid, *she has a good heart*, you hear me on that? And kids can go from zero to sixty, and then back again when things get intense. I just don't want you to underestimate the problem. Keep her in school, no excuses there, and get her established in a daily routine. Don't spoil her or treat her like she's sick. Can you bring her back day after tomorrow? Same time, three forty-five? I'm going to want to see her three times a week right now, she'll be my last appointment of the day. Monday, Wednesday and Friday. You can do that?'

'I can.' Olivia wondered how she'd pay for it. She was going to have to talk to Hugh. 'Can we really bring Winston to these appointments? You brought it up, and she's going to ask.'

'So long as he doesn't pee in my waiting room. I have a soft spot for goldens. I had one when I was a kid.'

'He'll shed.'

'Hell, I shed.'

'I'm really scared for Teddy. I don't like to admit it, but my gut says something's really wrong. I know I told you earlier that it started out in California, with the divorce, and since we moved it's gone from bad to worse.'

'Was Teddy scared in California?'

'I don't know. She just told lies.'

'Interesting. And what's different now?'

'Now, like you say, she's scared. And all the things that have been going on ... okay, to be honest, I'm worried about what really happened, the day Amelia died.'

Dr Raymond folded his arms. 'You're afraid Teddy had something to do with it?'

Olivia shook her head. 'I don't think she did. But I can't help but wonder. I'm scared for her. Teddy was standing right there by the bathtub. Amelia's head was under water and Teddy was

225

holding onto her feet. None of it makes sense.'

Dr Raymond ran a hand through his hair. 'We'll get to the bottom of that, but it won't be overnight. In the meantime, remember that Amelia was a grown woman, and Teddy is only eight years old, with no prior indications of violence. When you start having those kinds of thoughts about your little girl, I want you to watch how good she is with her dog. She adores Winston, right? Takes care of him? She's never done anything to hurt him, right?'

Olivia nodded. 'Right.'

'You hang on to that.' Dr Raymond thought for a moment. 'But you are going to have to steel yourself for the long haul. Teddy and I have a lot of things to sort out.'

'Yeah. Voices in her head and ghosts in the house.'

'Just remember that a ghost is a common, almost universal fear. So it's a very normal manifestation of other things that are bothering her. Once we get to the other things and deal with them, then the ghost will go away.'

THIRTY-SIX

Neither Olivia nor Teddy had much to say as Olivia backed the Jeep out of the Chambliss Place parking lot and onto the street. Even Winston was subdued. It was a mere three minute drive to the house, and Teddy sat quietly in the front seat, twisting her hands. Olivia had never seen her do that before.

They pulled into the driveway, just as dusk was settling to dark.

Olivia hesitated. She did not like leaving Teddy out here. Maybe it would be best to get Teddy settled into a hotel room and come back later, alone.

'Teddy—'

'Just hurry, Mommy, okay?'

Stick to the plan. She had agreed. 'Stay right here in the car with Winston, keep the doors locked, and don't open them until I come back.'

Teddy nodded and the look on her face broke Olivia's heart. She looked so much like the old Teddy, the little girl she'd been before the divorce.

'I'll be fast,' Olivia said.

Olivia went through the front door instead of the back, so Teddy could see her. She thought, as she often did, how odd the front door was, the awkward way it was hung, so that it hit the wall on the left and would not open all the way. She turned on the lights in each room she went through, leaving the shutters open so Teddy could see her from outside. And so she could see Teddy. She waved and thought she saw Teddy raise a hand.

The house had that same feel of *presence*, like it had since Amelia died.

Down to business.

Olivia dragged two suitcases out of the closet in the hall, bouncing them up the stairs to the bedrooms. She flipped the light switches as she went, hating the way the lights came on, those damned economy lights, just a glow at first, barely lighting the room, as they warmed up and grew brighter in tiny increments. The house felt different upstairs. Heavy with something she could not see. Almost like a fog. She was actually relieved to be going to a hotel.

She'd start in Teddy's room. The door was shut tight but the light was already on, she could see the line of brightness under the door. She hesitated, shook her head, and went inside.

Teddy had made her bed very neatly, her stuffed animals arranged around the pillows. A contrast to the carnage – every dresser drawer hanging open, underwear, tee shirts, jeans and socks in a snarl all over the floor, as if someone had ripped the drawers open in a fury and dumped them.

'Good God,' Olivia said.

Olivia knew that if she asked Teddy about this, she would blame it on Duncan Lee. She wouldn't mention it. She'd tell Dr Raymond, day after tomorrow, when she took Teddy back.

But there was anger here. Such anger. Olivia choked out a small sob and picked up jeans and tee shirts off the floor, stuffing them into the bag. There was something very wrong with her little girl.

Her own things she left on hangers, draping them over Teddy's suitcase. She looked up once at the attic fan. It took up a four by four section of the ceiling, the dusty monolithic motor looming behind the rusting brown grill. There was a

228

switch on the wall, and she felt the unexpected urge to turn it on. She didn't. She headed for the bathroom, packing up makeup and Teddy's favorite bubble bath. Amelia's things were still on the counter tops. Olivia tried not to look at them.

She was in a hurry, her packing was sloppy. The suitcases were heavy and awkward, and Olivia wrestled them down the stairs, the hangers with her expensive black sheaths, skirts and blazers slung over one arm. Dammit, she needed shoes. Back upstairs, fast, just that other pair, then running right back down on the slippery, polished wood, holding tight to the rail.

Olivia looked out the sunroom window at Teddy. Still there. Still okay. Winston sitting up front in the driver's seat.

There were clothes in the dryer, most of her lingerie that she washed on the delicate cycle in a little net bag. She wouldn't go far without clean bras and panties. Grab those and call it a day.

The basement door was open a crack, as if inviting her in, and Olivia tried to remember if she'd left it that way. She flipped on every light in the kitchen, and went down slowly, the light streaming in from behind, illuminating the paint chipped, open backed stairs. She held her breath until she found the switch about halfway down, and flipped on the light. A regular light bulb, this one. The basement lit up in a flick.

The dryer light was on, a red pinpoint glow that let her know the cycle was finished and her clothes were ready. No doubt the warning buzzer

229

had gone off the usual three times at five minute intervals while she'd been at work. The mundane normality made her feel better. The dryer door creaked when she opened it, and she reached in for the bag. The clothes were dry, and crackling with static electricity, emitting the faint sweet scent of the lavender fabric softener she used.

She shut the dryer door, and was heading for the stairs when she heard the thump.

Olivia turned around slowly, feeling a tingle of tension at the base of her spine. The noise had come from behind her, somewhere close, definitely right there in the basement. She looked from corner to corner. Stacks of damp, moldy boxes, the old washer and dryer Charlotte had left behind, perched on a platform of bricks along the back of the wall, collecting dust.

The thump came again, no mistaking it, just a few feet away. Olivia did not move. She held her breath. Waited. And once more, a thump, and she pegged it now, coming from the dryer. Had something got trapped inside?

She knew it would keep her awake that night, the thought of some bird or squirrel, maybe even a stray cat, a small one, a feral kitten. Coming in from outside through the dryer's vent, and getting trapped inside. Suffocating slowly, afraid in the dark.

Except there was no vent, not now. The dryer was disconnected and stacked and covered with that peculiar mix of greasy basement dust, shoved up on bricks against the wall.

Fuck it. Olivia crossed the room and opened the dryer door.

She dropped the clothes. Not a snake, no, the way it was coiled there in the bottom of the dryer gave that impression, but no snake had a buckle, no snake was bright red. It was a belt. A long, red leather belt.

And the memory of Teddy's voice flashed through her head. *There's a ghost there, Mommy, you have to believe me, there's a ghost. He's going to hang Winston from the attic fan with a red leather belt.* And then Dr Raymond. *It's not Winston anymore. Now it's you. She's convinced that Duncan Lee is going to hang you with that red leather belt.*

'Jesus,' Olivia said. She turned and ran up the stairs.

Two things happened, all at once. Every single light in the house went out, and a dog began to bark.

THIRTY-SEVEN

Olivia realized what a terrible thing it was, to know, and to believe. Teddy had been facing that alone. She muttered half sobbing apologies to her daughter as she went up the stairs. She made herself go slow, she made herself hold the rail, she even reached out for the switch and cried a bit when her fingers tracked the plastic nub that was clearly in the on position. One light bulb might go out like that, but not every single one in

231

the house.

The joy she felt was unexpected and exhilarating. It was the house that was fucked up, not her little girl. Dr Raymond had known right away that Teddy had a good, compassionate heart. And whatever bad presence there was in this house, whatever this thing was, it had been *after* Teddy. Charlotte had been right all along.

Whatever this thing was that was after her daughter, Dr Raymond was right. Step one was getting out of the house. Olivia realized, with the perspective that people get when the bottom truly drops out, that the jobs and the moves, the arguments with Hugh and the pressures of money, these were nothing. Nothing, so long as she and her little girl were safe.

The barking dog was frantic now, hysterical. It sounded like the stray she and Teddy had seen the other night. Winston picked it up. Olivia knew his sharp, panicked yelp. Two of them now, barking their heads off.

The basement door was shut tight, though she had left it wide open. Olivia banged her head into it in the dark, tripping on the top step, and bruising the crap out of her shin. She slammed her fist into the wood and jerked the knob and it opened easily. She scrambled up into the dark kitchen. She'd left the Jeep's headlights flipped on, and she could see the arc of light like a homing beacon outside.

But the back door off the kitchen was stuck.

Olivia kicked it hard, and turned the knob. Yes, yes, she'd unlocked it, and it came open an inch, then wouldn't budge. This had happened before;

232

she always had trouble with this door. Her hands shook and she trembled all over, but she just needed to keep her head, and pull, not push.

Then she heard him. The dog. Whining right at the door, could it be Winston? Out of the car? Or the stray? The dog started scratching, frantic, almost throwing itself at the door, and Olivia heard a crack and a sprinkle of glass. The kitchen window had shattered. All hell was breaking loose.

Olivia kicked the bottom of the door again to jolt it loose and pulled hard, felt the door give reluctantly, felt the blessed rush of air. Out she went, not bothering to close it behind.

And she saw him, the dog in the moonlight, loping toward the fountain. And seeing him up close for the very first time, she recognized the unusual brindle markings, and knew, before the dog even turned its head and looked back at her, that this was Hunter, Emily's dog. Which was ridiculous of course, because Hunter had to be dead, dead for years and years. She was just rattled. No time for this now.

Olivia knew she ought to go slow, that she could stumble and twist an ankle in the dark, but she ran anyway, to the headlights, to the car, high on the joy of freedom, now that she was out of the house.

The doors to the Jeep were shut, just as she'd left them, so it took her a minute of staring dumbly to understand. It was as if she were outside her body observing the hysterical panicked woman who opened the door of the Jeep and found the front seat empty. No daughter, no dog.

The woman cried, and ran to the fountain, around the house, and down to the street. She even went back into the house. The lights worked again, and she went through every room, mouth in an almost comic oval of disbelief before she opened her cell phone and dialed 911.

But Teddy and Winston were gone. Not a sign of either of them, just like all those years ago, when Emily and Hunter disappeared.

THIRTY-EIGHT

In a very tiny space in the back of Olivia's mind she was aware of the news crews gathering in little clusters outside her house. Of the television station that had set up a yellow canopy supported with white poles right on the curb. She could hear how the cars on the street outside slowed as they passed in front of her home. She was aware of the neighbors gathering in the corners of her yard.

Inside the house every light was on, and there were temporary but powerful spotlights rigged up outside. The driveway and the streets were crammed with cop cars, blue lights flashing, yellow police tape. She was grateful for the activity, what little of it she could absorb. She would have liked to be involved somehow, to help, it was her baby girl, but she was held captive by the noise in her head, the effort it took

234

just to breathe, as if she were in the grip of a silent tornado while everyone around her was still.

She was familiar with the clinical symptoms of shock, so she understood why she shivered and felt like ice, in spite of the blanket that the uniformed police officer who responded to her call had wrapped around her shoulders. Officer Rodriguez had radioed in for detectives and backup within ten minutes of listening to her panicked explanation.

She'd drunk up all the water they'd brought her, though Rodriguez had needed to help her with the glass, and she was still thirsty, but could somehow not find the words to ask for more. She felt a constant buzzing at the base of her skull, and she knew it would be unwise to try and stand.

Teddy's name seemed to pulse with every beat of her heart, and it took all of her concentration to sit on the couch, to go from one terrible thought to the next. Olivia knew what was coming. She had lived through this before. She did not want this pain, not again. She would live it now as a mother, which meant that this time it would be so much worse.

Her own mother had kept a journal, after Emily and Hunter disappeared. Olivia had read the tear streaked pages years ago, curious about the way her mother's handwriting had changed over the days, months, then years. Olivia had tried her hardest to forget that chronicle of the no man's land where her family had dwelled, had done a pretty good job, actually, because now, all she

235

knew for sure was that she was now in a place so dark, so arid and comfortless, that it would take everything she had to survive. And for Teddy's sake, she had to survive.

When Olivia was a little girl, she had been ashamed. Her family was different, her parents had to struggle just to make it through the day. They were isolated from the rest of the world, exiled to a public place of pain where people watched their every move, hungry, some of them, to feed voraciously upon a tragedy that could be held at arm's length, some just curious, and others, lots of others, clueless but well meaning and concerned.

Her mother and father spent years learning how to recreate a normal place for Chris and Olivia to grow up in, to compartmentalize their time, juggling the search for a missing child with the need for a family to build a new life, the basic realities of eating, sleeping, breathing in and out. Holidays had to be reconstructed, new traditions set, all the while meals needed to be cooked, there was laundry to fold, a mortgage to pay. Her father had cried like a baby when he had to go back to work.

All of it with the shadow of Emily, always there, but not there.

They stopped celebrating Christmas at home, going instead to a beach in South Carolina. Olivia and Chris were given a sum of money each year to buy a gift for Emily, ribbons and tissue paper to wrap it up, and Olivia wondered now – where did all those presents go? What had happened to Emily's clothes, her record collection, the pink frosty lipstick in her top dresser drawer? She could not remember. She drew a total blank.

The first goal is not to get lost. The sentence her mother had written came like a whisper in the back of her mind. No pills from doctors or friends trying to help. Stay away from alcohol. Keep your head clear and don't fall away. Wait for the moments when you feel numb – they will come. Welcome them. Your mind will know when you need relief.

Someone shouted outside, and Olivia turned suddenly, looking out the window with an electric current of hope. Someone had found her. They'd found Teddy. An unmarked car was pulling up in front of the house. A fair haired young woman and a pear shaped man got out of the car. Olivia craned her neck, waiting for them to lead Teddy out, biting the knuckles of her fist, feeling tears of relief running down her face.

The pear shaped man walked with quick jerky steps, and stopped to talk to one of the uniformed officers, a look of intense exasperation on his face. He waved the young woman off toward the back of the house and headed up the walk. Olivia opened her mouth, then realized that Teddy was not in the unmarked car. Her daughter had not been found. She sank back down on the cushion of the couch, and put her head in her hands. She was shaking and shaking hard. What made her think Teddy was there? Why had she been so sure?

It was clear, as soon as the pear shaped man entered the house, that the rank and file police officers were wary of him, the tension rose the minute he walked into the living room. He headed straight to Officer Rodriguez, but he was watching Olivia. She knew he was watching. She was not close enough to hear what he said.

He was interrupted by the ring of a phone, pulled it out of his pocket and listened, and Olivia stood up, hanging onto the arm of the couch. His comments were no more telling than *yes*, *no*, *okay*. He jammed the phone back into his suit coat pocket and came across the room.

'Mrs James? Teddy's mother?'

Olivia blinked. Swallowed. 'Yes.'

He gave her a hand which she shook. His grip was tight and hard. 'Sit back down, please, Mrs James. I'm Detective Donnie Withers, and I'm in charge of Teddy's case. I realize you're upset right now, ma'am—'

'That call you just got. Have you heard anything? Have you *found* her?'

'No, ma'am. Look, I'd like to ask you some questions. And I need to go over this timeline with you, okay?'

Olivia let the blanket fall off her shoulders. She felt she should know what this man meant by timeline, she needed to say this would be okay, but her mind refused to work.

'Mrs James?' Withers raised his voice as if Olivia were deaf. 'Mrs James, I need your help here. You want me to find your daughter, right?'

Olivia managed a nod. Sat back down on the couch.

'Look, I'm going to be blunt. If this is a stranger abduction, not a runaway, not a custody fight, then I've got about a three hour window to find your little girl. That ticking you hear is your daughter's clock running out. I don't find her in three hours, then, statistically speaking, Teddy is dead.'

Olivia felt a surge of vomit rise in her throat. She ducked her head and took slow breaths.

'And I've got to tell you that nothing about this whole scenario makes much sense.' Withers shifted his weight to his left foot. 'Now, if you think your daughter got upset maybe, and ran away, that changes the entire course of the investigation, and I expect you to be up front with me about that right now. Or. If there's some kind of funny business going on between you and your ex, I expect you to tell me that too.' He moved closer as he spoke, towering over her while she trembled on the couch. 'I've got one thing I'm worried about, and that's your little girl. If you lie to me, ma'am, that constitutes obstruction of justice and I *will* make sure the DA's office comes after you with everything they've got. Which means jail time if you fuck with me on this.'

Olivia wanted to stand up again, she was not quite sure why, but her knees were weak enough that she didn't think she could stay on her feet. She knew that there used to be an Olivia who could deal with a man like this, who might even punch a man who implied such terrible things. She thought of the detectives all those years ago who had looked long and hard for Emily, the one who had shyly asked if the family would like a black lab puppy when his own dog had whelped.

239

None of them had talked to her parents this way. She should not put up with being treated this way. But she was afraid to make this Detective Donnie Withers mad. If she made him angry, would he look for her little girl? If he suspected her, how could he do what he needed to do? She was at the mercy of this pear shaped man. She needed to think, but her mind refused to clear.

She was aware suddenly of Officer Rodriguez edging closer, till he stood beside her, and she knew that he was angry at Withers, and that he at least did not suspect her of these terrible things.

'Sir,' Rodriguez said. 'Protocol allows for a female officer to be called.'

Detective Withers went white around the edges of his mouth. 'I've *got* a female officer, she's out back. Go ask Tellers to come in, why don't you.'

'Yes sir,' Rodriguez said.

Withers settled on the edge of the chair across from Olivia, scooting it close. 'Mrs James, do you think there is any chance your daughter just ran away from home?'

Olivia felt it suddenly. A weird ripple of ... nothing. The numbness, as promised. 'No,' she said. 'Teddy was strapped into her seatbelt, the dog was in the Jeep. I'd just seen her out of the window and waved. There would be no conceivable reason for her to run away.'

'No trouble at school?'

'None.'

'But you did just move here?'

'That's right. But Teddy was happy in school, Detective Withers. My daughter did not run away.'

'I find it odd that someone would abduct her and take the dog.'

'So do I. On the other hand, it might be the only way she would go. If she was tricked somehow.'

'You mean lured away?' he said, nodding. 'That's the only thing that makes any sense. Is she a naïve kind of child? Young for her age?'

'No, she's smart for her age, and she and I have been over all the stranger danger stuff. On the other hand, she *is* just a little girl.'

'Maybe this was someone she knew.'

'We don't know many people, Detective, we haven't been here long.'

The front door opened and a man in forensic overalls walked in, letting in a rush of air that ruffled Teddy's school papers, scattered across the fireplace mantel where Teddy always left them instead of taking them upstairs, as instructed, to the little desk in her room. It bothered Olivia, the way some of the papers were hanging over the edge.

Withers put his hands on his knees. 'At least that narrows the field. We've liaised with the LAPD, and they've already sent officers out to notify your ex-husband, Hugh James, of the situation with your little girl. They confirmed just a few minutes ago that Mr James was at his office working. He asked us to notify you that he is on his way here. He's catching the first plane out.'

'Hugh had nothing to do with this.' Olivia felt the compulsion to straighten up the papers. A ridiculous compulsion, she knew that, but she

241

also knew that the very act of straightening them up would somehow make her feel better. The urge was ridiculously strong, but she had to fight it. Standing up, straightening those papers, that would seem like odd behavior, like a mother who did not care that her little girl was gone. She had to be careful. People would be watching her. Withers would watch her. She was on the tightrope now.

'Evidently your ex says the same about you.' Withers opened up a notebook. 'Let's go back over the timeline here. You say you saw Teddy, in the car, before you went down to the basement to get your clothes.'

'Yes.'

One of the papers drifted down to the floor, math problems, marked over and erased with three problems circled in red.

'How could you see her in the dark?' Withers bent over and put the paper on the coffee table.

Olivia stared at Teddy's math paper. 'The headlights of the Jeep were on and so were the lights inside the car. I figured Teddy was reading. She had a new Nancy Drew book. The book was still in the car, by the way. Which means she left it behind. That's not good. She takes her books with her everywhere she goes.'

'I agree, it's worrying. Why wasn't Teddy in the house with you? One of the officers tells me you were packing up suitcases. Where were you going, Mrs James? On a school night at that.'

'We were going to spend a few nights in a hotel.'

'Why was that, ma'am?'

Olivia reached across the coffee table and moved the math paper so it was centered, and not hanging off to the side.

'Mrs James? Did you hear me? Why were you and Teddy going to a hotel?'

'Detective, I'm sure you know my best friend died here yesterday afternoon.'

Withers nodded, shoulders tense. 'Wainwright, Amelia. Why was she here?'

'She just came ... to visit.'

'What happened?'

'I came home from work, and I found her ... she'd been taking a bubble bath and she drowned in the tub.'

Withers sat forward. 'As of now there's not an official cause of death, pending autopsy results, Mrs James. And you must know it's hard to believe that a healthy, grown woman would drown in the tub. And I have to say that what's happened with your daughter here puts that death in an even stranger light. The two incidents have to be connected. Do you have any thoughts on that?'

'No. None of this makes any sense.' Olivia was aware that tears ran down her cheeks, which was odd. She felt nothing.

'Ma'am, I get you're upset. Do you need me to stop this interview?'

Olivia looked back up at Teddy's papers on the mantel.

Withers flipped a page in his notebook. 'Tell me why you were packing those bags. Did you feel threatened by something?'

Olivia fought the urge to laugh. She bit her lip.

Stupid, stupid, it was nerves, that was all. Withers would think she was insane.

'Mrs James? Were you running away?'

Olivia looked down at the floor. 'Teddy and I were both pretty shook up by Amelia's death. We – Teddy was afraid to be in the house after Amelia died here, and I decided that it might be a good idea for both of us just to spend a couple of nights in a hotel.'

'Was your daughter here when this death occurred?'

Olivia shook her head. '*No*. Teddy was with my sister-in-law. Charlotte picks her up after school and Teddy stays at her house till I get off from work.'

'Do you have a number for her, ma'am, so we can confirm?'

'Yes. Of course.' Olivia tried to think. Her mind blanked. 'I can't ... think of it now.'

Withers seemed not to be surprised. 'Do you have it written down somewhere? Maybe on a list of emergency numbers somewhere?'

'Yes,' Olivia said. 'On the refrigerator.' She stood up, but he waved her back to her seat.

He leaned forward. 'Officer Rodriguez says that before Teddy disappeared you were in the basement and you heard thumping noises. Is that right?'

Olivia nodded.

'Any chance the noise was coming from the outside? What section of the basement did it come from? North side or west?'

Olivia had to think. 'It wasn't the driveway side. It was out the back. I thought the noises

244

came from inside the house.'

'Always hard to tell, that kind of thing.' He looked back down at his notebook. 'So then you started up the stairs and all the lights went out. All over the house.'

'Yes.'

'All of them. You're sure of that.'

'Yes.'

'Was it like somebody flipped the breakers?'

'I ... it could have been that.'

'They went out all together, not one by one.'

'Yes.'

'Ma'am, where is the breaker box for this house?'

'Outside. By the back door.'

'Interesting. Because they're usually in the basement of old houses like this.'

'This one's outside.'

'Which means anyone could access the breakers from outside the house. Now you say that when you found your daughter gone, you went back in the house to look for her, thinking she might have gone inside. Because you left the front door unlocked. And all the lights worked then.'

'Right.'

Donnie Withers seemed to consider that for a moment. 'But you didn't flip the breakers? You didn't go into the box?'

'No.'

'Tell me again when the dog started barking.'

'Right when the lights went out.'

'So it happened at the same time. Lights out, and dog.'

'That's right.'

'It would make sense for the kidnapper to cut the lights and then go for your daughter, and set the dog off.'

'Yes. That would make sense.'

He shut his notebook. 'Okay, Mrs James. I understand you've given us permission to search anywhere in the house.'

'*Of course.*'

'I'm going to leave an officer posted outside and I'm going to ask you to leave for the night.'

'But ... *no.* What if Teddy comes home somehow? What if she needs me and I'm not there? What if there's a ransom demand?'

'Ma'am. You've already told our officers that you've got roughly sixteen hundred dollars sum total in your accounts. If Teddy was abducted, it wasn't for money.'

Olivia put her face in her hands. The numbness was ebbing, and the waves of worry were coming, coming fast.

'Now here's the thing, ma'am. In the last twenty-four hours this house has been the scene of a death and an abduction. And in my experience, grown women don't drown in bathtubs, and little girls don't disappear with their dogs. I want a forensic team here. I'll let you know when you can come back home. Officer Teller can drive you to the hotel, or anywhere else you want to go. I'm afraid we're impounding your car.'

Olivia covered her hands with her mouth, because it was welling up inside again, this horrific compulsion to laugh. Did Withers really think

246

she would be worried about the fucking car?
That she was in any condition to drive?

It was her last coherent thought for the night.

THIRTY-NINE

Detective Teller was the blonde girl Olivia had
seen arrive with Withers. Olivia was trembling,
and Teller put a hand on her shoulder to steady
her as she stumbled down the front porch stairs.

Olivia stopped mid step. 'Wait, I need to go
back in.'

Teller took her elbow, and steered her away
from the door. 'Whatever it is, it can wait.'

Olivia jerked away. 'I have to go back and get
Teddy's school papers. They're on the mantel, it
will only take a second.'

Teller's face was full of an avid sympathy
Olivia recognized.

'Her papers will be fine, Olivia, don't worry
about them. I'll keep an eye out on them for you,
okay?'

'Don't patronize me.'

Detective Teller's face went red. 'I'm not
patronizing you. I understand how upset you are.
You should know that Detective Withers is very
good at his job. He can be rough around the
edges, but don't take it personally. His mind is
always on the work, and he's three steps ahead of
everybody else. If anybody can find your daugh-

ter, he can. You should be grateful he's the one on the case.'

'Grateful?' Olivia took a step backward. 'You're twelve. Don't tell me to be grateful. And let go of me, I can walk without your help.' Olivia closed her eyes. Be careful, she told herself. Don't antagonize the police.

McTavish was just pulling up when Olivia hit the last step. He parked the Cadillac at the edge of the curb and loped up the driveway, opening his arms. *'Olivia.* I can't believe this. I'm so sorry.' He looked over her shoulder at Detective Teller. 'Donnie Withers on this?'

Teller nodded.

'He put out an amber alert?'

'Rodriguez took care of that from the get go, Modello,' Teller said.

'What about CASKU? Withers should call them now, while the trail's still hot.'

Teller shook her head. 'You know he won't work with the FBI. He'll handle it himself.'

'Stupid fucker,' McTavish said.

'Hey, come on,' Teller said. 'Donnie's good, even if you don't like the guy.'

'Yeah? Because I hear through the grapevine your precious Donnie's been treating her like shit.'

'Pretty fast grapevine, you got some friends on the force?'

'Good night, Detective Teller. Your babysitting duties are officially over.'

'Donnie said—'

'Donnie Withers can suck my dick. Come on, Livie. Come with me.'

* * *

Olivia was vaguely aware that McTavish leaned across and fastened her seatbelt for her before he backed into the street, and began to drive.

'I know what CASKU is, McTavish. It's the Child Abduction and Serial Killer Unit with the FBI.'

McTavish ran a hand over his chin. Watched the road.

Olivia stared out the window. 'The OVC is the Office for Victims of Crime. That's the Justice Department. Then there's the National Center for Missing and Exploited Children, NCMEC – aren't they the ones that post the success stories? I know one of them does. And AMECO. That's...' Olivia stopped talking. She could not remember what she had been going to say.

McTavish was cruising the neighborhood. She had always loved the little bungalows in Bearden. So pretty. Were there children inside? Sleeping in their beds? Did their parents know they weren't safe?

'You know, McTavish, they didn't have all those organizations when Emily disappeared. We were kind of on our own, back in the day.'

McTavish took her hand. 'We've got a lot more smarts now, Livie. More resources, more experience. We'll find Teddy. *I'll* find Teddy. This is not going to happen to you again.'

'Your fingers are nice and warm,' Olivia said.

McTavish pulled the car to the side of the road and cut the lights. Took both of Olivia's hands in his.

'Listen to me, babe. Please. I know there's

249

stuff going on you haven't told Withers. I know you're upset, and it's hard to think straight. Can you pull it together and talk to me? Whatever it is you know, it could help me find Teddy. And honey, you need to believe me when I tell you that underestimating Detective Donnie is a big mistake. He's a prick, but he's a smart prick.' McTavish waited. Sighed when Olivia did not respond. He turned the engine off, and twisted sideways to face her in the dark. 'I know there was something funny going on, the day that Amelia died. Tell me everything, so I can go out and help them find your little girl. Otherwise I'm going out with Rodriguez to knock on doors, which is the bottom of the barrel when it comes to leads.'

'McTavish? I need you to do something for me. I need to go back into the house. Teddy's school work is on the mantel, and I need to get that and take it with me to the hotel.'

McTavish sighed. Gathered her in his arms. 'Olivia,' he whispered. 'Please, just please, *try*. Try and think with me, okay?'

Olivia liked the way he smelled. She pulled away from him, absently rubbing a thumb across his wrist. 'Honestly, McTavish. It's awfully hard to explain.'

'Try me, babe.'

It was time consuming, telling him everything. Hard for Olivia to organize her thoughts. Any interruption stopped her cold and she had to go back to the beginning to get her head straight, and finally McTavish said nothing, kept still, and listened. They sat together for a very long time.

After a while, Olivia put her head in her hands. 'You don't believe me,' she said. 'I don't blame you. I don't believe any of it myself.'

McTavish rubbed his chin and looked away. 'It's not that. It's Jamison. He's afraid to be alone right now, he's afraid to be asleep. But when he does sleep, he wakes up screaming. And he says that name over and over, that name that you and Amelia found.'

'Duncan Lee?'

'Decan Ludde.'

FORTY

McTavish hadn't wanted to leave her at the hotel, but Olivia had insisted. He had to find Teddy for her. *He* had to do it. Someone she could trust.

Hugh, flying out of LAX on the redeye, had called while she was being interrogated by Withers. He'd texted her to say he preferred to stay by her side at the house, but if that wasn't okay, he'd get a room at the Crown Plaza downtown. He'd been in flight when she tried to call back, so she'd left him a message. That she wasn't at the house. That she'd taken a room at the hotel.

Olivia had taken a shower but not washed her hair. Not even washed herself, just stood under the water, too tired to lift the soap. She'd tried the bed for a while, distracting herself with the drone of cable television, studying the ceiling tiles, the dust caked in one corner, the shape of what might be a dog directly over her head. When the knock came, at the hotel room door, she was on her feet in an instant.

It would be a police officer. Good news or bad?

But it was not a police officer. It was Charlotte. Standing in the hallway, face swollen and red with a tissue crumpled in her fist.

'McTavish called me,' she said, when Olivia opened the door. 'He told me to come.'

Charlotte tried to step forward to give Olivia a hug, but Olivia pushed her back.

'You stay away from me, Charlotte. And when my little girl comes home safe, you stay away from *us*.'

'God, Olivia.' Tears ran down Charlotte's face. 'Don't do this. I know—'

'You know nothing. Or everything. If you. And my *brother*. Hadn't started this.'

'Don't blame him. Don't blame Chris.'

'Why not? He's the one who brought it home. I never want to see you or Janet, or any of you. Ever again.'

Charlotte's chest was heaving. 'You don't mean it, but I'm upsetting you, so I'll go. If you need me, Livie. You know where I am.'

'Yes, I know where you are, Charlotte.' And then she had a thought that made the nausea boil. 'Have you talked to the police?'

Charlotte nodded. 'They came to the house.'

'*Charlotte*. You didn't tell the police about Teddy being there, when Amelia died?'

'I picked Teddy up after school that day, Livie. I was late and I picked her up at the corner of

252

Westwood and Sutherland, it happened just like you said.'

Olivia put her back against the wall. Covered her face with her hands. 'Thank you. Thank you for that.'

'We're family, Livie, like it or not. Like marriage, for better or worse. You can't be alone right now. You're not – you're not safe.'

'Safe? It's Teddy that's not safe. And I'm *not* alone, Charlotte. I have Teddy. I have Teddy and I'm not alone.'

Charlotte sobbed. 'Oh, God, Olivia—'

'*Go.*'

Olivia folded her arms, listening to the echo of soft crying, growing fainter as Charlotte stumbled down the hall. She waited just long enough for Charlotte to go away. She had to get out of the room.

She settled in the lobby in a deep leather chair, outside the first floor dining room. The scenarios of what might be happening to Teddy paralyzed her – it would be better if she could somehow turn off her brain. The three hour time limit Detective Withers had pointed out was long gone. Teddy was now statistically dead.

Sometime in the early morning hours Olivia dozed, waking to the clatter of plates – the hotel staff setting up the breakfast buffet. Olivia jumped up, feeling cold, trying to make sense of where she was. She had overslept, dammit, and if she didn't hustle Teddy would be late for school.

And then she remembered. It all came back.

253

Teddy would not be going to school that day.

She punched numbers into her phone, got hold of Detective Teller, who told her in too many words that Teddy had not come home. Teller was so friendly and so sickeningly sympathetic that Olivia knew that she had been instructed to befriend Olivia, gain her confidence, form a fucking bond. *No new developments to share*, was how Teller put it. What did she mean by *share*, Olivia thought.

She sat back down in the leather chair, watching the hotel staff moving in and out of the dining room. She smelled coffee, wondered if she was hungry. It was hard to tell, really, but she did not think she was. She knew from before that there was no shame in eating when your child disappeared, but even wanting a cup of coffee made her feel the shame all the same.

She had just decided to try and call Hugh, when she saw him come into the hotel lobby through the double glass doors.

He wore jeans, a white oxford shirt, expensive slip on loafers, a charcoal blazer, cashmere, she'd bought for him as a Christmas gift five years ago. She and Teddy had shopped together.

His energy was as controlled and precise as a sniper shot, and a man in a work shirt pushing a trash cart stepped out of his way. The desk clerk took a sideways wary stance when Hugh dropped his black leather carryall gently to the floor and set the oversized leather wallet where he kept airline tickets and travel paperwork on the wood partition.

'I'd like a room. Non smoking, king bed, but if

254

that's not available, I'll take any damn thing you've got.' Hugh took a credit card out of the inside pocket of his blazer. His hair was thick and wavy and even after a night on a plane it looked good. Olivia had always loved his hair. The gray was more pronounced these days, but she liked that too.

She ought to call out, to tell Hugh that she was there. But she froze. Hugh needed to check in first, didn't he? So should she say something or wait? Why couldn't she make the smallest decision now without this agony of details in her mind? Why couldn't she *think*?

She watched Hugh tap a finger on the counter while the desk clerk consulted a computer. Hugh could never be still.

'Look, my wife is here, Olivia James. She told me what room, but I can't remember. Can you look it up?'

Ex-wife, Olivia thought to herself. It was odd of Hugh not to remember the room number. He wrote everything down, he remembered details.

'I'm sorry, sir, I can't give out that kind of information.'

Hugh just nodded. 'I'll call her cell.'

Olivia stood up and waved a hand in the air. 'Hugh? I'm over here.'

He turned and caught sight of her. He looked familiar yet different, face thinner than ever, that sharp beak of a nose. He'd lost weight, and he looked years older.

He crossed the lobby in a sort of lope. *'Olivia.'*

'Hugh, I'm sorry, I'm so sorry, I didn't keep her safe.'

She let him hug her, and it felt very much like he was holding on to her for dear life. She was sobbing now, in the lobby, in public, and that embarrassed them both.

'Anything?' he asked.

'No. I talked to Detective Teller fifteen minutes ago. Nothing new, no leads, except a fresh oil stain in the driveway that didn't come from my car.'

'Let's talk upstairs.'

She nodded. Waited for him to finish checking in, then they went to the elevators hand in hand. She led him to her room, motioned him inside. He sat his bag down, looked around and blinked.

'Where are your things?'

'I don't have anything. It's all at the house.'

'We'll go later and get what you need.'

Olivia hugged her arms to her chest. 'I don't want to go back there.'

'To the house? I don't understand.'

'You better sit down, Hugh. I have a lot of things to explain.'

He sat with his hands on his knees and both feet flat on the floor and listened to every word she said, with no comment and no interruption, eyes narrowed like they did when he was thinking. Telling Hugh was a sort of test. He was highly intelligent and annoyingly logical and he had a way of sorting things straight. Slice and dice, they called him at work. Olivia thought that if Hugh looked at her like she was crazy, she might accept that verdict. She wasn't sure she cared.

She was not at all prepared for his reaction.

'I want to go to the house. If there's a ghost there, let's root it out.'

'You're humoring me?'

'I don't believe in ghosts, Olivia. But you seem to right now and something strange is going on. So I say we face it off together and rule it out in your head, then go to the next logical step. Olivia?' He took her hand. 'It's going to be okay, sweet. Why are you looking at me like that?'

'Just thinking how ... how useful you are. So what is it, Hugh? The next logical step?'

He ran a hand through his hair. 'Hell if I know. But we've got two deaths. Amelia – and God I'm sorry about that, sweet. Your brother. And two disappearances. Your sister, twenty-five years ago. And now—' His voice cracked. 'Now our baby girl. There's some common denominator here that we're missing. The police are following the conventional route. I say you and I focus on this.'

Hugh stood up and began to pace, just as there was a knock at the door. Olivia and Hugh both froze. They stared at each other, thinking there was news now. Good or bad.

Olivia looked out the peephole. 'It's Mc-Tavish,' she said, opening the door.

He was in the clothes he'd worn the night before. 'Livie. Nothing yet on Teddy but—'

'What the hell are *you* doing here?' Hugh said, moving across the room.

'Looking for your daughter, asshole.'

Hugh blinked. Took a step back. 'Of course. Sorry. It's just – how did you know where to find us?'

'Livie didn't tell you they impounded her car? I'm the one who dropped her off. Look, guys, we've had a little thing come up. Maybe a lead, maybe not. Officer Rodriguez was up at the crack of dawn today, canvassing up and down your neighborhood, Livie, and he got a hit on the dog.'

Hugh went up on his toes. 'Winston? You found Winston?'

'No, the other one. The German shepherd. Teller told you about the oil stain in the driveway, right? It's not much of a theory, but Rodriguez and I were thinking about something Livie told me last night. That she and Teddy kept seeing this stray dog around their house. And we were thinking if somebody was watching the house, maybe it's not a stray. Maybe it's his dog.'

Hugh folded his arms. 'What are you saying here? Mr Stranger Danger is watching my wife and my daughter, and he takes his dog along, while he's peeping?'

'Like I said, it's a theory. Anyway, Rodriguez was doing door to doors, asking about Teddy and Winston, strange cars around the house, and about a stray German shepherd. And early this morning he gets a hit. Seems one of the women in your neighborhood has seen it too.'

'Who was it? The couple next door?' Olivia said.

'No, a woman who lives a few streets over. A Patsy Ackerman.'

'Patsy Ackerman?' Olivia said.

Hugh took her arm. 'You know her?'

'I know *of* her.'

258

'She lists her occupation as artist,' McTavish said, 'but she's also the local *woo woo* woman.'

'Woo woo woman?' Hugh said.

McTavish rocked back and forth on his heels. 'She's a renowned local psychic. She's pretty well known.'

'Listen to me, McTavish. Charlotte said my brother was working with Patsy Ackerman, right before he died. I know it's early, but can I talk to her? Will you go with me, to see what she has to say?'

'We can go now if you like.'

'Oh, this is great,' Hugh said. 'My little girl disappears, and the only thing anybody comes up with is a mysterious dog, a haunted house, and the local version of one-nine hundred-psychic around the block. Jesus Christ, Olivia, and you say Los Angeles is full of shit.'

'Just this once, Hugh,' Olivia said, 'would you not be a total prick?'

'Fine, Livie. But I'm going too. We can get your suitcases from the house, and stop and say hi to Mr Duncan Lee.'

FORTY-ONE

McTavish drove. Olivia winced because Hugh was holding her hand tight enough to hurt.

Patsy Ackerman lived three blocks over from Olivia's place, a ranch style bungalow set back

259

deep into Forest Hills, up a narrow winding street. The house had been built at the end of the nineteen forties – cheap housing for soldiers returning from war. Olivia was well aware that what went for cheap housing then was top of the line now. There would be hardwood floors, a central hearth that ran the length of the living room, heavy plaster walls. Lots of upkeep with the wiring and plumbing.

There was no car in the driveway, but Olivia looked with hope at the tiny garage set in the hill at the bottom of the house. A single door, narrow, windows murky, but there might be a car inside.

They parked on the street, and climbed the walk to the front door. The house was set on a hill, the yard tiered and overgrown with ivy. Heavy shrubbery blocked most of the windows. The back and side yard were encircled with a black iron fence that strained to hold in the hedges and flowers and trees. It gave the house a hideaway effect, like a charmed fortress. As if the person inside might be hiding, or afraid.

'Let me,' McTavish said, moving ahead. He had to knock three times, the last rather hard, before the door finally opened.

'Enter the wicked witch,' Hugh said, softly, in Olivia's ear.

But this was no old crone. The woman's face was turned away, so it was hard for Olivia to make out features, but she saw the shine of long blonde hair, and noticed the interested way McTavish cocked his head.

The woman's voice was deep and it carried. 'I've already talked to you people once today, and I don't know anything else. I saw the dog. End of story. Please leave.'

'Ma'am, we're talking about a missing child. Her name is Teddy, she's only eight. This is her picture. Look at it, please.'

'I don't do readings anymore, and you people made me very unwelcome when I tried to help in the past. I get it. I went away. So return the favor and get off my porch.' She was already closing the door when she stopped. Walked back out of the house, shouldering past McTavish, to stand and stare at Hugh.

She was not what Olivia expected. She was not old, but she wasn't young either. Late forties, early fifties maybe, impossible to tell. Her hair was shoulder length and that right shade of blonde that at her age meant expert hairdressing. Her eyes were large and blue, but red rimmed and clouded with the kind of exhaustion that Olivia recognized. The woman was an insomniac, like she used to be.

Tired though she was, her face was strikingly pretty even with the frown and fatigue. She wore a black sweater and jeans, and slouchy high boots with flat heels. In her ears were tiny pearl earrings, just like Olivia's favorite pair.

She put her hands on her hips and glared at Hugh. 'So here you are. *Dammit.* I don't want to be involved in this.'

'I don't know you,' Hugh said.

'No,' said Patsy Ackerman. 'But I know you. You'd better come in.'

There was something very dominant about this woman, and the three of them went in meekly, like children who suspect they've been bad. They stood awkwardly in the living room, Olivia staring, taking it all in, the marvel of the house.

'They *said* you were an artist,' Olivia said.

Hugh walked to the fireplace, inspecting the mural over the mantel, the hand painted tile. 'That's an understatement.'

And it was. Even the wood step that led up to the kitchen was adorned with a hand carved fleur de lis.

'Call me Ack,' the woman said. 'And come with me. There's something in my studio that I want you to see.'

The kitchen made Olivia catch her breath, because it was the kitchen she had wanted all her life if only she'd been able to imagine it fully, to put it into thoughts and words. The countertops were some kind of poured concrete, stained a charcoal black, embedded with hand painted tile. The walls were French blue and terracotta with accents of green and red, and the mural on the wall looked as if you could open the painted stone doorway, that it would lead to another room. The porch off the kitchen had been gathered in, and you stepped down to an indoor terrace of stone floors, plaster walls, and open beams of aged timber on the ceiling. A wood stove had been built into the corner of one wall, and before it was a small table and an espresso maker, and baskets with tomatoes, an eggplant, yellow squash. Cut flowers were piled in the sink.

Another doorway led to the left, and Patsy Ackerman *call me Ack* led them into a room that gave Olivia the feel of an enchanted nook. A

262

leather loveseat, much worn and cracked, was against the far wall of the tiny room, there was a small fireplace, bookshelves with art supplies and books and bits of painted things on the walls. An easel and backless stool were set to the side of a floor length window that looked out to a gazebo in the back.

And pinned to the easel were ink portraits, three or four, with one charcoal drawing in the center, clearly a work in progress. All of them unmistakably Hugh.

'*Careful, Hugh, you better watch out.*' A squawky voice, coming from the corner near the window. And Olivia noticed for the first time the giant bird, the iridescent green, blue and yellow feathers of a parrot sitting high on a perch.

'That's Elliot,' Ack said. 'And you, of course,' she said pointing, 'have to be Hugh. I've had your face in my mind for three nights straight. Haven't got more than an hour or two of sleep in one go.'

'*Be careful, Hugh,*' the parrot said, raising a claw.

Hugh cocked his head at the bird. 'What does he mean by that? How does he know my name?'

Ack settled in the chair in front of her easel. 'I was hoping you could tell me. He's been chanting it for the last ten days.'

McTavish picked up one of the pictures. 'Why haven't you drawn a mouth?'

Ack rubbed the back of her neck. 'It worries me too. That's just how I see him. I don't know.'

'I would sue you,' Hugh said. 'If I could figure out what for.'

Olivia looked at the ceiling and sighed. 'Don't mind him, he's from California.'

'Yes, my darling, and this is all nice and lovely and creepy, but this woman could have researched you, and found our marriage records, and drawn all this ridiculous stuff.'

'Spoken like a true narcissist,' Ack said, looking up at him with a mean little smile. 'And don't forget the part where I taught my parrot to say your name. You came to my house, remember? That *was* you on my front porch?'

'Ma'am,' McTavish said. 'You told my officer this morning that you'd seen a stray German shepherd, hanging around Teddy's house? You know which house I'm talking about, right?'

'The stone cottage with the double chimneys. Yes, I know which one. I've only seen the stray a couple of times.' She looked over at Olivia. 'I actually thought it was your dog. I couldn't figure out why you kept the golden retriever in and the shepherd out. I got the impression he was some kind of guard dog.'

'And you saw him day before yesterday? Do you remember what time?'

'I take a break at lunch time, and go for a walk. So maybe a little before one.'

'About the time Amelia died,' Olivia said.

McTavish frowned at her. 'We don't have an official time of death. Were there any cars parked in the driveway, ma'am, do you remember?'

Ack nodded. 'Yeah, I was thinking it over, after I talked to your guy. There was a Jeep in the driveway, the one that's been there the last few weeks.'

'My car,' Olivia said.

'Was that the only one? Was there a car you didn't recognize? Maybe parked on the street, around the corner, just in visual range of the house.'

'Could have been, but nothing I remember.' She looked over at Olivia. 'So you live in that house?'

'Yes, why?'

'Interesting, that's all.'

'But it's more than interesting, isn't it? I'm Olivia James, and my brother, Chris, used to live there. Wasn't he talking to you before he died? Didn't he come to you for help?'

Ack looked down at her feet. 'Yes, he did, but he told me he was keeping our discussion confidential. Which is one of my requirements for my clients.'

'So he *was* a client?'

Ack shook her head. 'Look – what do you want me to say? I'm sitting in a room full of strangers who call me the *woo woo* woman.'

'How did you know that?' Hugh said.

But Ack kept her attention on Olivia. 'Your brother was in way over his head. But *he* opened that door. Don't make the same mistake, Olivia.'

'My brother made a bargain and he paid for it. My daughter, Teddy – she didn't do anything wrong.'

'You sound aggrieved, Olivia. Like somebody broke the rules. Like this thing we're talking about plays fair. And that's the one thing I could never make your brother and his buddy Bennington understand. This thing doesn't play fair.

265

It just plays.'

'Is it a demon?' Olivia asked. 'Teddy called it—'

'Don't.' Ack stood up and waved her hands. 'I don't want that name in my house. I *live* here, this is my refuge, don't track your mud in here.'

McTavish ran a hand through his hair. 'Demons don't kidnap little girls.'

'That's true,' Ack said. 'As far as I know, demons are a myth. I don't believe in demons and I hope like hell they don't believe in me. People create evil all on their own, they don't need any help. But I'll tell you this free of charge, Mister Hugh. Be careful, because something out there knows *your* name.'

Hugh clapped his hands. 'Bravo, bravo, drum roll please, here comes the not so veiled threat. How about a protection spell? Maybe you'd like to sell me one of those.'

Ack folded her arms and grimaced. 'Don't talk to it, Hugh. Don't challenge it. Don't listen to it and don't let it lure you in. Whatever you've got going on there, Olivia. Over in that house. Whatever it is, it's off the charts.'

'There are charts?' Hugh said.

'Enough,' Ack said. 'This is my studio, I haven't had my coffee, and I don't like your brand of rude. I've warned you, I've done everything I can do—'

'Have you, really?' Olivia said. 'Did you help my brother when he came to you for help? Because you can tell me it was all his fault as much as you like, but you went to the Waverly yourself, didn't you? I've googled you on the

266

Internet. You did a ghost hunting there fifteen years ago, right?'

Ackerman folded her arms. 'So what?'

'And Chris told you, didn't he, that's where all this started for him?'

'He told me.'

'And it's bad there.'

'It's *sad* there. The problem is that a place like that ... eventually it gets noticed. Think of it like a watering hole in the jungle, where everything comes to feed.'

'My little girl is missing and she's eight years old. You're a psychic, Ms Ackerman. Do you see anything? *Please*.'

'It doesn't work like that, I'm sorry. It doesn't come on demand. And anyway, I'm not that kind of a psychic. I'm a medium. And I can't seem to talk to the good things. I can only talk to ... the dark. Be glad I can't find your daughter. If I could find your daughter, she'd be in a really bad place.'

FORTY-TWO

'Well, that was creepy as hell,' McTavish said, as the three of them settled back into the car.

'Have you done any background checks on this woman?' Hugh asked. 'Is there any chance she could somehow be involved?'

McTavish shook his head. 'Unlikely, and yes,

I've checked her out. She is what she says she is. Whatever that may be.'

Hugh looked out the window. 'I would think that alone would be suspicion enough.'

'Look, let's stop by the house,' McTavish said. 'The forensic guys are done, and it will be okay for you to go back inside, Livie. You can get your things. And I'd like another look around without Detective Donnie breathing over my shoulder.'

'It's looking over your shoulder, or breathing down your neck,' Hugh said.

They looked at him.

'Sorry. I want to see it too,' Hugh said. 'The house.'

Olivia rubbed her eyes. 'I don't guess either of you are going to listen to me when I tell you the house is a very bad place. You guys will just think I'm nuts.'

McTavish touched Olivia's hand. 'Livie, you knew Amelia. Do you think there's any chance she killed herself? She was pretty upset about that little girl, what was her name, Marianne?'

'Amelia didn't kill herself. Amelia made a deal.'

'A deal?' Hugh leaned close from the back seat. 'What kind of deal?'

'Never mind.'

'Olivia?'

But Olivia folded her arms. She was not going to talk anymore. She should be outside, going through the neighborhood looking for Teddy. Or maybe she should stay there, stay in the house. Wait for Teddy there. Wait for something, God

268

knew what.

Of the three of them, Olivia knew she was the only one who hoped nothing would happen, that whatever was there in the house would stay in the background. But she knew it would be there. She knew it would watch. She was like Teddy now. She believed.

The driveway was empty and McTavish frowned.

'What is it?' Olivia asked him.

'There ought to be a patrol car out front. Teller said Donnie was going to have someone watch the place.'

'They took my Jeep,' Olivia said, as McTavish parked the car.

He shut the door of his Caddy very gently. 'They had to. After what happened with that little girl who went missing in Florida—'

'Please don't,' Olivia said. 'Not now.'

Hugh stepped backward from the walk, taking in the depth and breadth of the house. 'I forgot how pretty it is here, Olivia.'

'Don't let it charm you,' Olivia said.

But it was already too late. Hugh was bewitched. Olivia knew he was imagining them all together again, she and Teddy, Hugh and Winston, living together in the storybook cottage house.

'And no mortgage payments,' Hugh said. 'What do the utilities run?'

He'd be thinking about going out on his own again, Olivia knew it. All those nights they'd discussed it, Olivia thinking that if he did go that way they could live anywhere they wanted, unable to control the buzz of excitement in the pit

269

of her stomach. He'd drawn up business plan after business plan, but never pulled the trigger.

The door was locked, and Olivia handed Hugh the key.

'Aren't you coming in?' he asked.

'In a minute. You guys go ahead.'

'You want to wait out here, it's okay,' Mc-Tavish said. 'Just tell us where your stuff is.'

'I've got a couple of suitcases out in the hall. And I—' Olivia put her hands over her face, felt the tears spill over her fingers. 'I was going to ask you to get Winston's food bowls.'

'Of course we'll get Winston's food bowls. And his squeaky toys. He's going to need them when we find him. And we will find him, Olivia, he and Teddy, we'll get them back.' Hugh gave her a quick hug, and went inside the house, McTavish following.

It was a tedious thing, waiting, and Olivia was glad when Hugh and McTavish came out with suitcases and dog toys and piled them into the trunk of the Cadillac. But then they went back into the house, and were gone for a long time.

Olivia decided to go inside. She could go and get Teddy's school papers. She knew her obsession with the school papers made absolutely no sense, but she would take her comfort where she could find it.

She felt oddly self conscious, walking into her own kitchen, everything familiar but strange. She fingered the broken shards of glass from the window. It would need to be fixed or boarded up. She listened for the men, and heard them. In the basement, for God's sake. Olivia wished they

270

would not make so much noise. That they would be quiet, that they would be quick, that they would get out.

She went into the living room, walking quietly, so as not to disturb. Teddy's papers were right where she had left them, and she gathered them up, reached for the one on the coffee table as well, adding it to the stack. She had folded them in half and was just cramming them into her purse when she began to feel it. The foglike sensation that permeated the house. Whatever it was that watched them, it was watching now.

Olivia went to the top of the basement stairs. She had to make Hugh and McTavish leave the house, leave right now. She could hear them talking, tapping the basement windows, checking the dryer vent. One of them actually laughed. Stupid, stupid, stupid. She knew that whatever watched wanted her attention, but she pretended she did not notice. She would ignore it. It was not there.

Hugh was first back up the stairs, holding her net bag of lingerie in one hand, and from the other, dangling the red leather belt.

Olivia stumbled backwards. 'Hugh, dammit to hell, put that down.'

'Is this it? The famous red leather belt?'

'Don't touch it, Hugh, why did you have to pick it up? Get rid of it, *get rid of it.*'

'Bring it on, baby,' Hugh bellowed. 'You think you're going to threaten my *daughter*? You think you're going to threaten my *wife*? I'll hang *you* from the attic fan, you disgusting—'

Upstairs a door slammed very hard. None of

271

them said anything for a full minute.

'A door doesn't just shut like that,' Hugh said. Finally.

Olivia backed toward the kitchen door. 'Put that fucking belt down and let's go. Please.'

McTavish grabbed the belt out of Hugh's hands.

'What are you doing?' Olivia said.

'Taking it outside. To the garbage.' McTavish headed out the back. 'Let's just throw it away and be done with it.'

'Fine by me,' Hugh said. 'I'm going upstairs to see what slammed that door.'

'The hell you are.' Olivia grabbed his arm and pulled him toward the back door. 'Let's just go. Please. Who cares why the stupid door slammed?'

The grind of a motor starting up made them both go still.

McTavish came back in from the driveway, looked from Olivia to Hugh. 'What is it? Did the door slam again?'

'Listen,' Olivia said.

They were quiet, all of them, barely breathing.

'It's the attic fan,' McTavish said.

Hugh leaned close to Olivia, raised a hand to barely touch her cheek. He was whispering. 'We are by God not putting up with this.'

He turned and headed through the sunroom, and Olivia heard his step on the first stair.

'He's right,' McTavish said. And followed.

Olivia hesitated. She admired Hugh very much, but she knew he was wrong.

But she went upstairs behind them. It was fear

272

and not courage that made her go. She did not want to be alone. Not even outside the house. Outside was where Teddy disappeared.

She went up the stairs slowly, hanging onto the rail, careful in case something pushed her, or tried to make her fall. The noise of the fan dominated the house, and Olivia remembered how impossible it was to sleep with that kind of racket in the hall outside the bedroom doors.

McTavish was staring up, and Hugh was flipping the switch. On. Off. On again. Nothing happened. The fan continued to run.

'Where's the breaker box?' Hugh said.

'Right next to the back door. I'll go,' McTavish said. But as soon as he turned to go back down the stairs the attic fan stopped. He looked over his shoulder at Hugh. 'Turn it back on again.'

Hugh worked the switch but the fan stayed dead. 'Could be a short, maybe a loose connection.'

Olivia folded her arms. 'Right, Hugh. And a loose connection slammed the door, and wrote the names in the bathroom ceiling.'

'Let me see those,' Hugh said.

The three of them piled into the bathroom, and this time Olivia led the way. The stepladder was folded into the bathroom closet, and she got to it before McTavish did, set it up and began to climb. She wanted to see for herself. If the names were written in blue chalk. If she really had remembered it right.

'Let me go,' Hugh said.

'Just hand me the flashlight. It's under the sink.'

McTavish held the ladder steady, which Olivia really did not need. Hugh handed her the light. This time she knew exactly where to look.

Just like she remembered, the newer names in blue chalk. And now, one more added to the list.

Olivia dropped the flashlight, and the front cover smashed. She could barely catch her breath, and she was glad of Hugh's hand, helping her back down the steps.

'Olivia? What is it? What did you see?'

'Nothing, it's just ... a panic attack. I need to get out of here. Please.'

Hugh caught her up in both arms. 'What did you see, Olivia?'

'I told you, nothing.'

But McTavish was already climbing the ladder, shaking the flashlight, miraculously getting it to work. He paused for a moment, then poked his head back out of the ceiling. 'It's your name, dude.'

'Mine?' Hugh said.

'Written upside down in blue chalk. H-U-G-H.'

FORTY-THREE

The rest of the day was spent in uneasy alliance, with Olivia, Hugh and McTavish winding through the neighborhood streets around Olivia's house. The focus was on empty apartments and unoccupied houses up for sale. The economic bust had hit the area hard and there were plenty of candidates for their search. Having McTavish there made things official, it opened doors, and landlords of the tiny, run down complexes brought forth keys and let them into little cubbies that smelled of ancient meals and bygone cats.

McTavish had fliers with Teddy's picture and everyone, from the man with a cigarette hanging out one side of his mouth and a CAN YOU SEE ME NOW ASSHOLE orange vest, to the teenage boy with a skateboard tucked under one arm and a patch over one eye, gave the picture a serious look and promised to be on the watch.

Olivia imagined Teddy behind every scratched metal door, but the rooms were always empty, with no sign of her little girl. She felt as if Teddy were drifting further and further away.

McTavish put a yellow swatch of police tape on the door of every place they searched, and they ran across other doors with bits of tape. Detective Withers not only kept a list but marked every place the police had checked. Olivia felt a stir of respect.

At five thirty McTavish got a call. He'd gotten several throughout the day, and each time Olivia and Hugh went silent and tense.

'Anything?' Hugh said, when McTavish snapped his cell shut.

'No news. But Donnie has finally agreed to let me come into the magic circle, and he needs me to run a few things down. Look, Livie, you look like death warmed over and it's starting to get

275

too dark to search. I'm going to drop you guys off at your hotel, okay? I'll call you if I get anything. And I'll call you if I don't.'

Hugh headed for the car. 'Not the hotel. Drop us off at Naples, and we'll get a cab back. Stop shaking your head at me, Olivia, it's past time you had something to eat.'

Olivia stood on the sidewalk in front of the restaurant. Even from outside she could smell olive oil and garlic. She folded her arms. 'I told you, Hugh, I don't want to eat here. Why can't we just get something at the hotel?'

'Come on, Olivia. This is a good place for us. Put it down to nostalgia.'

But Olivia was crying. 'I can't go in there. It's the last place I took Teddy, before—'

'Even better,' Hugh said, guiding her inside. 'I want you to tell me about the last night you spent with Teddy. What she ate and the little things you talked about, and I want you to picture her happy and safe and home again.'

'I can't do this.'

'Yes, you can. I know you can.'

They sat across from one another in a red upholstered booth along the side of the restaurant, one down from the table where they'd had their first date. The waiter who had waited on Olivia and Teddy just a few nights before took their order – Veal Marcela for Hugh, lasagna for Olivia, and a half carafe of the house Chianti wine. Olivia waited for the waiter to ask about Teddy, to notice she wasn't there, but he didn't. She would not have known what to say if he had.

The bread was warm and soft in the middle and Hugh buttered a slice and handed it to Olivia, and topped off her glass of wine. She noticed he only had a half glass he ignored, and said no to the waiter when he tried to fill it up.

'This is a lucky place for us, Olivia. You came here every birthday when you were a kid, it's where we had our first date. This was the first place you brought Teddy when you got to town. What did she talk about that night? Did – does she like her new school?'

'She's got a crush on her teacher. She's made a couple of friends and there's some kind of lizard in the class.'

'A gecko. She told me when she called.' Hugh pointed to a booth across the room. A bigger one, that seated four instead of two. 'See that booth over there?'

'Yes, Hugh, I see it.'

'I want you to see what I see.'

'Hugh, what—'

'Go with me on this. Because I see you on the left side and me on the right. And Teddy is sitting beside you bouncing up and down because we just took her to the bookstore and let her buy every single book that caught her eye, and there are eighty-seven thousand, three hundred ninety-seven books in the trunk of the car.'

Olivia tried not to smile. 'Eighty-seven thousand.'

'Eighty-seven thousand three hundred ninety-seven. And we had the devil of a time fitting them in. A lot of them are hard covers, so it was one hell of a bill. And let me tell you another

277

reason that Teddy is smiling. She's got her daddy back.'

'Hugh, for God's sake.'

'Please, just listen. I want to come home, to you and to Teddy. We'll live anywhere you say. Right here in Knoxville, just not in that fucking haunted house.'

'No argument there.'

'We can find one of those godawful bungalows you love so much, or some house so old and decrepit that you can't resist falling in love. And we'll nurture it, and love it, and take our time fixing it up, because we'll be broke anyway after buying eighty-seven thousand, three hundred ninety-seven books. But we'll all stay together and never move again no matter what, and I'll go into business for myself or flip burgers at McDonald's, or be your assistant while you build your financial empire.'

'That might be nice. My current assistant is a bitch.'

Hugh smiled at her, that old smile he gave whenever she'd made him laugh. He took her hand across the table and leaned very close. 'I'm going to find Teddy and bring her back home. That's what daddies do. And I'm hoping that when I do that, you'll let me come home too. And that we'll stay together, no matter how hard things get, no matter how mad we get, because that's just the way life goes, and families stay together no matter what.'

'You bring my little girl home safe, Hugh, and I'll be yours for life.'

FORTY-FOUR

There was a very bad moment in the lobby of the hotel when Olivia saw Teddy disappearing around the corner into the hotel gift shop. She had called out, and started to run, held back by Hugh's firm grip round her shoulders. He had shaken his head but not argued, led her gently into the gift shop, so she could see and know for sure that the little girl was not Teddy. Olivia had tried to tell the girl's parents to be careful, that their child was not safe, but he had hushed her and pulled her away, throwing an apology over one shoulder as he forced Olivia to the elevators.

'I'm sorry,' Olivia said, as they stood outside her hotel room. She fished her card key out of her purse, touching Teddy's school papers.

'You have nothing to be sorry for,' Hugh said.

Olivia looked up, expecting him to come in, to tell her that neither one of them should be alone at night, but he kissed her gently on the cheek and turned away.

'If you need me, or you hear anything,' he said, 'I'll be right down the hall.'

Olivia shut the door in his face and put the chain lock on. She kicked her shoes off and pulled the spread off the bed, propping herself on the pillow and wondering if her mind would ever be still enough for sleep. She attached her cell phone to the charger and set it on the bedside table. There was a ballpoint pen and notepad with the hotel logo. She turned the lamp on and closed her eyes a moment, thinking to make a list of new places to search. She fell asleep with the pen in her hand.

The light hurt her eyes almost immediately, which was strange since she only had the lamp switched on, and it was a three-way, with the setting on low. And it wasn't really lamplight, it was more like the sun, shining so hard her eyes watered, and she had to squint. The front door to the stone cottage was unlocked, which was lucky, and she went inside, only this time it was like it used to be when she was a little girl and she didn't feel afraid. The old upright piano was still there and the living room was just like it had been when she was growing up. She was drawn immediately to the woman who sat with her back to the door on the old, nubby green couch.

'*Mama?*' Olivia said. 'But you're dead, how can you be here?'

'I thought you needed to see me, hon.'

Her mother smiled and Olivia thought how pretty she looked. She had on that chocolate linen dress that Olivia remembered. Olivia had loved that dress, her mother always wore it when she went somewhere special.

Her mother held out a hand. 'I'm sorry, honey. You've had such a hard time.'

Olivia settled at her mother's feet and let the tears come, sobbing hard in her mother's lap. Her mother stroked the top of her head and let

280

her cry it out.

And when she was done, Olivia sat up on her knees, and looked at her mother, content just to see her face.

'You have to go now, Olivia.'

'I don't want to go.'

'It's time.'

'Why can't I just stay here, Mama?'

'Because you gave Hugh the key to the house.'

FORTY-FIVE

Olivia was running down the hotel corridor when the call came through. It was Hugh's number that flashed up on the screen.

'Olivia? Darling?'

There was static on the line and in the background, the barking of a dog.

'Oh, God, Hugh, tell me you're not in that house.'

'Yes, but I'm leaving right now, heading down the stairs as we speak.'

'But—'

'You were right, you know. There is something here. It whispers at you, over your shoulder. It's ... vile.'

'Don't *talk* to it, Hugh.'

'Talk to it? I tricked it, Olivia. We're all going to be safe, we're all going to be okay. I know how to get Teddy back. Oh God, poor little baby.

It's a horrible thing, this—'

'Hugh. Get out of there, get out of the house.'

'Darlin', I'm on my way. I'm going to get our baby right now. She's alive, Olivia. *She's alive.*'

He sounded so happy, Olivia thought, he was laughing, damn him.

'Where is she, Hugh? If you know, tell me now.'

'It's not something I can *tell*, Olivia. It's hard to explain. But I'll get to her, I can do this, I swear.'

'Hugh, what's that noise?'

'It's the attic fan. Shit.'

The phone showed *connection lost.*

Olivia called 911 first, reported intruders without shame, and gave her name. The dispatcher wanted her to stay on the line but she refused, and rang McTavish instead. He didn't pick up. It was a bad time not to have a car.

FORTY-SIX

When Olivia made it down to the hotel lobby, there was an airport shuttle in the circle drive out front, discharging a tired looking woman in a charcoal gray dress. When the driver tried to wave her away, Olivia opened her wallet and offered him everything she had in cash – sixty-eight dollars and thirty-nine cents. He took all of it, even the change. When she asked him to drive

282

fast because it was an emergency, he said he'd do his best. As far as Olivia was concerned, his best was slow, and she chewed the inside of her lip and twisted her hands as he drove.

The police were there ahead of her. One patrol car, lights flashing. Parked on the curb out front. Hugh's rental car was in the drive.

The shuttle driver eased to the curb and looked at Olivia over one shoulder, then handed back the cash.

'Good luck, ma'am.'

'Thanks,' Olivia said. Then she was out on the curb and running up the driveway, noting as her stomach sank that every single light was on in the house. It was always like that, all the lights on, when the bad things happened. She was beginning to read the signs.

The front door was wide open and Olivia ran into the living room, stopping when she saw the uniformed cop on the stairs. His gun was drawn and he was crouched in the protocol firing position.

'Stay right there, ma'am. Don't move.'

'But—'

'I mean it. Don't move.'

He was in his thirties, with brown hair, and the spooked look in his eyes made Olivia think he might well fire his gun. In the distance, she heard sirens.

'Who are you, ma'am, and what are you doing here?'

'I'm Olivia James, and this is my house.'

'I'm going to need to see identification. We've had a report of intruders.'

'*Mike, I could use your help up here.*' A man, upstairs, another cop. Sounding panicked, sounding like trouble.

'*I'm* the one who made the call. Look, my husband was here, Hugh James? We were talking on the phone and he said ... he said there was someone in the house, and then the phone went dead. Is he here? I saw his car out in the drive, and I'm really worried that something happened to him.'

'Can you describe him, ma'am?'

'Five nine, slender, thick dark graying hair – likely wearing a charcoal blazer and loafers. Come on, you...'

'Yes, ma'am. We've found him.' The officer straightened from his crouch and came down the stairs, watching her. He did not holster his gun. 'I'm going to need to see that ID.'

Olivia's fingers were trembling and it was hard to get the driver's license out of the plastic slot, and Olivia finally handed him her entire wallet. He studied the picture on the license, the name, and the address that matched the house. The officer holstered his gun, and Olivia took a breath.

'You've found him,' Olivia said.

The officer pointed to the couch. 'I'm going to ask you to sit down, please, ma'am, we've got an ambulance coming—'

She ran past him, heard him shout something to his partner. She scrambled up the steps, noting that two of the spindles on the railing banister were splintered, one entirely broken off. Olivia recognized Hugh's shoe as she turned the corner to the landing, a brown loafer, on its side against the woodwork. And Hugh's Blackberry, up against the wall as if it had been kicked away.

There was another police officer in the hallway, and he was shouting something at her, but there was so much noise in her head she could not make out the words. And he could not move, he was holding Hugh by the legs, trying to relieve the pressure on Hugh's neck as he dangled, hung from supporting struts on the attic fan with a long, red leather belt.

Olivia ran for the stepladder in the bathroom, thinking how handy it was to have it right when she needed it, and she held Hugh's legs while the officer climbed and cut Hugh down. She could hardly hold Hugh when he dropped, but there were three of them now, one of the officers had him by the shoulders and it was awkward but they caught him and did not let him fall. Olivia worked the belt off Hugh's neck, one of the officers started CPR, and there were more sirens and more men thundering up the stairs, and Olivia held Hugh's hand, limp now but still warm, and turned away from the wide eyes, still hemorrhaging blood.

More paramedics arrived, shouldering Olivia aside, and she stood and watched them working. It was hard not to hope, but she knew as soon as she'd seen all the lights on inside the house. Hugh was gone. Just like everyone else.

She was aware when the paramedics gave up, she could feel it, sense it from the things they said, the way they slowed, the way they avoided her eyes. She walked to the end of the hall and picked up Hugh's Blackberry. It was set on record. She slipped it into the pocket of her jeans and sat down suddenly, legs splayed out in front of her, like a child.

'Ma'am? Ma'am, are you okay?'

Olivia pulled her legs to her chest and rested her head on her knees. The nausea was sudden and intense. She breathed slowly, and squeezed her eyes shut tight, and tried not to vomit.

A paramedic guided her down the stairs, arguing over his shoulder with someone about whether or not to take her to an emergency room before Detective Withers arrived. No one asked Olivia's opinion, which was just as well. She didn't have one.

She sat obediently on the living room couch, puzzling over Hugh's last words about Teddy until Donnie Withers had a uniformed officer come and take her away.

FORTY-SEVEN

Olivia was not sure of the time, for some reason she thought maybe three a.m., and her endurance was crumbling fast. She kept waiting for it to stop, the repetitive questioning. The interview room was metal tables and worn linoleum, rank with old sweat and fear.

She was distracted, having trouble concentrating on what Detective Withers said. Her body ached for sleep, but when she closed her eyes, she saw Hugh, swinging from that red leather belt. She was very aware of Hugh's Blackberry, still tucked into the pocket of her jeans. Detective Donnie would go ballistic over the Blackberry. He would confiscate it and Olivia might never know what Hugh had taped if she handed it over to the police. From moment to moment she expected Detective Withers to insist she turn her pockets out.

Instead, he questioned her and watched her. She'd stood up at one point when she thought she'd heard McTavish in the hall outside the small, airless room with the door shut so tight.

Olivia listened to the voices in the corridor, an angry man, then a woman laughing in a mean sort of way. Not McTavish. It was the middle of the night, McTavish would be home asleep. Or maybe Detective Withers would keep him away. She wanted to ask for him, but knew it would complicate matters beyond belief. But she was alone and hungry for even a glimpse of a familiar and sympathetic face.

'I want to go back to my hotel,' Olivia said.

'We're almost done here, Mrs James. Please sit back down.'

Olivia sat. Clasping and unclasping her hands. Withers had said he was almost done. She just needed to hang on a little bit longer.

'It's the dog, that's what's got me bothered,' Detective Donnie said.

Something about the offhand way Withers asked the question made Olivia wary, brought a cold edge of anxiety to the back of her neck. She told herself not to worry. That her state of mind was working for as well as against her – she might have trouble thinking straight, but she was also shielded from this man's perceptive smarts by his expectations – her twitchy distractedness would be put down to shock, grief, and extreme anxiety for her child.

Olivia clenched her jaw. How much longer would this go on? How long before she could go back to her room? What if she just got up and left?

'What *about* the dog, Detective? I don't know what you want from me. I don't get what you *mean*.'

Detective Donnie smiled as if that were exactly what he'd been waiting to hear her say. He opened a file and put two police reports on the table, lining them up side by side with care so that she could read them both.

'The description of the mysterious dog you saw the night Teddy disappeared. It's an exact match for the description of the dog that disappeared along with your sister, Emily, all those years ago.' He picked up a swatch of paper. 'German shepherd, tan and gray, black face, brindle markings. Unusual description for a shepherd, and it strikes me, you know? That this dog you saw looks exactly like your family dog, Hunter.'

Olivia gave herself a moment to think. 'Except for the limp. The one I saw had a crippled back leg.'

'True. Except for the limp. It's my experience, Mrs James, that a good liar sticks close to the truth when they start to spin a tale.'

Olivia felt the heat rise in her face. Her cheeks going red. 'You're saying I made up this dog? For what possible reason?'

'I'm saying it's time you told me what really happened the night Teddy disappeared. Come on, Olivia, for God's sake, this is your little girl, and we have two people dead at your house. Tell me what's going on.'

'I'm not the only one who saw the dog,' Olivia said. 'One of your own officers found a neighbor who saw him.'

'You mean that Ackerman woman?' Withers curled his lip and gave her a mean little smile.

And Olivia thought, yes, that Ackerman woman, who had somehow become her last hope. That Ackerman woman was going to have to help her somehow, because there wasn't anybody else. Withers was useless, useless, all his efforts spent questioning her, instead of finding her little girl.

'I want to go back to my hotel,' Olivia said.

'Call me,' Withers said, pressing one of his cards into her sticky palm. 'When you can't stand it anymore, when you're ready to tell me what happened to Teddy, when you want some peace in your heart.'

Olivia knew, then, that Detective Withers had given Teddy up for dead. It took all her strength just to get to her feet.

'I want to go back to my hotel.'

When the uniformed officer dropped Olivia off outside the lobby, she went to Hugh's room instead of her own. The police had been there, ransacking the room, while she and Detective Withers had talked. Hugh's briefcase was in the center of the bed, canted to one side, flap open.

Hugh loved that briefcase, a vintage reproduction mailbag he'd bought through the J. Peterman catalog. It had cost him the earth. Olivia noticed the jumbled look of the papers inside. The police had gone through it thoroughly, leaving the contents askew – Hugh was habitual and organized, he would have been so pissed. His phone charger was in the briefcase, in a zipped compartment, so the police would be on the hunt for the Blackberry. Olivia plugged the charger into the phone and an outlet by the side of the bed, her hands shaking hard.

She went into the bathroom, splashing water on her face. Avoided looking in the mirror. She touched the handle of Hugh's toothbrush, the razor he would no longer need. She knew she was preparing herself, gearing up for whatever Hugh had recorded. She left the clean white shirts hanging in the closet, and put on the soiled one Hugh had worn on the plane because it smelled of the shaving soap Hugh always used. She was ready now.

Olivia sat on the edge of the bed, working the Blackberry, bringing up that final video. She took a deep breath and pressed play.

The screen filled with Hugh's face.

His mouth was open. Olivia could see the back row of his teeth. His scream mingled with the grind of an engine. He was in the upstairs hallway of the house, right under the attic fan.

Hugh's head jerked back. As if he were being

dragged.

'No. *God damn you.*' He flopped sideways, like a fish on a hook. '*Love you. Olivia. Love you, love you Teddy, love you love you.*'

The angle of the camera showed the right section of hallway at the top of the stairs, and the outside of Olivia's bedroom. Olivia could see, right at the edge on the left, when Hugh suddenly swung up in the air. She trembled hard, the tears rolling down her cheeks. *Hugh*, she tried to whisper, but she could not talk. Her chest was hurting, her throat tight and dry.

Hugh laughed abruptly, and dropped to the floor. '*You're not going to win, you son of a bitch.*'

The red leather belt swung into view, dropping in front of the camera from the ceiling fan.

'*Son of a bitch,*' Hugh said. '*You son of a bitch.*' The last was a sob.

Olivia jammed her fist into her mouth.

The lights in the hallway began flashing on and off. Olivia could hear a dog in the background, barking hysterically. Hugh was up in the air again, as if lifted by a giant, invisible hand. He made a noise in the back of his throat, a harsh gurgling moan, suddenly cut off. Hugh's feet cycled frantically, then stilled, dangling heavily, loose. The loafer on one foot was half off, and it fell from his foot, rolling sideways.

The dog stopped barking. The lights in the hallway switched off one more time, then back on. Olivia held the screams in her chest and watched another six minutes of the shoe in the hall before turning the video off.

291

FORTY-EIGHT

Olivia wakened the next morning to the patter of rain. She had spent the night curled up in Hugh's bed, grateful for the light of the bedside lamp, cold, but unable to crawl beneath the covers, unable to get up and go to the bathroom when she felt the urge. Eventually the numbness had come, and she had slept.

It was dark out, a little before six a.m. Too early to knock on Patsy Ackerman's door, but she could sit outside the woman's house and wait.

It took a day and a half of off and on vigilance before Ackerman, exasperated, agreed to meet with Olivia the following evening to talk things out, if she'd please for God's sake go home and stop leaving messages on the phone.

Olivia headed for Ackerman's house right at dusk. It was still raining, hard and steady, but traffic was thin, and it took Olivia twenty minutes to get to Bearden from the hotel downtown. She was still staying in Hugh's room, sleeping in his tailored white shirts, wondering how long his credit card would last and if she should be the one to shut things down. She knew he'd made her executor of his estate.

Olivia was stronger now. Armed with information. Full of purpose, and frayed but steady hope.

She took the long way round, passing Forest Heights and turning left on Westwood. That way she did not pass by the house. She hit a dip in the road and water sprayed from beneath her wheels, and she took the Jeep slow and steady on the curves. Hugh had warned her how easily a Wrangler could flip. McTavish had applied pressure and she had her Jeep, two cars now, her own and Hugh's rental. She'd have to take the rental car back, eventually, so many things to do ahead, details, but not now. Teddy was her focus. Find Teddy. Anything else was noise in her head.

It was dark enough out, with the rain falling, that Olivia could distinguish the glow of light from inside Patsy Ackerman's house. She parked out front, tucked a large brown envelope into Hugh's briefcase, which had now become her own. She wedged it securely in the pouch next to her laptop, where Hugh's Blackberry nestled, safe and secure, and snapped the flap into place. The leather should keep everything safe from the rain for the few seconds it would take to dash to the house.

Ack had been watching for her, and she opened the front door just as Olivia made it up onto the porch.

'Right on time,' Ack said. 'Come in.'

Olivia ditched her wet shoes and left them on the mat by the door. She was dressed for comfort. Favorite worn jeans, and Hugh's black cashmere sweater. She wore thick socks which felt slippery on the dark pine floors.

'Thank you for this,' Olivia said.

'Sure. You've been camped on my doorstep for the last two days, so it was either this or call the police.'

Olivia looked at her feet.

'Any news on your daughter?'

'Nothing yet.'

Patsy sighed, and looked away. 'Sorry. Really. Look, let's do this back in the studio. I've got espresso on the boil, that okay with you?'

Olivia nodded. It was somehow easier not to talk.

The studio had been cleaned up a bit, and there were none of the sketches of Hugh on the easel. Olivia wondered what Ack had done with them. She did not want to know.

The parrot gave Olivia the benefit of his noble profile, then tucked his head under one wing. He was quiet today, almost sleepy. Maybe it was the rainy afternoon.

Ackerman was wearing gray sweatpants and a Vandy football jersey, and she too had on ridiculously thick ugly socks. She sat down on the leather loveseat in front of the coffee table and waited for Olivia to set everything up. Ackerman was different today. Edgier maybe. Focused. Like me, Olivia thought, when I see a client at work.

Olivia turned the Mac on, then took the bootleg copy of Hugh's autopsy report out of the envelope and handed it over.

'McTavish got that for me this morning.'

Ackerman began to flip through the pages.

'You'll see that two of Hugh's fingers were

294

broken and his left thumbnail was torn out.'
Olivia settled on the couch beside Ack, tilting the
computer screen. Then she was up again, walking to the window, looking out. 'There's a circle
of contusions on his right ankle,' she said, over
her shoulder. She looked out at the magnolia
tree, watching the droplets of water slide off the
heavy waxy leaves. 'One of his ribs was cracked.
Left side again, like the fingers. Death caused by
hanging. Strangulation, a slow asphyxiation. He
didn't break his neck. If you look, you'll see the
medical examiner made a note of that.'

Patsy Ackerman set the papers to one side of
the coffee table. 'You saw him? Right after it
happened?'

'Yes. I helped cut him down.'

'But you saw where it happened?'

'Yes. In the upstairs hallway of my house. He
was hanging from the support struts over the
attic fan from a red leather belt, just like ... just
like the threat.'

'What else did you notice?'

Olivia turned away from the window. 'Two of
the spindles on the railing in the hall were broken
in half. And one of Hugh's shoes had fallen off.
It was sideways by the wall.'

'And that's when you picked the Blackberry
up?'

'Yes.'

'And you haven't shown it to the police?'

'No.'

'He recorded it? The death?'

'Yes.'

Ackerman rubbed her forehead. 'Bear with me

295

a minute, I'm trying to picture this.'

'You don't have to picture it, you can watch.'

'Start it up then. You can go in the kitchen, if you'd rather. You don't have to see this right now.'

Olivia settled down beside Patsy Ackerman on the couch, as far to her side as she could go. She owed it to Hugh to watch, as many times as it took, felt compelled to watch the video time and time again, taking note of how long those legs had kicked, timing exactly how long Hugh had suffered at the end of that red leather belt.

She slid the disc where she'd copied the video into the slot on the side of her laptop, waited for the program to open, then hit play.

Ackerman caught her breath. 'Do you know what that noise is? In the background?' she asked.

Olivia found talking almost impossible. 'Attic fan,' she managed.

'But it was off when the police arrived?'

'As far as I know.'

'I'll be damned,' Ackerman whispered, sounding like a scientist at a microscope. She gave Olivia a quick glance. 'I keep thinking I hear a dog barking in the background. Do you hear it too?'

Olivia tried to say yes, but had to settle for a nod.

Ackerman watched the rest of the way through, sobbed softly, and held Olivia's hand.

'Take it,' Ack said.

Olivia tried to wrap her fingers around the tiny

little cup but could not seem to grip it in her hands. It was too hot. It was burning her palms, but she could not seem to force the words and explain. She shoved the cup back at Ackerman and looked down at her knees.

'It's okay to cry,' Ackerman told her. 'I'm crying. I've got tissues.'

Olivia laughed. Tissues, the one thing she always had. Tissues in her purse, on the front seat of her car, in the pockets of her jeans, and a motherlode of used ones wadded beneath the pillows of the bed in Hugh's room at the hotel.

Olivia wanted to turn the computer off but it was hard to move. Crying was impossible as well. She had cried enough. Everything was tight now in her chest and she could not imagine being able to even make a noise. There were things to do. Things to do.

'Well?' Olivia said, when she could finally speak.

Ack roamed around the room, talking softly to the parrot, then looked back at Olivia. 'What exactly do you want from me?'

'Want? I don't know. Help? I just – I want to know what I'm up against here. I want to know how to get my daughter back.'

'If I knew how to get your daughter back, don't you think I'd have told you by now?'

Olivia leaned forward and shut the computer down and began to pack up her things. That was it then. No hope here. She would try something else, God knew what.

'Look, don't go,' Ackerman said softly. 'Try that espresso. I got some very nice beans from

Sumatra. It's free trade coffee, expensive but good and guilt free. No farmers were exploited in the brewing of that coffee.'

Olivia stood up, slung the briefcase over her shoulder.

'Look, Olivia, I just don't know *how* I can help.'

Olivia nodded. Headed for the door.

'Let me think about this. We could meet again tomorrow.'

'No. Thanks.' Olivia went through the studio, the kitchen, snatched up the soggy shoes she had left by the door. Putting them on was a struggle. Ackerman was talking to her, but Olivia shut it out, though she finally had to sit on the floor like a toddler to get those shoes back on her feet.

Outside, it was raining even harder. The drops pelted Olivia's head and ran down her face, and turned the leather of the briefcase dark. She'd left the car unlocked, thank God. Was Ackerman watching her from the house? She had the vague impression that Ackerman had said goodbye and closed the front door.

Her hands were damned unsteady, and it took three tries to get the key into the ignition. She turned the heat up high, and the wipers on, and rested her forehead against the steering wheel. It felt good, how quickly the car warmed up. She focused on nothing more than the rhythmic drone of the wiper blades, and breathing slowly in and out.

What the fuck was she going to do now?

She was alone. She had no right, really, to ask anyone else to help. Not with everyone dead,

Hugh, Amelia, Chris. Hugh had said Teddy was alive. She had to hold that in her heart. Teddy was alive. Olivia would not give up.

So she would go to the house and take this presence, this evil thing on face to face. If it had a face. Would it offer her a deal? How did that happen, exactly? Would she agree? Chris had. So had Amelia. What kind of arrangement did Hugh make? He said he had tricked it, then wound up hanging from the red leather belt.

But she could go down fighting, if nothing else. She didn't have to win.

When the passenger door opened it was so unexpected that Olivia banged her head into the top of the steering wheel. She had not noticed Patsy Ackerman walking down the front lawn to her car in the dark and the rain.

'What are you doing?' Olivia asked.

Ack had a dark hoodie on over the sweats, and had jammed her feet into those same pirate boots she had worn the day they'd met. 'The question is what are *you* doing.'

'Taking a moment to pull myself together before I go back to my hotel.'

'Don't lie to me, I'm psychic, remember?'

'I thought you only talked to dark things.'

'It didn't always used to be that way. And besides, your thoughts are pretty dark now.'

'Look, get out of my car will you? I want to go.'

'That's fine, go ahead. I'll go with you. Come on, Olivia, I know exactly where you're going and what you think you're going to do, and I'm not going to let you. Anger can make you very stupid. You just saw what happened to Hugh.'

'Thank you so much for your concern. Now get the fuck out of my car.' Olivia braced her hands on the steering wheel. 'No? Fine then. *Come with me.* You'll be sorry.'

'I already am.'

Olivia drove slowly, with great precision and care. Anger could be magnificent. People always underestimated the power of a good hard rage. The trick was to control it, rather than let it control you. It was a skill you could learn but you did have to work at it. Olivia was working at it right now.

Ack grabbed the door handle and leaned forward when Olivia turned into the driveway of the house. Olivia parked sideways at the top of the drive, facing the sunroom window, right where she'd parked it the night Teddy disappeared. She left the headlights on, just like she had that night, and the light glared off the windows. She could see that the broken window in the kitchen had been boarded up. Who had done that and when? Had it been like that the night Hugh had died? She could not remember. No matter how hard she tried.

Olivia kept the engine running. It was a stupid fear, but she could not get rid of the idea that if she turned the engine off in this driveway it might not start back up again.

'Hugh did exactly this,' Ack said. 'Went in angry, spoiling for a fight. You see where it got him.'

'My little girl is missing. What else am I supposed to do? There isn't anyone out there to help me.'

'Yes there is.'

'Who? You've turned me down. There's no-body else left.'

'I wasn't talking about me. But you aren't alone with this. Help is constantly being offered, the universe will send you help, if you recognize it. If you ask.'

'I don't get what you mean. And *you* won't help. I've asked every way I know how.'

'I haven't turned you down, Olivia. I'm just ... I failed. I was meant to warn Hugh and—'

'You did warn him.'

'Not well enough.'

'All those pictures you drew, without a mouth? He was silenced?'

'To say the least.'

'Fine. Let them silence me now. I can't just sit around and wait anymore. I have to do some-thing. I don't even know if ... if Teddy is alive. If there's even a point to this anymore. At least Hugh. He's dead. At least he doesn't have to worry anymore.'

Ack put a hand on her arm. 'I don't get what you think you can do, Olivia. Don't you under-stand that whatever this is – it's just playing games.'

'But why us? Why my family?'

'Imagine this, Olivia. Imagine that you are alone and in the dark and you are lost and in pain and you're afraid.'

'You mean like now.'

'Fine, like now. And you see a light. What are you going to do?'

'Go to the light.'

'Exactly. But you're the light. Teddy is the light. Your brother was the light. Dark things want help – but the only way for them is to go back to ... how should I put this? Pure self. Pure energy. Back, if you will, to the source. So it's stuck. Because help, real help, means a sort of death. So whatever it is ... it comes in pain and it seeks relief and every manifestation is a cry for help. But the end of pain is the end of life and it fights to grow and live. Release is death, so it never lets go.'

'Is that supposed to make some kind of sense to me, Yoda?'

Ackerman gave her a small half smile. 'Put it this way. This thing is having some fun, but it's also *really* angry. It wants to live. So it's drawn to innocence and good and it goes for the weak.'

'Children. The Pied Piper.'

Ackerman nodded. 'Something like that. The light doesn't need the dark, but the dark needs the light.'

'Whatever that means. All I want is my little girl.'

'Look, I'll commit. I'll help. But I'm not magic, Olivia. All I can do is my best.'

Olivia took a deep breath. 'I get what I'm asking, you know.'

'Yeah. I wonder about that.'

'What did you mean, before, when you said you used to be able to know the good things, when you said you were psychic? Has it always been this way for you? Only talking to dark things, like you said?'

Ack rubbed a hand over her face. 'No. It didn't used to be like this.'

'What happened? When did it change?'

'Fifteen years ago. At the Waverly. That's when it happened to me.'

'The Waverly? The—'

'Body Chute. Yes. You begin to see a pattern here, right?'

'Like Chris. And Bennington. And Jamison. So what do we do first?'

'We? I meditate and plan and ask for help. One's mental state is crucial and you have to have a plan.'

'Meditate? That's it?'

'Whatever has latched onto your daughter, to your family, don't you get how strong it is? So be patient for God's sake, and let me get prepared.'

'But what am *I* supposed to do? Do you want me to talk to Bennington? He and Chris were in on this together, before Chris died. Do you know how to get in touch with Bennington?'

'Yes, and if you want to talk to him that's fine, but I don't think he's going to be much help. He's a victim, just like you. The best thing you can do, Olivia, is hold tight. Right now just drive me back to my place, go back to your hotel and *stay out* of this house. I don't like even being in this driveway, after dark.'

Olivia put the car in reverse, and faced it out to the street. She had just started down the drive-way when Ack twisted sideways and looked back.

'Shit.'

'What?' Olivia said. But she saw it. The light

in the kitchen had come on. 'What do you want me to do?'

'To do? I want you to get the hell out. That light is an invitation.'

'Maybe you're right, maybe it's *my* invitation. Maybe I can make a deal with it, just like everybody else.'

'Yes. Like everybody else, like your brother, Chris. And look what happened to him.'

'He paid the piper, but his little girl is alive.'

'Yes, but is it over? Did it stop? Do you think he'd have made the deal if he'd known what would happen to you?'

'I don't know. I think he was desperate.'

'Exactly. And when you're desperate, Olivia, it has you right where it wants you. And I can promise you one thing, speaking as one who's had some experience with the dark – paying the piper is always going to be too high a price. So take me home, Olivia, and sit tight. I'll be in touch.'

FORTY-NINE

Olivia was in the hallway outside her hotel room, just swiping the card through the lock, when she heard the soft voice call her name. She had been vaguely aware that the elevator had dinged, doors shuffling open and closed, aware of the footsteps behind her, someone in soggy shoes, saturated like hers by the constant downpour of rain.

The voice was girlish, sounding just enough like Teddy to make her blood pound, even though she knew better.

'Aunt Olivia?'

Janet held a hand out, and Olivia took a step backward. Olivia felt ashamed even as she did it, she knew it was unfair, but she blamed her, blamed Chris's little girl. Unfair and unkind, and she made herself smile and open the door to her hotel room wide and invite the girl in.

Janet was trembling, perhaps a combination of cold, nerves, wet. Her jeans were soaked, the ragged bottoms streaked with mud, and her navy blue hoodie was plastered to her body like a second skin.

'You're soaking, hon,' Olivia said. 'Come on, peel out of that jacket, let me get you a towel. Why don't you take those wet things off, you can borrow something of mine.'

Janet pulled the hoodie back off her head, but would not take the jacket off. Her hair clung in sodden strands around her face. Her eyes were bruised looking, her face broken out, angry red in patches on her cheeks and skin. She clutched the towel Olivia gave her in bunched up fists.

'Come on, Janet, sit down.' Olivia pulled a chair from the wall.

'I'll get it wet.'

'Don't worry about that. How did you get here? Does your mom know where you are?'

Janet settled on the edge of the seat cushion, hunching her shoulders together. 'I walked some

305

and took a bus. Mom thinks I'm doing a study date with a friend. I had to talk to you, but Mama wouldn't let me come. Because of what happened to Teddy. Because you were so upset. I'm so sorry, Aunt Olivia.'

'Thank you, honey. To tell you the truth, I don't know which end is up anymore.'

'That's one reason I had to come, Aunt Olivia. I need you to really listen to what I have to say.'

'Okay, but let's get you out of those wet things first. Let me run you a hot bath, and you can cuddle up in this bathrobe, and if you're hungry—'

'Please, Aunt Olivia, don't *mom* me. Please just listen to what I have to say.'

Olivia sat back on the bed.

Janet squeezed the towel in her fists and looked at the floor. 'I've been praying a lot, Aunt Olivia, for Teddy, and trying to talk to Daddy in my dreams. I can't know that he hears me, but I think he does.'

Olivia felt her shoulders sag. She felt she should hug Janet, wet and muddy or not, do something to comfort her. But she didn't. She just sat there on the edge of the bed, thinking about what Teddy would be like at that age, wondering if Teddy would be lucky enough to get to that age. Bad thoughts, but she could not keep them out of her head.

'I came here to warn you, Aunt Olivia. Because I think it must be trying to talk to you, isn't it, trying to get in your head?'

'What's trying to talk to me?'

You know what. Why won't anybody tell the truth about this thing? Duncan Lee, Decan

306

Ludde. Whatever you call him. The Piper. Don't pretend you don't know.'

'I *do* know what you mean,' Olivia said steadily. 'But I don't hear it in my head.'

'Are you sure?'

'I'm sure,' Olivia said. But was she?

'Because I bet it talked to Uncle Hugh. And it talked to Daddy. And I know it talked to Teddy. And all of them are dead.'

'Don't say that. Teddy isn't dead.'

Janet folded her arms, and Olivia realized her niece was looking at her with pity. 'It doesn't play fair, Aunt Olivia. There's not going to be any mercy for Teddy, haven't you figured that out?'

Olivia felt the strength go out of her arms and legs. 'Is it talking to you, Janet? Did the Piper tell you that?'

She shook her head. 'I don't listen anymore. Daddy taught me to block it. But it can be hard.'

'What does it say, when it talks to you? How does it work?'

Janet twisted the towel in her fists. 'It starts slow, Aunt Olivia, but it's always there, it waits and it *presses* on you, and after a while you start to know if it's around. It even has a name for the first stage. It calls it the *awakening*.'

Olivia wrapped her arms tightly around her chest.

'And if you listen even a little, then it's like it's got a foot in the door, and it gets stronger and stronger and sometimes it feels like a friend, but it's *not*.'

'Is it a voice in your dreams?' Olivia asked.

307

Janet tilted her head sideways. 'Sometimes. Or in your mind. But it can talk out loud, right behind you, or beside you. Sometimes it *breathes* on you. It's scary and weird. But the more you listen, the more attention you give it, the stronger it gets. Teddy told me it used to sit on the end of her bed, and sometimes at the table in the sunroom. She said you couldn't see it and Duncan Lee said it was because you were stubborn, and you refused to look. That no one can see it unless they agree. It has to be a choice.'

'Teddy *told* you that?'

'It's why we had the séance that day, when you and Mama got so mad. I knew Teddy was in trouble and only Daddy could help. Mama doesn't see it either. Or she pretends it's not there.'

'How long—' Olivia's throat was tight and it was hard to form the words. 'How long has Teddy been talking to this thing?'

'Do you remember the year before Daddy died and you came for Thanksgiving? You and Teddy, but not Uncle Hugh?'

Olivia nodded.

'Teddy was upset because you were moving again and she was going to have to go to a new school after Christmas break and not have any friends. She was crying in the night, after everybody was asleep. I heard her, she was in the living room all curled up. She said she wished she could live in the same house all the time like I did and go to the same school. So I told her about him. About Duncan Lee. I told her he could be her friend no matter how many schools she went to. That she would never have to start a

308

new school by herself again. He could even protect her, if somebody gave her a hard time. Because new kids always have to deal with bullies.'

Olivia stood up, and Janet flinched, so she sat back down. *'Why? Why did you tell her those things?'*

Janet stared at the floor, and her voice dropped to a whisper. 'Because he told me to. He said I had to say it, to keep my sisters safe. I didn't have a choice, Aunt Olivia – he says he gives you choices but that's a lie. He has a friendly voice, Aunt Olivia, but the things he says are *sick*. And bad things happen if you don't do what he says. So it's my fault. Everything bad that happened. Daddy and Teddy and Uncle Hugh.'

Olivia crouched down beside her niece, took the towel and wrapped it around her shoulders. Janet stayed tense and tight when Olivia tried to give her a hug. Please just cry, Olivia thought. But Janet pulled away.

'Listen to me, Janet. I don't blame you, and you shouldn't blame yourself. Whatever this Piper does – none of it is your fault. Teddy is eight years old and you're barely thirteen. You're children. This thing is taking advantage, don't you see that? And every time you feel guilty, every time you think it's your fault, every time you feel afraid, you're playing right into its hands. I know you feel like an adult, but you're not. This Piper thing is not your responsibility. It's somebody else's job.'

'Whose job, Aunt Olivia?'

'Maybe mine.'

'That's what Daddy told me too. But I wanted

309

you to know. I wanted to tell you I'm sorry. I needed to confess.'

'I understand, Janet. You can't keep something like this all to yourself. And it helps me to know what I'm up against. But I'm worried about you, now. Does it still – does it still sit on your bed and try to talk to you?'

'No. Not since Daddy taught me what to do. He told me never to listen, to say no out loud and ... and if it bothered me to ask him for help. He still helps me, Aunt Olivia, even since he's dead. I ask him to send me signs that he's watching over me, and he does.'

'What signs does he send?'

'Feathers. It's what I asked for. To send me a feather, so I would know he was there. And he does. There was one on the floor of the elevator, just a minute ago.' Janet dug into her jacket pocket, pulled out a tiny fluff of white and put it in Olivia's hand. Olivia held it up, the kind of feather that drifted out of goose down pillows. There were pillows like that all over the hotel.

'Do you believe me, Aunt Olivia? That Daddy can send me feathers? Don't lie.'

'I don't know,' Olivia said. 'But I have a story to tell you. About a phone call I got. I think your daddy would want you to know about it. So you can be sure in your heart he's okay.'

Olivia was only a little surprised that Janet took a phone call from her dead father in stride. Olivia made sure to tell her that Chris was in a good place, and watching over them all. She did not mention the warning, because it was not the

310

kind of thing her niece needed to hear.

And though Janet would still not take a dry set of clothes or a meal, she seemed different, lighter, relieved. Driving home, with the heater on full blast to keep her niece warm, Olivia had the sense that she had taken the weight from Janet's shoulders, and put it on her own, which was the way it should be – this was Chris's child, and Olivia was the adult. She told herself that information was what she needed, that knowledge was power no matter how upsetting it was. She told herself that Teddy wasn't dead.

But she was tied up tight with anger at the thought of her little Teddy, recruited like fresh meat. The anger felt good. She just needed to remember to be angry for both of them, two vulnerable little girls. Not to put the blame on a thirteen year old kid.

The Piper didn't play fair with anyone. She needed to keep that in mind.

Charlotte's car was not in the driveway when Olivia pulled up in front of the house.

'Good,' Janet said. 'She's probably at Kroger, getting groceries. I can sneak in. You won't tell her, right?'

'No, I won't. But you should tell her yourself.'

Janet shook her head. 'She'll only worry – she doesn't understand, but she knows enough to feel scared.'

'Just don't talk to it, Janet. Do what your daddy said.'

Janet looked almost old when she turned to Olivia, the reflection of raindrops on the windshield shadowing her face. 'That doesn't really work, all by itself. You have to pay toll to the troll, Aunt Olivia. I wouldn't be safe if Daddy hadn't died.'

The next morning, Olivia woke with the disturbing sense of a conversation interrupted, and the vague echoes of an unfamiliar voice in her head. She sat up, propped on one elbow, the hotel room grayish with early morning light.

She swung her legs over the side of the bed, shoulders going tense as the memory came. *An awakening*, is what the voice had said. A man, the voice was male. *Time for your awakening, Olivia.* The voice had given her a bad feeling, distinct and chilling, like a snake crawling up her back.

It had to have been just a bad dream, her dark imagination taking everything Janet had said to heart. Olivia pulled her tee shirt off, and stood in front of the mirror looking over her shoulder. Her skin had reddened, up and down her spine, as if she'd been scratching it in her sleep.

Was it really as simple as Janet had said? A simple acquiescence, opening the door a crack?

'Is this what you meant when you warned me about the Mister Man, Chris?' She was talking to the dead now, just like Janet. 'Were you talking about the Piper? Because you started this, didn't you, Chris? You brought this thing into our *home*. You think it's okay to save your little girl and not mine? You think I even want to live without my Teddy, that I wouldn't hesitate to trade my life for hers? You did it, didn't you, Chris? You made a deal. And if that's what it takes, then so will I.' Olivia stood up and opened her arms. 'Come and get me, Piper. I want my little girl back.'

FIFTY

Bennington Murphy had been a pain to get hold of. Olivia had spent the last two days leaving message after urgent message, never catching him home. But miraculously and at long last, when she woke up that morning, she had a message from the front desk that a Bennington Murphy had called, and would meet her that day at noon. He lived in a small town called Valden, in the far south-eastern edges of Tennessee, and according to MapQuest, it was going to be a two hour and fifteen minute drive. Olivia was leaving an hour early in case she got lost.

She was heading across the hotel lobby, brief-case slung over one shoulder, debating whether or not to show Bennington the video of Hugh's death, when McTavish came in through the re-volving front door. Olivia dropped her briefcase and froze. A tissue fell out of the side flap of the briefcase to the floor.

'Livie?' McTavish bent down absently and returned the tissue, then took her hands and squeezed. 'Nothing on Teddy. Where are you heading?'

He was looking at her jeans. She had not been

into her office since Teddy disappeared.

'Five days now,' she said.

'I know.'

'Five days.'

'Look, I know I've caught you on your way out, but can you sit down with me a little while? We need to talk.'

'I'm meeting someone, but I can give you a half hour. You want to go up to the room?'

He led her toward the dining room. 'Let's do the breakfast buffet. I'm starving. Livie, I can feel every little bone in your hand. Have you been eating at all?'

'I eat a bag of salt and vinegar potato chips every night and drink a beer and fall asleep.'

'That's it?'

'It's the jumbo bag, economy size. And it's the only time I'm hungry.'

He led her into the dining room. 'Whatever works.'

The buffet had everything that Olivia liked – shredded hash brown potatoes, melon slices, corned beef hash. McTavish helped himself to sausage links, biscuits and gravy, and Olivia sat down at a table with a glass of orange juice, thinking that if Hugh had been there, he'd have had the salmon and brie. But Hugh wasn't there. Hugh was gone. Just like everybody else.

A waiter brought coffee in a silver pot, and waited for Olivia to signal when to stop pouring cream. She began her new routine by lining up the salt and pepper shakers, then organizing the various sugars and artificial sweeteners, by color, in the bowl.

McTavish sat across from her and frowned, putting a napkin into his lap. 'Don't you want anything other than coffee and juice?'

'What I want is to know if Teddy had anything to eat today. If she got breakfast. If she's hungry, or ... you know.'

McTavish rubbed his forehead. 'I know.'

He knew, Olivia thought, but he was still able to eat. She watched him cut up sausages and wolf them down.

'Sorry kiddo, but I've been working twenty-four seven, and eating burgers from a bag, and this is the first hot meal I've had in days.'

'What did you want to talk to me about, McTavish?'

'Several things, but first off, I just needed to see you in person and make sure you're okay.'

'I'm as okay as I can be.'

'Yeah, I know, but Jamison. He's staying with me right now – and by the way he keeps asking about you, he seems to think you're going to be moving in too. You could, you know. It would be better than being alone.'

'I'm not leaving the hotel until I find Teddy. I'll go home with my little girl.'

'I'm not going to argue with you about it, Livie. Just know the offer holds. The main thing is, Jamison was up last night with nightmares, and he was frantic. He kept saying you were in some kind of trouble. I tried to make him understand that it was Teddy who was missing, but he kept talking about you.'

'I was in the hotel all night.'

'Yeah, I know, I called and confirmed, sorry, he

was pretty frantic. I had to promise I would check on you in person this morning. He's acting really weird, and he's hard to calm down.'

'What does he say?'

'It's not anything I can really make sense of, Livie. He's been anxious for weeks, but last night it was different. Last night he seemed scared, and worried about *you*.'

'As you see. Fine.'

'I thought you might be staying with Charlotte.'

'Charlotte and I are ... complicated right now.'

'Do you think there's any chance—'

'None. She had nothing to do with this.'

'You're probably right. She checks out okay.'

'You guys have been investigating Charlotte?'

'We've been investigating everyone. That's one of the things I wanted to talk to you about.'

Olivia leaned forward in her chair. 'You've got a suspect?'

McTavish put his fork down. *'No.* Sorry, but no. The thing is. Donnie Withers is looking really hard at you right now.'

'Yeah. He made that very clear the night Hugh died.'

'Livie, look—'

'You know what this means, if I'm the best he's got? Me? It means he's got nothing, it means he can't find my little girl. It means he's getting nowhere, if the best he can do is come up with bullshit like this. And it's my take he's given up on Teddy. He thinks she's dead.'

'He's got some legitimate concerns.'

'Such as?'

'You expect me to just tell you?'

'Hell, yes, I expect you to tell me.'

'Yeah, okay, twist my arm. Here's the thing. He's found out about that hospital report my ex-wife made.'

'Annabelle?'

'Yeah. About her suspicions that there was something odd going on between you and Teddy. That Teddy might be at risk.'

'Put it in writing, did she?'

'Yes, ma'am, she did. So give him his due, he does his homework. He goes to Teddy's pediatrician in Los Angeles, and finds out that the physician on record is a PA named Amelia Wainwright. Your friend, Amelia, who died by drowning in the bathtub in your house. And you were the one who found her. Lots of water on the floor, like maybe she was thrashing around or there could have been a struggle.'

'McTavish—'

'Let me finish. It gets worse. Then we get Hugh. Dead by hanging, and you're the one who called it in.'

'Is he honestly saying I strung Hugh up?'

'No. He doesn't think you could have overpowered Hugh, or that you're strong enough for something like that. And it's clear that Hugh put up a hell of a fight. So it's either a murder by persons unknown or suicide—'

'Suicide? Did you see that hallway? Hugh was fighting for his life, his finger was broken, and so were his ribs.'

'Yeah. I got to say the suicide idea is pretty thin ice. But here's the thing, Olivia. One, you got

317

laid off from your job eighteen months ago and you've had a rocky time since, financially.'

'Me and the rest of America.'

'True. But Teddy is Hugh's beneficiary. He left life insurance. And if something happens to Teddy, it all goes to you. You see how it all adds up?'

'Yeah, to a big fat crock of shit.'

'They tracked down the airport shuttle guy, so you've got an alibi for when Hugh died. But Donnie, he's thinking maybe an accomplice.'

'Am I following this? I am slowly killing Teddy, I murder her doctor when she figures it out, then I make Teddy disappear, and then kill Hugh for the money? Don't you think that sequence is a little out of whack?'

'Not if you were really smart. There's another thing that Donnie is puzzling over.'

'God. What?'

'That report you gave the night Teddy disappeared. Your description of the mysterious German shepherd hanging around your house. And the physical description, brindle markings, all of that. It dovetails exactly with your family dog that disappeared when Emily died.'

'I know already. Donnie was obsessing about it the night Hugh died.'

'Livie, when someone is lying to the police, they often describe something they know, and just substitute. Like if I were asking you to describe an assailant, and you were lying, you might just sit there and describe me. People do it all the time, describe the cop sitting right across the table. So he's thinking, it's a really weird coinci-

318

dence unless you're lying. And if you're lying ... that kind of opens everything up.'

'And you, McTavish? Do you think I had anything to do with this?'

'You know better. But I have to admit you were really funny about things when Amelia died.'

Olivia looked down at her hands. She reached for her coffee, but her fingers were trembling too hard to pick up the cup.

'Another thing. Hugh's Blackberry is missing. Do you know where it is?'

'In my briefcase.'

'*You've got it?* Why didn't you give it to the police?'

'I found it that night. When he died, when the paramedics were working on him. It was on video record and I knew that if I gave it to the police they'd take it away and I'd never see what was—'

'Are you telling me you have a video record of Hugh's death?'

Olivia nodded.

'*Son of a bitch.* You're saying Hugh had the presence of mind to record the whole thing?'

Olivia nodded.

'And you didn't tell anyone?'

'I told Patsy Ackerman.'

'Patsy Ackerman? Why didn't you tell me?'

'Because I thought it might get you in trouble for withholding evidence.'

'There isn't going to *be* any withholding evidence. Give it to me. Right now. What's on there?'

'I told you, Hugh's death.'

'Then how did it happen? Was there someone there?'

'Watch it yourself, McTavish, it's pretty weird shit. If you can sort it out let me know.' Olivia opened her briefcase and took the phone. Slid it to McTavish across the table.

He put his head in his hands.

'McTavish?'

'Olivia. I can take this in myself, or you can hand it over through an attorney.'

'Which should I do?'

'I don't know. Look, let me take it. Let's see how it plays. There's nothing incriminating on there?'

'You mean a video of my secret lover killing my ex? No, nothing like that.'

'Do you have a secret lover?'

'Just you.'

'I'm not secret, babe. Donnie has tossed me off the case three times already, and I've got no official standing.'

'You should know that Hugh wanted to get back together. He asked me if he brought Teddy home, would I take him back. In the nature of full disclosure, I told him yes.'

'Of course you did. Manipulative bastard. And if I bring Teddy back, you're going to marry *me*. Look, Livie. There's something else. Donnie has been looking back into the disappearance of your sister, Emily. The coincidence – girl disappearing with family dog – he was thinking that was what might have given you the idea for what happened to Teddy. If you set all this up. But when we were looking into it, we ran across a

320

guy.'

'A guy?'

'He's a snitch, said he had information about Emily years ago, but when the cops pursued it, it didn't pan out. He couldn't have had anything to do with her disappearance himself, he was in jail at the time, he just said he *heard* something. Like they do. The case got a lot of press, cops figured he was just cashing in. So we had somebody talk to him, just to cover every lead, but he made ridiculous demands and it didn't go anywhere. Soon as he was out of jail, he killed a guy, so he's back in again, only this time he's on death row. So Donnie sends a guy out to talk to him up in Eddyville, and he's still saying he's got information. Says he knows what happened to Emily, and he knows where she is. But he's not going to talk without a reprieve. Which we all know he ain't going to get.'

Olivia shook her head, gripped the arms of her chair. 'McTavish, you don't think ... you don't think Emily could still be alive?'

'No, Livie, I don't. I think we're being played by a sociopath. But I wanted to let you know what was going on.'

'But think about the way he worded that. He knew what happened to her. He knows where she *is*.'

'Sure. He put it that way on purpose. That's how these guys work.'

'I used to sit on the front porch every afternoon after school and wait for Emily to come home. Did you know that?'

'We all knew that, Livie.'

321

'I don't understand how all of this can be happening right now. I don't know ... I don't know what to do.'

'We find Teddy.'

'Right. But it's all so confusing. It's like some kind of maze in hell.' Olivia snapped the latch on her briefcase. 'Look, McTavish. I've got to stay focused. I've got to go, sorry, there's somebody I need to see.'

'Who?'

'Bennington Murphy.'

'So you got him on the phone then?'

'Yeah. I'm going to see him today.'

'There's nothing spooky there, Olivia. His wife is a school teacher, they've got two kids, he's a computer IT guy, works out of his home. Regular suburban dad. Married late, though, wife is ten years younger, his kids are grade school age.' McTavish looked down at his sausages.

'You stay and eat, McTavish. I'm sorry, I need to go, I can't sit still right now.' Olivia motioned to the waiter for the bill. 'Breakfast is on Hugh, I'm using his credit card right now. Until you guys haul me off to jail.'

'I don't get what you think you can accomplish with Bennington. I don't see how he connects.'

Olivia slung her briefcase over her shoulder. 'See, the difference between you and me is this, McTavish. You're looking for a bad guy. I'm looking for ... something else.'

'*What* else, Livie?'

'If I knew, honey child, I'd tell you.'

FIFTY-ONE

The rain had stopped, and the route to Valden was a flat stretch of interstate, an easy drive. It just didn't feel easy.

Because it was inside Olivia now, locked down tight in her heart, the fatigue, the urge to give up, the acidic burrowing of despair. Tired. The word played constantly in her head. She envied Amelia, she envied Hugh, she envied her brother – anyone who was dead now, whose battle was over and done.

Olivia had always thought that the one thing a parent gave a child was unconditional love. Unconditional love of one's children was easy after all. But now she saw there was one more thing required, and it was a hard thing. The stubbornness never to give up, the grit to keep hoping. She was beginning to think that getting older was all about wearing down. When she looked at people she had not seen for years, friends and family who had aged, what always struck her was not additional weight or wrinkles in the skin. What struck her was how tired they looked. Maybe age was nothing more than fatigue.

Valden, Tennessee, was more a pit stop than a city. There was a Dairy Queen and a worn down Citgo, but no cute town square or vintage houses. Most of the people there worked at a manufacturing plant fifteen miles away, line workers and managers engaged in the process of turning sawdust into the kind of pressed wood used to make crappy but affordable furniture, and all of them damned glad to have a job. She wondered how Bennington wound up in this godawful place. She wondered if maybe he was hiding. She could only imagine what Hugh would say about a town like this. Unless, of course, it was a place he wanted her to live. Even Hugh would have a hell of a time talking *this* place up.

Olivia double checked the scribble of directions she'd written on a scrap of complimentary hotel stationery. She watched for the split in the road and turned right, finding the stone marker announcing the entrance to *WINDERMERE ESTATES*. She did not know what she expected, but it wasn't this. The houses looked newer and the trees smaller as she wound her way back.

Bennington's house was a two story with beige aluminum siding and trim, shutters and front door painted robin's egg blue. It was the shrubbery that reminded her of Patsy Ackerman's bungalow – the neglected snarl of honeysuckle hedges, forsythia bushes and dogwood trees that formed a barrier to the street. A dirty white Ford Focus was at the end of the oil stained driveway, so Olivia parked by the curb.

The sidewalk was plastered with dead leaves that had fallen in the rain and dried to the walk like a second skin. A small limb was down from a struggling magnolia on the side of the house. It

324

looked like it had been there a while.

Olivia started up the driveway, then stopped when a flutter of black caught her eye. She walk-ed into the yard, the soil soggy and drenching her shoes. She found the feathers between two pear trees, a lot of them, mangled and smeared, as if the bird had died. She thought of Janet, pulling the fluff of a white feather from her pocket and putting it in Olivia's hands, saying it was a sign from Chris. Olivia's shoulders went tight, but she shook it off and headed back up the drive.

The sidewalk on the front stoop was cracked. A doormat said *WIPE YOUR PAWS*. Olivia rang the doorbell, trying to look into the windows but foiled by the tight seal of blinds. She rang again, and was checking her mobile for the time when she heard a scuffle of wood and the door swung wide.

'Bennington here.'

The first thing Olivia noticed was the smile.

Bennington was fair, like Ack, his fine corn silk hair banded in a loose ponytail that hung an impressive way down his back, but two blondes could not have been less alike. Bennington was soft all over, sunny and lamblike to Ack's black boots and angled cheeks and her lone wolf air of pain.

'Olivia James.'

They did not shake hands.

'Come on in.' He opened the door with a cer-tain reluctance, and Olivia stepped into the house. He herded her to a room to the right of a tiny foyer. 'This is my little sanctuary. Sit any-where you like.'

She only had a moment to see a bit of the house. The thin carpeted stairs that led to the bedrooms on the second floor. The way the hall ran straight back to what was surely the kitchen. And to the left, a living room, plaid nubby couch against the back wall, old boxy television on a stand in the corner next to a fireplace, and book-shelves jammed with paperbacks, the overflow stacked like piles of coins on the floor. It was quiet inside the house, except for the tick of the living room clock, everything economical, comfortable, and as normal as a pair of Wal-Mart jeans.

Bennington waited, smiling, for Olivia to go first, then closed the door behind them. Olivia wondered why he shut the door, if there was anyone else in the house.

The sanctuary had a layer of dust that rivaled her own office clutter. The entire back wall was a command post for computer geeks, screens, boxes, wires, a lot of it shoved aside and gathering dust. Olivia sat on the velveteen green futon pushed against the right wall, and Bennington pulled a little stool from behind a desk and faced her over a wagon wheel coffee table. The desk, the windowsill and the coffee table were littered with crystals, some pinkish, some clear, a lot of them blue. A feathered dream catcher hung in a corner of the room.

'I'm so sorry about what happened to Chris,' Bennington said, leaning back in his chair. He had a sleepy aura of contentment, as if his mind was on other things.

Olivia turned her cell phone off and held tight

to the purse in her lap. 'I don't think my brother died peacefully in his sleep.'

Bennington nodded sadly, head cocked to one side. 'Of course he didn't. He died in agony. Strangling slowly, unable to move or call for help. I think it might have taken a while. My biggest fear is I'll go the same way.'

'So you know.'

Bennington actually laughed. 'Sorry, it's not funny, of course, but it's either laugh or cry. But yes, I know. I know all about it, my dear.'

'What are we going to do?'

He folded his arms and settled back in his chair. 'Would you mind telling me your side? Your end of the story. Then we can go from there.'

Olivia nodded. She'd come for information, but she was perfectly willing to give to get. 'It started with a phone call. From Chris. Nine weeks after he died.'

Bennington raised an eyebrow and scooted his chair closer. *'Interesting*. I had no idea. He actually called you. After.'

Olivia nodded.

'What did he say?'

'He ... he seemed like he was reassuring me. Telling me that everything was going to be okay, because he'd paid the piper.'

'He actually used that phrase? Paid the piper?'

'Yes.'

'Maybe he *thought* he'd paid the piper. My guess is the piper didn't agree. That's been my experience anyway. But go on. Then what happened?'

Olivia sat on the edge of the futon, and put her hands on her knees. Thinking she would just give him the highlights, there were private things to hold back. But once she got started it was hard to stop. It seemed essential that he know everything, so she purged it all, every last detail, the way the radio came on in the middle of the night, playing 'Heart and Soul', the way Amelia's eyes had rolled back into her head, about her missing sister Emily and the death row convict who said he knew where she was. She told him things she had not even told McTavish. The blue chalk, the names in the ceiling, her original fears about things Teddy might have done, her relief when she found out Teddy was still the innocent daughter she'd always been, tangling with something that was over her head. Tangling with Duncan Lee. Decan Ludde.

Bennington's head snapped back when she said the name.

'Decan Ludde?' he repeated.

'Yes. He's mentioned in the original accounts of the Pied Piper of Hamelin.'

'You've done your research then. I'm impressed.' Bennington put a finger to his chin. 'Would you like a cup of tea?'

Olivia said she did to be polite.

She waited in the little office while Bennington disappeared into the back of the house, twining her fingers in the handle of her purse, listening for the comforting whistle of a tea kettle. Instead she heard the ding of a microwave oven, and a kitchen cabinet slam.

Olivia wasn't good at waiting. She realized

328

she'd been holding her breath when Bennington came in carrying two blue mugs that said *Tennessee Bank & Trust*.

'It's Oolong tea. I made it with lemon and just a bit of raw honey. I hope that's okay.'

'Perfect,' Olivia said. She took the mug and poked her nose into the steam that rose from the surface, then set it down, untasted, on the coffee table next to a rock that had been split open to reveal the glitter of mica inside.

'My turn then,' Bennington said, settling back on the stool. He held the hot mug without a flinch, drank while the steam rose in his face. 'We all had our reasons, you know, that night we went to the Waverly. It really was just a lark. Well, a haunted sanatorium, with a reputation for ghosts, and it was close to the hotel. How could we possibly resist? I had my dad's car, the three of us had ridden up together. We were feeling the freedom. We were dead serious about our wrestling match, so we weren't going to get wasted, and naturally it was lights out at nine, which worked for us, because we snuck out of the hotel at ten. We were way too keyed up to sleep.' He looked away. 'Hard to remember now how excited we were. Have you been there? To the Waverly?'

'No,' Olivia said. 'I've looked at the website.'

'Hell of a place.'

'Patsy Ackerman says it's like a watering hole in the jungle where the dark things come to feed.'

Bennington laughed, choking on his tea. 'You are in touch with Ack? Is she willing to help on

329

this? Chris thought he was wearing her down, but then he died. She won't return my calls.'

'She's preparing. Meditating.'

'More like working up her nerve. Look, I don't blame her. She had her own experiences there. And when I think back on that night – we were so young. Arrogant, stupid, taking on the world. You could almost say we got what we deserved. And like I said. We had our own private reasons, all three of us, why we had to get a scholarship. Jamison – escaping a smother mother who was going to keep him tied at home while he went to college unless he could pay his way. No dorm rooms or fraternities for him. And Chris, so worried about college money, your dad under so much pressure when his business took that dive.'

'What do you mean?'

'You didn't know?'

'I was five years old that year.'

'Right. Your parents were in deep then, money troubles. Chris wanted to work his way through, not ask them for tuition. And then there was me.'

'Money troubles too?'

'You could say that. It whispers to you, you know? Talks to you over your shoulder, offers you your fondest dream. And all you have to do is pay the piper when he comes to call.'

'Like the *Godfather*.'

'Exactly. And all hell breaks loose – literally – when you refuse. In my case, well, I had a girlfriend and she was pregnant, and her parents were pressuring her to abort. But we were in love. We wanted to be a family. And I knew that there would be no college for me with a baby on the way, no help from either set of parents, so I needed that full ride. Then I could have a crack at getting my computer science degree, and supporting a family properly. So yes, I wanted it bad, maybe worse than either Chris or Jamison.'

'Then what happened?'

'Oh, then. Then we got exactly what we wanted. Whatever you say about the piper, he holds up his end. He just expects you to do the same. And the price, for all of us, was unbearably high. Jamison had the accident, and wound up a vegetable living with his mother after all. Your sister Emily disappeared, and Chris was so eaten up with guilt he wouldn't use the scholarship, he would hardly even come out of his room. It was touch and go whether he finished his senior year. And then there was me.'

Olivia waited. She'd told him everything. She wanted to know.

'Me. Well, I got my scholarship and I used it, I went to school. And the wedding was planned, the parents actually coming round. We even had a name picked out, Allison, because Shelly just knew it was going to be a little girl. The pregnancy was perfectly healthy, perfectly great. Then Shelly went into early labor. Only she didn't know it was labor, she thought it was just back pain, and by the time we got her to the hospital, things were pretty far gone. The baby was too far down in the birth canal for a C section, but in considerable distress. Cord around her neck. So, our little Allison. She strangled as she was born.'

'Strangled,' Olivia whispered.

Bennington looked away. 'Strangled slowly, I have dreams about it. But. We lived. Chris, Jamison, me. We paid and paid hard, but then life went on. Until Chris stirred it all up last year, and the piper was on the hunt for all of us again. History repeats. But you could hardly blame him, your brother, with his daughter so sick.'

'Janet.'

'Pancreatic cancer. She was definitely going to die, she'd have been lucky to get another six weeks. So Chris made a deal and Janet was miraculously okay. All those test results strangely incorrect. Then Chris died, and he died hard, but as a parent ... as a parent, I'd say the piper was pretty fair with him. There were two other children, the piper could have taken them all. That seemed to be worrying Chris for a while. But in the end, the piper was merciful, and only took Chris.'

'And you? What did it want from you?'

'Oh, I was a fool. My business went to hell with the economy. My wife got laid off from her teaching job. The house, the cars, the health care. We were losing it all. The Cobra insurance payments alone were double my wife's unemployment payments. So all I asked for was work. And I got it. Caught up all the bills, and actually have a healthy savings account. But I haven't paid the piper yet. I'm still waiting, to see what he wants. One thing you can say for him, he keeps his end of the bargain. I think he enjoys it. Making me worry. Making me wait.'

'But what are you going to do?'

'Well, what can I do? Patsy Ackerman is no

magic bullet, no matter what your brother seemed to think. I'm waiting for my bill to come due.'

Olivia put her head in her lap because she did
not want him to see her cry.

She heard the stool squeak when Bennington
got up, felt the futon cushion sink as he sat close.

'You have two choices, Olivia, I'm sorry to
say. You can simply accept what the fates deal
you. Teddy lives, Teddy dies, Teddy never comes
home, just like your big sister Emily never did.
Or you can make a deal. Teddy can come home
safe. Maybe even Emily can come home safe.
Maybe you can have them both. But if you do
that—' He put a hand on her shoulder, the slightest touch, then pulled it away. 'If you do that
you'll have to pay. And you and I both know the
price will be high. The question is – is there a
price too high for the safety of your little girl?'

Olivia looked up. Rubbed the tears out of her
eyes. 'And if I decide to do it. To make a deal.
How do I make it happen? What do I do, just go
to the house and wait?'

'You could. But you say it never talked to you
there. Maybe it can't get to you at the house.
Maybe you have strong defenses. Who the hell
knows? If you really want to do this, you should
go to the source. Go where it's really strong.'

'The Waverly?' Olivia said.

Bennington nodded.

'What would you do?' Olivia asked.

'For the life of my child? I have two daughters,
Olivia. Two sweet baby girls. I would do anything to keep them safe. Anything at all. If it was
me, I'd make the deal.'

333

FIFTY-TWO

Olivia was halfway home when she took a random exit to fill the Jeep up with gas. She pulled into a new Weigels, set the gas nozzle running, and went to the ladies' room. Caught sight of her swollen eyes and blotchy face when she looked into the bathroom mirror while she washed her hands.

She got a cup of coffee, which she secretly found cheaper and better tasting than Starbucks, wondering, as she always did, if there was something wrong with her coffee palate. She truly did love Starbucks, God knows the ambiance was better. But the coffee just wasn't as good.

Olivia remembered to turn her phone back on as she belted herself back in the Jeep. There were three missed calls and two messages, both from McTavish. Olivia's stomach dropped, and her heart began to pound. It had to be Teddy. It had to be. Alive or dead? Her fingers shook so hard she could barely manage the phone, and she bounced her leg up and down waiting for McTavish to pick up. Which he did, on the second ring.

'Olivia? Where are you?'

'I'm at a gas station about an hour south of Knoxville, why? What's going on, McTavish, have you found her? Do you have Teddy?'

'No, no. It's not that.'

'It's not that. It's not that? What the hell else is there?'

'Olivia, did you go and see Bennington this morning?'

'Yes, I told you that's where I was going.'

'Was he home when you got there?'

'Of course he was home, we had a twelve o'clock appointment.'

'Olivia, listen to me. I made some calls after you left this morning. Something strange is going on. Bennington's wife just started a new teaching job, took over from a colleague on maternity leave. But she hasn't shown up for the last four days, and she hasn't called in. I got in touch with her sister, who said she was getting worried, because the two of them talk several times a week. She thought her sister was just busy, with the new job and all, but she was surprised because normally they'd be talking about it. But she hasn't been able to get her sister on the phone. And both of Bennington's sons have been absent from school for—'

'It's daughters, McTavish. He has two little girls.'

'No, he doesn't. He has two sons, seven and nine.'

'McTavish, I just talked to the guy, and he told me about his two little girls.'

'He was there? At the house?'

'I just spent two hours talking to the guy. Over a cup of Oolong tea.'

'Hang on a minute, let me pull up the description on his driver's license. Okay, big guy, six two, weight two sixty, black hair, brown eyes.'

'No. Blond hair. Blue eyes. Your description is wrong.'

'I don't know who you talked to, Olivia, but it wasn't Bennington Murphy. Look, give me a description of the guy you talked to. I'm heading down there to have a look, but I need to call this in to the local police.'

'But—'

'A description. Come on, Livie. We need to move fast.'

'Right.' Olivia took a breath. Gave McTavish everything she knew.

'Look, Livie, is there any chance you'd go back down there?'

'What, back to Bennington's house? But what should I say?'

'No, no, don't you dare go back to the house. Just go to the front of the subdivision and wait for me. If something happened to these people, this might be the guy that did it, okay? In which case, you need to be on hand to talk to the local police.'

'Sure. Sure I will.'

'But you'll be smart? You won't go near the house. You promise.'

'I promise,' Olivia said. It was hard to talk, her mouth felt like cotton. 'What do you think is going on, McTavish?'

'I don't know yet. But something is off about this. I'll be heading down there after I talk to the local guys and give Donnie Withers a heads up. In the meantime, you stay smart and you stay safe. Keep your phone on. I'll find you. I don't know who you talked to in that house, but I don't like the sound of this.'

McTavish hung up first and Olivia stared at the phone. She would go back, just as McTavish asked, she would stay safe, she would not go alone to the house.

FIFTY-THREE

Olivia had to sit at the gas station for a few minutes before she could drive. And while she was sitting it occurred to her. That Bennington and his wife, his two little boys. They might be in that house. She'd had a sense, hadn't she, that someone else was there in the house. Maybe she could help. She needed to go.

She drove steadily, hands gripped so tightly on the wheel her fingers were white. Once, her head went suddenly light and she veered out of her lane and into another, but there was almost no traffic. No cars around. Lucky. She took deep breaths and tried not to think.

It was strange, turning back to Windermere Estates. Everything looked the same until she inched slowly down the street where Bennington lived, and saw two cars marked *Sheriff* parked in front of the house. She pulled to the curb, a couple of houses down across the street, and got out of her car. Put her cell phone in her pocket and walked to the edge of Bennington's ragged lawn. The front door slammed open and a man in a local sheriff's uniform ran out onto the porch, turned sideways, and vomited in the flower bed on the right hand side of the porch. Olivia went back to her car.

It wasn't long before the beehive was alerted. The fire truck came first, even though there wasn't a fire. Then the paramedics. Another sheriff's car, and afterward, an entire fleet of state police, the yellow tan paint of their sedans glistening in the sun. Olivia waited to be noticed. It didn't take long.

Olivia sat sideways, driver's door open on the Jeep. She was too nauseated to finish her coffee, but she handed it to McTavish, who guzzled it down cold in one long gulp. He wiped his mouth with the back of his hand. He was white around the mouth, but steady, like always. Calm and steady.

'Hawkins said you did great. With your statement. They found the tea cups just like you said, he didn't wash up or anything, so they're hoping for prints. Guy like that. He'll be in the system. This won't be his first time.'

Olivia looked over her shoulder at the sound of tires on gravel. Coroner's van. Not in any hurry.

Olivia picked at a thread on her sweater. 'I was completely fooled. He knew everything about the family, and he looked so sweet. Kind of shy.'

'You're lucky Mr Sweet and Shy didn't kill you.'

'When will they bring the bodies out?'

338

'It'll be a while. You might as well go home, Olivia. Hawkins may want some follow up interviews, but you're done for now. You're a broker, your prints are in the system already, they'll be able to sort it out.'

'And they're dead? All of them?'

'The whole family. Bennington, his wife. The two boys. Even the family dog.'

'You went in there. You saw it. Where were they?'

'Basement.'

'They were down there, the whole time I was in the house?'

McTavish nodded. Gripped her shoulder. Hard. 'Jamison warned me. God knows how he knew.'

'Really? You think God knows?'

McTavish kissed her gently on the top of the head.

'You saw them, right?' Olivia said. Of course he had. She knew it. She could see it in the way he held himself, the distracted way he talked to her, the echo in his eyes.

'I saw them.'

'Can I look?'

'No. And you don't want to, I promise you. And we don't want your DNA contaminating the scene where the bodies are.'

'Surely they don't think I—'

'Of course not.'

'Okay. But you have to tell me. I need to know what happened to them. I need to know how they died.'

McTavish propped his arm on the top of the car. Shoved his sunglasses on the top of his head.

His hair was getting shaggy, it needed a cut. There was sweat along the edges of his hairline.

'The dog died in the kitchen. We found him at the back door, so we think that's where this guy got in. The door had a window, the glass was broken. There was glass in the dog's fur. We think he was defending the house. Dog was shot in the head.'

'In the kitchen?' Olivia said, thinking of how the Mister Man had offered her tea. How he had shut the door to the little sanctuary, as he called it. What if she had wandered out into the kitchen? Asked to use the bathroom? What would have happened then?

'Then he takes the family down to the basement. You can see signs around the house where he rounded them up. The kids were in the living room, playing video games. Bennington upstairs, looks like he'd just come out of the shower. Wife in the laundry room, putting in a load of clothes. He herded them all down to the basement. No sign of struggle, we think he had them at gunpoint. Maybe had one of the kids, with a gun to the head. Probably said he wouldn't hurt anybody, if they just cooperated. That's what they always say.' McTavish grimaced. Looked away.

'He had them sitting in chairs. In a sort of half circle, like they were watching a show. The wife and the two boys.'

'Did they suffer a lot? The little boys?'

McTavish shook his head. 'I'm sure they were scared, but they died quick. So did the wife. Shots to the head, close range, one two three.

340

Things didn't go so well for the dad. Killer used one of those heavy duty orange extension cords, strung him up over an open beam, and hung him right there in front of the family. Like they were all gathered there to watch him die.'

'I hope the kids died first,' Olivia said. 'So they didn't have to watch.'

'What the hell did the two of you talk about for two hours?' McTavish said. Something almost like suspicion in his eyes.

She was tempted. To tell him everything. To talk it out, to tell him she had to make a decision. That she was trying to find a way out but was thinking she'd have to make a deal herself. Ackerman had told her to wait, but Ackerman was dragging her feet. Ackerman was afraid.

Olivia knew that she loved McTavish when she decided to shut him out. When you came right down to it, Olivia thought, you were always and ever alone.

'See you, McTavish,' Olivia said, giving him a gentle kiss on the mouth. It felt a lot like good-bye.

FIFTY-FOUR

Olivia tried not to think on the way back, to concentrate only on the droning effect of the road. But the noise of it was strong in her mind. The long blond ponytail, the soft pudgy hands, the gentle look of a lamb. Offering her tea. She had sat and listened to the microwave ding, the slam of cabinet doors, while the dog lay in a pool of dried blood where it had died at the kitchen door. What kind of dog was it, she wondered. She could only picture Winston, which didn't help her state of mind. And the bodies, stiff and still in the basement while everything inside the house gathered dust.

It was dusk when she got back to Knoxville. She was tired and she wanted a hot bubble bath, the new familiarity of her hotel room. But she drove to the house first, not to go inside, just to look.

Every single light was on. Like they always were, when the bad things happened.

What would happen if she went inside?

Before she could make up her mind, her cell phone rang. McTavish again.

'Olivia? Listen to me. Are you back in Knoxville yet? Are you at the hotel?'

'No, I'm headed over there right now. God, what now, McTavish?'

'Look. Olivia.'

She waited. Heard him breathing.

'I'm going to give you the heads up, okay? Go somewhere else for the night.'

Olivia felt the bottom of her stomach drop, the feeling getting all too familiar. 'Why, McTavish? What's going on?'

'Donnie Withers is going to be sending some-one out to pick you up. He doesn't have a warrant out for your arrest, not yet. He's going to bring you in for questioning, as a person of interest, and he can keep you, Livie, for forty-eight hours without charging you. You can't avoid this, understand. Don't do something stupid like run. But we can delay it. If he doesn't know where you are, and he doesn't have an arrest warrant, he has to find you. So we have some time to prepare. If you're hungry, get something to eat. Take a shower, have a good night's sleep. And be ready, be mentally prepped. My advice is to get an attorney and then let them handle the arrangements with the police.'

Olivia felt cold all over, and she began to shake. 'Again, McTavish. Why?'

'Livie, listen to me. The teapot was there, the mugs were on the coffee table in that little office, exactly like you described. One of the cabinet doors was even open part way in the kitchen, right where the teabags were kept. There was a spoon on the counter, a jar of honey, everything exactly like you said it would be.'

'So what then?'

'There aren't any prints except yours.'

'I don't understand.'

'One of the tea mugs has your fingerprints all over it. The other one, nothing.'

'No prints at all?'

'Like it was fresh out of the dishwasher.'

'Whoever the killer was, McTavish, I saw him. I *talked* to him.'

'But you get it, Livie, that to someone like Donnie Withers, that just doesn't make any sense. And he doesn't get why the guy would go back there four days *after* he did the killings just to have a cup of tea.'

343

'But if I was in on it somehow, why would *I* go back? Look, this guy was in the house with me, he had to have left something, some kind of DNA track, down by the bodies, by that kitchen door.'

'Yeah. And we got fingerprints there. Prints of a guy with felony hits that would turn your stomach, but he ain't no blond guy with blue eyes. He ain't the guy you described. Donnie's pegging *him* for the murders, and he wants to pick him up, but technically it's not his case, and there are jurisdictional problems that are slowing things down, even though for once everyone seems to be cooperating. But we're going all out on one thing, which is picking this guy up.'

'Then what does he want with me?'

'He thinks he's got your accomplice.'

'What?'

'Yeah, I know it sounds crazy, but Olivia, it looks strange. Donnie's trying to make sense out of the whole mess. He's got bodies piling up under suspicious circumstances, and one person making money on the deal out of life insurance, and that would be you. He figures if he gets you locked up in a little room, you'll flip on this guy and tell him where he is.'

'And Teddy?'

'He's looking for her body, Livie. He doesn't think she's coming back alive.'

'So they've written her off?'

'Not written her off. Looking for her killer. Livie, hon, I know you didn't do this, but you have to admit, it's looking pretty strange. No matter what Donnie does, I'm finding Teddy for you and I'm not stopping till I do. Livie? You there?'

'Here. Okay, McTavish.'

'I don't have to tell you not to let anybody know you got a heads up. Donnie made sure I was out of the loop, but I've got a lot of friends. It's after six, that's why Donnie is doing it now. It will take you some effort to lawyer up. Find a place to spend the night. Don't use your credit card, don't leave a paper trail. In the meantime, I know a guy who knows a guy, and I can get the legal end going for you, if you'll trust me on this. She's expensive, by the way. The lawyer. But—'

'I'll give her the mortgage to my house.'

McTavish actually laughed. 'Livie. You dog. You won't do anything stupid, right? I did the right thing, giving you a call?'

'I guess that depends on how you define stupid, McTavish. But yes. You did the right thing. And I get how much you're doing for me here.'

'The main thing is we find your little girl. Detective Donnie may be distracted with his Mister Man hunt, but I've got my eye on the ball. Livie. I just want to tell you—'

'Don't tell me anything right now, McTavish. Let's see how this all plays out.'

FIFTY-FIVE

Olivia was too upset to be driving around after McTavish called, but she knew better than to stay by the house. The police would look for her there. It was her home.

She headed down Kingston Pike, looking for familiarity and comfort, and turned into the local Barnes & Noble. She bought a cup of coffee that was not as good as the gas station coffee but came in a prettier cup. She sat in one of the green striped upholstered armchairs, and set her purse on the little coffee table, and sat still, trying to think.

The first thing that came to mind was Hugh, and the way he had made her laugh, saying he would buy Teddy 87,397 books. She could use Hugh here, right about now. For all his faults, she missed him.

But it was peaceful in the bookstore, and she did not feel so alone. And it was surprisingly busy, tables filled with people hunched over computers, the café tables full, the smell of baked chocolate cookies, and the whir of the latte machines. With so many people out of work right now, it had become a hot place to hang out.

Olivia understood now like she hadn't before, how boxed in her brother Chris had felt. Had

346

Decan Ludde brought these same pressures to bear on Chris till he had no options but to make a deal? The choice for Olivia was clear. Do nothing, and live in the uncertainty loop of hell. Teddy would never come home. Or she would turn up dead. And Olivia herself might spend the rest of her life in jail. Dodging the police for one night was perfectly fine, but after that, she'd have to give herself up. She wouldn't get Teddy home by running away.

No Teddy and a lifetime in jail. These were the threats. These were her malign troubles, provoked. Was she going out of her mind, or could Decan Ludde make good on these threats? She felt like a rat in a maze with nowhere to go – just the Pied Piper leading her on.

And she knew him now, this Pied Piper, sure to her core that he'd been the man without fingerprints inside Bennington Murphy's house. She had met the elusive Decan Ludde – unexpectedly blond and mild looking, watching her and sipping tea, urging her to make a deal while the bodies of Bennington and his family decomposed beneath streaks of their own dried blood.

It had not gone well for Bennington, this making a deal. What good was a high paying job to support a family that was now dead? Patsy Ackerman was right, the price was too high.

And what other choice did she have?

Making a deal was the only play she had left, and it would have to happen before Donnie Withers hauled her off. Patsy Ackerman would have to stop meditating and prepping and working up her nerve. Patsy Ackerman would have to get her into the Waverly, where Decan Ludde invited her to go.

Before she left she had one small thing to do.

Olivia went to the children's book section, and found their selection of Nancy Drew. She could not afford 87,397 books but she could afford one, and she would pay in cash. No paper trail for Donnie Withers. She studied the titles, looking for one that Teddy had not read. Selected *The Secret of the Ninety-Nine Steps*. Teddy would love having a new book to read. Because Olivia was bringing her little girl home. No matter what the cost.

FIFTY-SIX

There were lights on in Patsy Ackerman's house, and the bungalow looked so homey, there in the dark, so safe and pretty, that it made Olivia homesick for the days when she had been a little girl, and the stone cottage where she'd grown up had made her feel safe and secure. Maybe it had never been safe. Maybe safety was an illusion that helped you sleep.

Patsy Ackerman was slow to come to the door, but did not seem surprised to see Olivia on the step.

'I see you got my message,' Ack said.

'What message?'

'Your cell phone was off, so I left you three

messages at the hotel. Just to call me, you didn't have to come.'

'Can I come in?' Olivia said.

'Of course. I'm not sure what it means—'

'You're not sure what *what* means?' Olivia said.

'Sorry. Come on back in the studio and I'll explain.' Ack led her through the kitchen. There was something simmering in a crock pot, and the scent of stewing onions and roasting meat.

Elliot the parrot was lively, stretching his wings and skittering up and down the bar of his perch. 'He's dancing,' Ack said. 'He loves the Backstreet Boys and one of their songs was on the oldies station this afternoon. It got him all stirred up. He'd love it, if you'd applaud.'

Olivia clapped her hands. It was full dark now, the dark pressing into the French windows that led to the backyard.

Ack paused in the doorway, watching them, arms folded. 'Elliot woke me up last night. Usually, when his cage is covered at night, he's very quiet, he just sleeps. But last night he got really agitated and started talking. About your daughter. He said Teddy's name.'

Olivia turned with a hand over her mouth.

'Let's see if I can get him to repeat it for you.' Ack headed to the cage and opened the door. She held a finger out to Elliot, inviting him out and onto her shoulder. 'Tell us, sweetie. Tell us about Teddy. What do you have to say?'

Elliot tucked his head into his wing.

Ackerman chucked to him softly. 'What's the matter, baby? Do you have something to tell me,

349

little man?'

The parrot teetered on his perch. *'Teddy, three fifteen, three fifteen. Teddy, three fifteen, three fifteen.'*

'Good baby. Good boy,' Ackerman chucked. Kept her finger out, but Elliot backed further into his cage. 'He's upset.'

'So am I,' Olivia said. She moved closer to the parrot. 'What does that mean? Teddy, three fifteen?'

'Three fifteen, three fifteen,' Elliot said.

'We get it, baby, three fifteen.' Ack shrugged, and closed the cage. 'I don't know. It could be a time. It could be a date.'

'March fifteenth is two days from now.'

'Yeah. Or it could be three fifteen a.m., or three fifteen in the afternoon.'

'Are you drawing, do you have any pictures in your mind, are you getting anything else?' Olivia said.

'No. Sorry, this is it. And I have no idea what Elliot means.'

Olivia sat down on the edge of the worn leather chair. 'It sounds like a deadline to me.'

'A deadline? Why would you say that?'

'Isn't it what makes the most sense? I'm being pressured, Ack. I'm being warned.'

'About what? To do what?'

'To go to the Waverly.'

'What? That would be crazy. You shouldn't go within a mile of that place.'

'Yeah, well, before you say that, let me tell you about my day. Because I think I've had a personal invitation.'

'From who?'

'Duncan Lee. Decan Ludde. The piper himself, whatever you want to call him. Look, will you take a drive with me? I don't think it's a good idea for me to be here, at the house.'

'Why the hell not?'

'The police are going to be looking for me. To question me, and they'll start at my hotel. And if they find out you've left me three messages today, the next place they'll come is here.'

'*Why* would they take you in like that? You didn't have anything to do with what happened to Teddy, anybody with a brain can see that.'

'Look, please, just come with me, in the car, okay? I'll feel safer that way.'

'Let me get my boots.'

Olivia headed back out into the neighborhood, took a side street and wound up on Papermill Drive.

'I don't think I can talk about this and drive, do you mind if we just pull over for a bit?'

'Okay. No, not there,' she said, as Olivia started to turn into the weedy parking lot of a defunct Mexican restaurant. 'Go up the hill there, to McKay's Used Bookstore, their parking lot is always full, you won't be conspicuous there. Why, is that funny somehow?'

'No, I just hide out at bookstores a lot.'

Olivia signaled left, passing the pool supply store as she went up the hill, and headed around to the back of the bookstore, away from the lights. They would be nicely hidden there. She understood now, why Patsy Ackerman and Ben-

351

nington Murphy lived behind a tangle of greenery. Hiding was becoming automatic to her now, a new way of life. Hiding from things that could find you in the dark.

Olivia turned the engine off on the Jeep, unbuckled her seatbelt, and faced Patsy Ackerman. There were no streetlights behind the bookstore. Both of them were shrouded in dark.

'So. Ack. Let me tell you about my day.'

And when she was done, Patsy Ackerman put her head in her hands and Olivia could not see her face, could not tell if she was trying not to cry. Ack crying made her nervous.

'Bennington Murphy. Another one dead, and I can't help feeling like some of this is my fault.'

Olivia put an elbow on the steering wheel. She felt matter of fact and curious and wondered where her compassion was. 'You didn't kill him, you didn't shoot their family dog. So why is it you're at fault? Because you didn't help? Do you feel guilty because you didn't help either Bennington or Chris?'

'Oh, God. It killed their dog too?'

'Yeah. It left his body at the kitchen door. And you know as well as I do that whoever actually killed that family, it was all because of the Pied Piper. It was all because of Decan Ludde.'

'Yes, I agree.'

Olivia took a breath. 'So you think I'm right? That's who I was talking to, there in the house?'

'Yes. In some form or another. No fingerprints, right? It doesn't come breathing fire, Olivia. Not when it wants to lure you in.'

'So now I have a choice.'

352

'It isn't a choice.'

'Of course it is. I can save my daughter. How can I say no?'

'Somebody *has* to say no.'

'And suffer the consequences.'

'Life *is* consequences. Nobody gets away from that.'

'If the consequences mean my little girl dies, then I'd rather make a deal.'

'Yeah, look at Bennington Murphy. He gets his finances taken care of and his entire family is dead.'

'Amelia made a deal and Marianne Butler is alive. My brother. He got his little girl healed. He may be dead but Janet is okay.'

'Really? Does Janet look okay to you?'

'She looks alive. She looks like a girl who does not have cancer.'

'Maybe she never did. Or maybe she *did*, Olivia. Life is like that, it's good and it's bad. You have to accept that.'

Something in her voice made Olivia cock her head. 'You aren't telling me everything, are you, Ack?'

Ackerman pulled a knee up, and gave Olivia a sideways look. 'No, I'm not. There's a reason I didn't help your brother, or Bennington Murphy, or anyone else who's asked me over the last fifteen years.'

'Does it have something to do with when you went to the Waverly?'

'Yeah. Because after that night, I started having dreams. Visions. Being led, like always, to what I'm supposed to do. Only this time, I don't

353

want to do it.'

'What are you supposed to do, Ack? How could you just leave my brother out there, Bennington out there, to go up against something evil like this, when you have ... gifts that would help.'

'Because it's not *them* I'm supposed to help.'

'I don't get it.'

'No, of course you don't. I don't get it either, really. Because what I keep getting, over and over, what the universe keeps telling me in its unique and annoying way, is that I'm supposed to help *it*.'

'*It?*'

'The Pied Piper. Decan Ludde.'

Olivia leaned back against the door.

'Yeah. See what I mean?' Ack said. 'See why I haven't been bending over backward to make *that* happen.'

'But didn't you tell me that the dark things, entities, whatever you call them, like Decan Ludde ... They're afraid, and in pain, and that's why they go to the light. Isn't that the compassionate viewpoint?'

'Sure. But did you forget the part about what happens when they accept help? It means to all points and purposes, they die. Decan Ludde doesn't want to die, Olivia. You can take my word on that.'

'How could you even do that? How could you help that thing?'

'I don't know. I've been waiting for a plan, and nothing.'

'Fifteen years you've been waiting for a plan?'

'Hey, I didn't say this was something I was anxious to do. But it won't leave me alone. I've got Hugh on my doorstep. Dead. I've got your brother and Bennington begging me for help. Dead. Now I've got you, and I can tell you're on your way to the Waverly—'

'So I'm next up. Dead.' Olivia shrugged. 'If Teddy comes back alive, I don't care. Wherever she is right now. It can't be good. It even promised me ... it promised me that Emily would come home.'

'Your long lost sister? The one who disappeared like Teddy did, twenty-five years ago?'

'We never found out what happened. Do you know how hard that is? I keep waiting ... thinking it might be possible. She could come home. It happens sometimes.'

'Decan Ludde is just upping the ante on you, Olivia. Sure you don't want to wait for an even better deal?'

'I don't think there is going to be a better deal,' Olivia said. 'Three fifteen sounds like a deadline to me. Look, Ackerman. I'm going. Come to the Waverly with me. They know you there, you're a respected psychic. They'll let you in. We can go up to Louisville tonight and go first thing in the morning, in daylight, not the dark.'

'Do you have any clue how hard it is to get into that place? Every curiosity seeker, nutcase and ghost hunter in the country is banging on the doors. You have to make arrangements, you have to schedule a tour. They're booked for the next six months.'

'You checked?'

'Yeah, I checked. The only way to get in there now is to do what your brother did. Trespass.'

'I'm going to be arrested tomorrow,' Olivia said. 'But I've got some free time tonight. If you're ready. If you want to face it. Don't you think it's time to stop running from this? Aren't you tired of living under a shadow? Maybe we were meant to do this together, you and me.'

'You'd say anything to get me up there. The only thing you're worried about is Teddy, not me.'

'True.'

'But you're good, Olivia. You should be in sales.'

'I'm in the mom business right now. I can take you home or I can take you with me.'

'Look, give me some time—'

'I'm out of time, Ack, and I'm scared as hell that Teddy is out of time too. For all we know three fifteen means tonight, or tomorrow afternoon. And I'm going to be in police custody very soon. If you haven't come up with a plan in fifteen years, you won't come up with one tonight. Just drive up there with me, okay? Show me how to get in. You want to wait in the car, you wait in the car.'

'I'm not promising I'm going in there with you, Olivia.'

'Fair enough.' Olivia started the Jeep, and backed out of her parking place, heading back down the hill. The Papermill exit was right by the interstate and five minutes later they were on their way.

FIFTY-SEVEN

The Waverly Hills Sanatorium was located in the southeastern edge of Louisville, and from Knoxville, it was a solid four hour drive. By eleven eleven p.m. Olivia and Ackerman were just a mile away. Ack looked at the clock on the dash and snorted.

'Well, we timed it perfectly, didn't we?' she said. 'We should be heading into the tunnel right about midnight.'

'If it matters to you, we can get a hotel room, and go in the morning. Early, before it opens.'

'We can't go in daylight, Olivia. There are security cameras and volunteer security guards, workmen all over the place doing renovations. They'll be there tonight too, but it will be a skeleton staff. We'll have a better chance in the dark. If we're going to do it, let's get it done.'

'So you're coming in with me?'

'Yeah,' Ack said. 'I'm coming in. If for no other reason than my butt is getting tired of being jolted around in this Jeep. You got any shocks on this thing?'

'It's one of the older models. You get used to it.'

'*You* get used to it, I just want out. I've been nauseous the whole way. Look, there's a Pilot station a couple blocks from here. Let's stop for coffee, before we face our doom.'

'Are you being funny or serious?' Olivia said.

'I haven't decided yet.'

Even the pictures on the website had not prepared Olivia for how big the sanatorium was. Spotlights on redbrick and white concrete, several stories high, a monster. An institution. Inaccessible behind a gate that was padlocked and brightly lit. It stretched out like a castle, and Olivia realized the size was a serious advantage. The grounds took up acres, and even with an army of security guards, there was simply too much property to watch.

'Don't stop here, Olivia, keep on going. If I remember right, there's a dirt access road in the woods behind the north wing. You don't happen to have a flashlight do you?'

'I've got this little pig light on my key chain. Teddy gave it to me for Christmas, but it makes little oinking noises when it's on.'

'Perfect,' Ack said. 'We're like a couple of goof butts out of an Elmore Leonard novel. Do you get that we're totally unprepared?'

'Do you get that I'm totally out of time? And you're prepared for this, Ack. You've been prepping for this for the last fifteen years.'

'Yeah, but ... wait, go back, Olivia. There it is. There's the road, see, on the right?'

Olivia backed up and went right. The dirt road doglegged, then wound through the woods on the north end of the estate, and Ack had Olivia follow it for three and a half miles before she was satisfied they had driven as far as they could.

'We'll go the rest of the way on foot. How good are you at climbing fences, by the way?'

'As long as there isn't barbed wire, I'm not too bad.'

'There didn't use to be barbed wire. Let's hope there's not now. Don't look like that, Olivia. This is a huge place, we'll find a way in. Just like your brother did, twenty-five years ago.'

'Yeah, but I never really got it till now. How incredibly big this place really is. What part of the sanatorium should we concentrate on? Does it matter? Will one of the outbuildings do?'

'We're going where your brother went, Olivia.'

'The Death Tunnel?'

'Or you could call it the Body Chute. I'm not sure which is worse.'

Olivia sat forward, looking out the windshield at the grounds. 'We'll never find it in all this maze.'

'It's easier than you think. Come on, turn off the engine. I've got my cell phone, you got yours? In case ... I don't know, we get separated or we need to call somebody.'

'Let's not get separated, okay?'

'Yeah, okay. Come on, Olivia. If we're going let's go.'

'But how will we ever find the Body Chute in the dark like this?'

'Easy enough. We'll go in through one of the vent shafts. They come up about every one hundred feet. Look for a big concrete cylinder, two by three. They'll stick up about two feet above the ground. I hope you don't have claustro-phobia,' Ack said.

It was chilly out, with patches of fog drifting along the leaf covered ground. The only sweater Olivia had was Hugh's black cashmere, and she put it on with a muttered apology. Ack wore a sweatshirt and jeans and her usual pirate boots. She took a rubber band out of the pocket of her jeans, and pulled her long blonde hair into a ponytail. Olivia looked at her and shivered, thinking of Decan Ludde.

A half moon gave them just enough light to make their way, with the pig light ready when needed. In the end they did not even have to climb. They walked along the side of the chain link fence and found a weak spot that bowed inward along the ground. They went under instead of over, smearing their bellies with grass stains and dirt. Olivia's sweater caught on the fence, ripping a flap in the back. She asked Hugh in a whisper not to mind.

After that, Ack took the lead, wandering for so long at the edge of the woods that Olivia began to suspect she was losing her nerve. But then Ack stopped, and Olivia saw the concrete open-ing that was swallowed up by ground. A vent shaft, right into the Body Chute. Ack went for-ward and looked down into the hole, then glanc-ed over her shoulder at Olivia.

'Decision time. You really want to do this? Once we're down there, I'm not exactly sure how we're going to get back out. With any luck, we can follow the tunnel into the main building.'

'And get arrested for trespassing.'

'Maybe. Maybe not, if we're smart.'

'I'm up for murder, that's the least of my worries now. And you're a well known psychic. You can talk your way out.'

Ack shrugged. Took a breath. Swung her legs over the ledge. 'I'll go first. Wish me luck,' she said, and jumped.

Ack disappeared, and Olivia heard the thud of her feet hitting the ground beneath, and her shout that yes, she was okay, not to worry, it was no more than a ten foot drop.

Olivia stood very still. Somehow she'd thought she'd be the one going first, that she'd be talking a reluctant Ack in. But once Ack's head disappeared down the hole, it dawned on her that it was one thing to trek through the woods, and another to go into a tunnel. Underground. Into a place called the Death Tunnel, or, worse still, the Body Chute.

Was it possible that Teddy was in a place like this? Teddy could be anywhere, and there were limitless possibilities of bad. Maybe Teddy was in a dark place. Maybe Teddy would be in a dark place till Olivia found her.

Olivia went to the edge of the concrete and flashed the little pig light. 'Ack? Where are you? You okay?'

The blonde head appeared beneath the halo of light and the pig light made grunting noises. 'Don't shine that thing in my eyes, dammit. You coming? Because quite honestly I don't think I can climb back up and this would be a hell of a crap time for you to change your mind.'

'I'm coming,' Olivia said. She swung her legs

over the side of the concrete lip, slid as far down as she could on her butt, then jumped, landing on her feet but rolling sideways on the packed dirt floor.

'Shit shit shit,' Olivia said.

Ack bent over her. Olivia could smell the coffee breath.

'You okay?'

'Bruises and a banged up ego.' Even when she whispered, Olivia's voice echoed, and it was cold down in the tunnel, she could almost see her breath. 'I think I have to go to the bathroom.'

'You went at the Pilot station,' Ack told her. 'It's just nerves. Come on.' Ack gave her a hand up.

'What now?' Olivia said.

'Hell if I know. Let's walk.'

'Which way?'

'That way,' Ack said. 'Toward the main entrance. Look, see the tracks there? That's how the rail car came through. Bringing the supplies in.'

'And the bodies out,' Olivia said.

'Yeah, well, I wouldn't dwell on that.'

They hugged the left side of the tunnel, single file, with Ack going first. The rails took up the entire right side. Ack told Olivia to keep the light going, and to point it just ahead at their feet.

They walked for about a hundred yards. The farther they went, the darker it got, until they were close beneath another shaft, which let in blessed fresh air and moonlight. The tunnel was an oblong, tube shape, their footsteps raising little puffs of dust on the dirt floor. There were

362

things written on the walls sometimes. Olivia saw *ALICE* then *help* then decided not to shine the light on the walls anymore.

Their footsteps made muted echoes, and Ack moved steadily for another hundred yards before she gasped, and took a step back, running into Olivia, who was too close behind.

'What?' Olivia said, shining the light.

'Shine it over there,' Ack said, pointing. 'Okay. There. And there. Okay. Okay, it's gone.'

'What was it?' Olivia's heart was thumping hard. 'I don't see anything.'

'I just ... I felt it. Someone took my hand.'

'What?'

'Don't forget who I am, Olivia, or what I do. It wasn't ... unfriendly. Just lonely, I think. There's a lot going on down here, remember. It isn't all—'

'Don't say it,' Olivia said. 'Please. Don't say his name.'

Ack laughed softly, in the dark. 'You do know, don't you, Olivia, that there are plans to turn this place into a four star hotel?' She turned and headed forward down the chute, and Olivia hesitated for only a second before she followed. She was glad she was not here alone. But she wasn't sure she was glad the person with her was Ack.

And as they continued to walk, Ack began to whisper. 'Livie? Keep walking, but listen. Are you listening?'

Olivia nodded her head, then realized that Ack could not see her. 'Yes,' Olivia whispered. Her throat was going dry.

'I want you to keep the light just ahead like

you're doing, okay? Just like that. But also, do you see ahead of us, on the right near the rail track? About ten feet up ahead. Keep walking, don't stop.'

Olivia kept walking, and kept the light just ahead of Ack's steps, and looked onto the right, up ahead, straining to see what Ack saw, in the dark.

'No, I don't see anything, I just – oh. *God.* What *is* that?'

'What do *you* see? Keep going, Olivia, keep walking.'

'It's weird looking. Like a mist with something dark inside. It's moving. It looks like...'

'What, Olivia? Because to me, it kind of looks like ... shadow legs.'

Olivia took a breath, and stopped. 'Yes. It looks like that to me too.'

'Keep going, Olivia.'

'I don't—' Olivia felt the start of tears in her eyes. 'I don't want to follow that thing.'

'You have to.'

'Why?'

'Because there's something just like it behind us.'

Olivia gasped and made a noise deep in her chest, and Ack took her hand. 'Keep moving, keep moving. *Come on.*'

'We can't go back,' Olivia said.

'No. We can't go back.'

'What is it?' Olivia whispered.

'Maybe it's just ... an escort. Maybe it means we're going the right way.'

'I want out of here,' Olivia said. 'I'm sorry,

Ack, but I want out.'

'I don't think getting out is an option for you, Olivia.'

'What the hell is that supposed to mean?'

'I've been thinking about this, and it occurs to me, that maybe this entity, whatever it is, maybe it's after *you*.'

'*Me?*'

'Because it's all around you, Olivia. Think about it. Everything that's happened, it always seems to connect back to you.'

'I don't think I'm that important, Ackerman.'

'But you're always on the sidelines, aren't you? Meanwhile your sister disappears, your brother wrestles with this thing his whole life.'

'This thing is Chris's fault. He's the one who brought it back. He brought it back from here.'

'Very possible. And also possible that this was an opportunity while it was hunting you.'

Olivia stopped, but Ackerman pushed her along.

'I know you're scared, Olivia, and I'm not trying to make it worse, I just want you to be prepared. To be strong if you get ... targeted. You can't just stand on the sidelines with these things. Keep going, come on, the only way out is forward, there isn't any other way. Think of your little girl, and keep walking, Olivia. Keep walking, okay?'

'What's that up ahead?' Olivia whispered.

'I think we're almost to the entrance to the sanatorium. We've been going uphill for a while now. It looks like – wood doors. I can't see from here but—'

Olivia shined the light up ahead. Double doors, heavy wood, with metal braces across in three places. Bolted tight.

'We're trapped,' Olivia said. Her breath was coming faster. It was getting hard to breathe. 'Look at it. Look at that ... that *thing.*'

Because the legs were taking shape now, taking form, still hard to make out but there seemed to be a head, and a torso and legs, only the torso was bent, as if the thing was traveling on all fours, instead of two.

'Olivia, you have got to calm down,' Ack said.

'I can't help it. I'm scared, dammit.' Olivia stopped, and Ack held her hand and Olivia held the light and they watched the thing solidify as it moved in the dark.

Once it got to the doors, it paused for a long moment. Olivia felt her heart beat harder still, and it was hard to catch her breath. It stood, finally, upright at last, and turned as if to face them, growing very tall. And more distinct. More detailed. Like focusing a camera lens. Long blond ponytail, lamblike demeanor, chubby, soft fleshy hands.

The man Olivia had met in Bennington Murphy's house. The man-thing Teddy called Duncan Lee.

'Hello, Olivia.' A singsong in its voice. Sounding breathy and kind. 'I see you took my advice.'

'It's you,' Olivia whispered.

It held out a hand. 'It's me. I've been with you off and on for such a long time. Did you know that Teddy could see me, looking over your shoulder? Teddy. Three fifteen.' He smiled. 'I

366

don't think I ever told you my name. Teddy likes to call me Duncan Lee.'

'I'm sure you have a whole *host* of names,' Ack said. She wasn't whispering. Her voice was strong. Somehow she managed not to sound afraid.

'Ah, Ackerman. Always so brave. I thought I had you then, fifteen years ago.'

'Not brave. Just lucky. Live or die by a quirk of fate.' Ack held a hand out. 'I've come to see you home, Mr Lee.'

'Such ego, dear Patsy.' It spoke to her softly. 'But I am home. I am home in the tunnel, I am home in your studio when I whisper to your bird. I am home in the little stone cottage where Teddy and Olivia live.'

'You could spend all night spinning lies,' Ack said. 'Playing on all our fears. But aren't you tired, of being so alone? Aren't you tired, of living in the dark? Do you have any memory, any feeling at all, about letting go of all your pain, and closing your eyes—'

'To die? Only humans let go like that. Only humans get so scared they can't live. Do I look human to you?'

'I'm just offering you peace,' Ackerman said.

'*You* offering *me* peace? My, what an ego it has. And you?' Decan Ludde seemed to grow taller. He held out a soft white hand. Solid. Solid as any man. 'Take my hand, Olivia. That's all you have to do, you know, such an easy easy thing. Take my hand and say yes, I want Teddy home safe. And she will be. Home safe. Do you love your little girl? You have to make your mind up now, Olivia, three fifteen, three fifteen. Time to take my hand, and this will all be over.' He tilted his head, seeming to sway sideways.

Olivia lifted her hand. And the noises started. Snuffling and moans, and someone wailing her name. *Olivia. Olivia.* Then *mommy* coming from the other side of the door. Ackerman was talking to her, but it was hard to hear.

'Is that her?' Olivia said. 'Is that Teddy, on the other side of the door?'

Decan Ludde looked at her and smiled. 'I keep my promises, Olivia. If you ever want to see Teddy alive and well, you need to *take my hand.*'

But it was hard to hear the whisper of his voice. A noise like a freight train, coming behind them, then a voice, booming into the tunnels, like a recording from the 1920s, an old fashioned newsreel, as if they were taking a tour.

'*As you can see, these sanatoriums are real hospitals, with hundreds of beds,*' the voice said. '*Modern medicine offers many new treatments, like UV Therapy. Meanwhile, while they heal, patients make crafts to pass the time. Look at those beautiful baskets!*'

And Olivia realized that Ackerman was no longer holding her hand. 'Ackerman? Patsy? Are you there?'

'*Rest and relaxation in the sunlit solarium, and look, classes in typewriting.*'

'Take my hand,' Decan Ludde said. 'Take my hand and find Teddy. Take my hand before three fifteen.'

'*Children of patients are cared for here, and even have their own schoolroom.*'

Olivia heard it again. *Mommy.* So faint she could not be sure she really heard it. Maybe she only wanted to hear.

'Up here on the roof, sick children are exercising in the sun and the fresh air. Playing while they heal.'

'Is that where she is?' Olivia said. 'Is she in that children's building? Is Teddy in there? Where is she, I have to know.'

'Take my hand,' Decan Ludde said. 'If you want her home *safe*. They all come home eventually. Emily. Teddy. They come home one way or another. But if you want them home *safe*, you must do your part.'

Olivia lifted her hand, but pulled it back when she heard running footsteps, and a scream that sounded like Ack. Then the little pig light went out. More snuffling noises, and dark. And something breathing on the back of Olivia's neck and a whisper from Decan Ludde.

'Take my hand, Olivia, take my hand.'

She felt the oddest sense of recognition, like she'd known him all her life. Taking his hand would be such a relief. No struggling anymore. She had not understood how much she would want this, how good she knew it would feel.

She was crying now. She had to do it. Make the deal. The only way to save her daughter. She opened her eyes and saw a light, and then a form, and then, her phone was ringing. Her phone was ringing, and she took it out of her pocket. *Call From Teddy* lit the screen.

'Hello,' Olivia said, in a whisper.

'Mommy. Mommy. Mommy.'

369

Not Teddy. Not Teddy's voice. The timbre was masculine and slow, as if it were mocking her. Mocking her pain.

'*Mommy.*'

Then a hand, grabbing her arm.

'Olivia?'

'Patsy?'

Patsy was pulling her away from the door, away from Decan Ludde, who was smiling, smiling, holding out a hand.

Olivia felt warm breath on her neck and turned. Not Patsy, with that hand on her arm. Something dark with masses of hair. She jerked away, closed her eyes. Screamed.

'Make the deal, Olivia. Say yes and Teddy can come home.'

And that was all Olivia wanted, really. Just her own little Teddy, home safe.

'*Oh my dear.*' The voice was so gentle. So knowing. 'Don't you see it yet? We've wanted you for such a long time. We've had our eye on you since you were a very little girl. We had our eye on you since before you were even born. Think of all the people you love who are gone now, just because they thought they knew better. Because they tried to keep us out. All those people who got in the way because they were jealous. Because they weren't the one.'

'What do you mean?' Olivia whispered.

But on some level she felt it. That she was the special one, she always had been, and there was something evocative about the feeling it gave her, knowing she was chosen. She felt the urge to accept, to give in, to take that hand that beckoned her on. If she gave in now it would be easier. She would find peace in her heart. Just the thought of it made her feel warm, bathed in relief.

She took a hesitant step forward, thinking that Teddy would not have to be sacrificed, her little girl could be safe, feeling a sense of rightness about this, what other decision could a mother make? But then she stopped, an old image, a memory, alive in her mind. Teddy at the playground, wearing little pink denim overalls, she could not have been more than two or three. She had been coming down a circular slide on her belly and moving too fast to stop herself from landing sideways in a heap on the ground. Teddy scrambling to her feet, looking wildly around for her mother, and as soon as she saw Olivia, heading straight toward her, chubby little baby arms held out.

Olivia had felt important then too, but it was nothing like this feeling. Then she had felt the tie between mother and child, but there had been no ego involved, only a sense of responsibility and love.

And Olivia knew then, by instinct if nothing else, that whatever the piper offered would guarantee the worst possible outcome for Teddy. That there were things in the dark so much worse than death.

She was ashamed suddenly. Of how angry she had been, how much she had blamed Chris. Bennington had made a deal to take care of his children, twice, and been left with no children at all. Chris had saved Janet, who was now consumed with anger, guilt and fear. Marianne

Butler's mother was convinced a demon had possession of her child and for that Amelia had drowned thrashing in a tub, her eyes rolled back in her head. What had Amelia seen and thought in the moments before she died?

And Hugh. Brave and canny, crafty and wise, so sure he'd tricked it, only to hang by the neck from the red leather belt. Smarter people than she was had tried with the piper and failed.

There was good and bad in life, and the thought filled Olivia with dread, because she knew what it might mean, for Teddy. Life was consequences, for having children, for falling in love, for having hope. Happiness meant people you'd lose one day. There wasn't going to be an easy way out. In real life, there never was.

'No,' Olivia said to Decan Ludde. Who began to waver like a mirage in front of her eyes. 'No. I won't make the deal.'

'Olivia.' A woman's voice, wailing. Patsy Ackerman. For real this time. 'Olivia, help me.'

Then a scream, a thud, and a dragging noise, and Olivia could not help herself, she ran. She ran to the door, tried to open the bolts, whatever was behind her was dark and bad and she pounded on the door screaming, making all the noise she could, sobbing and begging someone, anyone, for help.

And when the doors opened by some miracle, and Olivia stumbled through, she told herself she was going for help, she was not running away, she was not leaving Patsy behind.

The volunteer security guard was everything she could have hoped for. Burly, tall, face gone chalk white when he unbolted the door to her screams. She would have had no way of knowing how much courage it took. How it had happened before, noises, cries from behind those doors. Noises and screams that turned to heavy watchful silence the minute the bolts were undone and the door opened wide.

The guard picked Olivia up when she collapsed at his feet, and settled her into a well lit room where he spent most of the hours of his shift, with a phone where he could call all the volunteers working security that night.

He listened patiently when she was able to talk, gave her a cup of coffee to settle the hysteria. He gave her his jacket, and he called for help.

Something kind in his eyes reminded her of Chris. She had been angry with Chris. So angry. She could not be angry with him anymore.

FIFTY-EIGHT

Olivia spent a long time in the well lit room where the security guard was. He stayed with her when the other guards went down into the Death Tunnel to look. He wanted to search for Patsy Ackerman, everyone there knew her name, here at the Waverly she was legend. But Olivia cried whenever he got too far away. He was sturdy and not that tall, balding a bit. But something about him made Olivia feel better. So to keep her from

373

crying, he stayed.

But no one could find Patsy Ackerman, so they had to call the police. Olivia wondered if she would go to jail for trespassing or if there would be a fine. She did not care. Anywhere was better than here.

She looked at the time on her cell phone, and watched the clock until three fifteen a.m., wondering if Teddy's time was up.

She had the strong feeling that no one really believed anything she said, did not believe that Patsy Ackerman was actually there with her, inside the Body Chute, until they finally found the signs. Olivia was able to identify everything. Patsy's cell phone. Patsy's purse. One black pirate boot, the heels scuffed and torn as if Patsy had been dragged. But no sign of Patsy herself. No blood anywhere, but a hank of long blonde hair further down the tunnel, hair torn out by the roots. They set up floodlights, and called for extra help, and they searched the rest of the night and the whole next day. No other signs of Patsy, anywhere. No signs of Patsy at all.

FIFTY-NINE

Olivia was waiting in her hotel room when the police came. The manager of the Waverly, called out by the Jefferson County Sheriff's Department, and known to be tough on trespassers, had taken one look at Olivia's face and decided not to press charges. It was the Waverly, after all, one of America's most haunted places. Strange things happened at the Waverly. Not all of them good.

Olivia had driven herself home, looking from time to time at the passenger's seat, almost expecting to see Patsy there. She found a long blonde hair on the dashboard, and as soon as she made it to Knoxville, she went to Patsy's house, broke a pane out of the kitchen window to get inside, put bird seed and fresh water in Elliot's little ceramic bowls. She turned off the crock pot, and put it straight into the refrigerator, as if she had hope that Patsy might come home again.

The bird would not look at her, or acknowledge her, but sat on his perch with his head tucked beneath a wing. Olivia wondered if he were in mourning. Animals knew things, certainly this one did. She wondered if Patsy had family. If someone responsible would come. She told Elliot she would look out for him, but he would not look up.

Olivia had gone back to her hotel and taken a shower, changed her clothes, then sat on the bed with the pillows propped up and the television on. She recharged her phone and drank a beer and ate salt and vinegar chips, and wondered what would happen next. She watched the clock until three fifteen the next afternoon, dozing now and then, then waking suddenly, checking the clock, wondering over and over if Teddy's time was up.

When the knock came on her hotel room door,

she jumped, and swung her legs to the side of the bed, pausing a moment to catch her breath. She looked through the peephole and saw Donnie Withers and McTavish. She wondered if they would put her in handcuffs. She wondered if McTavish had found her a lawyer yet.

Olivia opened the hotel room door. 'Hello,' she said. Her cheeks felt stiff.

'Mrs James?' Withers said. McTavish was looking at her strangely.

'Yes. I'm ready,' Olivia said.

'Mrs James, can we come in for a moment?' Donnie Withers said.

Olivia shrugged. 'What's the point of coming in? I'm ready to go.'

'I'm not here to arrest you, Mrs James. Just the opposite. We've picked up the guy who killed Bennington and his family. He's a habitual felon with a history of violent home invasions, and he confessed for the favor of an orange soda and a box of Keebler Oatmeal Cookies. There's no question. He was working alone. There's a theory he's been targeting your family as well. We're trying to find the car he ditched, match it up to the oil stain in your driveway, but at the moment, he's clammed back up and we're not having much luck.'

Olivia cocked her head sideways. 'You didn't come here, together like this, to tell me that.' She took a step backwards. 'Oh, God. You've found her, haven't you? You've found Teddy.' The tears were coming but her breath was not. She could not seem to get oxygen.

'We've found something, ma'am. We just

don't know what.'

'I don't understand. What do you mean? *Tell me what you mean.*'

Withers looked at McTavish. 'You tell her. Better coming from you.'

'Olivia. Honey, it's not Teddy. It can't be Teddy, the body is too far decomposed. Sit down here, sweetie.' He took her hand and looked into her eyes as if he weren't sure she understood what he was saying.

'Not Teddy?' Olivia said.

'No.'

'But you said *body*. You said *decomposed*.'

'One of our guys went back to interview that man I told you about. The one on death row.'

Olivia nodded. 'The one who said he knew where ... oh. He knew where Emily was? Is that what you mean? You've found ... oh *shit. Shit, shit*, it's starting now, isn't it? Just like he said. He warned me, Decan Ludde warned me. They'll come home one way or another. *One way or another*. That's what he said.' Olivia screamed and scratched the sides of her cheeks, drawing blood. 'No. No, I change my mind. I want her to come home alive. *I want her to come home alive.* I should have made the deal.'

McTavish put his arms around her, sat beside her on the bed rocking her back and forth.

'Oh, God, McTavish. I just wanted ... I just wanted to come home. I was so homesick. And now I don't care anymore, I just want Teddy. I want to hear Winston squeak his toy, and I have to tell him to hush because Teddy is asleep in bed waiting for me to kiss her good night. I want

Emily to come home. I want Hunter. I want all of us to be the way we were when I was a little girl before Emily went away. I just want to go home, McTavish, and I can't for the life of me figure out where it is. Where's my home now, McTavish? You tell me that. You tell me where it is.'

McTavish was patient, letting her cry it out. At one point Withers mumbled something and went outside to wait in the hall, with the air of a man who has seen these things more times than he'd like.

And in due time she grew calmer. She laid her head on McTavish's shoulder, and closed her eyes, thinking she might like to go to sleep. But he wouldn't let her. He would not let her sleep.

'Olivia. I think there's a really high probability we've found Emily's remains. I know you were just a very little girl back then, but we have some things we'd like you to look at, for identification. Do you think you can come with me? Do you think you can do it? There isn't anybody else.'

Of course there wasn't anybody else, Olivia thought. Not now, now when she was so alone.

'What day is it, McTavish? The date?'

'March fourteenth.'

'And what time?'

'Six thirty.'

'How many hours till three fifteen?'

'Olivia. You're not making any sense.'

'Oh, you're so wrong about that. I'm the *only one* making any sense.'

'Donnie's waiting, out in the hall. Do you think

378

you can do this, Olivia? If you want to wait—'

'It would be better to go now. Sure, of course I'll go.'

He took both her hands. 'Olivia. If it is Emily, and I'm not saying it is. Wouldn't it be better to at least know for sure?'

'Where are we going, McTavish?'

'We're going to the river.'

SIXTY

Dusk was thick as McTavish pulled his Cadillac into Sequoyah Hills Park. Tudor mansions lined up next to one level ranch houses, and smaller bungalows, prime Knoxville real estate that backed up onto a green space that Olivia had always thought of as a little swath of heaven. The parking lot was a gravel rectangle, and filled with patrol cars, lights flashing, a scene that was becoming familiar enough to Olivia to make her tired. The park was a stretch of meadow and green grass, with large leafy trees lining the edge alongside the river. People walked there, let their dogs run there, went fishing, or sat on green metal benches to enjoy the day.

'We used to come here a lot when I was a little girl,' Olivia said. 'We used to throw a tennis ball in the water for Hunter. Hunter loved to swim.'

McTavish opened the door for her, and led her out.

'What is it I'm going to be looking at here?' Olivia asked.

'The thing is. We've been dragging the river since early this morning.'

'Oh.'

'We found something a few hours ago. They're not ready to move it yet, but ... they're pretty sure.'

'How could they be sure?'

'Just come with me, okay?'

They had a bit of a walk, and they went hand in hand like lovers. When Olivia had been a little girl at the park, running in the grass with Hunter, she had seen her mother and father walk hand in hand, and she always thought she'd come to the river with the man she loved someday. Be careful what you wish for, she thought.

The uniforms were knotted at a lovely spot. Next to a green metal bench and a shade tree that looked out over the water. An open bundle of wet blankets was plastered to the ground, but McTavish led her to the bench and told her to sit down.

'Let me check and see if they're ready for you.'

He wasn't gone long. Olivia was aware that she was being stared at. Someone was putting up a floodlight. McTavish came back with plastic baggies. Inside one, a small heart shaped necklace, tarnished and covered with algae. Inside the other, a rotting dog collar, with a hook where the tags used to hang. Olivia reached for the baggies and he let her take them. She held them up, and studied them, but she knew. Inside, she knew.

'My sister had a necklace just like this. A little heart with a small pink stone, an amethyst. Jamison gave it to her on her fifteenth birthday. She wore it all the time. I mean, there isn't a stone in there now, but you see that little thing there, on the heart? That's where the stone used to be. And Hunter had a collar like that. A circle of leather, just like this. But he had tags. I guess ... the tags are gone. Where did they find these, McTavish?'

'We snagged bodies, in the river. Wrapped together in a blanket. They were down really deep, but it helps when you know where to look.'

'Will you let me ... I want to see them. See what's left.'

'It's not a good idea, Livie.'

'It's not up to you. And I've been waiting a long long time.'

He ran his hand through his thick hair, and grimaced. 'Sit here another minute. Let me see what they say.'

Olivia looked out at the water while she waited. Heard a horn, and saw the lights of a barge inching closer.

In the end, they decided she had the right. Mc-Tavish led her to the wet blankets she had seen, lying in the grass. They had found the bundle, snagged on a rock, in the deepest part of the river, where the channel branched and opened. A bundle of gray wool army blankets, rotting, taped tight with duct tape, and tied with rope that had long disintegrated. But the tape had held.

The blankets were open on the grass, and Olivia saw the skeletons in the floodlight, while

381

moths dodged in and out. One of the skeletons was human, and there was no flesh, just long hair, dark brown, Emily's shade, so much like her own, winding through the shredded fragments of rotting clothes. Another skeleton lay beside it, close enough that it looked as if the two skeletons had died in a hug. A dog. Olivia saw the teeth, the canine fangs, the long nosed snout. Emily and Hunter, buried together, floating in a blanket in the river just three miles from her house, decomposing quietly in the water after all these years. What had happened to them, Olivia wondered. How exactly had Hunter and Emily died? And would Teddy die the same way?

Olivia looked at her watch. Counting the hours until three fifteen.

Or perhaps it was a date. Tomorrow was March the fifteenth. Tomorrow was three fifteen. And Decan Ludde had promised Olivia that everyone was coming home. Emily was home now. The promises were coming true.

The police had taken a cheek swab, to compare DNA, and the medical examiner had confirmed that the human skeleton was female, mid to late teens, and that the other was a canine, likely a German shepherd, with a break in the left hind leg that occurred shortly before death.

McTavish took Olivia back to the hotel room, sat holding her hand, telling her things she did not want to hear. The man on death row had known Emily's killer. He had met him in jail, a monster with a predilection for children, boy or girl, it didn't matter which, he just liked them

382

young. The monster had talked about Emily one night, gently reminiscing. How opportune it was, how she had walked right into his arms, how he felt it had always been meant to be.

All because her dog had gotten out. Hunter, sensing something off, smelling the predator who watched the girls inside the house. The monster had heard the barking and the growls and gotten back into the car, wary and annoyed. He'd been after the little one, asleep on the couch, thinking he could snatch her up fast and bundle her off, but the dog had scared him away. He'd actually been in his car and on the street when the dog came barreling out of the fenced backyard and into the road, and he had hit him, okay, accidentally on purpose, he hated dogs like that. The other one had run after him, the big sister, too old really, but hey, why not. Crying over the German shepherd as he lay whimpering in the road. It had been so easy. Bundling the dog in the car, putting it in the girl's lap, weighing her down, always planning. Promising to drive them straight to a vet. Of course, he hadn't. He'd taken them to a place he had ready, well, he tried, but when he made a wrong turn the girl went nuts, got hysterical, and the dog bit him, and it was a big fat mess, and he had to shoot them both. There were scars, see there, on his biceps and leg, well, look there, under the tattoo, and see where the dog had actually bitten off a chunk of his ear? He'd gone back, actually, that little one was still there, all alone now on the couch, and God knows he'd earned it, actually paid in blood, might as well scoop her up in the net. But

383

it was too late. Cars in the driveway and lights on all over the house. Time to cut his losses. He'd been smart that way. He'd bundled the bodies up in a blanket, anchored them well, and dropped them off in the river and moved on to the next town. Nobody had ever found him out.

Yeah. He was a bad one. And he liked them young. And he had such a knack for getting the kids to go with him. They used to call him the Pied Piper, because of that.

McTavish had not wanted to leave Olivia alone in the hotel room, angry that she would not come home with him, stung when she refused to let him stay.

But she could not be with him, be near anyone – it somehow made too much noise in her head. She wanted nothing more than to lie fully clothed on the bed, and to be absolutely, utterly still.

Her family had been normal and happy for such a short part of her life. But she liked to think about it. Liked remembering what it felt like, back in the day, it was an ideal of happiness she always held in her mind, an ideal she had been spending her entire adult life to try and create.

Olivia's parents had dutifully attended the intimidating beautiful Presbyterian church on Kingston Pike. They went as a family each and every Sunday, and after Emily disappeared, Olivia's parents had gone from Presbyterian light to devout. Olivia found the services tedious as a child, and as a teen she had rebelled at the hypocrisy of all religion. Hugh had been Jewish, and their marriage had been a comfortable if lazy truce of no services of any kind except on major holidays.

Over the years, Olivia settled into the conclusion that the various religious denominations were a sort of market bazaar of spirituality, offering various paths to the same place, with some taking you on more twists and turns to get where you wanted to go. There was no religion she agreed with completely, though perhaps that was too much to ask for the mere individual. She relied now on an inner guide, a sort of chiming she felt inside when she was deciding about right or wrong or what happened after death.

It was this instinct that had given her the wisdom to turn the Piper down – if wisdom it had been.

Now she was in trouble, and she did not know where to turn. There was no help for her in organized religion, no history of trust. Ackerman, maybe reliable, maybe not, had disappeared into the labyrinth of nightmare tunnels beneath Waverly Hills, and Olivia held herself to blame, but had no clue what to do about it.

If Ack was right, and help was there for the taking, who was she supposed to ask?

So Olivia decided to hedge her bets. She called on Mother God, and Father God, and spiritual guides, angels, Buddha, her mother, her father and Chris.

And afterward, she did not sleep well, but she did sleep, finding herself moving into a numbed sort of detachment that made her wonder if she was breaking apart completely or gaining strength. The only thing she felt sure of was that there were bad things to come, and she needed all the help she could get.

SIXTY-ONE

Olivia slept little and woke early, restless now, in the hotel room bed, thinking that she had promised herself to stay until Teddy came home, and wondering if this would be her last night, if Teddy was coming home, one way or another. She drank coffee at the buffet downstairs, and had a glass of juice, then went to the river because she had nowhere else to go.

She sat on the bench near the spot in the river where Emily and Hunter's bodies had been found.

Olivia put her head in her hands. It was true, what Decan Ludde had said, it had wanted her all along. All these years since Emily had disappeared, she had thought in terms of bad things watching the people she loved. But the bad things had been watching her. She had an image of herself, just five years old, hair damp from a bubble bath, tucked into fresh pajamas, sound asleep on the couch. Completely unaware of the predator watching from the darkness, edging into the sanctuary of her house.

It had taken her sister, killed Emily, killed the dog, both dying to protect her, both dying to keep her safe. And then the piper had come back for her, as she slept unaware.

She had been lucky. Her parents had come home in time. A difference in traffic, a flat tire, a stalled car ... a last minute errand on the way home and the piper would have had her for his own.

Was it true what Decan Ludde had said? Had she been marked from birth? The unfairness of it made her grind her teeth. What was she supposed to do? How could any normal person fight a thing like this?

Olivia put her head in her hands and closed her eyes. She was tired. So very tired. So ready just to give up and let go.

'Help.' She said it out loud. 'Please.'

She sat for a long time on the bench, listening to the sound of cars going up and down the road, distracted by the footsteps of a jogger going by, when noises in the water made her look out over the river. A boat had gone, leaving a wake, the water slapping gently on the rocks and bits of driftwood right at the water's edge. There was a breeze here, right by the water, the wind humming in her ears and blowing back her hair.

Something in the water caught her eye. Something dark, bobbing in the current. She looked at her watch. Two forty-five. It couldn't be. Too early. It couldn't be.

But she was up on her feet, and going to the edge, watching to reassure herself it was driftwood. Maybe a blue heron fishing for lunch. There were a lot of herons here.

A red cardinal fluttered close, and landed on

the arm of the bench. The whir of cicadas rose and fell.

The thing in the water was not driftwood and it was not a heron. Whatever it was, it was moving. It was swimming. It was coming to shore, right where she was, and she watched, trembling all over, till it got close enough to recognize. A dog. A dog, swimming in the river, coming straight for her, snorting and huffing like dogs did when they swam.

'Winston,' Olivia whispered.

But as the dog got closer, she could see that it was not a golden retriever. This one was a German shepherd. It came up on the rocks and shook itself and Olivia held out a hand.

'Hunter?' she said.

Tan and silver brindle, even wet, she knew her own dog.

'Hunter?' she said again, holding out a hand.

The dog shook itself again, then climbed nimbly up the rocks and ran past her into the grass. Olivia watched, then decided to follow. She needed to touch the dog and see if it was real, but it kept moving, hesitating every few steps, until the obvious dawned on her, and she realized she was being led.

The dog limped. Left hind leg. Olivia noticed that. She noticed everything. That it was warm out, and sunny, and that because it was the middle of the day there was no one else in the park. The dog kept going, across the wide grassy area, heading for the line of houses. He was going quickly now, and Olivia had to run. She looked at her watch. It was three minutes after three.

388

And it hit her. The exact words of the warning. Not three fifteen. But three fifteen, three fifteen, repeated twice. Three fifteen on March fifteenth. That was the deadline. It was happening today. Teddy had twelve minutes to go.

The dog was loping now, and Olivia ran, and ran hard. Out of breath, but running, she would run till she died if she had to. How far, she wondered. Twelve minutes left, how far?

The dog veered left, to a house that was under renovation. A huge place, two levels, with a wide tiered terrace that looked out over the river. The dog scrambled up the gray slate steps, and Olivia followed. No workmen today, just a concrete mixer, and a dump truck. Plastic drink bottles, most of them empty, lying on their side, but a half full liter bottle of Mountain Dew forgotten on a brick wall, remains of a workman's lunch. Nobody on the job today.

The back door was gone, heavy plastic nailed in place to keep the weather out. But the plastic had been there a while, and there was already a hole, the plastic shredded on one side, and the dog disappeared into the house, with Olivia following. She stopped inside. Wood floors copiously tracked with sawdust, and the stairs leading up to the second floor, where all the rooms were intact.

Olivia heard noise over her head. The dog had gone upstairs.

Wet dog prints on the carpet led to the master bedroom suite. There had been a fire, that's why the house was being redone. No furniture but a bed frame, and a couple of sagging dusty boxes, and the smell of smoke and some kind of chemical that had turned the wheat colored carpet brown.

The room was nicely proportioned, not as big as the masters in newer houses, but there was genuine smoke stained molding around the trey ceiling, a blackened fireplace in a sitting room area, which was clearly where the fire started, and a bathroom off to one side. His and her sinks and a Jacuzzi. An impression of marble with pinkish swirls.

Olivia went through the bedroom, calling Teddy's name. She looked at her cell phone. Three twelve. Teddy had three minutes left. Olivia pulled at her hair, wondering what the hell she was supposed to do.

And then she saw it. A tiny little painting of a bed and breakfast in Savannah, Georgia, oddly placed on the dressing room wall. There had been other pictures, Olivia could see the marks where they had been hung on the wall. But the homeowners had wisely taken them away. Not left them to be found by anyone wandering through the plastic door to their house. All the pictures but one. There had to be a reason for that.

Olivia took the picture off the wall, and there it was. The control. One of those horrible little keypads with numbers and symbols and a red dot of pulsing light that signaled an intruder. It had probably come with a six page booklet of instructions, but it was the entry to a safe room. Lots of people had them in California. Evidently the rich people in Knoxville had them too.

And as she picked up her cell phone to call the police, Olivia checked the time. Three fourteen. Three fourteen on three fifteen. If her theory was right, Teddy had one minute left.

Nine days. Nine days locked away in a safe room without food, without water. Olivia would call the police, who would call the owner, and they would all of them be too late. It might take hours to track down the code.

And then she remembered, almost like a voice in her mind, what Patsy Ackerman had told her. That there was help when you needed it, if you looked, if you tuned in. And she remembered Hugh, in the restaurant, swearing he would buy Teddy eighty-seven thousand, three hundred forty-seven books.

Eighty-seven thousand, three hundred forty-seven. Books. Or a five digit code?

Olivia punched the numbers into the pad, there was a loud click, and the door swung open. Just like magic, just like that.

The first thing she noticed was the smell.

Winston was on his side, and Teddy lay on the floor beside him, the two of them making her think of those two skeletons in the blanket, lying side by side. Winston whimpered but could not seem to lift his head. Teddy's eyes were open to little slits. But they were moving, just under the lids, as if she were in a dream.

No water, no food, no bathroom. Both of them lying on a concrete floor. Nine days without water, water that comprised two-thirds of the human body weight. Water needed for every basic human function – blood circulation, respiration, and without it, the blood slowly thickening, the heart working harder. Teddy and Winston looked like little old men, as if they had aged together in that barren concrete room, eyes sunken, flesh contracting and wrinkling as the skin lost elasticity and the body literally shriveled in on itself.

Olivia ran down the stairs, remembering the bottle of Mountain Dew. Sugar water, fast, and then help.

Back up the stairs as fast as she could go, calling 911 on her cell as she ran. She could rub the liquid on Teddy's lips, maybe coax a little down, but Teddy needed glucose and IVs and all the help she could get.

She ran into the bedroom thinking she could do this, it was going to work out, she could pull it off, Teddy was going to be safe.

Teddy was here, Teddy was alive. Olivia rubbed liquid on her daughter's dry cracked lips, cradled her in her arms, holding up her head. She dipped her fingers in liquid, over and over, rubbing it on Teddy's gums, prying the teeth open, wanting to pour liquid in, but knowing Teddy could choke. She had to be on time. She had to be on time.

Beside her, she felt Winston twitch, heard the low weak growl from the back of his throat just as she felt a hand on her ankle. Olivia screamed and jerked away.

'Olivia.'

A whisper, though when she turned, there was no one there.

'Olivia. One more chance.' She did not know

where the voice was coming from. Maybe she was crazy. Maybe it was in her head.

'They won't make it, you know, if you don't come to me. I heard you when you said you'd changed your mind, Olivia. I heard you invite me back. I've wanted you such a long time.'

'No,' she started to say.

But the words would not come, because the piper, whatever he was, had grabbed her by the throat.

Olivia clawed at her neck, unable to breathe, held in the grip of a strength and rage that gave her a new awareness of how small she was, how feeble, how weak, how helpless. She shut her eyes but would not give in. She felt like she was falling, was aware of voices and words she could not make out.

And the sirens came, loud and close, and voices, human voices, men in a hurry and footsteps and the clatter and commotion that humans always make.

The grip was off her throat. She lay on the floor beside Teddy, hands touching the swelling muscles of her neck, aware of the concrete beneath her back, the human smells of the room. She could not talk when the EMTs began firing questions. But she could breathe. She could breathe, and she was grateful for that.

The paramedics worked their magic with the grim look of professionals who would do their best, but held out very little hope. Once the IVs were in, Teddy was whisked away on a stretcher. Olivia looked at Winston. He was too weak to move, but he watched her, aware, and Olivia imagined the deep brown eyes sending her gratitude and love no matter how it turned out. She saw a tech bend over the dog, shrug his shoulders and tell someone she could not see that he wasn't a vet, but he'd do what he could.

Someone helped Olivia to her feet. Guided her down the stairs. There was no sign of Decan Ludde, or Hunter, her beloved protector and dog. She checked the time. Four forty-five. The deadline had come and gone.

Olivia followed the EMTs down the stairs, feeling a pit of cold in her stomach at the way they took care to keep her close to Teddy, insisting she be right there in the back of the ambulance. She puzzled over their terse medical codes involving respiration, hypotonia and hypervolemic shock. They were having trouble with Teddy's IV, tiny shriveled veins collapsing. A burly man with an iron gray crew cut encouraged her to talk softly to Teddy, and hold the delicate hand, and Olivia could not help feeling that he was thinking of final moments in a life, and giving her a chance to tell Teddy she loved her, to tell Teddy goodbye.

Teddy's hand was unresponsive, small and precious, and Olivia held it tight, thinking how Emily and Teddy were home at last.

The ambulance turned a corner to the hospital and pulled to the emergency entrance out front. Olivia had an odd and sudden sensation, as if she had passed through cobwebs, followed by that familiar voice in her ear.

'See you in your dreams, Olivia.'

SIXTY-TWO

For the first time, in a very long time, Olivia was able to celebrate her birthday at Naples Italian Restaurant. Even as a little girl, her birthdays made her secretly sad. Tonight she looked out at all the smiling faces, like she did every year, and realized that it was fear that made her anxious, fear that made her sad. Fear of change, of the comings and goings of the ones you love, of the way she so often felt left behind. Wisdom was acceptance, and freedom from fear, but for Olivia, wisdom felt a long way away.

The mysterious bruising on her chest and throat had faded slowly and finally healed, her flesh supple, lightly freckled, pale. But her voice was not the same. A husky note could not be shaken off, and there were twinges of pain, like a memory, whenever she talked too loud. She felt like she had been marked, branded for the rest of her life. *We knew you before you were born*, Decan Ludde had said.

Patsy Ackerman came to her in dreams sometimes. Long blonde hair turned completely white. Always silent. She never spoke. The last time Olivia had gone to Patsy Ackerman's house to feed Elliot, the back door had been wide open, and the parrot gone from his perch. Where, kept

395

her up at night.

Teddy bounced up and down in the seat opposite, making the booth shake, making Jamison grin. He looked at Olivia across the table and Olivia caught a glimpse of something knowing, something that spoke of the man Jamison might have been, the boy her sister Emily had loved all those years ago.

Charlotte was there, with all of Teddy's cousins. Just minutes before, Olivia had watched from the parking lot as Janet had picked something up off the sidewalk, on her way into the restaurant. Janet had straightened, looked over her shoulder at Olivia, held up a small black and gray feather, and given Olivia a strangely satisfied smile. As if they shared in secrets nobody else could bear.

Teddy had a recurring dream where her daddy came home, and she would wake the next morning, crying, hugging Winston who slept, as always, in the middle of her bed. She did not remember what had happened the night she disappeared. Dr Raymond said it was a memory that might never come back. The only thing Teddy remembered was being afraid, and crying, with Winston in the room, until Aunt Emily had come to hold her hand, and sit with her, and keep her and Winston safe.

McTavish sat beside Olivia, his arm resting on the top of the seat, cradling the back of her head. They liked the idea of moving in together, but for now Olivia did not want any changes in Teddy's life.

Teddy handed Olivia a package. 'Open this

first.'

But McTavish waggled a finger. 'No presents till after dessert.'

'Just this one,' Teddy said. 'I want her to open mine first. It's from me and Winston, see, I put his paw print right here. *Please, please, please.*'

'Okay,' Olivia said. 'Don't chant.'

'Let's fill that wine glass up and put a smile on your face,' McTavish said, topping off Olivia's glass.

It was clear from the copious amount of tape that Teddy had wrapped the gift herself, and there was indeed a muddy smear on the front where Teddy had put Winston's paw to make a print. Olivia had to work to get to the box. Teddy was too excited to wait till all the paper came off.

'It's an iPod,' Teddy said, leaning across the table. 'Do you like it, Mama?'

'I love it.'

'McTavish took me and Jamison to shop. I thought you could listen to it at night when you can't sleep. You can curl up with it in bed.' Teddy looked sideways at McTavish. 'Mama never sleeps at all. She reads or wanders all over the house.'

'It's perfect, Teddy. Thank you. All of you. Thanks.'

'Now she'll just have to figure out how to make it work,' McTavish said, giving Teddy a wink.

Teddy snatched the iPod up across the table. 'Here, I can set it up for you, Mama. Let me.'

Olivia balled up the wrapping paper, and stuck it in her purse. McTavish took the pink sticky bow and stuck it to the top of Olivia's head.

'It's you that's going to be embarrassed now,' Olivia told him. 'I'm going to wear it like this all night.'

'I keep forgetting how shameless you are,' McTavish said, and there was something in his grin that made Olivia's cheeks turn pink.

'Here, Mommy.' Teddy was out of her seat, helping Olivia put the ear buds on. 'It gets Internet radio. You can have music from all over the world. This is a station from France.'

Teddy adjusted the volume, and Olivia tilted her head, waiting for the music to come through.

Heart and soul, I fell in love with you
Heart and soul, I fell in love with you
Baaaby...

Olivia grabbed the edge of the table.

'Mommy? Is something wrong?'

'I'm fine, Teddy. I feel good. This is a happy night.'

Olivia had just a moment to hug her daughter before the waiter arrived, with plates that steamed with lasagna, and pasta with meat sauce, Chicken Marcela, another basket of warm bread, and the second carafe of house Chianti. Olivia sat on the edge of her seat while the plates were sorted out.

She still felt it sometimes, the compulsion she'd had when she'd reached for that ghostly hand, and she sometimes felt the lure, that yearning grief for her childhood home, thought she heard the piper whispering in her ear. But when the urge got too strong, she had only to touch her throat, to listen to the hoarse damage in her vocal cords, and it was enough, it was, to keep her safe.

She wondered, if she turned her head just right, would she get a glimpse of them, the good things and the bad? Did Decan Ludde still watch, was her family close – Chris and Emily, maybe her mom and dad? Did Chris know she had forgiven him, and wasn't angry anymore? Was Hugh watching from across the room, smiling at Teddy from another booth?

Where were they now, Olivia wondered. Maybe they were right beside her. Maybe they had always been there.